CRESCENT CITY RHAPSODY

Also by Kathleen Ann Goonan

Queen City Jazz
Mississippi Blues
The Bones of Time

CRESCENT CITY RHAPSODY

KATHLEEN ANN GOONAN

AVON BOOKS, INC.
An Imprint of HarperCollins*Publishers*
10 East 53rd Street
New York, New York 10022-5299

Copyright © 2000 by Kathleen Ann Goonan
Interior design by Kellan Peck
ISBN: 0-380-97711-7

Library of Congress Cataloging in Publication Data:

Goonan, Kathleen Ann.
    Crescent city rhapsody / Kathleen Ann Goonan.—1st ed.
      p.   cm.
    I. Title.
PS3557.O628 C74 2000
813'.54 21—dc21   99-042227

First Avon Eos Printing: February 2000

AVON EOS TRADEMARK REG. U.S. PAT. OFF. AND IN OTHER COUNTRIES,
MARCA REGISTRADA, HECHO EN U.S.A.

Printed in the U.S.A.

QPM 10 9 8 7 6 5 4 3 2

www.harpercollins.com

For Skylar, Jazz, and Sean:
The best is always yet to come.

Acknowledgments and Thanks

For his constant emotional support as I wrote this book, I am grateful, as always, to my husband Joseph. He also maintains my website at *www.goonan.com*.

To Jennifer Brehl, my astute and patient editor, my heartfelt thanks.

Sean Stewart's thorough critique helped immensely, as does the Edge group in general.

Thanks to Joseph Kirschvink of Cal Tech for his permission to quote the material in "Break in Four Sections" from *Nature*, Vol. 370, and from the Internet, and to the Auckland group doing research on biogenic magnetoreceptors—Michael M. Walker, Carol E. Diebel, Cordula V. Haugh, Paricia M. Pankhurst, John C. Montgomery, and Colin R. Green—for their permission to quote their paper on the subject, which appeared in *Nature*, Vol. 370. Thanks also to Dr. Jon Dobson of the University of Florida for permission to quote his paper in this same section.

Thanks to Dr. Adam Eisenberg of Northwest University for use of his definitions of electromagnetic pulse, signal, and telecommunication taken from the Internet, and to Dr. John Broderick of Virginia Tech for his idea about vacuum tubes.

Many books were exceedingly helpful in shaping my creation of the workings of the Biocities postulated in my books, including but by no means limited to *The Biology of the Honeybee* by Winston, *The Honey Bee* by Gould and Gould, and *Chemical Communication* by Agosta.

All of K. Eric Drexler's books on nanotechnology, including *Engines of Creation*, *Unbounding the Future*, and *Nanosystems*, and several books which extrapolate from this concept, such as *Nanotechnology*, edited by B. C. Crandall and *Becoming Immortal* by W. M. DuCharme, Ph.D., are central to this future history.

The vision and scope of Marshall Savage's *The Millennial Project* is central to this book.

Two classics of *voudoun* culture, *Divine Horsemen: The Voodoo*

Gods of Haiti by Maya Deren and *Dancing Spirits: Rhythms and Rituals of Vodun, The Rada Rite* by Gerdes Fleurant, guided me in this sector.

And finally, Hasse's biography, *Beyond Category: The Life and Genius of Duke Ellington*, and Ellington's own fascinating *Music Is My Mistress* provided the backbone of the musical framework of the book, but jazz biographies of Mingus (*Beneath the Underdog*, Mingus), Coltrane (*Ascension*, Nisenson), Sun Ra (*Space Is the Place* by John Szwed), and books such as *Thinking on Jazz* by Burliner and *Bebop and Nothingness* by Francis Davis, along with countless other books, provided critical insights regarding this uniquely American art.

And thanks to my father, Thomas Goonan, for imprinting me with jazz from infancy, and my mother, Irma Knott Goonan, for supporting me in every endeavor I have attempted.

To Dance is to take part in the cosmic control of the world.
—Maya Deren,
Divine Horsemen: The Voodoo Gods of Haiti

rhapsody

a literary work consisting of disconnected pieces

an instrumental composition that is irregular in form like an improvisation or free fantasia

—*Webster's Third New International Dictionary*

Rhapsodies by Duke Ellington:
New Orleans Rhapsody
Creole Rhapsody
Rhapsody, Jr.
Swanee River Rhapsody
Rock 'n' Roll Rhapsody

CRESCENT CITY RHAPSODY

Opening Note

The baseball-sized objects exploded as they hit Earth's atmosphere.

All burned to cinders except one.

PRELUDE
Swiftly; With Gravity

Marie | New Orleans | 2012

Marie always knew she would be murdered. Not knowing the details kept her on edge for many years.

In a way, it was a relief when it happened.

Involved in stock reports, Marie felt rather than saw the sky's gradual blackening; welcomed the slight breath of breeze on her sweat-sheened skin; heard thunder rumble with the distant, primal pleasure she always felt during late summer when storms deluged New Orleans daily.

There was little traffic on her small bricked side street this time of day. As usual, the beat of desultory blues rose from street musicians to her office on the fourth floor of the town house that had been in her family for generations. After their usual noontime skirmish, the appetizing smells of hot spices and garlic vanquished the sweetish, sickly smell of spilled beer that cooked up from the bricks around 9 A.M. like steam. Since the corner restaurant had been there for over a century, and the beer for longer than that, these smells were a part of the cycle of the day for Marie and, she liked to think, for a long line of Maries.

Her immediate background was one of wealth and opportunity. With the coming age of nanotechnology, Marie didn't see why this could not be the lot of all.

Some disputed that such an age was coming. They didn't know that it was already upon them. The public was told that molecular

2

manipulation was a distant pipe dream. Their ignorance, in Marie's opinion, was deliberately fostered to make it easy for those in control to shape the future as they pleased. Nanotech research and advances were the property of the military and of their quasi-private research arms. Stealing classified information from such places was defined as espionage.

Marie's grandmère had raised her to believe that education and information were basic human necessities—after food and shelter. And Grandmère drilled into Marie that she had to be better than her own mother, a wild teenager who metamorphed into a beautiful jet-setter and died of an overdose when Marie was ten. But like her Grandmère, whose rum smuggling had established the basis of their fortune, Marie quickly realized that she would have to run with her lights off in dangerous waters. If she had to operate an amateur spy network in order to further the dreams she had inherited along with her money, so be it.

But Marie didn't have to depend on foreign governments to provide her with enemies. She had plenty right at home. A recent murder trial had put away one of the most powerful members of the old-boy network, clearing her playing field considerably. The *Times-Picayune* ferreted out the fact that she personally paid Sharbell Dighton III, the attorney who accomplished this tricky feat, a small fortune to represent the victim.

Money was no object—at least not as long as Marie continued to invest wisely. She had a knack for it, and it was a necessity. It was her responsibility to take care of her people. And, according to Grandmère, dead for ten years now, all oppressed people.

It was not always easy to discharge these responsibilities.

Even wearing shorts and a halter top, Marie sweltered in the muggy afternoon as she sat low to the floor in a canvas sling folding chair, her favorite seat when working. Sipping strong, sweet coffee watered by melting ice, she absently noticed that the rough bricks of the wall behind her workspace lacked their usual slice of sun.

A visitor to her high-tech loft might have been surprised at its elegant hard-edged simplicity, but visitors were few. Rare tropical plants flourished in Chinese pots. French doors leading to a balcony stood open. An aromatic herbal scent pervaded the air, leavened by hot wind that banged the green shutters hooked back loosely against the streetside bricks. Though Hugo, her bodyguard and longtime friend, hated her practice of leaving windows and doors open, she could not stand being separated from the weather. At college in Chicago twenty years earlier, she had left her windows open during the coldest nights, a practice that created a daily argument which soon fell into a mannered sequence of feints and parries. But today Hugo wasn't here to play the game.

Marie's computer screen was an arc of about sixty degrees of flat silverish flexible material resting on the floor, a crescent of information. The apex was about four feet high. Marie like to keep a lot of information visible. Sometimes, like today, it looked like the jumble of a messy desktop, a dada collage of bright colors and odd shapes. She held the keypad on her lap. The top border of the screen shone with *voudoun* symbols: a snake, a drum, and the spirit of love, represented by concentric nesting hearts. Not that she knew anything about *voudoun*, though her name and heritage were intimately related to the practice. She was not superstitious; her rather scattered scientific and mathematical background precluded that. She had no truck with her family background of *voudoun*, though her grandmère, a true believer in the hybrid of African religions and Catholicism, had sternly tried to bring her around until her dying day. The images on Marie's screen had been designed as a gift by a believing friend, of which there were many in New Orleans, and she used them because they were beautiful.

The path beneath the snake branched to include files on every person of any importance in New Orleans—and many who might seem to lack any distinguishing qualities. This information had been committed to computer only in the past few decades. Before that, such facts had been held within the minds of a long line of Marie Laveaus.

New Orleans had never been as Marie envisioned it would be in the future. Grandmère's stories emphasized that there was no golden past to return to, unless one idealized New Orlean's continental origins. Marie could see the possibility of something better—something completely different—glimmering in the distance. She was often described as cold and ruthless by her enemies. And perhaps that was true. She didn't mind. The ability to inspire fear was a necessary adjunct to power.

A stock trading program ran on auto in the upper-right-hand corner, using the latest complexity-based algorithms. Although she had a stranglehold on local politicians that she was certainly not going to abandon, Marie had diversified from her family's traditions. Her wealth now came from discreet investments in the most promising of new small companies specializing in some essential facet of nanotech, though generally the application was not called nanotech, but by a much more specific name. Her holdings were an international patchwork, for one country might ban what another allowed. Since around 2005, the possibility and dangers of true self-replication had been taken much more seriously, and every possible avenue that might lead to such a development was closely scrutinized—and often snapped up and classified. But because this process was usually accomplished by appointed government committees, and because developers had powerful lobbies, many loopholes were naturally overlooked. Over the last few years, Marie had observed a pattern emerging that perhaps few people had the time or inclination to fully realize, one based not on scientific development itself, but on the commerce spun from it. She believed that it wouldn't be much longer before self-replication, the simultaneously pursued and feared watershed, would become a reality.

Once that happened, all bets were off. The floodgates would be loosed. Control over matter, on a very discreet scale, would be possible. But it seemed just as likely that molecules that could create others like themselves might engender a chain reaction until all available matter was used up, and the Earth and all living creatures were reduced to simple lifeless forms of matter.

It was a terrifying vision.

Yet, unlike most people—at least those who ventured an opinion in a public venue—Marie did not fear the development of a viable nanotech. She took a keen interest in it. There would be some point, she believed, that humanity would pass a point of no return, beyond which everything would be unimaginably changed.

She planned to be there. And she planned to take her city with her.

Marie looked away from her stock information, the varied ways in which sales, calls, and puts were progressing. She enlarged several pictures of her daughter and set them in motion so that Petite Marie danced, stuck out her tongue, played quietly in the corner of this very room, unaware that her actions were being saved.

Beauty had blessed—or cursed—most of the women in Marie's family, quadroons and mistresses and then the free businesswomen who had laid the foundation for Marie's present fortune. One of them had been the sister of the famous second Marie Laveau, *voudoun* queen of New Orleans, and the name had made its way down through several rings of cousins before alighting, solitarily, on Marie.

Until, that is, her own daughter, Petite Marie, had been born.

Marie always felt that her own face was too strong for beauty, her nose too straight and long, her chin too determined, her eyes too clear of the romantic rubbish that had ruined her mother's life. But the ancestral pattern of beauty was reasserted in Petite Marie. This was quite obvious, even though she was only five years old. Her dark eyes were round and large; her skin, the color of gold-kissed mahogany, held a constant deep pink blush over her cheekbones. Her irascible hair flowed in a black kinky stream down her back, resisting combs, causing a daily temper of screams and threats. She was wild, merry, a delight . . .

And she should have arrived in Paris by now. Marie blanked the videos and rubbed a cramp at the back of her neck. She could easily verify her daughter's physical location. She could beep up Petite Marie, or Hugo, or Al. She could check the satellite position of the jet, her own private jet. She restrained herself. Al, her husband, was greeting their daughter. He was giving her presents. Too many presents. Al's nasty yappy little white dog was bouncing around like a Ping-Pong ball, adding to the din. Soon they'd remember Mom, staying behind to work. Alone. Any minute—any minute they would call.

At least Hugo was with Petite Marie and would remain during the long visit she would have with her father. Being a dwarf did not seem to handicap Hugo's ability to do anything, including being a body-guard *nonpareil*.

Marie clipped back the braids dangling in her face with a brusque gesture as she studied a constant feed of red, green, and yellow lines tangled in one quadrant of her screen. The lines paused; knotted in an odd rhythm. Scrying these signs was like watching the surface of the sea, divining not only that there were fish below, but their size, depth, color, direction of travel. This twinge signaled something different. And therefore important.

She called up specifics. Someone—somewhere—had sucked down a big chunk of a rather interesting small company working on artificial, trainable neural pathways. The company was called Consciousnets. She glanced at their annual report, then asked for their bills of lading for the last six months, quickly analyzed the raw materials, and told two different analysis programs to figure out who was behind this purchase.

Leaning forward, suddenly eager, she set up the process that would acquire snips of Consciousnets from here and there, gradually, in a process that might take hours or days and initially be distributed to a range of buyers with no discernible connection.

Sheer gauzy curtains billowed into the room as a gust of wind brought her back to the present. Why didn't they call? Al's stubborn face, that face she'd found so attractive years ago and still did, damn him, appeared on the corner of her screen as she spoke his name. She almost said, "Call," but hesitated. No, she'd give them a few more minutes before pestering them.

Al wouldn't live in New Orleans. He claimed it was too dangerous. Marie thought that was just an excuse; he was simply homesick. All his communication to her since he had returned to Paris had the same content. She could almost hear his delightful accent as she glanced again at his smiling brown face: I've lived in your country; now you live in mine. Come to Paris, to my worn, pleasant rooms piled high with books, forgo your heritage, honor our marriage, become *civilized* and leave your obsession with the future in a haze of flowering spring trees and strolls along the Seine and my delightful cooking.

His cooking! The lazybones had given up his trendy new restaurant on Royal Street once they'd married. He had the staying power of a midge. He always hoped to lure her to Paris; she saw that now. He pined and moped so that she sent him back, for a month's vacation that turned into half a year, and then he and Petite Marie pined and moped for one another. Well, they'd have a good time without her. Marie had work to do. And unfortunately he was right about the danger. But that was everywhere. It followed her. It would follow her anywhere. Her family was relatively safe—as long as she wasn't around.

The brief jump of a fake siren below her window startled her, then the sound stopped abruptly. Just kids playing. Uneasy, she rose, crossed the dark polished wooden floor, strewn with Petite Marie's toys, kicked aside a puzzle piece with her bare foot, and stepped out onto the balcony. Marie ignored the cozy tableau of wrought-iron chairs ranged around the small table where she took her morning coffee and grasped the railing so tightly her knuckles whitened. She should have gone with her daughter. She hadn't realized that she would miss her so *much*. Tall palms in massive pots bent in the wind, their fronds clicking. A riot of red geraniums and yellow hibiscus were sheltered by an ivied brick wall. For a second Marie scanned the street for the bulletproof limo that would bring Petite Marie home from school, then caught herself. Just as well the little one had left for a while. She had started to complain about Hugo sitting at the back of the classroom each day. It was an elite school and the administration had insisted that, with all the wealthy people sending their children there, their security was already fine, thank you. Money, as usual, had prevailed. Some parents objected to the bodyguard as an everpresent reminder that violence could burst into their children's classroom; others welcomed him.

Well, surely she could stand being away from her child for a month or so. Though danger to both of them would be lifelong, so much so that she'd put off having a child for many years, she had lately been able to make certain provisions that very few people in the world could afford. Provisions for alternatives that very few even knew existed, pulled together as they were from so many sources. . . .

Marie took a deep breath. She'd give them another five minutes before she called. She watched the street show below as she had all her life, though today it held little interest. Two jugglers, in shimmering purple and yellow clown suits and masks sparkling with obsolete computer circuits, spun pins through the air in intricate rhythm. Their huge mirrored shoes flashed with the last ray of sunlight as black clouds boiled across the sky. The French Quarter was locked into a curiously uneven anachronism, based solely on the desires of those who lived there. Solar cars, where limited street access existed, were fine; they were noiseless. Other exterior trappings of technology, such as satellite dishes, were banned. On the other hand, she was free to land a small helicopter on her specially reinforced roof any time of the day or night. She could pretty much do as she pleased, being on the board of just about everything imaginable and having plenty of money to contribute—and plenty of secrets to reveal should the lure of money prove inadequate.

A blast of cold wind hit her, and on either side of her head, massive hanging pots of ferns pirouetted in unison, a row of dancers schooled by the wind's wild grace. Though the crowd around them was dispersing beneath the first fat drops of rain, the clowns juggled on intrepidly.

Maybe she *would* go to Paris. Al was quite wily, in his way. She smiled despite her worry. *Could* she hold the invisible reins of the city from halfway around the world? Al thought her despotic, old-fashioned. No, she told him earnestly, these are my people; this is my home. I have great plans for my city.

Your city! She could hear his snort even now.

A razor's edge of rain hissed up the narrow street, chilling her with sweet cold wind and ozone. It swept across her tin roof with a pounding roar and steamed briefly on the street bricks below. The two black musicians dashed for cover, leaving rain-sheened chairs. Tourists huddled beneath store awnings.

The phone's ring was faint, but she turned, gladness blossoming. It must be them. Petite Marie was safe in Al's Paris flat.

Then a glint from the street caught her vision, an odd motion of one of the clowns. She paused because he was pointing one of the pins at her . . . and the whoop of the fake siren filled the air.

Paralyzed, Marie had a second to experience her heart pounding in terror, heard her own cry in the roar of the storm as if it were that of someone else, felt rough bricks skin her face and arms as she spun to the floor of the balcony from the force of the bullets. Above her one of the fern pots exploded in a shower of dirt and shards.

She heard the soft beep that signaled the shutdown of her vital functions, which would call *them* . . . even now, *they* were on the way. A minute, no more.

Among her ragged thoughts a thread of gratefulness spun briefly— at least Petite Marie was safe. The timing was perfect.

Then she died.

THE FIRST MOVEMENT

electromagnetic pulse (EMP): A broadband, high intensity, short-duration burst of electromagnetic energy. *May be caused by nonnuclear means.*

signal: Detectable transmitted energy that can be used to carry information.

telecommunication: Any transmission, emission, or reception of signs, signals, writing, images and sounds or intelligence of any nature by wire, radio, optical or other electromagnetic systems.

—From *Federal Standard* 1037C

Semiconductor devices fail when they encounter an EMP because of the local heating that occurs. When a semi-conductive device absorbs the EMP energy, it displaces the resulting heat that is produced relatively slowly when compared to the time scale of the EMP. Because the heat is not dissipated quickly, the semiconductor can quickly heat up to temperatures near the melting point of the material. Soon the device will short and fail . . . It should be noted that in EMP tests not all electronics and systems at risk were initially destroyed. Some items did not fail in the first test or even the second.

—Adam Eisenberg, Ph.D.,
http://www.geocities.com/CapeCanaveral/5971/emp.html

First Solo

The Radio Astronomer | Southwest Virginia | 2012

Zeb downshifted to take a curve on the two-lane blacktop; the creek had flooded the road, leaving a sheet of ice in the bend. The back wheels of his Ford pickup held steady and after the ice he resumed his previous speed. He had gone into town for a Thanksgiving party and he shouldn't have.

He would never be able to socialize happily, but a certain excruciating amount of it always seemed to be called for. At least he didn't go off the deep end anymore; thanks to medication and the hard work of Sally, his older sister and always his champion, his flights of manic intensity had been under control long enough for him to settle into a life of being a professor of astronomy at a rural state university. Not the glittering academic life his parents, dead for many years now, had envisioned for him, pushed him toward; far short of what all indications had been during his adolescence, when all doors were open, when every major university wooed him. The courses he taught didn't begin to scratch the surface of what he knew; he was an astrophysicist. But it was a predictable life; even, generally, a satisfying life. It had been purchased at the cost of closing the floodgates to the infinite. It was enough. If he was deliberate and firm, there was a reason. He lived with a certain amount of satisfaction at just being able to function predictably. Most people took this state of mind for granted. It was a privilege for which he'd had to fight.

Nobody else was on the road. It was Wednesday night, and everyone had gone over the river and through the woods and were at Grandma's now. Sally was expecting him for dinner tomorrow in Roanoke, a sixty-mile drive. He was looking forward to seeing Annie, his niece. In her second year of college, she was beginning to be able to ask intelligent questions. She was majoring in nanotechnology. Seemed like a real scattershot major to Zeb, but then he tended to keep entirely immersed in what was happening farther than the eye could see. Annie was a bright kid. Zeb only hoped that she would not suffer as he had, that his genetic weirdness would not be echoed in her.

Across a snowy field that seemed to glow faintly, an old white farmhouse threw patches of colored light onto the snow through a window—an early Christmas tree. Behind the fields rose dark ridges, trees blackly sawtoothed against a slightly lighter sky. Zeb cracked his window and lit a Camel. The blast of cold air felt clean and good.

The party had been stuffy. Zeb stood out, as usual, felt clumsy and big in his heavy boots and plaid wool shirt. He explained to his hostess when he arrived that he was dressed to go up on Angel's Rest later and check the antenna, but he still felt out of place. He sat gingerly on one of Dr. England's delicate chairs, wishing he could smoke, while she and her husband passed out eggnog. He didn't see anyone else smoking, though. England had urged him to drop by when she saw him in the supermarket this morning; probably felt sorry for him, he thought now. He just hadn't known how to say no. He didn't want to insult her. Parties with mathematicians and physicists were tolerable, because it only took a few minutes to start a heated academic argument, but these people were all with the arts. They were nice, but he heard snippets of conversations around him filled with concerns he knew he would never be able to fathom. He took a sip of eggnog and looked around, wondering if he could slip into the kitchen and pour it out and wondering how long he had to stay to be polite. He decided it didn't matter. He would just leave. He stood to go.

Then Terri had come in the door.

She was dressed nicely, as usual, he saw, as Judy England took her coat. A black dress. Pearls.

"Zeb," she said, seeing him.

"Stay away from the eggnog." After a long moment, he added, "How are you doing?"

Her eyes were slightly merry at that; a small victory, pulling two whole sentences out of him.

"Fine," she said. "Wonderful." Her hair was ashy blond, but he knew that she had it done once a month because a lot of it had turned white when she was thirty. The year she'd married him.

"You look good."

"Thanks."

Their talk was small, but it always had been. After three years of marriage, she decided she needed more words. Now she was married to a sociologist. Jim was from New York. He talked a lot.

"Well, I should go." Zeb gulped the eggnog and frowned. It really was wretched.

She put one hand on his arm. "Take care. Are you still living in that—old house?"

He knew she'd narrowly avoided calling it a decrepit old shack. He nodded.

"And do you still spend all your time studying that radio astronomy data?"

She'd hated that. Apparently, she had thought it some sort of bachelor pursuit that he would outgrow, even though he had been forty when they got married. He didn't spend as much time looking at the stars through telescopes as she had imagined he would; *that* seemed much more romantic to her. But stars and space had a lot more to say than could be seen in the visible spectrum. Zeb spent his time online, traveling, or teaching. He had no hobbies or outside interests; he didn't watch television and he didn't go to the movies and he didn't read fiction. He still wondered how two such dissimilar people had ever considered marriage. Then she smiled—just a bit—and he remembered.

"Pretty much." He looked at his watch. "Tell Jim hi."

He had hurried out into the cold air gratefully. He took his gloves and hat from his pockets, pulled them on, checked the chains on his truck tires, and got in. The bed was full of sandbags for traction, but he left a little too quickly and the back wheels fishtailed on the icy unplowed side street. That's right, he thought. Hurry away from your latest failure.

Now, safe in relatively unpopulated territory, he finished his cigarette, tossed the butt out the window, and cranked it up. It had taken him an hour of careful driving to get to the lower slopes of Angel's Rest. A student's father owned the field they built their antenna in. It had taken most of the fall to put it up. Zeb had agreed to check the constantly incoming data over the break. Of course he was up there as often as time allowed. He loved the thing. So big, so seemingly primitive, yet the same kind of homemade setup with which the existence of pulsars had been discovered.

He put on his turn signal for no one and swung between two fence posts onto a frozen dirt road beneath an unbroken crust of icy snow. He pushed the four-wheel drive button and shifted into low. The newer trucks did all this on voice command, but he preferred his old dependable model, a real antique from 1971 with no sensitive computerized

15

components, bought for fifty bucks from a widow whose husband had kept it pristine, and repaired it with parts foraged from junked trucks he kept on the slope behind his house. He'd bolted on a global positioning system that put maps on a small screen next to the radio; that was the extent of its modernization.

As the truck labored up the mountain, a doe leaped through his headlight beam, as if she'd been waiting for a car to show her a good crossing. A clump of snow fell from a fir bow and his wipers whirred. If Terri had been here, she would have played classical music, but he preferred the sound of the wheels grabbing the snow, the steady smooth growl of the transmission. The raw data. It had its own poetry. Or, if not poetry, at least a kind of honesty.

Far below he could see the few lights of Pearisburg. The truck slid a bit when it coasted onto the bald, a huge swipe of treeless space at the end of the ridge. He grabbed his wide-beam flashlight and stepped into the profoundly silent night.

The stars arced overhead in vast splashes. He crunched through the snow, which reached midcalf. The dipoles and wire cast long shadows in the moonlight. He experienced mild pride. His students had done almost all the work of getting the grants to finance the project—and the physical work as well.

He grappled in the back of his truck for the push broom he had brought and set the flashlight on the hood. He set to work pushing snow off five large solar collectors. They were tilted, and most likely the snow would melt enough to slide off tomorrow, but he might as well do this now. It took the better part of an hour and was quite a hike in the snow. By the time he finished, he was drenched in sweat.

That done, he walked over to the small prefab recording shack, dialed the combination, and opened the door. He switched on the overhead bulb.

Recording pens powered by solar batteries moved slowly across scrolling paper. One of the many things this project was supposed to do was give the students an appreciation for the raw data, untranslated by any computer program and operated without any computerized components. They had even scrounged old vacuum tubes from ancient equipment. He hoped that this would give his students a greater understanding of the electronics involved. Hands-on experience had helped him immensely, and he had great respect for learning the basics. There was so much fancy software now that a lot of students no longer truly understood how the data was generated in the first place. This setup would be useful in his teaching for many years to come, long after the current crop of students moved on, as long as they could keep it here.

The wind picked up and something outside vibrated in a high whine. The paper folded slowly as it fell into a box beneath the moving pens. He carefully tore off those in the box. He would take all of these records with him for the students to analyze. Glancing through the tiny window, he noted that the valley was dark. Some kind of power failure. He felt a mild ping of smugness. He was a fan of self-sufficiency. His house was heated with wood and his hot water heater and generator were solar-powered. His property looked as if he were operating a full-scale communications empire. Several radio towers and a few more satellite dishes were scattered across his several acres.

He looked back at the pens, which were scribbling wildly. That was odd. He watched, wondering what sort of malfunction might be occurring, knowing that the beauty of the setup was that there were very few interfaces. This was directly from space, this scruff, as it was called.

Suddenly the pens stopped moving. The seconds ticked past and the lines were completely flat. Then the pens scribbled again. Stopped. Each time the interval during which the scribbling occurred was longer. Each data section was not any sort of configuration he had ever seen before. Radio interference from towns was pretty sparse here, but it could happen. He pulled up the lone stool, perched on it, and watched.

He watched for two hours, propping his back against the wall. He dozed off at one point and woke, shivering. He decided he should warm up in his truck; he didn't know how long this would last.

As he crunched out to the truck, he decided to set up some way to heat the observatory, as they were calling the little shed; someone less self-sufficient than he was might get stuck up here overnight. There was a cell phone, but he liked backups. He was responsible for the students' safety.

He climbed into the cab. The truck wouldn't start. He swore, got out, and opened the hood. He hung the flashlight from a hook on the underside of the hood and checked all the connections. Recent tune-up. Water in the battery. Hoses tight. He had just filled the gas tank this morning. Nothing wrong that he could see.

He took the flashlight, slammed the hood, pulled his down bag from behind the seat, and tramped back to the shed. It would be a long, cold night.

When he got back in, he noticed that the radio sky seemed to have returned to normalcy. He watched the pens move in slow sweeps. The lights were back on in the valley. The plastic floor was not long enough for him to stretch out on. Maybe it would be better in the truck. Sighing, he tramped back out to the truck. He turned the key one last time. No luck.

Then he remembered: He had replaced the starter last week with a new solenoid-type starter from the dealer, because he was out of junk starters.

The truck sat at the top of a bowl-shaped depression. Maybe it would jump-start. The worst that could happen was that it would be stuck at the bottom of the hill instead of the top.

He let off the brake. The truck slowly gathered momentum. After a minute, he popped the clutch and the engine caught. It *had* been the starter. He just didn't like those computerized components. Too fragile by far.

Gingerly shifting into first, he went into a controlled slide and started up the hill on a different track, hoping that he had enough momentum to get to the top. The truck slid sideways for a few feet, then plowed up the hill. He reached the crest, next to the recording shed, and circled around until he was back in the tracks he had made on the way up.

He took the truck out of gear, set the brake, and turned on the heat full blast. Leaving the truck running, he went into the shed and took the data from each roll, making sure he had the last few hours of information.

After he finished getting the papers, he turned off the light and locked the door behind him. He had already planned to be back on Friday. Now he thought he might return tomorrow.

He stacked the papers in a box on the floor of the truck and climbed into the cab.

His house was on a low ridge halfway between Angel's Rest and town. It was about 2 A.M. when he turned into the long driveway. His two collies, Pleiades and Zephyr, rushed from the porch to meet the truck.

Exhausted, he staggered into the yard, tilting his head to look at the stars. Puzzled. Intrigued. What the hell was going on? After a few moments, they flashed and twirled like the Van Gogh print Terri had put on their bedroom wall. He felt giddy; euphoric. That was a bad sign. He needed his medication. Sally kept urging him to get one of the new time-release implants, but he was shy of having stuff in his body. It put him in mind of shrapnel.

He and the readouts survived the dogs' greeting and he crossed the porch and opened the door. The collies rushed past him and bustled around, barking. He turned on lights and set the readouts on a huge heavy table in the center of the living room, pushing aside a stack of books to make room. The ornate Warm Morning Stove he had bought at a junk store in Newcastle was almost out. He stuffed a few newspaper twists, some kindling, and two big logs on top of the still-glowing ashes, closed the door, and opened the dampers. The fire roared and snapped for a few minutes before settling down.

His farmhouse was over a hundred years old. After years of steady work, the house was as habitable and as up-to-date, communication-wise, as he wanted it to be. The living room, where he spent most of his time, had been three rooms. He had taken out the walls and put posts in strategic places. Two old comfortable couches and several big armchairs sat here and there, facing not one another but various flatscreens, some wall-mounted, some stand-alone. Bundles of wires ran every which way beneath various rugs, which made the room look as if it might be infested with large snakes. Electronic gear was stacked on scattered tables, lights winking at seeming random. The walls were covered with books and CDs. The wide plank floor beneath his feet was scarred and dark.

He went into the kitchen, turned on the propane burner, and made himself some coffee, which he drank black. He picked up his vial of pills; put it down. Best to take the next one tomorrow morning, his regular time; that's what they told him to do if he missed a pill. He scrambled eggs in a cast-iron skillet and carried his snack back into the living room. Bannered across his mail screen was a message from an old friend in Washington: WOW!

He heard from Craig at least once a month. They'd done a few papers together, but Craig moved in higher planes than he did; he was internationally known and taught at Harvard for a portion of each year. They'd met at Stanford during the heady year before Zeb had crashed.

Crash was the word for it. He would literally be walking on air for days on end, forgetting to eat, absorbing books, lectures, raw data. He was there on a scholarship, studying graduate physics, though he was only eighteen. He was the darling of the physics department. He spent most of his time submerged in challenges he chose himself, discussing them with heated intensity in the lounge, arguing points, picking up insights. He would come down from a week of this utterly wrung-out, sleep for a day or two, and drag himself out of bed with no energy. The world looked dull and stupid; completely impermeable. He couldn't understand how he could have been so excited, how it had all clicked so precisely. Then it would start to build again, until he once again was in the realm where he could fill pages and pages, disks and optical spheres, with pure thought. He was lit. He was burning.

And he burned out.

He couldn't even remember the depth of his despair when the darkness took a long time to lift and then longer and longer. He had cut his wrists. Why? Such an action was completely unimaginable to him today. But back then . . .

Sally was pregnant then with Annie. She'd still flown out to California. Their parents were dead. She was his only hope. His college HMO would pay for only the most rudimentary of treatments. He lost his scholarship. All was in fragments—not only his thoughts, but his life. He was like two different people. Three. More. They were not finely delineated. But he was, most definitely, mentally ill.

Sally got him back in shape. Brought him home, took him up north to an expensive clinic, talked to people who might have an inkling of what was wrong. Different than simple schizophrenia. Some sort of neuronal firing malfunction, possibly stress-related. Many medications were tried. He was now on medication generations removed from those.

He was satisfied with the path he had taken. Terri had compared him to Rimbaud, some French poet who had burned like the sun and then never wrote again. He felt that comparison was rather unfair. He was still capable of thought. He still published the occasional paper. At first he chafed at the medication, for it was clearly holding him in, barring him from the higher realms he knew existed. But living in this slow way, he could savor life. He was happy. Before, he had never been happy. He had merely been extremely excited.

He eased into a chair. The dogs sat next to him, panting. The room was warm now. He ate his eggs. "Wow," he directed verbally, and the wow file opened.

He read: WHAT THE HELL'S GOING ON? WHY THE BLACKOUT? GOT A CLUE? CRAIG.

Blackout?

He tried to log on to the Internet, but now, apparently, the phones were down. Craig's message had come through an hour ago—probably about the time he came down from Angel's Rest.

Clearly some news was called for. "SNN," he said resignedly.

The alerted screen was filled with static. Satellites must be out.

Zeb found a local station. The announcer cast worried glances toward the camera; her voice quavered at times. ". . . have radio information broadcast from Washington in the past half hour. An apparent high-altitude electromagnetic pulse of unknown origin has caused communication failures. Many satellites are out of commission. A plane crashed in the fog at National Airport, killing everyone onboard. Emergency crews are working overtime to get phones working. Expect temporary lulls in service and please do not panic. Floyd and

Montgomery counties are presently without power." She paused for a moment as someone handed her a paper. "We repeat: There has been no known hostile action on the part of any country. There have been no reported nuclear explosions. We have just received a—"

Static filled the screen once more. Zeb sat back in his seat. Thinking.

The most likely source of an electromagnetic pulse would be a nuclear explosion in the atmosphere. Depending on the power and location, it could do a little damage to communications and power systems—or a lot. A 1962 explosion of a nuclear weapon over the Pacific blacked out Honolulu for half an hour and triggered burglar alarms. But if there had been an upper-atmosphere nuclear explosion, Zeb thought that there would be a lot more war hysteria.

Zeb constantly monitored and taped radio transmissions from their West Virginia telescope, using a vacuum tube amplifier he built in high school, still perfectly good.

He was pleased that his computer system was still working, but of course it had the best shielding he could afford. He called up the profile of the last few hours of radio broadcasting. That was one advantage of vacuum tubes—they were unaffected by radiation.

He converted that information to a simple time chart; printed it out. He took books from his long table and piled them on the floor to make room to unfold the antenna printout, which he checked against the time chart. Same pattern.

Except that it was reversed. During the times that the little blackouts occurred, his pens had recorded. They had stopped during the brief intervals broadcasting worked.

Something had happened. He saw here evidence of a pattern that would have been washed out by a solar flare.

This was no solar flare. That much was certain. And there had probably been no nuclear explosions.

An intelligent source had created this pattern. There was no way it could happen at random. No way in hell. He could think of two possibilities: humans, which was the more reasonable. Or some interstellar source.

Maybe someone—or something—was communicating with them at last. Or at least communicating in their general direction. The idea of aliens had never excited him much, though; they seemed to him a pulp pipe dream. He was much more interested in the mechanics of time, space, stars, and planets. The information he had here would be fodder for the alien-seekers, certainly. But of course there was another explanation. There had to be.

*   *   *

21

He was startled awake by the ringing phone and realized that he was stiff and cold. He'd fallen asleep in the chair. The fire was out.

"Phone," he said. Then: "Hi."

Sally's voice issued from the screen, but not her picture. He had picture capability, but few others did. Her voice was pitched higher than usual and she spoke rapidly.

"Thank God you re all right, Zeb! They just got the phones working again. Most of ours are ruined, though. I've been so worried!"

"Calm down," Zeb said. "Is everything okay there?"

Her deep, shaky breath was audible. "Yes. Yes, we're fine. The power was off for about six hours, but it came back on this morning and I put the turkey in the oven. I hope it doesn't go out again." She paused. "Are you still coming?"

"What time is it?" he asked groggily.

She sighed. "I guess you were up all night. That's no good for you. You need to keep on an even keel. It's noon. I'm a nervous wreck. Maybe we should stick together. The stores have been ransacked, but I've got lots of canned goods."

"Why don't you and John and the kids come down here?"

"Down *there*?"

"This is the best place to be if there's a problem, Sally. I've got heat, the woods are full of deer and wild turkeys . . ."

"I was thinking you should stay *here*," she said rather grumpily.

They were silent for a moment.

Zeb shifted in his chair and a spasm shot through his back. "I'll be there in about two hours. Then we can decide what to do. Okay? And I'll bring the dogs in case I have to stay—"

"The *dogs*? They shed all over everything."

"Brad will be very happy." Brad was ten and wanted collies of his own, much to his mother's dismay. "See you soon, okay?"

He got his stuff together quickly. He looked at the printouts for a moment, then packed them up too. They contained valuable information. In fact, they probably had rare information. Most radio telescopes, heavily computer-dependent, would have been knocked out by the pulse. Apparently a lot of satellites had been knocked out. Except maybe those in the Earth's shadow, depending on what the source had been. But then they wouldn't have this information either. As he picked up the box, he wavered. He didn't really know what conditions were like out there.

Still, it might be best to take them. He looked around and grabbed a Virginia Tech tote bag. He slipped the printouts inside.

He was starting to walk out the door when he remembered Craig. He went back and wrote a message that would be sent whenever traffic allowed. KIDS MADE A DIPOLE ANTENNA. PRETTY INTERESTING FOOTAGE. STRANGE CONCLUSIONS. TALK TO YOU TONIGHT. He was pleased when the message zipped off.

Both dogs fit in the cab with him. Pleiades got up as close as possible to the window, crowding the dash, staring forward, his brown eye on Zeb's side, his blue eye on the window side. Zephyr cowered on the floor, preferring to pretend that she was not zooming down the road faster than she could possibly run. He stuffed the printouts under the seat.

He made it to the interstate, then realized he had forgotten his medicine again. "Damn!" he said and smacked the steering wheel with his hand. The dogs looked at him.

He decided to keep going. He was halfway there. There were some old pills in Sal's medicine cabinet; they were probably still good.

The road was crowded, considering that many vehicles depending on computerized components might well be incapacitated. The pulse's effects must have varied quite a bit. Both the north and south lanes were bumper-to-bumper, moving steadily but slowly. Emergency flashers lined the road every few miles where wrecked vehicles were being cleared away.

The trees and hills coming toward him assumed a strange, graceful rhythm, entering him in a cadence like music.

The distance between inner and outer dissolved. He was the trees, the traffic, Ironto Mountain, the green exit sign. He was the data; he even had it memorized; he realized, there in his photographic memory, the silences and signals blazing in a strange ratio. Like a message; a signal. Sure, it would happen again. If the ratio of signal to silence held. But not soon. Maybe in another month. If he thought about it, he could work out the exact dates. He was positive.

Damn. Damn. No one knew. Well, a few people probably knew, but not many. And he didn't really know anything either. He wished he had stayed home so he could mull things over with Craig. His excitement began to grow.

The trees, the cars, the gray sky. Flowing. Drawing him along. Glowing with a lovely light. He sighed. Only twenty more miles. Then he would have to forsake this beauty, this utter, piercing harmony. He would have to take his pill. The doors to the infinite, when they opened, let in such a bright light. It would be nice if it was always this way. But he knew that after a long, trackless time of perfection, which was usually seventy-two hours more or less in the dull, time-bound world, it would all turn to shit.

The sky drifted toward him, in warping skeins of wind-driven flakes. Traffic slowed further. He pushed Pleiades aside and opened the glove compartment, keeping his eyes on the road. He rummaged around until he felt his little recorder. Good. He took it out, clicked it on, started to talk. When he was like this, he had to write, usually equations. Or talk. Talking was the next best thing.

The smell of Thanksgiving dinner filled Sal's house. The dogs pushed their way inside, and Brad screamed in delight and embraced them, ignoring Zeb. John and Sally and Annie hugged him. There was a fire in the fireplace. It was all one thing: perfection unparsed. What Terri had wanted, maybe, with him. He stared into Sal's eyes and smiled. A big smile.

She looked at him suspiciously, her long blond hair escaping from her ponytail, her apron spattered. "You need a pill, Zeb."

He nodded, smiling. "I guess." Amazing how bright everything was in here; how buzzing with sound and energy.

"Hey, Zeb!" John, his brother-in-law, shook Zeb's hand vigorously. "Hell of a day for the TV to go bonkers. I was looking forward to the Purdue game." He rubbed his large bald head ruefully and his ruddy face creased with a half-worried smile.

Then Sally was there with a pill and a glass. "Scotch?" Zeb asked hopefully.

"Water," she said sternly.

He swallowed it only because he knew it would take several hours to kick in. Several hours of ecstasy. He noticed Annie looking at him thoughtfully. "What's up?" he managed, his head filled with images, which would translate, if he had a pencil in his hand, to equations that would express the projected periodicity of the signal. He thought, vaguely, that perhaps he should ask for one.

"I was thinking," said Annie, looking startlingly like her mother at her age, with those clear blue eyes, that curly blond hair, "that right now a DNA-based drug is in the planning stages—"

"A *nano*drug, right?" asked Zeb. Everything was prefaced by "nano" in her world. He usually tried not to make fun of Annie's solemn belief in the coming power of nanotechnology, but sometimes that was difficult.

"Time to eat." Sally herded them into the dining room.

"We have some serious matters to discuss," said John as they sat down at the table. "What do you think of the blackout?"

Zeb was not in a cautious mood. "I think that it's a deliberate manipulation of the electromagnetic field of the Earth by some intelligent entity."

Brad looked at him. "Do you mean aliens? That's what all the kids are saying."

"I told you to stay inside. And don't feed those dogs at the table," said Sally.

"I'm *not*. I dropped it."

"I'm sure Uncle Zeb meant no such thing," said John, passing the mashed potatoes.

"He missed his pill," said Sally.

"Now wait a minute," said Zeb, getting irritated. He turned to Annie. "What do you think?"

"I think that it's a good opportunity to stress the development of organic-based nanotech communications, at least for backup. I'm sure my friends would think so too—if the Internet was working better. I just got logged on again when you got here, but I got bumped right away."

John shook his head, smiling faintly. "She and her friends see the world through a haze of nanotech."

"What's wrong with that?" demanded Annie. "Nearly free manufacturing! All you need is the raw materials and everything is assembled. No more factories. And no more poverty. That's just the beginning."

"You're becoming a Marxist," complained John.

Zeb was beginning to chafe. As he ate, the numbers and ratios began to fade, along with the urgency. He told himself it didn't matter. He had the data. He could work it out the long way, the hard way, when he got back. And he could also recall it, though it was more difficult under the influence of his medication. The neurons simply didn't fire in quite the same way. It made a difference. An important difference, he tried to remind himself.

"So everyone is saying that it's a solar flare," he said.

"Why do you have this other idea?" asked Annie.

"I have readout data from the antenna my students built up on Angel's Rest. Remember when you saw it last summer, when they were working on it?"

Annie nodded. "Well, then, how or what do you think is causing this?"

"I really don't know. I just know it doesn't fit the profile for a solar event."

None of them had any idea of how quickly things might change, thought Zeb. They'd had a scare, a small one. But it was over, apparently. Time to forget. Particularly if it was a natural, uncontrollable event. Solar pulses might come in waves, so they would be worried for a while, but that was all. Soon everything would be back up and running, where the damage wasn't too serious. Some places might take months to get back on track, or longer, but it would all seem as if it was in the natural scheme of things.

Until the next pulse.

Talk turned to other matters. The pleasant clatter of silverware and crystal overtook his efforts to concentrate; Sally allowed Zeb a glass of wine and they grinned at each other.

"A toast," he said. He looked around at all of them. "To—this."

"To this," they said, and Annie raised her water glass, and the dogs, sensing something, scrambled to their feet and watched. Zeb felt himself calming down. Shutting down, the other part of him said sarcastically.

Then the power went off again. John cursed and went outside to bring in more wood for the fireplace, and Sally lit candles.

"Time to go," Zeb said. The dogs hurried to the door.

"You're not staying the night?" asked Sally, surprised. "But—it's snowing, and—"

"I'm fine," he said, hugging her briefly. She always looked so harried. "Look, this isn't a new event, or pulse, or whatever you want to call it. It just takes a long time for all the repairs to get done. There was one event in Canada years ago—a solar flare—that took months to clean up. But I want you to promise that if anything happens again, you'll come to my place, all right? I'm not kidding—everything there is self-sufficient." Suddenly filled with urgency, he kissed them all good-bye. He looked long at Brad and at Annie; they, more than anyone, would feel the eventual brunt of this.

But—maybe he was utterly, completely wrong.

He fervently hoped so.

The interstate was deserted. The mountains looked strangely primitive without house lights twinkling on the ridges. The radio was blank, but halfway home it flared to life and Zeb found WKBW, a clear-channel AM station broadcasting information about shelters in Buffalo, New York.

He was puzzled as he turned onto his long driveway by tire tracks half-filled with snow. Not his. Who in the world would have come to see him? A student, perhaps?

His headlights showed that whoever had been here had left. But the door stood partly open.

After a minute, he climbed down from his truck. The dogs rushed past him into the house. Then Pleiades came back and stood in the door, as if to say, *Aren't you coming too?* Admittedly, his dogs would most likely simply greet an intruder, although they could seem vicious enough at times.

He walked to the house, reached inside the door, turned on the light.

He was stunned. The floor was covered with books; a chair stood upside down; file cabinets had been dumped. He was angry. And puzzled. What could they have been after?

Then he noticed that the few sheets of printout containing data recorded before the phenomenon occurred were no longer on the table. He was sure he'd left them there.

Who knew that he even had them?

Some people at the party knew that he'd been going to the antenna last night, but he seriously doubted that any of them would have given it a second thought or understood the possible significance. Some of the ten students working on the project might have told others about it, but again, that was unlikely to stir up any interest.

He slowly went to his e-mail setup. It had a battery backup, and the Internet was evidently working, but he didn't know what to say. Finally he just wrote: CRAIG, ANY NEWS?

After ten minutes, it bounced back. No such address.

He ran a search. It didn't take long. The results were not entirely conclusive, considering the state of everything, but he was reasonably sure that the information was true.

Craig no longer existed online.

Just past Manassas, Zeb passed the umpteenth all-night church candle vigil he'd seen on his drive up the Shenandoah Valley to Fairfax, Virginia.

He'd listened to the radio all day. There was a lot of talk about the end of the world, sin, and the best way to go about imploring God to reconsider. Very occasionally, he'd hit on some mention of the Emergency Summit that was to begin tomorrow. Astoundingly, from Zeb's perspective, official talk had changed from the solar flare explanation to "a previously undiscovered quasar," with occasional mention of an electromagnetic pulse. Excited talk from newscasters, mostly; curiously little from anyone in authority. Sound bites from various heads of state asking for order and doling out calculated phrases of soothing comfort.

Traffic was heavy for midnight. At least Zeb thought so, though he hadn't been to the D.C. area for about three years. The city must be filling up for the summit, and people weren't flying if they could help it. Zeb wouldn't have minded flying. He knew that nothing would happen again until the dates he had dropped off at Sally's on the way up, with the admonition not to let anyone she knew fly at those times. The first day was three weeks away, but he didn't know what might happen to him by then.

Ten miles of NO VACANCY signs prompted Zeb to turn abruptly into the Captain's Nest, a motel with a green blinking anchor, an artifact from long ago when Route 50 was a major corridor to Delaware beaches. He jumped from the cab into the shock of cold; traffic swished past on the wet road.

"Last room," said the elderly clerk, sliding a heavy brass key across the worn Formica counter.

Zeb opened #10 and left a copy of his tape beneath the pillow, the tape he had made on the way to Thanksgiving dinner in Roanoke, when he understood it all. He hadn't had time to reconstruct his reasoning yet. He had another copy in his pocket, had left yet another in an iron box buried on the slope above his cabin. The printouts were still underneath his truck seat.

In another fifteen minutes, he was on a quiet subdivision street. Most of the houses had turned off their holiday lights for the night.

Craig's wife sent him a Christmas card every year. He had known her in college as Craig's girlfriend, a quiet girl with long brown hair and heavy glasses, a math major. They had two children, one in college now. He had never met the kids. He had seen Craig fairly often since college at meetings, but had never been to this house.

He turned right onto Swan Lake Drive. He had ascertained that Craig's house was three houses from the corner on the right. He looked around to see if there were an untoward number of cars parked nearby, but it didn't look like it. He wondered whether to park farther away and walk and decided that might be a good idea. He thought again that he should have rented a car. Surely whoever had ransacked his house knew what kind of vehicle he had. For all he knew, a satellite had him under surveillance right now.

And, he reflected, he'd even taken his medicine.

He parked down the street. He sat in his truck for a minute after he killed the engine. It was cold; his unreliable truck thermometer showed twenty-one degrees. He hadn't called ahead. He realized that he had only the vaguest of ideas of what he hoped to accomplish here. A confrontation with Craig? Or maybe he would find that his old friend had suffered the same kind of indignities as he had.

Somehow he thought not.

The good homeowners had duly cleared their walks, but he walked gingerly because of ice. He saw no one. He stepped onto Craig's small porch and rang the doorbell.

A dog barked inside. He wondered how his dogs were doing at Sally's and rang again, holding the buzzer down. "Go away," a voice whispered at his elbow. He started. An intercom.

"I can't," he said. "It's Zeb. I need to talk to Craig."

"Craig's not here." Clara's voice.

"Where is he? Is he all right?"

There was silence again for a while. He buzzed again. The dog barked.

"Craig really isn't here," she said, sounding irritated.

"Look. I'm sorry I woke you up. I've just kind of stopped by for a holiday visit."

"Right."

He was sure she knew something. "Please. It's really cold out here."

He heard a snort. The chain rattled; she ordered the dog away from the door. She opened the door and yanked him inside by the arm. She shut and chained the door swiftly.

She turned, frowning. "I thought you lived without heat." Her hair was much shorter now and blond. She was not wearing glasses, and her blue eyes were much sharper than he remembered. She was wearing slacks, a turtleneck sweater, and heavy socks. "You look rather distinguished, despite the mountain man getup."

"Thanks, I think," said Zeb. "You look great. You were awake, I guess."

The dog growled. "Quiet, Zeit."

"Zeit?" Zeb frowned down at him. Zeit was a Doberman. Zeb had never cared for the breed.

"Spare me the jokes," Clara said. "It was my son's idea. He was studying German at the time. Come in and sit down."

Zeb followed Clara two steps down into a den that faced the backyard; a fire burned low in a stone fireplace. Zeit followed at his heels. Clara gestured toward an antique table that served as a bar. "Help yourself. The Dalwhinnie is excellent. That's what I'm drinking."

Zeb took a lot of water and a drop of whisky. He and Clara sat facing one another on deep leather chairs. Zeit's eyes as he assumed an alert pose before the fire did not leave Zeb's face. "So where is Craig?" asked Zeb.

"I don't know," said Clara. She leaned her head back against the cushion and stared straight ahead. "I often don't."

"Do you have a clue?"

"No. He just vanished two days ago. I know that he's safe, but that's all. He has very high security clearance." A resentful undertone entered her voice. "For all I know, they took him to one of those holes in the mountains. You know, those places where his family isn't allowed to go. Sometimes, Zeb, I—ah, what's the use?" Now she just sounded disgusted. "I don't know if I'm mad at him or at the government. It's had the same effect, I guess." She got up and poured herself another inch of whisky. Zeb noticed that despite her clear speech she

29

swayed alarmingly as she turned from the table, steadied herself, and walked very carefully back to her chair.

"You don't seem surprised that I'm here."

She sighed. "Look, Zeb. You may be in danger. Craig expected that you might come and he told me to tell you that—if you insisted. You seemed insistent. Believe me, you're lucky to get that much. He's told me nothing else."

"Not that my house was broken into and data stolen? Data that only he knew about?"

"Since he didn't break into your house," said Clara with a hint of anger in her voice, looking at him directly, "it seems clear that someone else knew as well. When was that?"

So she didn't know. "Thanksgiving."

"Oh. What was the data about?"

"Want to guess?" Zeb asked in a sarcastic tone.

Clara narrowed her eyes. Her mouth tightened. Zeit growled at him, raising his lips so that sharp teeth showed.

"Just joking," said Zeb with a faint smile. "I have collies. They're much better-natured. Look . . ." He hurried on when her grim expression did not soften. "I'm not sure how much you know about this, so maybe it's better not to tell you more. Endanger you."

She laughed briefly, and the dog put his head down on his paws. "Don't worry about *that*. I'm just trying to piece things together for myself. I'm sure it has some sort of bearing on what happened the other night. 'The Incident,' as they're calling it in *The Washington Post*. Craig just went around muttering, 'Out of the blue' while he threw things in a suitcase. A car came and picked him up. That's all I know. Except that he told me to tell you to lie low. Those were his words. Lie low. So whatever you know, you're right, Zeb. It's dangerous. For you anyway."

"And for you if I'm here," he said, eyeing the dog and rising as slowly as a tai chi practitioner. Zeit sprang to his feet, and Zeb felt lucky the dog didn't go for his throat.

"You have a place to stay?"

"I'll be fine. Mind if I leave by the back door?"

Clara knelt by the sliding glass door, pulling the curtain over her head, and threw an iron bar on the rug. She stood and slid the door open. "You're . . . better?" she asked hesitantly, looking up at him. She remembered, of course, his dramatic breakdown.

He smiled. "More or less."

He tramped through the snow of four backyards and looked between the houses at his truck. He considered just walking away from it, leaving it there, maybe coming for it in a few days. That's silly, he thought.

But even though he didn't turn on his lights at first, he had to—eventually. At that point, the car that nosed out from a space down the block and fell in behind him turned on its lights too. But it turned off before he reached the main road. Got the jitters, he decided. There was nothing he could do anyway.

A man was loading up the newspaper box at the motel and Zeb bought a *Washington Post*. Inside his room, the heating unit clattered. He shucked his boots and crossed his legs on the bed, shoved a thin pillow behind his back. The paper said that the summit would start tomorrow at a downtown hotel. Next he would get out his computer and log on. He had thought he ought to avoid it at least until he had time to set up some kind of decoy identity, but it didn't seem to matter now since they—someone—probably knew where he was.

He fell asleep on that thought, sitting up, the light on, fully dressed, clutching the newspaper.

When he opened his door the next morning at ten, he saw that another six inches of snow had fallen. Good. Traffic might be light. The Metro would probably be overloaded. But it was later than he had hoped. He hadn't set his watch alarm.

It was a gloomy day. He had no time for breakfast, though it wasn't good for him to skip meals. He thought about putting on his tire chains, but decided to risk going without. He could put them on later if he needed to. He shaved, unzipped his suit bag, and tore the dry cleaning bag off of his suit. He hadn't worn it since his wedding. He was relieved to find that it still fit. He stuffed eight or nine conference badges, scooped from a drawer on his way out of the house, into his pocket. This event would most likely use some sort of coded signal or bar code scan, but one of these nametags might be useful in a low-scrutiny situation.

He tossed all of his luggage into his truck cab, but didn't check out. He left the radio off as he pulled onto the four-lane road. The hysteria was wearing after awhile. He stayed on Route 50; it went straight into town. He didn't hit any congestion until he crossed the bridge. He could get no farther than the Vietnam Memorial and fortuitously snagged a parking place from someone just leaving. He checked his map; the conference hotel was only about ten blocks away. He left his down coat in the car. It didn't mesh with his present appearance. He put one of the tapes in a pocket and set out, aware that he was probably being followed.

He would have enjoyed the walk were it not for the sense of gravity

31

and responsibility that weighed on him. The gray sky spat flurries that melted on his face. The noise of traffic was muted by the snow, only partially cleared from the streets. Holiday decorations were out in full force, so it all might have seemed quite festive were it not for his worry.

Any astronomer of note knew most everyone else in that small category. Surely they all would have made some effort to get their speculations onto the Internet or to communicate it somehow. That would be anyone's first impulse.

But perhaps all speculations and speculators—if they came anywhere near the mark—had been dealt with as he had been.

As he walked, he became increasingly agitated about the situation. Maybe he should get a lawyer, even though he had never employed one in his life, not even for his divorce.

He was several blocks from the hotel when serious congestion confronted him. It was like New Year's Eve in Times Square. He pushed through the crowd. Many people were wearing headphones and then a woman appeared before him and offered him some for fifty dollars. "It's the summit," she said.

The tiny earphones nestled in his ears. He pressed onward. He heard that a session was about to start in the Magnolia Ballroom on the second floor.

Finally he squeezed against the brick wall of the building. Next to him was a gray metal door. He tried the handle, but it was locked.

Then it opened, just a few inches. A man stuck his head out and yelled, "Hey, back up, folks!" No one paid any attention, but eventually the man got the door open wide enough so that he and three others managed to slip through it. Just before it shut again, Zeb pried it open wide enough to make it through.

Inside was a corridor lined with ceramic tile. He walked briskly for a short distance, came to a stairway, and climbed to the second floor.

He emerged on red carpeting of oriental motif beneath a crystal chandelier. A lot of people were milling around, but at least there was room to walk. SNN was interviewing a woman about ten feet away; no one seemed to notice him. He grabbed a badge at random from his pocket that said DR. ZEB ABERLY, RADIO ASTRONOMY, VIRGINIA POLYTECHNIC INSTITUTE and pinned it to his jacket. He headed toward a ballroom that had one door open; it was standing room only. As he stepped inside, a guard said quietly, "Sir—"

He walked past, ignoring the guard, who followed, grasping his arm and looking at his badge. "Dr. Aberly, I must see your pass."

He felt in his pockets. "I must have left it in my room. I'll get it after this session."

"I must ask you to leave, sir."

"I'm sorry," Zeb said, his voice rising in spite of himself. "It is essential that I attend this session." He walked ahead, but the guard grabbed his arm.

Zeb shook him off and pushed through the standees, hoping to lose the guard, but another guard joined the chase. One of them grabbed his arm again and the other took the other side. Zeb struggled. "Let go of me," he said. As they pulled him toward the door, he began yelling, "They're lying! They're all lying to you! I have some real data!"

Heads turned, but in the eyes of those near him, he saw only irritation. In less than a minute, he was out of the ballroom. One guard kicked the door shut behind him. "Now, look," he said, "do I have to call a cop and have you arrested?"

Zeb knew he was out of control, but it seemed called for. He yelled again, "There IS NO QUASAR, don't you UNDERSTAND?" And then the SNN microphone was shoved in his face.

The announcer said briskly, "And here we have . . . Dr. Zeb Aberly from Virginia Polytechnic Institute. He seems to have become embroiled in a controversy. Dr. Aberly, did you say that there is no quasar?"

"He can't—" said one guard, but the other gave him a warning look. They released Zeb and stepped back. The announcer looked at him questioningly.

"That's what I said." He ran his fingers through his hair, suddenly aware of how rumpled he must look despite his earlier pains.

"And you are a radio astronomer, sir."

"That is correct. I'm a professor of astronomy. I have data that suggest that an—"

The lights went out.

In the darkness, he was grabbed once again and this time he fought harder. The emergency exit lights came on and a repetitious warning blare sounded. He was dragged bodily to the stairs and as the door closed he saw the lights come on again. The siren ceased. He felt what might be a gun in his side. "I'd suggest that you be very quiet for the next few moments, sir."

"Who are you?" he asked, but was jabbed again.

He was hurried down the stairs and down a corridor different than the one by which he had entered.

A shabby, dented gray car was in the alley, running. As the men pulled him into the alley, the passenger door swung open. Craig leaned over from the driver's side and said, "Get in, Zeb."

Startled, Zeb did so. Craig reached across him and slammed the door and they jounced down the alley, leaving the henchmen behind.

"I tried to keep you out of this, Zeb," said Craig. He had long ago traded in his heavy black glasses frames for some sleek, urbane, and stylish, but Zeb could only think of him as his old roommate, brilliant yet savvy, politically and socially, in a way Zeb had never been and never cared to be. His face, always somewhat childish, was at last beginning to reflect his true age. He was wearing an expensive-looking black overcoat, buttery kid gloves, and a cashmere scarf. The only mystery, thought Zeb, was why he was driving an old rattletrap.

"Then why did you try to steal my readouts?" he asked. Craig had chosen an alley perpendicular to the hotel and now they were in the clear.

"You still like Chinese food?" asked Craig.

"I guess. I should eat." Zeb felt in his pocket for his pills and realized that they were in his other pants. Second time in a week. Out of his routine. "What's going on?"

"Take a wild guess." Craig cut across three lanes of oncoming traffic. They careened through some scary-looking blocks, then he zipped into an empty parking space. "What luck. The restaurant is on the next block. Didn't you bring a coat? What kind of a mountain man are you?"

They got out. Zeb set a fast pace to try and keep warm. "Are we at war?" he ventured.

"Good wild guess," said Craig. "That's the general impulse, but there's a problem. At war with whom? Some entity that we have only a brief radio inkling of? Someone who, admittedly, tried to knock out our communications systems and defense satellites and did a damned thorough job of it too. Problem is, they haven't declared themselves. Now, we don't know who else besides you has the incoming radio profile. Down here." Craig steered him down some steps to a door with a half-moon window.

Warmth and the million mingled smells of Chinese food hit him—five spice, frying noodles, roasting duck. He was initially surprised to find the place packed, then realized that it must be lunchtime. An empty booth awaited them, with a small vaguely oriental-shaded light jutting from the wall. Craig didn't order anything; the waiter seemed to know him and brought tea and then hot and sour soup and then an array of vegetables, lo mein, and duck as he and Craig talked. Everyone around them spoke Chinese. Mandarin, he supposed, not that he could tell.

"I was hoping you'd just stay tucked in the mountains down there," Craig said, shoveling down noodles with his chopsticks. "I really had nothing to do with your house being ransacked. The word 'dipole' was a tag, particularly when the eyes were on every known astronomer."

"But you know about it."

Craig didn't say anything.

"And why are you feeding the public all this crap about a quasar?" Zeb put his ceramic soup spoon down. He never could eat when he was nervous. "Solar flare. Whatever. You and I know that it's not."

"You and me and the fence post, buddy," replied Craig. "And about a hundred people at the Pentagon, and maybe a couple hundred more around the world. Some people in your general situation. Not as many as you might think."

"Surely there's some plan to let everyone know—"

Craig shook his head. "Quite the opposite. Use your head. These dumplings are good. With that sauce. Eat, man. Now, just what exactly do you think people would do in the face of actual evidence of . . . well . . . just think. Massive civil unrest. Utter chaos. It's going to be bad enough. Think tanks are going all over the world to try and figure out how to cope once the . . . quasar . . . washes things out completely. I mean, who knows what that's going to be like?" Craig shrugged. "The main thing is to keep communications viable."

"So that it will be easier to perpetuate massive lies? Seems like what you want is the opposite effect. You have children, Craig. Don't you think they deserve to know the truth?"

Craig stared at him blankly. "What for? This is a matter of national—and international—security."

Zeb was flabbergasted. "You can't keep something like this a secret."

"Something like what?" Craig asked, his words slow with exaggerated patience. "This event quite resembled a solar flare or a nuclear-caused electromagnetic pulse."

Zeb nodded. "But it's what happened *during* the pulse effect that's important. The information that I recorded. . . . Look. An electromagnetic pulse—an EMP—does certain things to the ions in the atmosphere. I think that certain elements of the atmosphere were cleared away by the pulse event to make way for whatever was coming in."

"And what exactly do you think might have come in?"

"I don't *know*. All I know is that I have this information—"

"Which you need to hand over to the government. Here's the deal." Craig put his elbows on the table; clasped his hands; leaned forward. "We share with you and you become a part of our team. Like you said, this is war. At least, for the moment. An undeclared war, though; that's what makes it strange. There's still a chance that this has somehow come from a human source or a completely natural source. We're not going on the air and saying that an extraterrestrial intelligence caused the pulse. And that that's not even the whole story—that there was other information incoming at the time that in all probability was not picked up by any kind of receiver that had any kind of computer components in it. As if they only wanted certain . . . agents . . . to have it."

Zeb was getting irritated. "Are you intimating that I'm some sort of alien agent?"

"It's not me, buddy. It's the mind-set. It does seem to me that you're refusing to help. Why? And why *should* we tell the public anything more at this point? No matter how organized what you call the incoming information seems, that could be an accident. AI cryptology analysis engines need to get working on this pronto.

"But putting that aside, there are enough problems of international concern right now without everyone thinking that aliens might land. The technological infrastructure is a wreck. It's been Balkanized. Listen, Zeb. You're already marked because of what you did at the conference. So your alternative is to get a real good lawyer—and fast—because Plan B is to take the key and lock you up. Because you're nuts. There was a quick meeting after they couldn't find the printouts to decide how to contain you. There's a certain amount of hysteria in the air, Zeb. I hope it won't last, but I don't know. There are a lot of zealots when it comes to this kind of thing. I'm prepared to pull all the strings I possibly can for you. I can vouch for you. I know what you used to be capable of. Even a lot less of that is a powerful resource for us. But you're going to have to change your attitude. And pretty quickly too. Like in the next sixty seconds. I can convince them that you'll be useful. Come on, Zeb." Craig's eyes were honestly pleading. "Otherwise . . ."

The muffled buzz of a cell phone sounded from Craig's overcoat, which he had tossed onto the bench next to him.

"Your phone's ringing," said Zeb.

His eyes on Zeb, Craig took it out; flipped it open and shut. "Now it's not. I am not all-powerful, Zeb. Far from it. Say yes now. Just agree to this, all right? I have a new identity for you. The newshounds are going to be after you after that performance you gave. You are not to be found. *One way or another*. Do you understand? You can't contact anyone."

Many fears gripped Zeb. The overriding fear was deeply related to self-preservation. He knew that the wiser course would be to go along with Craig. Yet he could not. He knew that it wouldn't last long if he did. If only he could pretend, he could probably do some good—eventually. But he knew himself too well. He would soon begin to bluntly contradict people. This was something that the scientific community should be working on together. He was utterly opposed to the secrecy that Craig implied was so necessary. And if Craig tried to protect him, he would go down too.

"Is there a back door?" He whispered because suddenly his voice would not work.

Tears stood in Craig's eyes. "I'm sorry," he said. "Give us a struggle, all right? I'm going to be in trouble."

"I'm just going to the bathroom," Zeb said.

Craig shrugged, pulled a large packet from his coat pocket. He set the packet on the table and tossed his coat to Zeb. "Take this."

Zeb caught it awkwardly, and as he passed, Craig grabbed his arm and pressed a wad of money into his hand. Zeb stifled an impulse to laugh.

He pushed through the steamy restaurant, turning down a narrow hallway obstructed by boxes with Chinese writing on them.

He exited into a snowy netherworld, gray and shifting, the buildings on the next block obscured by sheets of snow. The heavy utility door slammed shut behind him. He pulled on Craig's coat, stuffing the money in the pocket without counting it. There was no one in the alley.

In front of him was a church, wire mesh covering soaring stained-glass windows. But the back door was unlocked.

He stepped into the echoing interior. He saw no one, but felt deeply comforted by a presence he had never been able to explain and had never wanted to, which he always felt in churches. Maybe it was just the memory of his mother, who had taken them to church until he had rebelled. A faint scent of incense lingered in the air. He was drawn to a bank of flickering candles. The light of the world. Truth. Knowledge. Transcendence. How far they had come since candles and faith were the only lights in the darkness.

But if Craig was right, they were entering the Dark Ages again. If Craig was right, there were few people who could stem the tide of ignorance. Especially if the government was actively on the side of ignorance and if the Internet was not functioning. He feared he lacked the temperament—the physiology—to be one of those who would become the inevitable underground. Maybe if he could contact them, they could band together somehow.

But already his world was drifting apart. An odd, diffuse, inappropriate joy edged his thoughts, even as he contemplated the bleakness of the situation. He could not contact Sally. He might walk back to his truck later, but it would surely be gone—and his pills with it. He would go to a hospital at some point and try to get more without revealing his identity. He should hurry. Once he passed a certain point, he wouldn't care.

He felt, as he stood in front of the steppes of candles casting flickering shadows, that the very architecture of the church was drawing his thoughts upward, outward. The abstract glass, dimmed by lack of sun, nevertheless lent definition to light as his neurologic architecture defined reality for him.

A new space of thought hovered round him. Speculations concerning the nature of infinity. What vast time had it taken for the disrupting wave to arrive at the Earth? Or if the origin was close, what vast time had formed up those capable of such a journey? He had grasped the edge of some of the particulars. He had the tape of his speculations—but that would be ruined, perhaps, when the next incident occurred. He also had the periodicity of his computer's lapses, which in any event would not have been difficult to find elsewhere. Unless somehow it was even now being erased from any kind of unlikely peripheral record such as he himself had unwittingly made.

The world would probably not change quite as quickly as he would. He had little to go back to. His dogs were safe with Sally. He would miss them greatly. But he might not be able to care for them very well in this new life.

He realized that he had passed the point of no return. Not because he was too far over the division's verge to care, but because he was not. He was still capable of making the decision. He would not go back. Not to his old life. Not to his old mind, the parameters of which he had carefully defined over many years to keep the light from flooding in all at once. Let it flood. The world he had staked a place in was gone. Overnight, in a blast of light out of the range of human eyes.

He put a coin in the box and lit a candle with a taper; watched it flare to life. He observed it for a moment: the blue core; the planelike whorling of the corona. There were mysteries in the sky. There always had been. There always would be.

If he hadn't been so afraid, he would have been elated.

He walked down the aisle of the church, found a door behind the choir pews, and stepped out into the silvering world.

Motive in a Fleeting Key

Late-night television. Condo in Rosalyn; exterior wall a sheet of glass; Key Bridge a necklace of lights spanning the black Potomac and Georgetown receding mounds of glimmering. S. Wayne Tell (the S. is for Sun, the first name he never uses) is thirty-two. A highly educated fellow. Doing top-secret postdoc work in bionan research and development that feeds directly to the National Institutes of Health.

Half-empty bottle of warm cheap Chardonnay; remains of a pineapple pizza in a box on the glass coffee table. He leans back on the couch, flicks between stations. David Letterman. He's always funny. Ancient now. And taped, not live. Live too undependable now. Wayne turns up the volume. New Year's, almost.

"Well, it won't be long now until they get here." Laugh. Everyone knows who "they" are. The aliens. Dave mugs earnestly at the camera. "What some folks don't realize is that they're already here. I have it on the best documented evidence that the following people are aliens. Study their pictures, folks, you can just see it in their eyes, can't you? President Rolnikov—now look at the way that lock of hair points straight up. He's either the Gerber baby, a spawn of Satan, or an alien. Now look at—oops, sorry, folks"—a picture of Letterman is shown for five seconds—"that's top-secret information, classified—" A wave of laughter—

Wayne turns off his television. It's sickening. People don't realize. They're being led to think that it's all a joke. Even now, weeks after the defining event of Earth's history. But he's been to Roswell. He

39

even got a visa to travel to top-secret alien landing sites in Russia, damn it. He knows what he's seen. Look, there, on his wall. A thousand feet of books about aliens, coverups, conspiracies. Double-stacked. How can there be any doubt? His own father abducted. Died with his own brothers and sisters and even his wife, who divorced him, thinking that he was loony. Wayne was his only friend at the end. Wayne has written letters to countless editors. A letter to the President, even. Everyone online knew the truth; everyone he hung with, anyway, before the Web went to shit.

And luckily, some of them had access to the Pentagon and other important vectors, like the NSA, and those more secret.

He leans forward, cradling the clicker in both hands. He's done the right thing. Sometimes he doubts it, but things like this make him sure. It had to be done. The momentum must continue. So that his father didn't suffer in vain. So that more don't suffer again.

So that everyone knows who the real enemy is.

Blued Duet

Marie | Tortola, British Virgin Islands | 2014

As soon as Marie stepped out of the heavy door of the Pink House and shut it ever so quietly, she was drenched in sweat. But she had to get out. She just had to. Alone.

Heat struck her like a solid force as she forsook the cool darkness of the thick-walled old house. Roadtown—on Tortola in the British Virgin Islands—seemed without inhabitants midday in June. Pastel-painted buildings—irregularly shaped, as if formed of white plaster by the hands of a child, then slapped with primary colors and set out to bake—lined the single black road. Missy, their young cook, had told Marie that they replaced a row of wood shacks swept away by a hurricane ten years ago.

In the time between her death and her bionan resurrection, it seemed to Marie that much had been swept away. Petite Marie, Al, and the infrastructure of the whole damned world. At times she felt as if she were clinging tightly to a palm tree, while anything that made sense was carried far from her on a storm surge so powerful that it was past understanding.

And she was still not healed.

Marie watched the ferry from St. Thomas buzz closer, filled with pastel blips which were tourists knocking back complimentary rum, and found herself resenting the fact that they were still alive.

But everyone else in the British Virgin Islands was happy. It seemed that the communication cataclysm sparked a powerful impulse to spend all the money one had on end-of-life-as-we-know-it sailing trips to the sunny Caribbean. They got here via coal-powered freighters or clipper ships with solar-energy-collecting sails.

Beyond the seaward row of buildings, a stony bank, studded with cans and bottles, sloped to a stone-walled waterfront. Bleached cars, missing windows and handles, flowered with rust, rested close to the buildings in exhausted attitudes.

Marie got about twenty yards down the street, which miraged away past Second Street as if more distant parts of Roadtown had been sacrificed to the sun in return for local solidity. She stopped, completely drained of energy, and took in the glorious colors of a half-finished mural on the side of a building. This entertained her for some minutes. With a start, she realized where she was, felt large and dangerously conspicuous, shrugged, and crossed the empty street.

Flies investigated four overripe mangoes in Joe Alinqua's sparsely stocked wooden fruit bins. He rose from his twisted lawn chair. "Hello, Miss Zena."

She opened her mouth, then closed it. She *was* Miss Zena here. Cloak-and-dagger stuff. As if it mattered. It certainly didn't matter to her.

Which was probably why Hugo didn't let her out alone.

"Interest you in some mangoes?" His home-rolled cigarette threw off sparks as he sucked on it. He didn't appear to care that she had been staring at the fruit with the expression of a stunned cow for several minutes. The way the orange splotches faded into green, in a sort of spotty pixillation, was quite fascinating.

"I don't know, Joe, they look about done for," she said, poking one. Yup, she was gaining the ability to kick right into conversation again. Big deal. That was some kind of syndrome, she remembered. Inability to speak until spoken to. So damned many ways for the brain to get off-track. "Got any more of those plantains?"

He went to the back of the shack to look. She unscrewed the lid from her plastic water bottle, took a swig, and recapped it. Heat was not good for the bugs in the water. They wouldn't do any harm if they made their bionan move before they got into her body; they were just useless. She congratulated herself, however, on remembering to bring them along at all. She still wasn't exactly sure how her appallingly expensive resurrection actually worked. Maybe she had when she ordered it up. She only knew what the results were, and they were strange and unsettling and unpredictable. Not as advertised.

She was supposed to have suffered something as mundane as a heart attack or stroke, but even trauma had been repairable—so those peddling the process claimed. A veritable cocktail of therapies combining the cutting edge of genetics, cell repair and regeneration, and life extension had been promised as an expensive hedge against death.

She squinted against the sun and yanked the wide brim of her straw hat lower, surprised as well that she'd had the presence of mind to grab it on her way out the door. "Yes, we're just full of surprises today," she said out loud. Her hair was just starting to grow back and she'd gotten a bad burn on her bald head a few weeks earlier. Missy had been extremely cross with her. "The sun here is *very* hot. Didn't I tell you?" she'd scolded in her faintly British-tinged accent. She'd smeared some sort of homemade pounded unguent on Marie's head. The stuff soothed and actually seemed to work. Aloe. Pointed succulent green spike-bounded tongues . . .

Her language exercise ceased as Joe emerged with a bunch of plantains. Mastering language was something toddlers excelled in. She'd had to work rather hard on it, but it was finally all snapping back into place. They said that some part of her brain had had to regrow. She couldn't remember the name for it. "Two dollars," he said firmly.

When she frowned, Joe shrugged uncertainly. Taking pity on him, she pulled several crumpled dollars from her dress pocket, not remembering when they had been deposited there, and gave him two. "Thanks," she said.

But that was the extent of her ability to speak—for a while.

She turned and looked down the street. It was dizzying. The buildings—shops and houses mingled—were all at funny angles, leaning into the street or swaying away, but never straight and foursquare. Then the concepts of "street," "Caribbean," "resurrection," "death," and "recovery" evaporated, leaving her defined only by the blobs of color surrounding her, patches of greeny blue flattened by a straight line on top, filling in between the other blobs of white, red, yellow, purple. It all spun away from her and she was left with darkness—

"Marie!" Her face registered a stinging slap. She gasped, feeling fleetingly proud to have categorized the sensation instantly. The darkness fled, coalescing into colors that once again were clear with the intensity of hallucination.

The shapes became Hugo. She recognized *him* well enough. She was still standing. One of those irritating momentary seizures . . . she was able to laugh, though.

"What's so funny?"

"Didn't you just blow our cover?" But Joe was now well back into his dark cavern and was probably completely uninterested in all this anyway.

Hugo stooped and picked up the plantains she'd dropped on the dusty road. He straightened. He tilted his head back and glared at her. "What the hell do you think you're doing?"

His face was stunningly aquiline; rather rectangular; handsome. His thick black hair was oddly straight, considering that his skin was so dark, but he said that was from the Spanish side of his family. He was a bit less than five feet tall. His shortness, he joked, came from the circus side. His body was top-heavy; his shoulders broad. His legs bore the brunt of his shortness. He was only a few years older than her. She could barely remember being without him; they'd been like brother and sister since she was ten. He was wearing a beautifully tailored linen suit so white that it made her squint. And the red of his sandals leaped right into her brain.

He had spent years trying to dull the intelligence in his startlingly pale green eyes. He wanted them blank and hooded and expressionless like those of Robert Mitchum or characters in espionage books so that, he said, people would underestimate him. She'd seen him practice this effect in the mirror when they were teenagers. At that time, her peals of laughter had not been appreciated.

Now, though, his eyes were not heavy-lidded and blank. Marie observed that he chose to throw away years of training to favor her with a glare brimming with anger, exasperation, and apology.

"Only idiots go out in this heat. Ever wonder why the streets are empty?"

Marie shrugged. "I got restless."

"Tell me, then. We can go for a sail or something." Her ketch, guarded by two French-speaking sailors who were very good with automatic weapons, was anchored in the harbor. So far it had not attracted her.

"It's not like that," she said and turned back toward the Pink House, rather dizzy.

The Pink House was not fancy. It would have been hard to outdo the other houses in Roadtown, many built during the insurance cash-in after the hurricane to satisfy bizarre sybaritic tastes no doubt previously unsuspected by friends and neighbors. Life-sized, brightly painted statues of the Virgin Mary and assorted saints vied with gilded plaster columns, which in turn might contrast oddly with a glass-and-beam stab at international style several feet away on the next lot.

The Pink House was small, modest, and solid as a rock, squatting several tiers above the main drag behind a high concrete wall with broken glass embedded on top. Easily defended, Hugo said. Bars on the windows. The tiny pool with the fountain in the interior courtyard wasn't good for much except her long, quiet, medicated soak in the middle of the heat. Everything was strictly to a purpose here.

That was the point. The pool, the thick walls, the privacy, the plainness. All for one purpose. Since coming here a month ago, after the most sensitive cell regeneration procedures of her yearlong resurrection had been completed, she'd gradually remembered scouting out this place five or six years ago. It was like that. Memories surfaced suddenly. She realized now that she'd never truly understood what it would mean to live here. At the time, it had seemed that it might be low-key, romantically local. A tropical vacation. She hadn't reckoned on an interlude of nightmares and regret. She hadn't reckoned on how it might feel if she wasn't able to leave.

She hadn't reckoned on Petite Marie and Al being dead.

Hugo unlocked the bright purple door and they trooped into the dark foyer. She kicked off her sandals and cool slate soothed her feet.

Hugo shrugged off his jacket, revealing the gun strapped to one side of his torso. The tiny palm trees on his shirt were darkened by patches of sweat.

Marie advanced into the full splendor of the living room. Two tall rattan stools tilted uncertainly in front of a bamboo bar, which had succeeded in shrugging off many large chips of a misguided coat of dull black paint, giving it a piebald mien. A magnificently ugly green Naugahyde couch hunkered on a pinkish terrazzo floor missing many stones, putting Marie in mind of a vast gap-toothed mouth. Facing the couch, in a halfhearted attempt at a conversation group, were two plump, massive red velvet art deco chairs that must have been new in the 1930s. The velvet on the arms was worn smooth, but much remained on the seat and back so one had the choice of sticking to Naugahyde or smothering and itching with the prickly velvet in the heat. A few end tables holding lamps and ashtrays and untidy piles of Hugo's books completed the picture. It lacked air-conditioning, of course. Hugo, surprisingly, was in favor of this. He said he needed to be able to hear what was going on outside.

Missy rattled some pans in the kitchen, and the smell of sizzling garlic wafted into the living room. Marie wished could enjoy Missy's coconut-based delicacies, but food didn't interest her.

Marie flopped onto the couch. She did feel better inside. It was at least twenty degrees cooler. Things seemed to move along in normal time, rather than pausing for long periods like a damaged video. "I want to go home."

Hugo went to the bar. She only saw his head over the top, then that too disappeared as he bent to rummage for his noonday beer. "You can't go home. Not yet. And I don't see that you've changed your appearance any. Wasn't that part of the plan? Confuse them, keep them guessing?" He hissed open a Greeny Man, local for a Heineken.

She had not foreseen the possibilities very accurately. The old Marie seemed to have had a large blind spot. No one could have predicted the communication breakdown, the pulses, the silence. But those who had sold her this resurrection program had not told her how difficult and painful it would be. She had not been frozen, since her team was available immediately. Instead, though clinically dead, she was immediately put on a heart/lung machine that circulated and oxygenated her blood. Then she was immersed in a cocoonlike bag filled with an organic jelly that seeped into the damaged parts of her body—her liver, her damaged lung. Experimental healers unavailable to the public spread throughout her body, taking from her DNA the necessary information for regeneration, using precise concentrations of enzymes and hormones to facilitate cell growth. She remembered only a continuum of images that, like dreams, had probably been interspersed with long periods of darkness.

Death had not been painful. Living was. And the most painful part of it had to do with the inescapable fact that her dearest ones were dead because of her.

"I think I need a new plan now," she said—to herself, evidently, as Hugo did not reply, engrossed in the intricacies of whatever was behind the bar.

She caressed the sinelike curve of a huge teal ashtray bearing the stylistic imprint of the sixties, shaped like a cartoon tear. She was supposed to touch and move as many things as possible, to the extent of actually using children's building blocks. This was spatial/tactile input. Smooth. Cool. Awaiting some long-ago smoker, dead by now, no doubt. As was she, in all ways except one.

A new plan. She wasn't sure what that might be.

But a signifying gesture seemed called for. "A gin and tonic would help me think," she said in the most authoritarian voice she could muster.

"Marie, you *can't*—" began Hugo, standing next to the television, which only Missy watched, with a book in one hand and a beer in the other. She met Hugo's frown with what she hoped was a commanding gaze. Seeing it, he sighed, set his book and his beer on the television, and stepped back behind the bar. "Maybe just a Lite?" he asked, raising his eyebrows hopefully.

"HUGO!" It was a roar. A rather pleasing roar. Unusual, but it was quite possible that she was growing a new personality along with a new brain. She'd had nothing alcoholic to drink in the past eight months. Not that she'd ever been a drinker. But right now she definitely felt driven to drink. Wasn't that what people did in the tropics, people prostrated by the heat, people who had suffered a loss, people who lived and thrived stubbornly, rebuilt and wonderfully new while all those they loved were dead, spattered about the room by a tiny bomb? And who were not found until too late because she herself had died, and things were not all that up-to-date in Paris, and Hugo himself had lain unconscious under rubble for more than a day? Her mouth trembled and she blinked.

No, no, she was through with all that. One could only cry for so long. And then dark loss stretched forever, completely uninfluenced by human pain. She stared out at the pool in the courtyard, through open french doors of incongruous polished mahogany. Beyond, in the small courtyard, bounded by brilliantly muraled plaster walls, the pool of chipped tiles bulged with hypnotically green water, as if its surface was pulled upward by a reverse gravity machine.

She was alive, stubbornly alive, she had to face that. Alive, most likely, for a very, very long time. Others, such as those who had killed Petite Marie and Al, would not be quite so lucky.

She would live, at least, to assure that. It was the only thing that gave interest to her life. A part of her knew it was idiotic and futile and small-minded that the thought of revenge gave her fierce joy. You must broaden your horizons at some point, Marie, she told herself, walking languidly toward the pool and shedding her clothes along the way. Dress, panties, that was all. They fell from a skeleton-thin frame. Tall as she was, she would probably now wear a size three. That is, if she cared to acquire clothes that fit, which she did not.

The hot sun struck her as she left the shelter of the eaves. The concrete burned her bare feet. She stepped down into the pool, which was not cool and not warm, just a soothing envelope filled with healers kept alive by special filters, healers so tiny that they were absorbed through her skin. It was the pool setup that was important about the place. It had been prepared for years, awaiting her, awaiting each new development, each of which was duly incorporated into the system. Awaiting her.

And Petite Marie.

Hugo touched the cold glass to the back of her neck. She gasped and extended her hand. He hunkered down and gave her the gin and tonic. A green cut lime floated in it.

"I'm sorry," she said.

He shrugged, and his lopsided grin did not disguise his look of anguish. With a grunt, he rose, wriggled onto a chaise sheltered by a sharp angle of shade, folded his hands across his lap, and apparently having regained self-control, rehooded his eyes. He could sit like that for hours. Marie had once asked him what he thought about during those times. "Acrostics," he had replied.

47

The gin was good. It released her mind. She'd never been very fond of alcohol, though the occasional bottle of fine wine was welcome. People said you drank to forget. That was handy. She hoped to. It might take cases of the stuff. Years. She thought of how ironic it was to have such a clear memory of loss while at the same time she had to work so hard to remember simple words. She took another resolute sip. "Bitter," "sweet," and "astringent" described it.

In the mural on the wall opposite black women carrying bananas from a strap around their foreheads and black men scything sugarcane segued into black men and women brandishing large curved swords with which they chopped at pale bland whites cowering in terror behind oddly scaled houses and trees. Haiti, she mused, as she did every day about this time, wondering if—no, hoping *that*—she was becoming gin-sodden. The previous owner had been Haitian.

"Know anything about *voudoun*?" she asked Hugo.

"Loas. Legba. Baka. Gad." His head was full of words.

"The last?"

"A guard," he said without a trace of irony, "in the form of a brown dwarf."

"Zombies," she said thoughtfully. "Maybe I'm a zombie now."

"I thought you were descended from *voudoun* queens," he said.

"Right, and their assembled ancestral knowledge waters my brain. Hugo, I know little or nothing about *voudoun*. Did you ever see me do anything with chickens except cook them in wine? And leaving a dead goat on the courthouse steps didn't seem like a very useful addition to all those lawsuits I seem to have been a party to. I've been too busy for *voudoun*. I do know that it's a real religion, not the cartoon that some people think it is. A mix of Catholicism and African spiritism. A New World hybrid. I seem to have a bit of spare time now. And I seem to be thinking odd thoughts. Funny thing about that. This process is anything but predictable. Anyway, I always thought that the other Marie Laveaus controlled New Orleans because they had the dirt on everybody. I thought *voudoun* power was just another word for blackmail." She set the glass on the edge of the pool and submerged her head. The water was deliciously cool on the bald spots. She bobbed back to her seat and took up the glass again. "Maybe there's more to it."

"A large part of the human brain seems to be mapped for irrational beliefs." Hugo took a long pull from the Greeny Man.

Marie gazed at the mural for a few more minutes. She raised one long, thin arm and compared it to the color of the people in the mural. "I want to be darker," she said.

"Your wish is my command." Hugo pulled his phone out of his shirt pocket and flipped it open.

"That thing working?"

"Got a green light. How dark?"

"The color of night," she said. "With a nice bluish sheen."

"One color of night, coming up." Hugo ambled inside while he talked. Before, she would have done this herself. Now these whims struck her, and she didn't care. Have it done, not have it done, what does it matter? Hugo had said something about changing a little while earlier. Maybe this would make him happy.

Hugo returned to the sunlight and took up his position on the chaise. "Done," he said. "Blackness special delivery. Jetpack, actually. A week, they said."

"Slowpokes."

"A lot of the time is going to be taken up by bouncing it around the world. Things aren't like they used to be. Only a few countries allow jets to fly into or over them now and they're under a lot of pressure to make it illegal. Flying without instrumentation is pretty difficult for pilots trained on pre-Silence technology, and nobody knows when a pulse will come or if it will cripple a jet in flight. After WorldSpan Flight 101 crashed into the center of Rome, a lot of governments decided that it wasn't worth the risk."

"I go away for a while and the whole world falls apart. Who's doing the skin work?"

"I figured—that lab in Costa Rica."

"Why not the one in Prague?"

"Some government agency put them out of business."

"Well. Thanks. How about some Ellington?"

"Oh, you want a party." Hugo grunted as he pushed himself out of the chaise. "Running me ragged."

"You need to keep in shape to do a good job," she said and could have bitten her tongue. Hugo's depression at losing Petite Marie was even darker than hers and much less accessible. He felt completely responsible.

He did something inside. Strange, haunting strains filled the air. Hugo emerged with bottles of gin, tonic, a tray of cut-up limes, and a bucket of ice. He set them next to Marie. "Knock yourself out," he said. "I am now your official enabler."

She concocted another drink. " 'Mood Indigo'? But it's . . . so muted. Not like that version with Ray Nance and—" She frowned, trying to remember.

"Not bad," Hugo said. "In fact, I'd say that music therapy is pretty good for you. The version you're thinking of was done in the fifties.

This one is the original 1935 radio recording. It's so striking because Ellington switched the parts of the trombone and clarinet. Put the trombone up high, the clarinet down low. It was a completely revolutionary use of these instruments. It knocked everybody out."

Hugo was the jazz expert. He was the one who'd slipped out nights, haunted the nightclubs, the blues palaces, the early morning jams, and more than once, Preservation Hall. Bunch of old fogies playing old fogie stuff, he loudly announced one morning at 2 A.M. swaying at the foot of her bed from too much to drink, then crashing over, waking grandmère who had made a horrified fuss while she and Hugo thought her strange, so very strange, that she would think that they would ever want to have *sex* with each other, an attitude that had never changed. But Hugo had infused her with something—his love of jazz and an ever-expanding knowledge of an art form that mirrored the changes in humanity that war and science had wrought in the twentieth century.

Marie's mind filled for a moment with odd fantasy. A retwisting of reality. Maybe it was born of the music itself, arising from the piano arpeggios that sounded tinny on the poor ancient recording, even as its original and stunning newness was still fresh. And the fantasy was analogous.

Maybe she could take knowledge and use it in a completely new way. Maybe she could put people—masters, as these musicians were masters—into a new situation, as the musicians had been thrown into the milieu of Ellington's environment, and the hothouse evolution of jazz. What emerged might be so new as to be unforeseeable, so powerful that it might be able to use the silences to catapult humanity to an entirely different level. Or solve the mystery altogether.

Why depend on some government to do so?

"This was his first band?"

Hugo nodded. "One of the earliest. Not the first."

"He had many."

"Right. Many orchestras, many bands, many trios and conjunctions of artists. But his genius was that he never tried to imprint yesterday's orchestra on today's. He used the unique musical talents of each musician in a unique way, accented their strengths. He even said that their limitations spurred his creativity. Sometimes I try to imagine what it must have been like. All those voices at his command, totally dedicated musicians who had made it to the top, people drunk not on liquor, because he had ways of harassing boozers if drinking interfered with work, but drunk on jazz, something utterly new, something the world had never seen before."

"Something that the world had never seen before," echoed Marie, her eyes closed, the music rearranging her mind instant by instant, but the instants were all related to each other and lovely, lovely, lovely. Distant in time, yet powerfully present. "That's the only thing to do, Hugo. Create something that the world has never seen before. Don't you think?"

"You think for me," he said companionably, then "Mood Indigo" was over and they moved on through "Take the 'A' Train," "Black and Tan Fantasy," "Solitude," and "East St. Louis Toodle-OO." "Which was actually 'Toddle—OO,' but the record company decided that didn't make sense," Marie heard from Hugo's court as the hot afternoon unwound slowly toward evening and the smell of chicken-coconut soup actually began to seem enticing to Marie and when she realized this she knew that Drink had worked; she had Forgotten.

For the moment.

"Why did you let me drink so much?" she moaned to Hugo the next morning as she lay on the couch.

"To teach you a lesson," he said. He had taken one of the velvet chairs. His legs stuck straight out. Today he was wearing a shirt covered with large orange flowers. They clashed hideously with the red velvet. Marie closed her eyes.

"You'd evidently forgotten the lessons you learned in Chicago. Remember that night you and your girlfriends went down to State Street?"

"Twenty years ago? You know I don't," she said. "Sadist."

"You didn't even remember the next day," he said. "And it seems to have worked out all right. The aftermath is keeping you from wandering down the street."

"Which was more interesting than this," she said, sitting up. A soggy washcloth fell from her head. "Where's the system?" Her computer. "I know it's around here somewhere."

"You're supposed to stay away from that stuff."

"Bullshit," she said. "I'm ready. I had a hole in my heart, not in my brain."

"Actually, Marie," he said softly, "you had a hole in your brain as well. A rather large one, relatively speaking. They used dumdums. That's why it's been so difficult for you. They had to re-create embryonic conditions in your brain so that specialized tissue would grow again. And after that everything had to be remapped, relearned. You probably don't even remember all those months. You had no control over any body functions. They thought that there was a strong possibility that you wouldn't ever remember who you once were. But apparently some important regions of your brain were damaged only minimally, and one day you just—woke up. Only for a few minutes, then for a few hours a day. During the first pulse, I thought we'd lose you when the power went out. But that's when you turned the corner. You had lots and lots of music therapy while you were regenerating. Almost nonstop."

"A lot of Ellington?"

Hugo grinned. "I guess there was a heavy concentration of Ellington and jazz in general. It stretches the mind. The therapists got in as much classical as they could slip past me. They had a lot of studies backing them up. Pretty ordered stuff and that's what you needed. But even they could see that the jazz made your brain activity jump for joy, as it were. Sorry. Bad joke." "Jump for Joy" was an Ellington piece.

After a long pause, Marie asked, "Why didn't you tell me?"

"Doctor's orders. You had enough to deal with. You've been doing pretty well for three or four weeks now. You've been deemed stable enough to do without an army of technicians and nurses."

Marie flopped back on the couch. Her stomach roiled. It had not been necessary to seal her in a metal cylinder to await the regenerative power of future technologies. She imagined being sealed in the metal cylinder. She sat up.

"We have to bury Petite Marie."

She thought she could hear his heart beating from across the room. Finally he said, "Why don't you wait, Marie? When you're better, you can decide."

"She's dead, Hugo. I can't bear to think of her being in that cylinder. Whatever's left." By the time Hugo had regained consciousness in the hospital, what was left of Petite Marie had been intercepted, finally, by Marie's Paris team. Not knowing what to do, they had put her in the cylinder and filled it with the fluid that would sustain life. But this was only supposed to work if the individual had been dead for less than forty-five minutes and was relatively whole. What had happened was a horrific travesty. Al had not wanted any part of it for himself. Per his wishes, Al had a funeral in Paris, attended by his mother, his three sisters, countless friends, and many hangers-on who were bitterly disappointed when his will was read.

"You might want the genetic material," said Hugo, and she knew it was an effort for him to keep his voice steady.

She wiped tears from both cheeks with the palms of her hands. "I've thought about it a lot, Hugo. Really I have. Sure, I could have some zygotes created. I could carry one of them to term. And then I'd have a baby that looked like Petite Marie. But she wouldn't be her.

She would never be her. Petite Marie is dead, Hugo. If ever I have another child, I don't want her to have . . . my dear one's face. It wouldn't be fair to the new child. Don't you see?"

She looked up and saw tears tracking Hugo's face. Marie rose. The washcloth fell from her lap to the floor. She sat on the wide arm of the chair and leaned over, awkwardly embraced him, rested her head against his as he cried at last.

Petite Marie's funeral took place two months later in New Orleans. It was just herself, Hugo, and the priest in the small old church on a November evening. Faint rock music from a block away came in through the open windows. Hugo had ordered vast banks of flowers, and the scent was overwhelming. The priest's intoning spiraled outward, echoed from the cool stones.

Her own death certificate was filed in the courthouse. Petite Marie's death certificate was in the courthouse as well. To her mind, the date on both of them was correct.

And Hugo was right. She couldn't come back yet. For one thing, her killers were still at large and did not know that she had lived. But even if that were settled, she realized, she wasn't sure that she wanted to return. She didn't even want to slip inside the town house in which she'd spent her entire life, though a secret visit would have been easy to arrange. It was the home of another person, another Marie, and was being kept for that dead person by one trusted housekeeper dusting, polishing, watering the plants.

The ride to the cemetery was cool, inside the black bulletproof hearse. It seemed to Marie that she was riding through a foreign country, though she knew every inch of the route by heart. Or someone she had once been did. Hugo stared out the window. Marie reached over and took his hand. He sighed and looked at her. "Stop blaming yourself," she said. She squeezed his hand, which sat dry and still within hers. She was aware that, against her wishes, Hugo had indeed saved the DNA of Petite Marie. It was stored, frozen, against the time when he, apparently, thought she might change her mind. She had decided not to tell him she knew. It was his way of dealing with his grief. Petite Marie had meant as much to him as she had to her and Al.

During the time leading up to the funeral, Marie tried to get interested in the workings of her city once again. Hugo had overseen them as best he could during her months in the South American clinic. Everything, from garbage collection to online public school education, was in an uproar. At Hugo's insistence, she got in touch with her lawyer, Dighton, the only person in New Orleans who knew she was alive, and together with Hugo set up some lines of command that would force order into the system and allow her to keep track of things from a distance. Dighton pointed out to her that there had been a hue and cry from certain quarters that if only Marie Laveau were still here, the pulse-caused pandemonium would not be so overwhelming. Not only that, her enemies were gaining power and dismantling all the good she had done for the city, taking advantage of the problems generated by the Silence; exacerbating and profiting from them.

She listened with distant interest. Her mind was elsewhere. What difference did her city—her past—make now? She read her obituary with satisfaction. Only one thing was on her mind. Revenge.

Yesterday afternoon had been fruitful after a week of frustration. On a quiet side street, deserted in midday, the painted wooden sign said MADAME NIGHTWING, COSTUMING. Hugo entered without knocking; Marie followed.

It was dark inside, so as to keep the fine silks and satins from fading. Bolts of fabric made the narrow stairway almost impassable. Everywhere she looked, magnificent stripes and patterns, brilliantly dyed, were piled from ceiling to floor on sagging shelves. Hugo interrupted Madame Clarissa Nightwing, an ancient, massive woman, as she stood at a drafting table sketching.

Hugo did all the talking. Marie stood well back in the doorway, her face covered by a fine veil, her hair free, her bare arms the color of night, with a tiny white spot on her forearm, like a reverse freckle. Nightwing gasped on seeing Marie and crossed herself. Marie never spoke a word, but gave herself an inner nod of satisfaction. The rumors would begin—now.

Hugo took out his wallet, flipped it open, and slowly counted out a large sum of money; set it on the table next to Nightwing's drawing. In a low husky voice, Nightwing answered his questions concerning who had commissioned the clown suits; how much they had paid. She did not know their names, but she had observed them quite closely. One had a scar across his cheek, the other wore a necklace with a scorpion carapace sealed inside.

She had been threatened with death by those men after the detail of the clown suits had come out in the paper, but that was nothing to her, she said with a toss of her head. They had told her not to talk. Did they think she had never stared death in the face before in this rough town, in her long life? Legba protected her. She stared knowingly across the room at Marie when she said this. She had not, of course, had any idea what the suits were to be used for. *Mon Dieu!* But she had not, she admitted, breathed a word to the police. Hugo said something in a sympathetic tone about there being certain lines one could not cross. Nightwing nodded emphatically and scooped up the money.

Hugo worked the streets.

The men were apparently hiding out somewhere in the Caribbean. Even those who had commissioned the hit might find this information difficult to come by. Marie's network was fine-tuned, based on a delicate web of *gris-gris* that stretched back for a century. Subtle, knowing pressures from Hugo worked through the system, forcing their aliases to the surface.

But that was all they had.

The limo bumped into the St. Louis #1 Cemetery and squeezed through the narrow roadways. It could not make the last turn. The driver opened her door and she stepped out. There, around the corner, was the Laveau mausoleum.

"I am the resurrection and the life," the priest said before they slid the small coffin inside, next to those of Grandmère and her mother. Marie thought, I am resurrected; I am alive, but what does it matter? Life must be filled with something to be of any interest or importance at all, and that was something that she did not have. Give me *that,* she called out to the invisible stars, to an invisible God. Give me *that*!

They slid the coffin inside. Marie turned and walked away, Hugo by her side.

BREAK

The Washington Post, May 4, 2013
Metro Section

The phone was down for the fifth time this month when Willie Smith dialed 911. He was unable to call the police or an ambulance when he needed them. As a result, he is suing Southern Bell for injuries he sustained during an armed robbery of Pawn-a-Rama, the T Street shop he has owned for twenty years. "I pay my phone bill," said Smith. "I expect service."

This is one of many such lawsuits clogging court dockets all over the country. Phone companies are increasingly using the defense that the interruptions are "an act of God."

Mr. Smith has also filed a suit against his HMO, which refused to provide him with nanotech devices that might knit the shattered bones of his hands and face in one-quarter of the time nature might take. The HMO, MidSouth Services, claims that these devices have not been fully approved by the FDA and that their efficacy is presently in doubt.

Mr. Smith's lawyer, Endine Singer of Candillio, Sweat, Bean, Magnifico, and Crumbed, alleges in a separate suit that HMOs are putting pressure on the FDA to slow the approval process, and that certain components that might help Mr. Smith have indeed been approved. "These little buggers are going to be expensive as hell. There's plenty of money on the move under certain tables in Washington to assure that they are. You can quote me on that." Ms. Singer's suit alleges kickbacks from HMOs in return for a slowing of the approval process.

Diminuendo in D.C.

Zeb | Washington, D.C. | 2014

The Post Office steps were magnificent. Zeb often stood at their foot for a time, as he did today, allowing a slow rearrangement of his perspective. Glowing white marble fanned out at street level and narrowed to an apex promising a concentration of energies, like a sort of lens. It was stimulating to let his wide thoughts flow upward and then focus at doorways dwarfing humans.

It was an excellent, crisp winter morning; the air so cold that he could not smell the smog; the sky intensely blue behind the white, white building. Yesterday it had rained and he spent the day in the library reading astronomy and physics journals curiously empty of any information relevant to the Silence. Still, they had sparked some thoughts.

Zeb drew his small notebook from the inner pocket of Craig's overcoat and tried to extract a pen or pencil from his shirt pocket, where he kept his enormous found collection. But his pocket would only hold so many and he'd stuffed them in tightly. When he pulled on one of them, they all came out and bounced across the sidewalk. He let them lie, like so many pickup sticks, and began to write.

He stood writing for well over an hour. Behind him at the bus stop, many buses had come and gone. He finished with a sense of release and accomplishment and closed the notebook. He had an impulse to climb the steps and look at the boxes, as he often did, rows of glass-fronted boxes with brass frames. Each the same, but with different contents. He was getting hungry. He reached into his pants pocket and felt the dollars some woman had given him. Enough for some coffee and a grilled cheese at a greasy spoon down the block. He woke up about once a month with a good deal of money in his pocket. Each time he thought he must have forgotten where it came from. Either that or someone was putting money in his pockets while he slept, which seemed to him an ironic twist on the paranoia he tried to fight when he was able to notice it.

He heard the idling of another bus behind him, and someone grabbed his arm. Come on, he heard, and he was pulled toward the open bus door.

"Hey!" He turned angrily.

"Get on, I said. Now!" It was Craig, his face tense.

"I'm not sure I want—"

Craig pushed him up the steps and the driver closed the door. Craig stuffed some money into the box and said, "Back of the bus." There were only a few people onboard, sitting behind the driver. He and Craig sat facing each other on some seats in the back.

"Now, look—"

"How did you find me?" asked Zeb.

Craig pulled a knife from his pocket, unfolded it, and before Zeb knew what he was doing, sliced the top button off the coat he'd given Zeb. He folded his knife, slipped it into his pocket, lowered the window, and tossed the button out. "Did you think I'd just let you go? I figured that you probably wouldn't like my offer."

"Any more of that stuff here?" asked Zeb, holding out his arms and looking at his sleeves.

"Not any more."

"Would you tell me?"

"Yes."

"Who else knows about it?"

"Nobody. We all operate in a pretty insular manner. And even if they did, I convinced most everyone that you're just a harmless idiot."

"Thanks. I guess. That means I don't have to be afraid of trying to get my job back? It would be real nice to have better access to up-to-date information."

"Then you wouldn't seem like a harmless idiot anymore, would you? Furthermore, without a dependable Internet, telephones, and transportation, not to mention the fact that each pulse sizzles the computer components in the big telescopes, there really isn't much up-to-date information. How many pulses since the first—three? But I don't have much time. Just listen. I'm trying to organize a countermovement. This is getting out of hand. You were right. I was wrong. The hysteria is growing. Something terrible has happened."

"What?"

"A hotel where an international radio astronomy conference was taking place was blown up."

"What?"

"Yes. Supposedly they were preparing a press statement about the incoming information. The information that you presumably got from your dipole antenna. That information proves, much more than the fact of the pulses, that this is being caused by an intelligent source. It's extremely organized; clearly a code."

"That's so. But . . . I just don't understand. About this suppression."

"When is the next pulse going to happen?"

"Next Tuesday."

"How do you know?"

Zeb opened his notebook and reached for a pencil.

"Just kidding," Craig said. "We don't have time. But how do you know?"

"Because the incoming information sets it up. The information that I recorded. It's not a secret I want to keep, you know. Want me to call *The Washington Post* and tell them?"

"No!"

"But why not?"

"Hoo! Top-secret classified, buddy. They'd be all over you. The problem is that they don't know what to make of it."

"That's a bunch of crap."

"No. Swear."

Zeb shrugged. "Well, especially if they're killing off everyone who might have a clue. Are you sure these people that are trying to keep this from getting out aren't just buying up stock in rail, steam, and zeppelin travel?"

Craig looked out the window for a few beats. "All right. I'm going to be honest with you. In my opinion, something very strange has been happening in my division. Not that we all know each other or anything. We're actually scattered throughout a lot of government agencies and a lot of us are abroad as well. Moles. But there's a kind of bizarre hysteria. A kind of Earth-first xenophobia. What makes people so nationalistically nuts? So that they tear apart whole countries based on ethnic background? This is kind of the same effect, it seems to me. The sacred ground of our ancestors we were here first mind-set. Racheted up to intense levels."

Craig leaned forward, put his elbows on his thighs, and clasped his hands. His mouth tightened and he shook his head back and forth a few times. His face was drawn and weary-looking; his eyes had a bleak cast. "I—well, actually, I'm sorry to say that I have proof that a small cadre of people in our government actually was responsible for the deaths of those astronomers. That's why I'm afraid."

The bus stopped and the door hissed open. Craig tensed and stared at the middle-aged woman who took a front seat. He kept watching her as he continued. "I began to suspect a few months ago. It was getting to be pretty clear that most everyone else shares a mind-set that I wasn't relating to. They were even developing their own slang. Anyway, don't think this is all necessarily your government doing this stuff. Well, it is in a way, I suppose. They have a lot of powerful resources at their command. They don't even have to put anything in writing. Carte blanche; national security at stake."

Zeb watched gray stone buildings give way to a block of small shops and restaurants. He tried to understand what Craig was telling him. "You know, I never said that aliens were coming. Did I? I think that I just said an intelligent source was strongly indicated. And who knows how far away they might be? Think about it. Whatever has reached us was probably sent ages ago."

"Yes, well that's your weak alien theory. Aliens might be fun and interesting. They might reveal something about the universe, something about ourselves. To these folks, especially now, that resembles the dilemma of the daughter of a fundamentalist Jewish sect deciding to marry the son of a fundamentalist Moslem sect. An open-minded attitude must be prevented at all costs. And a surprise attack would suit them. Mobilize the world. Remember Pearl Harbor? Rumor has it that Churchill knew what was going down. He didn't tell us because he needed us in the war. There might be a lot of idiotic scientific types who want to figure out what this intelligent source is, right? Try to communicate with them. Give those nasty extraterrestrials the upper hand. Give too much away. In fact, they have a plan to try and make the real picture seem like complete bunk. It will probably work unless there's something definitive and powerfully convincing opposing it. Verifiable."

The bus jerked to a stop. The woman got off and two men got on and took separate seats toward the middle of the bus. Craig leaned closer and spoke so quietly that Zeb lost some of his words.

"I have a small network. Very small. I've been trying to link up with others. They must be out there. It's not easy when everything is down. I wish now that I'd spent less time doing physics and more time playing golf." His maniacal laugh startled Zeb. Craig extricated a thick envelope from a pocket and tucked it into Zeb's coat pocket. "Least I could do. On short notice. Like I said, a lot in the pot. Don't go back to the Post Office. You go there at least twice a week. You might consider changing your habits somewhat too. Move to a different city, even. One of the ploys they might use is to try and put out the information that anyone who has the kind of information you have must be one of the aliens."

"What?"

"Sure. Witch hunt. Why the hell would you set up that antenna? Pretty damned clever the way you pretended from way, way back that you were nuts, eh? You just had to get to that particular part of the world and get your setup ready at the right time. You've been planning this for a long, long time, Zeb. I mean, we don't know how long you live, how long you've been here . . ."

Zeb stared at Craig.

"They're military for the most part, Zeb. They're not scientists. Money is pouring into their pockets. Plenty to siphon off without anyone noticing. Or even caring. And I've made myself part of it too, I guess. Take care. And save the other stuff. It's important. Wish I had more time, but I've got to go. Keep well. Hang in there." He rose, grabbed the overhead bar, clapped Zeb on the shoulder. The bus shuddered to a halt. The doors hissed open. Craig turned back. "And Zeb—"

He hesitated for a moment, looked at Zeb as if he had something important to add.

But he didn't. He dashed from the bus and into the door of an office building.

Zeb leaned back in the plastic seat, stunned, as the bus pulled away. He was not all that surprised, he told himself. Yet it was amazing. You'd think that "they," whoever "they" were, would want all the information they could get. Instead, they were suppressing it.

He jolted, unseeing, to the end of the line. The bus driver changed off, tapping him on the shoulder before he left. "Great day for a nice long ride, eh?"

Zeb wangled a transfer from the new driver, which was a minor miracle, and changed buses. He rode to a new part of the city. New for him, anyway, in his new mode of living. Near the zoo. He'd always liked Rock Creek. He stepped out amid a swirl of exhaust at the Sheraton Hotel. It was dark. Leftover Christmas lights shone out from restaurants and bars.

Everything was in a spin. New territory. New agenda. More danger. And he held some kind of key that could be deadly to him? The world seemed highly absurd.

He was tired, dizzy, dirty. He reached inside his coat, felt the envelope, teased it open without taking it out, and pulled a couple of bills from it. He stared at them. They were hundreds. He walked into the lobby and asked for a room. When the clerk told him they had no rooms available, Zeb put the three bills on the counter. He and the clerk, a young man with hypergroomed hair and too-stylish glasses, looked at each other. Zeb made his face say, *I am an important academic. A bit eccentric, perhaps*.

The young man did not seem to understand what his face was saying. Maybe it would be best to talk.

"I know I look terrible." He tried to smile. "My BMW broke down in Maryland last night and I had a heck of a time having it towed and getting here."

The young man nodded and slid him a key card. "How many nights?"

"Just one."

"You get change then."

Zeb had been showering in shelters with little privacy. He soaked in the tub for a long time. He looked at his filthy clothes lying on the floor. He couldn't believe he'd been wearing them. He couldn't bear to put them on. He ordered some from the lobby store and had them sent up. He wore pretty standard sizes, but these hung big on him and he had to send the pants back for a smaller size. He asked the boy who brought the clothes if they could spiff up his coat. The boy looked at it doubtfully, then said, "We'll try." Zeb had emptied the pockets already and handed it to him.

He had a large fine meal in his room. Lobster and steak. What had happened with Craig? Had Craig jolted him back to reality? What an odd reality to be jolted into. Hunted as a possible alien.

Finally he opened the fat envelope Craig had given him. He found $9,700 inside. A bum could live on that for a long time if he didn't waste it like he was tonight. He could buy a small business. A used car to sleep in. A trip to Paris.

A bus ride to the Valley to see his dogs and Sally.

There was a small packet of thin brown paper, folded. Zeb unfolded it and three diamonds slid onto the quilt. At least it they looked like diamonds. Maybe they were something else. Some kind of new information technology. That was the most probable thing. He rewrapped them and stuck them in the envelope.

Zeb considered getting a job. He felt unusually clearheaded. Maybe he just hadn't been eating right. But wouldn't he need a new Social Security number? Maybe he could just wash dishes somewhere or something. Some kind of cash job where people didn't ask questions. He really needed to think about everything. Maybe he should go to a clinic, get some medicine. Tomorrow he should call Sally, let her know he was all right. Enough of this hocus-pocus. Craig must be mistaken about all that nonsense. Maybe Craig was going nuts too. Or maybe he'd hallucinated everything Craig had told him. He flipped open his notebook, paged through all of his work. What did it matter?

His coat came back, mended and cleaned, with a new button, around midnight. He was impressed, but the boy said they had a lot of international travelers and everything was open twenty-four hours. "Even the barber shop," he said pointedly, looking at Zeb's clean, but lanky, shoulder-length hair.

Zeb lay down to sleep, but tossed restlessly for an hour. Then he got up. The sensation was familiar. Things were building again. It was almost two o'clock in the morning. But he had to walk.

He dressed in his new clothes. Mighty fancy for the street. But they seemed as if they would be sturdy; wool. Damned expensive. He looked at the tag he'd torn off and read that they were embedded with some kind of dirt-eating microbe. He laughed. They certainly wouldn't go hungry. His boots were still all right. He rolled up the extra pair of socks he'd bought and stuck them in his coat pocket, along with his notebook and the packet.

He sat on the edge of the bed and flipped on the TV. A replay of the midnight news. From reading newspapers, he knew that when broadcasting wasn't working, people could go to centers to hear and see taped news or subscribe to a taping service.

He saw a fire in Northwest, a murder in Maryland, a robbery on Wisconsin Avenue, and then heard "Police are investigating the death of a homeless man found on a bench at Dupont Circle last night at 10:48." The camera panned a gurney; the emergency crew shouted angrily at the cameraperson. "Hey, lady, the dead deserve some dignity!" But they'd gotten a distant shot of someone who looked a bit like Craig. It was hard to tell. But then the newscaster said, "He has been tentatively identified by police as one Craig Sinclair. The weather tomorrow—"

Zeb found it hard to breathe. He couldn't move. It had to be a nightmare. He had to be dreaming. The objects in the room became distant. Then they became menacing. The colors were bright but disconnected from objects, flat planes intersecting here and there. A black box, in front of him, with flickering pictures. A doorframe brightly lit from within. A pattern of interlocking snakes at his feet.

Why was he sitting here in these clothes? Where had they come from? He touched one hand with the other. Were they both his hands? But those were his boots. Yes.

He stood, shucked his coat, tore the strange shirt off, ripping buttons. He pulled off his boots and peeled off his trousers, kicked them aside. He found his real clothes on the bathroom floor with a sense of tremendous relief. Who had put them there? He was so dizzy. There wasn't enough air in the room. What was he doing here anyway? He dressed hurriedly and pulled on his boots without tying them. Maybe there was a fire in the building; that was why it was so stuffy. He grabbed his coat and ran out the door. He had to take the stairs because there might be a fire. That was what you were supposed to do.

He pushed the emergency bar on the ground floor and burst onto the street, hearing an alarm go off, sharp and loud, behind him. He saw that the police were half a block away, blue lights flashing, at the lobby entrance. Was that the clerk from the haberdashery shop they were questioning?

Zeb plunged off the sidewalk and stumbled down into the roaring darkness of the Rock Creek ravine. Holding on to a tree, he vomited. Maybe he had food poisoning. He washed his mouth with creek water and spit it out. If he wasn't sick before, he'd be sick now for sure.

He crawled up under the bridge, onto the concrete apron. It was a very high bridge, and the thunk of traffic as cars left the bridge and dropped down half an inch soothed him, along with the running of the river over winter rocks. He buttoned his coat, pulled a rock beneath his head, and fell asleep.

The next morning he walked into a convenience store ten blocks away. He warmed up a biscuit in the microwave and poured some coffee. He hoped they wouldn't be suspicious of the hundred-dollar bills he'd found in his coat, but he automatically felt in his pocket and pulled out a ten, change from the hotel.

He stopped and stared at the *National Inquirer* headline:

ALIENS RESPONSIBLE FOR BROADCASTING SNAFU; ALIEN CHILDREN LIVING ON EARTH

There was a picture of a big-headed bald child next to the headline, captioned:

IS YOUR CHILD AN ALIEN?

The woman behind him, holding a quart of malt liquor and a package of gummy spiders, nudged him. "People never get tired of believing in aliens, do they? Kinda like Santa Claus for adults."

"Mmm." Zeb patted his notebook, crammed into Craig's inner coat pocket. His picture of the transformed radio sky.

Was it the only one?

*   *   *

Tuesday morning did not so much dawn as develop, slowly, in tones of black and white. Zeb watched white breath puff in front of him as he walked over the Rock Creek Bridge, felt the bump and sway of the bridge through his feet as traffic passed him. The cold burned exhalations of cars smelled ashy. The rocks below had delicate skirts of white ice.

He did not have a watch. But it would not be long. Better to be out walking than inside the stuffy shelter. The sky released its first fat flakes of snow as he stepped off the bridge, headed south toward downtown.

He thought about the diamonds. He was hoping that they contained ionization information. The pulses and incoming information would have created a unique ionization situation in the upper atmosphere, which would yield a lot of clues about the nature of the transmission. Surely the diamonds were read-only. But how to read them?

The few lights burning in the windows of the massive brick apartment buildings edging Connecticut all went out at once.

By the time he got to S Street about twenty minutes later, Connecticut's wide swath was clogged with stopped vehicles. A cacophony of horns was a measure of the frustration index. Pedestrians swarmed around the cars. The door of a health food store stood open; inside Zeb saw that the shelves were empty. At a gas station a few blocks from Pennsylvania, he saw a man pull a gun from his pocket and wave it around as he exchanged shouts with another man wielding a crowbar like a baseball bat; Zeb crossed the street and continued his walk. He thought that it might be a good day to spend at the Library of Congress—if they didn't close it down.

But by the time he passed the World Bank, the streets were thick with stalled cars, people, and rapidly accumulating snow. Zeb's hatless head was soaking wet. A woman nearby pounded a pay phone with a rock. Coins gushed out, but she ignored them. "Fuck!" she yelled each time she bashed it.

Zeb sighed. Not the best day for a thoughtful stroll.

BREAK

The Washington Evening Star, January 15, 2015
Guide to Top Stories

In the wake of a massive power outage, the President declares the fourth National State of Emergency in a year. A-1

Officials estimate that it will take two to four weeks to restore telephone service, as long as another pulse does not set them back. A-3

World financial markets in chaos. The Stock Market's 80 percent plunge echoed in London, Tokyo, and Beijing. D-1

Food riots in Berlin leave 500 dead. A-22

The recently formed ENN, Emergency News Network, had its first test last Tuesday. A network of small planes and retrofitted steam vessels carry news to affiliated members. A-7

Latest Bicycle Courier listings for the Metro Area. B-1

Emergency propane, food, and water sources. B-2

Shelter locations. B-5

Newspapers make stunning comeback due to television and Internet failures. D-1

Freedom of Information test case denied hearing by Supreme Court; broad interpretation of War Powers Act cited. A-10

Divine Horsemen Glissando

Marie | Haiti | 2016

The messenger came at dawn, but Marie had been awake for hours.

Several years after Petite Marie's death, Marie's ketch was tied up at Port-au-Prince Harbor, home to Jean and Jacques, her French terrorist bodyguard/chefs.

She and her crew had not been in Haiti long. The trail of Petite Marie's killers, cold for a very long time, had been suddenly revived through a small carelessness that only someone as relentless as Hugo would have noticed. And it led to Haiti.

She generally slept little and lightly, and at 4 A.M., a beep alerted her that the Internet was available, which was quite rare in this post-Pulse world. She opened her eyes but did not move from the tattered couch where she had fallen asleep. Rain pattered on the tin roof of the mountain shack she had lived in for the past month, waiting for Hugo to cook his information. Or his informants.

Marie was not happy about being in Haiti. She had at last put the murders, which divided her life into before and after so much more powerfully than even her resurrection or the Silence, behind her. Because of her own nature, because of her heritage and because of her position, she should never have had a child. It had been deeply irresponsible. Hugo reminded her that her mother and her grandmother had both seen fit to have children. Marie said that they'd lived in different times and Hugo snorted, remarking on Grandmère's rum running.

Now anger and guilt consumed her once more.

The computer beeped again. A gust of wind rustled the thick tropical forest surrounding the shack.

She sighed. It would be wasteful not to use this opportunity.

Turning her left wrist upward, she pushed hard on what looked like a small tattoo of a snake, though she couldn't see it in the dark room. Beneath the snake was a hormonal delivery system that she was trying not to use. But if she didn't, she was not functional. She was either exceedingly angry or else she didn't give a damn.

It would take a few minutes to kick in.

She sat up and fumbled for matches; lit a kerosene lamp on the table next to the couch. In its soft glow, she unrolled her scrolled computer and pulled the touchpad into a suitable shape; made the screen portion a nice-sized square and snapped it with her finger to stiffen it. She touched the icon that would connect her to whatever satellite system had suddenly become operant and leaned back on the tattered couch.

Webwork was now a privilege of the very rich. Marie was an investor in SignalCycle, a company that continuously readied satellites in order to replace those that fried each time a pulse shot through the atmosphere. The pulse-sensitive components were kept in exceedingly pricey shielded boxes until needed. This effort provided only a sheer lacework of communication time, expensive and effervescent compared to the former powerful gridwork that was the glory of the recent millennium. But it was better than nothing—if you could afford it.

Regular telephone service was just as rare. Municipalities waged a constant battle against the Silence—*El Silencio*—but constantly replacing melted computer chips and transformers was terribly expensive.

The search was on for organic alternatives. And nanotech alternatives. Or, possibly, both combined: bionan. The changing tides of technology had shifted little in Haiti, which had exceedingly low levels of technology to begin with. It was an island—before and after—with rationed electricity and running water only for the rich. Its only wealth was a surfeit of anger at whoever was in power.

But Marie and Hugo weren't here for the stability.

Marie leaned backward and cranked open the wooden jalousies, amplifying the roar of a nearby waterfall. Though basically a diva of information, she didn't feel very divalike this morning. Still, she knew more about the silences than most civilians. Over the years, during active communication phases, she had ferreted out any number of interesting snippets from dedicated networks and from her international transcriptions of intercepted cellphone conversations. The collected information was shot through with spiders that responded to the frequency with which certain words were repeated. It did not take the word "alien" to trigger the spider's frenzy. Innumerable code words were being used. One thing in particular that had caught her attention was the attempted roundup of all children born nine months after the first pulse. This action was hotly protested and litigated by parents in the United States, though it received curiously little coverage in the news. Hardly any at all, in the fact, even considering that news services were in tatters.

Marie hated censorship.

A few bars of Strayhorn's "Lush Life" issued from her computer and she hunched over the screen.

Her spiders scored a hit, matching up a positive percentage of necessary attributes, and the opening page of Dento, Inc., a Japanese government-linked nanotech research lab, appeared. A list of the matches scrolled down the right side of her screen: nanotech, biotech . . . and Kita Narasake.

This astounded Marie.

She remembered Kita. A fellow student in Chicago many years ago, with whom she had traded e-mail, hence the record of her name carried through generations of computer changes. What was Kita working on?

After a second, the answer appeared.

Marie frowned.

Bees? Why the hell would she be spending so much time on bees?

Marie glanced through the jalousies. The rain had ceased, and drops of water with the brilliance of jewels clung to the eaves. On the opposite side of the ravine, the ridgetop flared with sunrise, which illuminated a line of pink flowering trees threaded through the dark forest. Her heart was filled with happiness—at least it seemed so; a certain feeling effervesced and infused life with what she could only think of as a steady glow. She was just barely able to remind herself that this state of intense joy was promoted by the hormones. Knowing this did not put a dent in the joy itself. Life was utter perfection. Precisely ordered hormones from Advanced Endocrine Research, Inc., urged her to believe that she was the target of the forces of goodness in the universe. They were her window into the amazing world of brain chemistry. Could she imbue herself with the overwhelming desire to paint, or sing, or write? Or torture, maim, and kill? Food for thought.

And fodder for investment. Something to add to her portfolio, along with a goodly share of the technology for creating the government-mandated solar roads and cars that would soon replace gasoline-based cars, and the land she had bought along the routes of the proposed North American Magrail System—NAMS. Perhaps the way in which she procured the classified NAMS maps could be described as illegal—marginally illegal, maybe, but lawyer Dighton said that the legality was debatable and he was willing to debate it for his usual exorbitant fees should anyone bring it up. Marie was at the edge of a cresting wave of new technologies. She had nothing to lose; she was fearless. The only thing she lacked, Hugo had once told her, was a moral footing. "You're like the mafia everywhere in the world, Marie. The end justifies the means."

"I'm hurt, Hugo," she'd replied with a slight smile and eyes cast down.

"Like hell," he had rejoined.

Marie reminded herself, with an effort, that no godly fingers pulled wisps of mist upward from the valley in tendrils, and looked back at the Dento, Inc., screen, which was covered solidly with chemical equations. Her spiders had searched beyond the smooth surface of the site and found another private Dento network that apparently spanned the world. She was in. She said, "Tell me what these equations mean," and a box on her screen obligingly appeared, containing the word PHEROMONES. It was odd that the waterfall was getting so much louder—

She jumped from the couch, heart beating, and reached beneath the cushion. The cold, heavy Luger felt reassuring. She crouched and peered through the jalousie slats.

A vividly painted ancient VW bug erupted over the rim of the steep driveway into the packed-dirt yard and halted. A tall thin teenager got out. Dreadlocks escaped from the red baseball cap jammed crookedly on his head. He looked around, walked toward the porch, set an envelope on the top step, jumped back in his car, and drove back down the mountain.

As per Hugo's instructions.

Marie wiped away the sudden sweat of fear, wryly reflecting that perhaps her hormones were not too strong after all. She had not imagined that a golden chariot had alighted in front of her house or that an angel had left a box full of miracles.

She stepped onto the dew-damp porch. Tiny yellow orchids, drooping from an overhanging tree, flailed in a sudden gust of wind. She tore open the envelope and read the note: SPECIAL DELIVERY PACKAGE IN TOWN. MEET ME AT NOON.

Hugo had found Petite Marie's killers at last. Or at least, the final clue.

Marie stumbled back into the house.

In the small kitchen, little more than a lean-to addition, she fired up the propane burner. She put on distilled water for tea and fumbled for the ceramic lid to the tea canister, but after lifting it up, she hurled it to the floor. It shattered in a very satisfactory fashion and she heard her own paroxysm of hysterical laughter rather distantly. Reaching into the jar, she grasped a handful of yerba mate and dropped it into the boiling water and wrenched the knob that turned off the gas. The water quieted. The clean scent of mate mingled with the rainwater air. She closed her eyes and Petite Marie danced in the blackness.

She strained the mate into a thick pottery cup with no handle and carried it to the bedroom, where she dropped cross-legged onto the straw mat covering the uneven wooden floor. From beneath the net-draped iron bed she pulled a stainless-steel briefcase. She touched index fingers to circles on either side of the latch, whispered "Open sesame," and the latch sprang open.

Rain thrummed anew on the roof. She surveyed the small stainless-steel vials strapped in neat rows inside the briefcase, then touched a pad in the center of the case and accessed a screen called DESCRIPTIONS.

They were doing amazing things with brain chemistry nowadays. Not many of such things were legal. Marie funneled money into small labs throughout the world through obscuring interfaces, in hopes of eventual paybacks. But the lab that had distilled #19 was not hers. She had come to possess #19 through a complicated trade. The function of the contents had to do with imprinting and ducks. God knows it was a very bad sort of stuff. It had only been mammal-tested on rats and on one adult lion, whose original wild mien had undergone an amazing change. Might there not be a market for completely docile large cats? The ability to coexist happily with humans would certainly create the ready cash to bring them back from the verge of extinction. Slightly altered, of course, but then nothing was perfect. Her contact claimed that its effect on humans remained a mystery.

Not for long. She smiled and pulled open the Velcro straps, took out #19, closed the case, and slid it back beneath the bed.

Balancing the bottle on the dresser's wavy veneer, she wrestled with a stuck drawer and pulled out a dress she thought of as formidable. Tight on the top, with a nice flamenco flare that started below the hips to allow for kicks. She pulled it on and looked at herself in the pocked mirror. Hugo was wrong. She *was* gaining weight. Practically all muscle. She worked out several hours a day with free weights.

She pulled her many long braids up into a twist and secured it with a silver comb of concentric hearts; sat on the bed and slid her feet into high heels. She clasped her hands and bowed her head.

Was this right? No jury, no trial?

What cared she? Petite Marie had had none either.

Slipping the vial into her pocket, Marie walked down the rickety porch steps, climbed into the Jeep, and headed down the mountain, narrowly avoiding two showy fighting cocks strutting in the rutted road two switchbacks below her shack. She waved to an old man on a porch as she jounced past, and he waved back. Sunlight broke through the mist, illuminating the valley. She crossed the tiny bridge at the bottom of the mountain and got on the main road to town, a two-lane blacktop with no painted lines. She drove very fast.

She parked on the edge of the market and made her way through it. In the colorful madness, she was little noted; in fact, she looked positively sober and conservative compared to everyone else. Little did they know, she thought, what madness danced within her brain. She felt it to be madness. It was not even a slippery slope. It was a cliff. She was poised on the edge, wings strapped on.

Embracing the new was another way to put it. Semantics were so useful.

The neighborhood near the market was growing raucous, even though it was before noon. Wild cries, even gunshots, were not apt to be particularly noted. She turned down a cobblestone alley. Her French terrorist chefs, lounging on dilapidated lawn chairs, sharing a bottle, appeared not to notice her and she appeared not to notice them. She turned in at the open door they bracketed and climbed narrow stairs to a third-floor apartment. Knocked in the silly code she and Hugo had devised when children. How far we've come together, she thought. He opened the door.

"Bring on the clowns," she said.

He grimaced at her terrible joke and jerked his head sideways, locking the door behind her.

The room held a folding chair, a battered couch, two chairs with ripped upholstery, and a massive iron table with a man chained to each end.

They sat on the floor and leaned against the furring strips of a wall that had lost most of its plaster. The tall one had a new red slash across his face. The short one had a cast on one arm. Both were heavily bruised. Neither could contain his shock at seeing her. The tall one shifted as if to jump and run and was restrained by the chain. The short one looked longingly at the window.

"Release them," she told Hugo.

Displaying no emotion, Hugo felt in his pocket and manipulated the radio key. Their fetters sprang open. "Don't even think about it," said Hugo.

"Make yourselves comfortable."

They looked at each other, rose, and slouched to the chairs. They were both sweating heavily. The hand of the tall one as it sat on the arm of the chair began to tremble. He clasped it on his lap within his other hand.

Marie said, "You know who I am."

Silence. Marie grinned slightly, though she felt as if she was falling into a bottomless pit. "No?" She strolled across the room, yanking the heart comb from her braids and tossing it to the floor, lowering her head so that her braids curtained her face. She clasped her hands behind her back. "Picture me . . . a different color. Somewhat lighter—perhaps—oh, all those descriptions are so tiresome. Like coffee with a lot of cream. And not only that." She stopped, turned, and whipped her braids back with a toss of her head. "Picture me standing . . . on a balcony . . . yes?"

The eyes of the short one widened. "But—you are"—he choked—"dead."

The tall one spoke more firmly with a deep, raspy voice. "It not be her. Not Marie Laveau. We kill her t'ru and t'ru. Though it be a mistake . . ." His voice trailed off as she continued to stare into his eyes.

"What do you mean, a 'mistake'?" snapped Marie.

"We supposed to . . ." The short one glanced at the man with the scarred face.

"Speak up now," she said, her voice like a whip.

"In the killing of Marie Laveau." said the cut-faced man, clearing his throat. "That we have admitted to that dwarf there. But that is all that we say."

"*Oui,*" muttered the short one.

"I am indeed Marie Laveau." Marie was practically hissing and they shrank back at the way she leered at them with, she hoped, her most ominous expression. "You did kill me." She straightened. "But I have certain . . . powers." She tapped her foot.

Both of the men looked alarmed.

"You killed me. And you know who killed my husband and daughter."

The cut-faced man swallowed hard.

"Well?"

"Yes, ma'am," they both admitted after Hugo shifted from one foot to another and cleared his throat in a suggestive manner.

She dropped onto the folding chair and stared at them. "I am of a mind to kill you both."

They said nothing. The short one picked some small thing from his pants leg and examined it.

"Do you agree that I would be within my rights?"

They glanced around.

"Well?"

"Yes, ma'am," said the short one with a Haitian accent, earning an evil look from his companion. "But—"

"But nothing!" She rose. Her dress swirled around her. She paced the floor, her heels clicking. "Do you dare to plead for your miserable lives?" She turned back, touched her cheekbone where the snake was. At least she hoped it was; she didn't exactly remember which side she'd put it on. "I am impossible to kill."

The short one looked away. The tall one said, "I do not believe in *voudoun*."

"You don't have much time left to believe in anything," Marie replied. "Enjoy your freedom of opinion. How about you?" she asked the short one.

He made the sign of the cross. She grinned. "Wise, but useless, I'm afraid."

The tall one jumped from his chair and she kicked him across the face. He fell to the floor on his back. That took about ten seconds. Hugo had his gun out.

"Get back to your chair," she said curtly. The short one was breathing in gasps. The tall one resumed his chair. He wiped away the blood that trickled into his eye from his freshly broken wound with the hem of his T-shirt.

"I want to try something new," said Marie. "Consider yourselves unimaginably blessed." She pulled the vial from her pocket, the vial containing Potion #19: IMPRINTING.

Hugo knew better than to disagree with her in front of the killers, but she could feel his shock. He recognized the vial, of course, as coming from the briefcase of bionan experiments, but he didn't know what it was. Just that, in general, it was something that could wreak strange changes.

"I've been told that you wouldn't say anything about who hired you," she said.

"Our names be mud we be talking," said the tall one defiantly.

"*You* will be mud shortly if you don't cooperate. This is a kind of truth serum." She tossed the vial up and down.

Hugo sighed loudly.

"Are there any glasses in this dump?" she asked.

"Some used Styrofoam coffee cups in the trash," said Hugo. "Next to the kitchen sink." His voice might sound neutral to their roommates, but she heard cold disapproval. *Get rid of the scum now. As soon as we know their bosses. Wasn't that the plan? Don't play this game.*

She strode into the kitchen and retrieved two cups from the garbage. She stood on squares of green linoleum peeling up from the floor, which was strewn with yellowed newspapers. An attempt to pry the porcelain sink from the wall had been abandoned, leaving it awry. Brownish water spluttered from the faucets into the cups. She poured several drops from the vial into each one, then stared out the kitchen window at the wooden wall across the alley, thinking of nothing. Blank, she thought. Joy gone. Dose getting low.

Should she?

She crossed her arms tightly, bowing her head. She could no longer imagine any love, any nonchemical joy.

But she was still alive. She would step into this new future. She would find new alternatives. She would be a player. She would take control as much as possible. To see the alternatives and then not make a choice was a choice in itself, the choice of passive acceptance. The world was changing very quickly.

So would these two killers. She picked up the cups, made herself tall, swept back into the other room.

"Drink all of this," she told them. "The only thing that I can guarantee you is that it will not kill you." A lie. "But he will in an instant if you spill a drop."

She handed a cup to each man. Nervously, both gulped their portion. Marie resumed the folding chair. She didn't really know how long this would take. For that matter, she didn't know if they would fall to the floor convulsing and die. She didn't really care. And Hugo would be ever so happy if that happened.

"Look at me," she commanded. "I want to hear the story of your life. The whole story. You first, Shorty."

Shorty licked his lips.

"Now," she said. "And call me Boss."

It was a bit of a stab in the dark. But the lab animals dosed with #19, or so said the sketchy abstracts that accompanied it, had developed a quick and enduring loyalty to the experimenters who interacted with them during the first few moments after they ingested the potion. It worked along the lines of genetic engineering, but rapidly, due to a combination of various enzymes, so that the brain chemistry situation that allowed ducklings to imprint on their parents would be—if this black market stuff worked—replicated in the brains of these criminals.

Let them think it *voudoun* if they preferred, and let them think the science that had resurrected her *voudoun* as well.

Shorty's voice shook when he started but soon smoothed out as he became lost in the telling. She was not surprised at the tale of poverty and beatings; the inclusion and power of finally belonging to a gang. "Look at me when you talk," she reminded him several times. "And you too," she said to Cut Face. His story was essentially the same, though he was from Jamaica, not Haiti.

But an odd thing happened as he finished his telling; stuttered out the names of his employers and all he knew about their network. His face worked; he began to cry. He fell to the floor and crawled toward Marie.

She was taken aback. Hugo sprang forward and kicked him in the side. "Get up," he commanded.

Instead, Cut Face moved swiftly as a snake and kissed Marie's shoe.

"Queen," breathed Shorty, as Hugo mauled an unresisting Cut Face back to his chair.

"Boss," reminded Marie, disconcerted. She stared down at the wet mark on her shoe.

"Boss," they both echoed, tears flowing. Shorty blew his nose on his shirttail. "Boss Queen," said Cut Face, his once blank eyes imploring as those of a punished child, "I and I deserve to die. Put mercy on we. We be talking now. We be telling Boss Queen de trut'."

"We are," Shorty agreed vehemently with sharp nods of his head. "You check this out, you will see. We are sorry. Sorry for the killing. But the little girl, she was not our fault. We cannot be in two places at one time. Not like you, Boss Queen. We will help to find them. We only know a name. Bensonberg. From Copenhagen. And you—you were a mistake—"

"Yes," she said quietly. "A mistake. You said that before. What do you mean?"

There was no pause this time. Cut Face said, "You, dey just be wanting to scare, to warn. Den dey would tell you—whatever dey want. We don't know what dey be wanting to tell you. But dey be killing . . . your daughter, your husband, so dat you be obeying them. We don't know how you be displeasing them. But the signal, the siren, it came out wrong. First siren sound is test. Den, dey supposed to call you, threaten you. If you don' listen, siren plays. We t'ot we had the order for to kill you. Please, Boss Queen—"

"They died—" Her voice shook now. "They died as a warning to *me*?"

Petite Marie—innocent, beautiful, completely unaware, and not a threat to anyone—was dead. As was Al, a wonderful, intellectual, loving man. Because of their organization. Because they wanted to *warn* her . . .

A sudden flare of rage woke every memory and flashed through her body like lightning, beyond her control. She understood in an instant the fury that caused people to slam fists through walls, the fury that caused unpremeditated murder.

Shaking, she turned and went to her bag, which was slumped on the floor by the couch. She opened it and pulled out her photoscreen. *"There!"* she said, in a low voice "Look! My little girl. Marie. *Look,* I tell you!"

She stretched the photoscreen larger with trembling haste. "See? There she is. Playing in the garden. There she is." Her words were staccato as she changed the image with a touch of her finger. "LOOK at her!" Her shriek was hysterical. "Here. Here she is at her first Communion. And there—there—" Her hands shook so hard she knew they saw very little. "With her father in Jackson Square. He's dead too. They're both *dead,* you vicious scumbags." She collapsed onto the couch, sobbing.

Hugo gently removed the photoscreen, touched the shrink tab, put it back in her purse.

"We be sorry," said Cut Face.

Marie looked at Hugo. "You got all the information you need from them?"

He nodded. "Bensonberg is enough. I've had dealings with him before."

"I think I will kill them now."

"Good. But Marie—"

"Give me your .44. Put the silencer on it."

"Marie, we can have someone—"

"I want to do it myself."

"Please, Miss Laveau," said the short one. "I be doing anything for you. But if you want to be killing me—"

"I do," she snapped.

The man with the cut face bowed his head. "Your will be da main thing."

Marie aimed at the man's head. At the last instant, her hand jerked.

A scream like that of a wild animal sliced the air. Blood spattered the wall, the floor, the tattered chair, and flowed out onto the floor. Marie staggered backward, shifting the gun to her left hand and shaking her right. A burnt smell lingered. Her ears rang.

Hugo hurried forward. "You hit his calf. I think I see bone." The man had passed out and was slumped forward. Blood pooled beneath his leg.

The short man stared at his companion, an expression of horror on his face. He looked back at Marie. His eyes were wide and pitying.

"You do da right thing. We deserve to die." Tears wet his round face. "Here. Shoot me too. She was a beautiful li'l girl. Not'in but a baby." He knelt and lowered his head to the floor. "Kill me."

Marie kicked him in the head—hard. He sprawled to one side, groaning. She kicked him again, again, again, until Hugo caught her arms from behind and twisted her away.

She was panting in hoarse gasps. She went and leaned against the scarred wall, looked through a window lined with jagged teeth of glass to the street. No one seemed to have noticed the shot or, more likely, no one cared. Or they were afraid.

She doubled up and hugged herself while harsh sobs ripped through her. "Why did I *live*? Why? Is there some kind of *reason*?" Hugo took her hand and led her to the couch.

"We all make our own reasons, Marie." Hugo squeezed her shoulder gently. "Maybe . . . maybe we'll find a reason again."

After a few minutes, she went into the kitchen, washed her face, and came back out dripping and cool with her head empty as a Tuesday church. Everything looked far away. The bodies of the injured men, the blood, slow-seeping now; the splattered table, chairs, and wall. "Let's go."

She kicked aside the silver heart-shaped comb, still lying on the floor. Then she closed the door behind her.

As they jounced back up the mountain in the dark, Hugo was royally pissed and made no bones about it.

"Why don't you just tell me what we're up to, Marie, before you pull these stunts? And slow down. I'm going to bounce out of the damned Jeep."

"Put on your seat belt," said Marie, splashing through a small creek that cut across the road. Another dose of hormones had done her a world of good. That was why she mistrusted them so. "You could tell me about your stunts, you know."

"What are you talking about?"

"Petite Marie. I know that you saved her." Marie was glad it was dark. Hugo couldn't see the tears that suddenly welled in her eyes.

"You're changing the subject," said Hugo, his voice rough. "What are we going to do with those . . . those *zombies* you created back there? I'm not sure that the one you shot will die. Furthermore, we have no idea how long the effects of that potion will last. What if they come to their senses at the wrong time?"

"Then their death will have been delayed for a while, that's all. They will have had time to enjoy life's splendors a little longer."

"Do I detect an undertone of irony?"

"You can if you want to." She sighed and downshifted to climb a steep muddy hill. A shower had passed, and clouds blew swiftly through the night sky, revealing a brilliant full moon. "I'm not sure I have a plan. Without those hormones, I wouldn't give a damn about anything."

The wet jungle shone to their right in the moonlight. The sweet scent of jasmine pervaded the air. Across the valley near the ridge, a fire burned.

"What's over there?" Marie reached a flat place and turned off the engine. The sounds of the jungle rose about them—the faint, distant roar of the falls; the whistles and chirps and occasional whoop of unseen, unknown creatures; the wind in the trees.

"No houses on the survey map," he said. "It looked to me as if the ridge is too steep to build on. But there are trails. Some kind of . . ." He stopped.

"*Voudoun* ritual," Marie said thoughtfully.

"Bunch of kids out drinking."

They stared at the small flickering orange light.

"Do you think—?" started Marie.

"Whatever it is, I doubt that strangers are welcome."

Marie spun the wheel and caused the Jeep to roar back down the mountain, careening around the switchbacks. "Damn it, Marie, slow down or let me out," yelled Hugo. The headlights illuminated a narrow swath of dripping jungle as they arced wildly. Marie slowed gradually, downshifting, and then they were at the bottom of the mountain.

"Here's where it gets tricky," she said.

"Oh," said Hugo. "It hasn't been tricky yet?"

The main road curved to the left, where it crossed the stream via a rickety bridge and headed into town. Marie turned to the right, where a wide path that might have been a road at one time vanished into the wall of forest. She shifted into first gear and cautiously advanced. Wet branches bent away from the windshield and whipped behind them.

Then the road bent to the left, to a small muddy beach. The headlights illuminated what looked like small whitecaps in a broad swift cut of water. Marie gunned the engine and the Jeep plowed through the creek, raising wings of water, then swiftly ascended the steep bank. Marie let out a triumphant yell.

"Yeah, we're alive," panted Hugo when they reached the top of the bank and turned onto the narrow track that led back into the valley. "But hey, I guess that doesn't matter to you much."

Marie smiled wickedly at Hugo. "You're signed up too, sweetheart, don't forget."

"After seeing how it's affected you, I am seriously considering taking my name off the list," said Hugo.

The weeds between the wheel tracks were a foot high, but they were definitely on a road. The jungle receded as they passed through what might have been, at one time, someone's cleared field.

They could no longer see the fire, but the road began to climb the side of the mountain. Marie was surprised to find her heart beating hard; what—afraid of death? She laughed.

"Keep in mind there's no door over here," said Hugo. He leaned forward, gripping the bar in front of him. Their progress was tanklike, slow and grinding. After five more minutes, the road widened out. Around a curve, perhaps fifteen cars were parked.

"Wouldn't have thought those would make it up here."

"Maybe they came before the rain," said Marie.

"It's never before the rain."

Marie turned the Jeep around and set the brake. "Ready for some action?"

"It's been kind of a long day for me." But he got out and followed her.

The wind freshened as Marie hurried up the narrow moonlit road, jumping water-filled ruts, feeling a lift in her spirit with the rising of the wind. The sound of drums came from the forest ahead, complex and deep. She ought to be afraid, she thought, but instead she almost felt like dancing, as if she were a child again, running down the street toward the sun-gleamed, barge-roughened Mississippi.

"You know, Hugo," she said somewhat breathlessly when he caught up to her, "it was rather nice of me to spare those two men today, don't you think?"

Hugo grunted. "You and I seem to have different value systems. Either that or your vocabulary is way too limited."

They rounded a turn, and suddenly the fire was visible through a skein of branches about fifty feet away. A very large man stepped out in the road and said something in Creole. Marie spoke French, but couldn't really understand his strange accent and grammar.

Hugo replied, gesturing at Marie. The man raised his bald head and stared at Marie thoughtfully with deep-set eyes that gleamed in the fitful light. He tilted his head. Then he gestured for them to follow.

"What did you say?" whispered Marie.

"I told him that you were Marie Laveau," said Hugo. "You know, that famous Voodoo Queen we've all heard so much about."

"Shit," said Marie. "They'll be expecting something from me. And stop smiling that way."

"What way?"

"That wicked way."

"This is an entirely innocent smile. Good God. Will you look at that?"

They crossed an invisible threshold into a scene of, Marie thought—despite her native skepticism—sacred beauty.

A banyan of mythic proportions was at the center of a clearing. It was surrounded by candles planted in the ground. To the beat of the drums, women and men dressed in white moved counterclockwise around the tree, casting long shadows.

To one side sat three drummers on camp stools; their drums were of different sizes and spoke in a complicated, intoxicating rhythm. Rising out of that rhythm was song.

An old woman with brilliant white long hair topped by a white kerchief and wearing a long white dress stood next to the drummers, resting her weight on a cane. She flung out lines of chanting in a powerful croak, throwing her whole body into her delivery, swaying on the fulcrum of her cane, making Marie fear that she would topple over each time. The dancers echoed her. The woman took a gourd from a young man standing next to her, sipped from it, and sprayed it from her mouth in the direction of the dancers. Behind her was a table made from a board resting on two plastic milk crates.

She saw Marie and motioned to her.

Marie stood as if rooted to the ground.

Hugo gave her a little push and she stumbled forward. She turned to glare at him, but he was staring at the treetops, smiling, his arms clasped behind his back.

Marie consciously straightened herself, held her head high, and stepped forward.

The old woman was quite as tall as Marie. Light glinted off her deep black face; high cheekbones and large eyes gave her fierce beauty. Despite the white hair, Marie saw no wrinkles. She regarded Marie. The drums slowed. She pushed down on Marie's shoulders and forced her to kneel in the dirt.

Marie felt two hands clasp her head firmly. Just the touch of another's hands can be soothing, she reminded herself sternly, but despite herself memories of Al shot through her like an explosion of light and she found herself sobbing uncontrollably. And angrily. It was as if a neurologic firestorm flared through her, creating the lost connections between her lost emotional past and her present life. She tried to struggle away, to free herself from the intensity, from the grief, but the woman's hands pressed ever more firmly and then a warm liquid was poured on her head. She tasted it. Rum, mixed with salt tears. Some sort of baptism?

Two men came to her side and helped her rise. Another came to her with a gourd and bade her drink. The old woman stared at her and Marie dared not disobey. She was reminded of her grandmère and of having her legs switched with a branch from the lilac bush. Men had not an ounce of power over her, but an old imperious woman . . . *mon Dieu*! She drank it all because they would not let her stop, swallowing the raw egg floating in what seemed to be rum.

The old woman assumed a bent-legged stance, her back straight, and began moving slowly round the circle. One of the men stared meaningfully at Marie and she imitated the woman, strutting behind her. She realized that but for the rum she would be paying more attention to the wearying aspect of the posture, but the drums carried her along. When the woman began to move her shoulders back and forth, she did so as well, and when the dance moved into a new and more active phase of shouting and leaping, she heard words coming from her mouth for a long time as her voice hoarsened.

She stopped thinking about anything except the sky and the tree and the circular motion. She danced around an inner ring of delicate white designs that some of the dancers were creating around the tree, letting flour trickle through their hands in a thin stream, shapes that reminded her of the intricate wrought iron of New Orleans.

Home. Al, never a guardian, always a companion, a partner, beckoning her to join him, as if through an open door in the sky. Petite Marie, descending through wreaths of stars. Her ancestors—her mother, grandmère, men and woman she'd never known, stretching in an ancient chain back to humanity's roots, to Africa. Though all around her seemed a spinning, pounding frenzy, she felt calm and expansive, as if she herself were an Eye seeing through unimaginable time and space, floating in it as if held within a warm phosphorescent sea, rising and falling on the waves, radiating power from her head, her hands, her hips, and every drumbeat pushed her through a transformation as precise as the unseen calculations that drove her computers.

She woke with a sneeze. The ground was hard and she was soaking wet with dew. She moaned and pushed herself upright. Sunlight spilled through the jungle. The clearing was empty. Except for Hugo. He sat with his back against the banyan. He had an acrostic look on his face.

"What time is it?" she asked. "Shit." She grabbed her aching head with both hands. "I can't believe I fell asleep on the ground."

"Passed out is more like it," said Hugo. He glanced at his watch. "It's about eight-thirty. Hungry?"

"Not exactly. Stop smiling that way. You're giving me a headache."

"I'm so sorry. I guess I don't know my own power. You were quite a hit. Too bad you can't remember all the fun you had. You have an invitation to visit the old lady."

"I'm not sure I want to see her again."

"Sure you do. She gave me her card." Hugo pulled it from his shirt pocket. On it was a hologram of one of the delicate heart-shaped designs that still surrounded the tree.

"Nice artwork."

"Those are called *vévé*," Hugo told her.

"It's too early in the morning to be such a know-it-all," Marie said. "Besides, there's no address."

"She told me where she lives. I thought you didn't know anything about voodoo."

Marie sighed. She pushed herself back to a large rock and leaned against it. Her stomach roiled. Her head pounded. "Grandmère took me to a ceremony on Lake Pontchartrain once. I'd forgotten all about it, to tell the truth. I must have been very little. I remember seeing a lot of legs dancing around before I fell asleep. I don't know. It was actually . . . well, not fun last night. But satisfying. In a strange sort of way. I guess I was in a trance. That's never happened before."

"Probably something else in the rum. Maybe a touch of hallucinogens," said Hugo.

"But the drums made a difference too," said Marie. "What do you think about that?"

"Surely rhythm organizes neuronal firing," said Hugo, getting to his feet and dusting off his pants. "What would your brain have looked like being scanned last night?"

Marie let Hugo pull her up. "Like a fireworks show," she said. "It seemed as if I were in touch with—this is going to sound silly, but it seemed as if I could feel Al, and—and Petite Marie. As if they were still alive somewhere, as if they still had some sort of presence."

Hugo coughed at that, but said nothing. He fell silent as they walked back toward the Jeep, and his silence had a strange quality. Marie knew it had to mean something.

She stopped walking and let him go ahead.

The jungle leaves made a music of their own in the wind. Through a gap in the trees, Marie could see other ridges off to the south, like lush green waves, stopped in their motion for a moment, and beyond them the deep blue line of the Caribbean. She had been talking about Petite Marie . . .

"Hugo?" she said.

Hugo stopped, and turned back to look at her. She read it in his face. Apologetic. Stubborn.

"You didn't," she said.

"Marie, please. I had to. Not only for myself. For you."

"And who did you choose to . . . to . . ." Words failed her.

"Missy," said Hugo.

"Why? *Why?*"

"To make you care again," he said.

"Did it. Ever. Occur. To you. That I don't want to care?" Marie sank to the ground. She knelt in the mud, bent over in pain, gasping, her arms wrapped tightly around herself. Hugo came and stood by her side uncertainly. Then he put his hands on her head, as had the old woman the night before.

This time she felt no lightning, no brilliant burst of timelessness.

She only felt his hands trembling a bit. She heard that his breathing was ragged.

She reached up and grasped one of his hands tightly. She turned to look up at him.

"It's done, then," she said, her fury gone. She did not own the stuff of Petite Marie. It had come from her and Al, another of the unique creations of life. "It's all right, Hugo. It's all right. Only . . . she'll have to be yours, I think. Your responsibility. I couldn't stand it. I'm no good at raising children." She hugged him, rested her head against his chest, heard his heart pounding.

Yellow and green birds flashed across the road as they drove into town for breakfast.

The next afternoon Marie fought the steering wheel as she and Hugo jolted along the rutted mud road on the coast. They were going to see the old woman. As they passed through each tiny village, a storm of raggedly dressed children ran alongside the Jeep, yelling, hands outstretched.

Even a day after the ceremony, all seemed strangely luminous to Marie. Her hangover had been cured by a dose of her hormones. But this was deeper than that somewhat artificial joy.

And therefore more dangerous. She would have to remind herself daily that this new child was not Petite Marie. She was Hugo's child. Period. She had told Hugo to think of a name. She had instants of dread, thinking of all that might go wrong. Cloning humans was still relatively rare, despite thousands of successes. All, of course, illegal from start to finish. And she didn't want to see the girl. They ought to have no links to one another. Hugo had given her the details. He had taken Missy to a clinic in New Orleans. She was three months pregnant and back in the Pink House in Tortola. She was very excited.

Hugo touched Marie's arm. "I think this is where we stop."

The cries of the children were high and sharp like birdcalls. Tin roofs glittered in the sun, and the shacks of scrap wood were small and crooked. The village had, perhaps, fifteen or twenty such houses. A tiny grocery boasted a faded pink Coke sign. Marie wondered what they did to make a living here. The foot of the mountain was scarred, scraped clean of vegetation. Steeper cliffs rose beyond, precluding cultivation. She pulled off the road on the ocean side and stopped the Jeep. Children crowded around.

"It's still about a mile away," said Hugo. "I think it's off that road to the left, out on the peninsula." The sea was luminous green close in and met the sky in a dark blue band. Ahead a gleaming white crescent of sand edged the road in mile-long sweep; beyond, she saw waves crashing against a cliff in a repeating flare of white foam.

"Maybe they fish," she said, getting out. The sun was hot on her bare arms and legs. She wore light shorts and shirt, a straw hat, and hiking boots. She surveyed the children. "Line up," she said in her best Creole, which was slow and awful. They giggled, but to her surprise, understood and obeyed.

She saw open-faced young boys of six and seven, their ribs plainly visible. Girls—some in ragged dresses, others in faded shorts—looked at her expectantly, their hair braided and clipped with plastic barrettes.

She went down the row and gave each of them a five-dollar coin, much more valuable than gourdos. She'd brought a lot for this purpose. A chorus of *mercis* enveloped her and the children rushed off exuberantly, yelling.

Marie looked back the way they'd come. She saw the other poor villages strung out along the curved coastline, could pick them out by their tin roofs throwing back sunlight. "This is such a waste," she said. She rummaged in the back of the Jeep and pulled out a heavy canvas bag.

"Others have tried to help," Hugo said, a warning tone in his voice as they began their walk down the faint grassy road that led onto the peninsula. The smells of salt and dried grasses mingled in the heat.

"Corrupt governments that had no intention of giving power to the people," she said contemptuously.

"Not anyone *nice* and *smart* like you," said Hugo.

"I'm not nice," she said. "I'm worried. Do you remember the Rasta we saw at breakfast yesterday?"

"It's not so long ago," said Hugo, because, Marie supposed, he couldn't say anything without being a smart aleck.

He had been sitting at the next table, eating cereal and fruit. He looked up, seeing Marie staring at his reddish dreadlocks as they stood waiting for a table. He motioned for them to join him. After a few minutes, Marie felt sufficiently emboldened to ask him what being a Rasta was all about.

He was very thin, as thin as the children in this ragged village. In an odd blend of Brooklyn- and British-tinged English, he said he was from Jamaica. His father had been Haitian. He had been born in New York City, but then his mother returned alone to Jamaica, where he grew up. He had come to Haiti to find his father, and still had not. But Port-au-Prince had been his home for five years now.

"We as Rastas are destined to free all life-forms. We have been reincarnated through seventy-seven bodies. We soon will free all beings. We are engaged in a jihad, a holy war." His eyes were serious. "It is a war against poverty and ignorance. We want to free those alive on Earth now. Not in some future heaven after death." He drank the last of his coffee, pulled a large spliff from his pocket and lit it. They were in a tiny restaurant on a side street with few customers. No one even glanced at him. He offered some to Marie and she toked. He offered some to Hugo and Hugo shook his head.

"How is this different from *voudoun*?" she asked.

He frowned. "*Voudoun* worships the past. It is ancestor worship. We live in the present. We hurt no living thing. We make no sacrifice. We will save all of life. I am a vegetarian, you see. We are all conquering lions doing God's work."

"Except that you have to be a man?" suggested Marie.

The Rasta shrugged. "I do not believe that. I am a teacher. I hold a classroom every weekday morning on Prince Street. I teach girls as well as boys to read and write. Good English. I would teach them good French too, but I do not know French. You look like a rich lady. Come by sometime and see what we do. Maybe you could give us some money, eh? Some books? Pay the electric bill, give us some computers?" He smiled faintly. "You think I am a hustler. But come by and see." He handed her a card. Hugo took it and put it in his pocket.

Now, as he walked the dirt road's fringe, Hugo said, "His name, according to his card, is Zion. Rastafarianism is a millenarian movement. It's not messianic. They don't believe that one of God's manifestations is going to save them and take them to heaven. I mean, Bob Marley said he felt like bombing a church once he knew that the preacher was lying. They are Marxist in their belief that organized religion is just a tool to oppress the masses, to make them feel as if being poor and downtrodden is a virtue and they'll be rewarded for their suffering in heaven. The Rastafarians believe there's going to be a golden age here on Earth. Like he said. And they really try to do something about that. You have to respect them for it. We can drop by his school—if that's what you're getting at."

They drew close to the old woman's house, which sat alone on the low headland. It was neat, though small, and painted with a faded mural. The most striking part of the mural was a tree whose branches twined around the corner. Instead of leaves, large pink hearts hung from the branches. An unpainted fence surrounding the house contained some chickens. In a pen of sagging wire fencing, several goats bleated. A large battered generator sat on bare dirt beneath a corrugated green fiberglass roof. Next to it were three red plastic gasoline containers. Surf surged across nearby rocks and filled the rusted remains of a car, leaving foam that drained back into sea.

Marie stepped up to the house and stood in the doorway. She knocked lightly on the frame and peered inside.

As her eyes adjusted, she saw hearts: hearts beaten from tin, hearts within hearts, in so many mediums that Marie was overwhelmed. Hearts cut from the mutlicolored newsprint of comics; hearts cut from plastic milk cartons. What seemed like a hundred heart-shaped stones, set on shelves and tiny tables, of salt and pepper granite; hearts struck from slate and shining in planes of flaked silicone. She saw a heart that was the knot of a tree, chain-sawed flat on the bottom so that it sat only slightly tilted on the green-painted wooden floor. And the woman who lived within this wealth of hearts had a heart-shaped face, as dark as Marie's, eyes alight, white hair like a lion's mane about her face. The heart woman looked even older than Marie had imagined as she advanced through the kitchen into the light.

"Come in," she said, her voice dry and papery as a discarded snakeskin. She wore a T-shirt that said something in Japanese and shorts that revealed strong sinewy legs. Her feet were bare.

Marie ducked beneath the low lintel. She took two bottles of very good whisky from her canvas bag and put them on the table next to a shell ashtray. The woman turned the bottles and squinted at the labels, then nodded to Marie to take a seat.

"I am Adele. Would you like something to drink? Lemon soda? Diet Coke?"

"Diet Coke, thanks." Marie pulled out a wooden chair and sat at the sea-green kitchen table, from which Formica peeled, and accepted the can of Diet Coke Adele took from a waist-high refrigerator. The old woman moved slowly, with a precision that Marie realized was pain-generated. It was hard to believe that she had danced with such vigor the other night.

Adele sat and pushed aside two copies of *The Journal of Jungian*

Studies that lay on the table. She plunked down two small glasses and struggled to open one of the whisky bottles. Finally she grimaced and handed it to Marie. Marie twisted it open and handed it back. Adele plopped whisky into the bottom of each glass; shoved one toward Marie. She took a pill from her pocket and washed it down with whisky. "Arthritis medicine. I do not think it does much good. So— you are from New Orleans?"

"Yes."

"Why did you come to Haiti?"

"Because my daughter was killed. I was looking for her murderers."

"Did you find them?"

"No. But I found those who worked with them."

"And do they still live?"

"In a fashion." Marie took a sip of whisky, then a sip of Diet Coke. She could hear the sea through the white-curtained window. She felt as if she had never been so far from home. She was startled at a movement on the kitchen counter. It took her a moment to register that the slow steady slide was that of a white boa, longer than what she could see since the end of him turned a corner, and big around as her thigh.

"What happened to me the other night?" Marie wanted to act nonchalant, but couldn't help staring at the snake.

"You were rid' by a l'wa. Agwe. God of the Sea. He spake through you."

"What did I—what did Agwe say?"

Adele looked thoughtful. She took a cigar from a box on the table and lit it. The smoke drifted out the window. It smelled good to Marie.

"He said that a golden age comes. A golden age and a golden city. Like Jerusalem. He wants to make this place. For all peoples. With the power of the heart. With the power of his lover, Erzulie. We celebrated the Silence that night. The Silence is good. Wipes everything clean."

"What does this have to do with me?" Marie leaned forward and the chair creaked. "I know that my friend told you that my name is Marie Laveau. And it is. But those Maries, those were my grandmère, my great-great aunts. They are not me. I know nothing of *voudoun*."

"Blood knows."

Marie looked around the room. Even inside, plants grew in great profusion, with huge deep green leaves and brilliant orange and purple blossoms. The walls were dense with scenes that Marie thought Adele must have painted herself. A three-foot-high chipped plaster statue of the Virgin Mary, her heart painted red with a golden cross in the center, stood next to the stove, staring at Marie with eyes of flat blue love. Photographs of children were lodged around a mirror frame. A vévé of shells and stones gave off a dull white glow on a warped dark oak table. Marie knew that they were supposed to have some kind of power.

"Your world is alive," Marie said. "My world is not." She was surprised to hear despair in her voice.

Adele reached over and grasped her hand with a strong grip. "Our worlds are the same world," she said. "Remember that. It is you who need to let life flow into your heart. It is waiting. It is all around you, the Being of the world, the gods and goddesses who come into us. It is stronger than anything. It is stronger than death. Love swallows death like a snake swallows eggs."

As she had the other night, Marie felt the current of the old woman's life flowing into her. She squeezed Marie's hand hard, as businessmen in New Orleans did, as if she were sealing a deal, and let go.

Marie did not buy this love swallowing death crap. It was all aching and empty and ragged.

Even with the new baby on the way. More so, perhaps.

She looked up to see Adele's shrewd eyes watching her. Beyond her, through the window, was the green line of the sea. Chickens clucked outside. "What are the sacrifices for?" asked Marie.

Adele became grave. "Christ bade us sacrifice in praise and thanksgiving. They are for love. All sacrifices are for love."

Marie decided not to engage in theological argument. "Who are these . . . these l'wa?"

"When they come to you, when they mount you, you change. You let go. You are empty and they move you. They speak through you."

"How do you know that I was—who?"

"Agwe. Because of how you looked, how you moved. Serious. You cried, but your face did not move. Ghede sometimes comes, for instance. Death." The woman sat straight, crossed one leg loosely over the other, let the cigar dangle from her lip. Her entire countenance changed. Then just as suddenly she was the old woman again. "Myself, I am a *servitour* to Erzulie. The Goddess of Love."

She rose and went to a small bookshelf; pulled out a well-worn book. She opened it, searched through some pages, handed it to Marie.

Marie flipped back to the cover: *Dancing Spirits: Rhythms and Rituals of Haitian Vodun, the Rada Rite* by Gerdes Fleurant. She read aloud, " 'The dance in honor of Agwe produces a state of ecstasy, a release of emotional conflict in contact with superior beings. Dunhan shows rightly that the lwa are beneficent forces in nature, and in Rada there are no bad lwa or evil magic as those concepts are understood in Western Society.' "

" 'No evil magic?' " Marie closed the book, holding the place with her thumb. "What about zombies?"

Adele shook her head. "Sorcerer stuff. People believe that evil magicians create them to do work, to pay debts. I have a ceremony to release them if such an act is claimed. I never have attempted to create them."

"I have zombies of my own." She thought of the two men. She thought of her memories of Petite Marie.

She thought of herself.

"Then you must release them to free yourself."

Marie shifted uncomfortably. Hate rose within her. It was not swallowed by the hearts.

"Let it go," said the woman in a cautioning tone. She rose, went to a low table arranged altarlike with various candles, pictures, pieces of lace. She picked up something, murmured some words that blended with the distant hush of waves, pressed it into Marie's hand, closed her fingers over it. It was cool and hard and smooth. As she brushed close, Marie inhaled her spicy scent. Marie opened her hand and saw a heart-shaped rock, and within the heart another heart stood revealed: a fossil whiteness, small but of certain shape.

"Find your own heart," the woman whispered. "Swallow death and live again."

This is too much, thought part of Marie.

But the new part of her considered the advice seriously. She knelt before the woman and kissed her hand, much as she'd been taught to kiss the ring of the Catholic priest.

"Thank you," she said and walked out into the strong sunlight.

That evening Marie walked down a long wooden dock in Port-au-Prince Harbor on the way to her boat. She'd cleared out of the mountain shack. Her business in Haiti was almost at an end.

Hugo was at her side. The mountains swallowed the last glow of sun. The wind was still and limpid water reflected boats, masts, and docks with smooth blobby distortions. Spray from a fisherman hosing down his boat drenched her right side; the coolness felt good before it was obviated by heat the next instant. Slow beats of Bob Marley, more of a god than ever, trudged through the humid air from several competing tape players. "Sucking the blood of the sufferers day by day." The chant of the centuries'-owned.

As she turned a corner and neared their slip, she stopped.

"Hugo. What's that on the dock?"

"Looks like a person. Asleep, maybe."

"Is he in front of our slip?" She walked faster.

Hugo pushed ahead. By the time she got there, he was leaning over Cut Face.

His leg was bandaged with a torn shirt. His eyes were closed and his face was beaded with sweat. Next to him lay a makeshift crutch of nailed-together lumber scraps.

Shorty was perched on the ketch's cabin.

"What are you doing here?" demanded Marie.

"We serve you now." Shorty's voice was matter-of-fact. "We do everyt'ing you say."

"How did you get here?"

"We follow da guards. Not dere fault. Dey talk about killing us, but dey let us come. Dey say you decide."

"Shit," said Marie. "I don't want you around. Just jump in the drink, all right?"

Shorty slid down from the cabin onto the deck of the boat. He made his way to the back and leaped into the harbor, where he began treading water.

"Is this some kind of joke?" Marie said to Hugo.

"I think the joke's on you."

Marie had hired some painters to change the name of the boat to the *Erzulie*. Below the name was Erzulie's vévé, a delicate heart design. "Not bad." She stepped onto the deck. "Get me a glass of wine, please," she said when Jean emerged from the cabin. "Why are those guys here?"

"Want us to get rid of them?"

Marie glanced over at Shorty, who was panting and sinking below the surface now and then.

"If he lasts two hours, fish him out."

"What about the other one?"

Marie was at a loss for a minute. Then she shrugged. "Just leave him there."

The next morning Cut Face was still alive, so she reluctantly allowed Hugo's doc to look at Cut Face's leg. He shook his head and said the fibia was broken. He took Cut Face to the small local hospital and had the surgeon put a pin in his leg, without consulting Marie. Medical care was utterly minimal on Haiti, so Marie figured she was giving Petite Marie's killer deluxe treatment and hated herself for it. Cut Face returned five days later, crutching along the dock, a big smile on his face. "I be back, Miss Marie."

Marie decided to work them to death. The next day she gave Cut Face money and told him to go to the market and lay in a supply of food. She watched him crutch down the dock and hoped that it was painful; his face told her that it was. He returned after eight hours pulling a wagon of packages roped to his waist. Shorty spent three days scrubbing every imaginable surface on the boat. She planned to have him strip down all the teak with 0000 steel wool.

She avoided them. The sight of both men made her ill.

The next day they paid a visit to the Rasta school. Marie followed Hugo through narrow streets in which the sun's power was magnified by the corrugated aluminum used frequently as a building material, supplemented by flattened tin cans, rotting plywood, and cardboard. Through jagged holes in the metal, around which sharp points of bent aluminum splayed like dangerous flowers, she glimpsed naked children playing on dirt floors. Skinny men, shirtless but wearing old dungarees, perched on the edges of tires that lay in fetid puddles, smoking cigarettes and gossiping. The air smelled of rotting fish and every corner held a compost of garbage.

Marie was completely soaked in sweat. Hugo, ahead of her, kept wiping his forehead with the white handkerchief he always carried, his jacket slung over his shoulder and held with his left thumb, his gun quite public. "Are you sure you know where you're going?" she asked.

"I think it's about two more blocks then we turn west," he said.

" 'Blocks'!" she hooted. "How do you figure blocks? This is a warren."

Hugo turned west when they came to a break in the shanties, onto a road of hard-packed dirt. Frame houses lined both sides, clad with distant memories of paint. Tilting second-floor balconies held ramshackle chairs and potted plantain trees heavy with green bunches. A few people sold rice, cold coconut milk, or homemade sweets from their porches.

"Here it is," said Hugo.

"I'm astonished." This house, though far from square, was freshly painted. A narrow cobblestone patio separated the front door from the street, shaded beneath the overhanging porch. The voices of children issued from inside. Next to the door, a neatly painted sign, bolted to the bricks, read NEW ERA SCHOOL.

Marie and Hugo stood in the open french doors.

Sunlight was tempered by lowered bamboo shades, and the air was stirred to a semblance of coolness by ceiling fans. The walls were thick plaster and the floors flagstone. Children of all colors and ages flowed through the large room. A small group was gathered around something on the floor nearby; Marie stepped closer and saw they were assembling a map of the Caribbean, laying the islands on a piece of oilcloth on which their outlines were traced, putting labeled names next to each bit of land. She bent over a bronze-skinned girl with long red dreadlocks and said, "What's that?"

"That little dot?" She looked about six years old. "That's Freestate."

Zion rushed up to Marie, his face beaming. "Welcome! I am so happy that you took the time to come! We are working on square roots over there and I had to finish the lesson."

"What's Freestate?" asked Marie. It sounded vaguely familiar.

Zion looked at her in disbelief. "You have not heard of Freestate? It is an artificial island about a hundred miles west of here. They are growing it from sea water. Here, we have a lot of schoolwork having to do with it. The entire sequence of growing the island, how it functions, how we are going to be able to colonize space from it . . ."

"Colonize space?" asked Hugo.

"Let us see how we can impress you." Zion looked around. "Michel? You have been studying sea cement? Tell our guests about it, please."

Michel wore only a pair of faded shorts. He greeted them with a wide smile. His English was, as Zion had bragged, very good. "Well, the colonization of space won't happen for a long time. Right now Freestate is slowly growing from materials from the ocean. Current is conducted by sea water between an anode and cathode, and minerals form on the cathode, starting a web of material. Here, I can show you a chart of how it happens." He went to a blackboard on the wall and started sketching. "See, the magnesium here is created by this reaction." He began a flurry of letters and numbers. Marie watched, fascinated, her knowledge of chemistry resurfacing.

"What's the next stage?"

"I'll tell you what the final stage is," said Zion, watching the boy with obvious pride. "It's a brotherhood—and sisterhood," he added hastily, "of m . . . humankind."

Marie smiled. "Did you teach them all of this?"

"No." He spread his hands flat in a self-deprecating gesture. "Some one from Freestate comes every few weeks and expands the curriculum. They have not been here for . . . well, a few months. We have missed them, but they are very busy, and after all they are doing this for free. We are trying to raise enough money for a field trip to the site."

"Tell me more about Freestate."

"It was started about fifteen years ago by a group that put all of their money together. The original plan was formulated in the late twentieth century, and many people contributed to the foundation. It helped that several of them were very wealthy and had strong opinions about taxes and governments. They preferred to use their wealth to create a country where they could see their taxes at work more readily. These are not ordinary people. There are several Nobel laureates and all their families. Most of them are very technologically adept."

"Does it involve nanotech?"

"I believe that there has been a lot of debate about that in Freestate. So far, it does not, but I wouldn't be surprised if they adapt some kinds of nanotech applications very soon."

"What were you talking about, going into space?"

"There are many stages to Freestate. Their ultimate goal is to be able to travel into space, and for that they need to learn how to live independent of outside support. The whole thing unfolds in different stages. One stage finances the next. There are lessons to be learned too. They are as isolated as they can possibly be because they wish to simulate the experience of space travel. They had already begun Freestate before the pulses, but since then their mission has become more urgent."

"I will take you on your field trip," said Marie, wondering in the next moment what possessed her to be so impulsive. Then she felt the l'wa stone in her pocket. Maybe it did have some strange effect on her after all.

"Oh!" Zion smiled. "Thank you!"

Hugo cleared his throat. "What?" asked Marie.

"May I offer a humble opinion?"

"I doubt it."

"I think we ought to check it out first. I really wouldn't want to be responsible for these children otherwise. Have you ever been there?"

"No," admitted Zion.

"Well?" asked Hugo.

"You're right," said Marie.

"I will forever treasure that singular statement."

"Get out of town."

Marie had lunch with Zion at the school, sitting at a small table in an alcove at the back of the building. The children had a garden in the small courtyard using, Zion said, French intensive methods. They ate a salad of sweet onions, basil, and tomatoes grown from it and made by the children. She was also served a glass of green liquid. Zion told her it was spirulina algae in fruit juice. "They bring it in from Freestate. They grow it there. It's full of protein. We drink it every day."

Marie smiled, suppressing her initial grimace, as she swallowed the thick liquid.

In the classroom, now set up as a lunchroom, the children ate lunch with no need of supervision, and some of them were in the kitchen cleaning up. "When we take the children, we will need to get permission from the parents," she told Zion, and he looked grave.

"Madam, the few of them that have parents who actually care for them, I will ask. Most of them live with distant relatives, and some with older brothers or sisters. Many of them live upstairs here."

"I didn't know you were running an orphanage too," said Marie.

"I never really thought of it that way." Zion shrugged. "It just happened. Where else do they have to go? What else do I have to do? I'm sure that the children do not think of it as an orphanage. That makes them sound pitiful. Instead, they are to be admired. We have a communal household. It has evolved gradually. They all have work that they do to make things run smoothly, even the youngest. We iron out problems at our weekly meeting." His smile was wry. "Sometimes the meetings are not much fun. I must say that I often take the role of benevolent dictator. They would probably leave out the word 'benevolent.' It is true that it doesn't work out for everyone. I feel as if I am always nagging. I have had to throw some children out. But it is an interesting experiment. It is the best way to build a new world. But a very hard way."

"It's curious, Marie," said Hugo, sitting on the side of her cabin bunk two mornings later, waking her from a sound sleep.

"I'm not," she said, rolling over.

"The people responsible for Petite Marie's death."

She sat up. "What time is it?"

"The right time to get up. For circadian healthiness. Five-thirty A.M. on a lovely bright morning—"

"I'm sorry," she said, rubbing her eyes and pushing herself back against the headboard. "What did you say?"

"I sent out feelers a couple of weeks ago after Cut Face and Shorty gave us that information. Of course, I had no idea whether or not it was true."

"And?"

Hugo shifted on the bed, frowning. "It seems that this goes to the highest level of international intrigue. Of course, most governments are pretty tightly tied to global corporations."

"Go on."

"There's a company called Small Minds in Sweden. They specialize in artificial intelligence."

"Cute name." Marie was beginning to feel sick to her stomach.

"The thing is that even though we can find the person who gave the orders and set things up, he was working—unbeknownst to him—

for a conglomerate that was doing top-secret work for the U.S. government."

"In Sweden."

"All over the world. You scared them, Marie. Seems that every time some obscure new patent was filed, every time some new product came out, you were there. Buying up shares. Getting control."

"They couldn't know," said Marie in anguish. She rested her head against the yacht's mahogany woodwork, felt the vibration of someone walking up on the deck. Through the open window she heard the sounds of the harbor awakening—metal clanging, seagulls crying, even the sizzle of bacon from the galley of the ketch next door, only a few feet away. "There are . . . certain individuals that are responsible?"

"A few," said Hugo. "The people that set up the . . . situation in Paris. We've got their number. A man in Zurich. Some sort of broker for that kind of thing. And a woman in Sweden. But basically, Marie, you were meddling in some kind of power play. They wanted you under their control. They wanted to use you to further their own ends."

Marie touched the heart stone she now wore around her neck on a chain. She'd had it set in silver and it had just been delivered the day before. The voice of Adele came back to her. *Let it go.*

"They still think that I'm dead."

"So far. Probably."

She did not hesitate. "Kill them."

"I've already sent Cut Face and Shorty to do just that."

She stared at him.

"I told them that it was your order. They left a few hours ago. Eager to do your bidding. Cut Face limping like a trouper. I hope that stuff doesn't wear off midtrip. I have to admit I was upset about it at first. Now I think it's just dandy."

"How—"

"I sent Jean with them."

Marie sank back against the pillow. "Why do I feel so—so strange about it?"

Hugo glanced at her heart stone and smiled very briefly. "Maybe that thing is working. Luckily, I don't have one."

"Hugo?"

"Yes?"

"I want to go home."

"But what about the visit to Freestate?"

"We can arrange to help them. There are children in New Orleans too." Marie had not mentioned the forthcoming child again, and neither had Hugo. Her initial excitement had vanished, and she was left with an emotional vacuum that she hoped would disappear at some point. She had cut way back on her hormones, and intimations of God in the Works had subsided entirely. Enough of illusions. The events of the last few days had jolted her out of her idiotic artificial euphoria. "I've been away too long."

Hugo said quietly, "Yes, you have."

A ketch stopped briefly at a secluded dock at Algiers, just across the river from New Orleans. A brown dwarf and a very tall, very black woman debarked, walked across an expanse of concrete to the ferry terminal, and bought tickets; the ketch continued upriver.

The dwarf wore a suit impeccably tailored of Caribbean-pink linen. The woman wore shorts and a halter top. She carried a large leather bag; her face was half-hidden by a wide-brimmed straw hat.

As the couple approached the ticket booth, she said to the dwarf, "This is ridiculous."

He said, "Specialty of the house."

The woman selling tickets was white. She looked up from her book briefly, made change, caused tickets to issue with a mechanical clank. "It'll be another twenty minutes." She returned to her book. But after a bit she looked over at the two, sitting in the glare of the dock light. The woman seemed oddly familiar. Maybe it was just that she was so striking. The ticket clerk found her place again. Then she remembered who the woman looked like and glanced back over at them. But the ferry was at the dock, and they had apparently boarded.

It was only a four-block walk from the ferry terminal to Marie's old town house. The night was hot and the streets were full of drunks and revelers. Live music blared from every doorway, a cacophony of dull bass runs mingling with tired dixieland. A woman vomited while holding on to a tree. A couple yelled at each other across the street.

"It's good to be home!" said Marie fervently.

They turned down a cobblestone street. Marie shuffled in her bag for a key, unlocked a wrought-iron gate, passed through the vestibule, and unlocked a green door. She pushed it open. After a moment, Hugo took her hand. "You have to go in," he said gently.

Two days later, the *Times-Picayune* gossip section reported that Marie Laveau, whose death certificate was filed in the courthouse, had been seen at the Café Monde on Saturday morning, eating beignets. "This is the third sighting of Marie this week, though the woman is clearly not Marie. Yet the resemblance is close enough to make people look twice. The EAR is offering a fifty-dollar reward—no, the EAR just checked its expense account. Better make that a cup of coffee on the EAR for information leading to pinning this impostor down!"

The police cordoned off her street for a few days until the crowd died down. Her apartment appeared to be inhabited. White curtains blew from open windows.

Sales in *voudoun* paraphernalia shot up.

Marie was not seen again for quite some time.

SECOND SOLO
Japanoiserie

Kita | Kyoto | 2016

Kita leaves the room whenever her assistants centrifuge insects. Bees, ants. Bees, this time. Having lived with insects for so many years, trekking through jungles and across savannas with various mentors while holding the initial pristine vision clear, she tries to think of something else when she knows their lives are ending in such unexpected velocity. She gets a can of coffee hot out of the machine, hides in her cubicle, catches up on six weeks of the exploits of Nan Girl, her favorite comic, which is about the only thing she has her news program automatically save and file, during its sporadic activations—but she usually ends staring unseeing at the screen, her mind filled instead with the past.

The London Zoo. A model hive of bees. Billions of them, crawling over one another, massed in pulsing, buzzing globs of gold and black. Her mother tells her not to be afraid, they are behind glass, but Kita has no idea why she ought to be afraid. She is eight, not a baby. The occasional sting of a honeybee when she runs barefoot through the grass is merely an annoyance. Elephants, giraffes, puffins, most of them nearly extinct in the wild, pale before this alien spectacle. The interactive says that they can see light waves that humans cannot. Their eyes—faceted. They attack enemies, contract with one another and grow their hives, based on something called pheromones, chemical communication cells precise and imperative. How? She remains pressed to the glass until her mother says we have to meet your father and sister now and pulls her away.

She remembers nothing else about that particular London trip.

A green light on her watch glows, no larger than a flea. It's over. She always sets the timer and it seems to help relax her, knowing that the bees are slurry, beyond it all. She touches it with her right forefinger and blots it out.

She walks down the hall, nodding at the guard, always stern and unsmiling. Security is tight at Dento, Inc., a thinly disguised node of government research. Her anticipation rises as she walks. No matter how many computer simulations one runs, there's nothing like getting your hands into the real stuff and mucking around. Leave it overnight accidentally and spawn a new industry. And time seems short. So very short. There are many communication alternatives underway, worldwide. Probably thousands, labs hoping to cash in with the next big thing. She only, and always wanted only, to save the round blue planet that contains her beloved jungles with endemic orchids, species of insects still undiscovered, miles of ants marching from here to there oblivious to human realms.

Until she kills them.

The lab door slides open. Her assistants share amused glances as they always do at her squeamishness. She is a bit different from them. Japanese, of course, but raised all over the world. She stands outside of their idea of one big happy Japanese family. Sometimes she feels a bit dishonest. They accept her. She benefits from this, was wooed from Copenhagen with this plush job offer. But she doesn't buy into their invisible social contract blindly, like they often seem to.

But . . . she loves Kyoto. It's good to be home. Easy.

Briskly, she says, "Well, are we ready?" Another day of trying to simulate pheromones that interact with an artificial medium—gel, liquid, gas, she still doesn't know what will be most efficient. But she knows there's something there. Something important.

Jump Joint Break

Kita | Kyoto | 2016

It was late afternoon. Kita hurried down a corridor at Dento, Inc. She needed to talk to Sui, but couldn't remember his code. She came to a widening in the corridor, expecting to see a secretary at his desk, but he was not there.

Kita dropped into his seat and ran her finger down the code chart on his desk, searching for Sui's number.

A man in a dark suit, wearing a visitor's pass, peeled off from an entourage and leaned on the desk. He smiled broadly.

"Do you speak English?" His accent was American.

Kita nodded absently, perusing the chart.

"How about dinner tonight?"

"I'm busy," she said and stood up.

"No, please. I'm all alone here in Kyoto. You're not married, are you?"

"No, but—"

"Well, come on. I want to see that new place—what is it? That pheromone bar place I read about in the guidebook."

In fact, Kita was a bit intrigued about it herself. She had been thinking about going soon anyway. The guy looked innocuous, and she'd had practice taking care of herself all over the world, practically since she'd been born. "All right."

Kita upended a vial of clear liquid and swallowed it. Too sweet. She grimaced as she set the vial down on the bar. A driving rhythm blasted from the huge flat speakers that formed the walls. The room was packed with dancers looking like models in a wind tunnel, hair blown this way and that. Kita touched the bar and got the wind information again.

FANS ARE NOT JUST AN AMBIENT QUIRK it read, in an attempt to translate Japanese to English. THEY BLOW THE PHEROMONES GENERATED BY YOUR MIND-RELEASE™ TO THE SYNTHESIZER PANELS, WHERE THEY ARE CONSTANTLY COMBINED WITH THE PHEROMONES OF YOUR FELLOWS AND SYNTHESIZED INTO MUSIC. THIS IS MUSIC DIRECT FROM YOUR MIND! TRIP HAPPY! REMEMBER THAT TO CONTINUE TO HAVE INPUT YOU MUST CONTINUE TO DRINK. WE HAPPILY WILL MIX MIND-RELEASE™ INTO YOUR FAVORITE COCKTAIL.

Kita wryly reflected that if she'd added her shot of Mind-Release, for which she'd paid the equivalent of fifteen American dollars, to a cocktail she might be enjoying herself more. She leaned against the bar and surveyed the scene.

The walls pulsed with psychedelic color. As the colors changed, so did the music, gradually, supposedly reflecting the group mood of the people in the bar. A mad little riff ran through it all, which she could have interpreted as her skepticism, had she not been too skeptical to believe that she wasn't at something analogous to a flim-flam show. She was irritated by the almost religious look on the faces of the others there. Luck of the draw, really—some of these bars were raucous, some were violent, and they were springing up everywhere, the latest fad.

But the ghost of her work was in that bar. In fact, she wondered if her company was somehow involved, making money on some of the components. Perhaps some node she knew nothing of had developed those wall panels. Maybe that was why this guy Jack wanted to check it out. His company, apparently, was interested in entering some kind of relationship with Dento.

And maybe the effect was real.

It gave her a glimpse of the future as a mood, a collective event intimately keyed to processes lodged deep within humanity.

It made her uneasy. She did not want to live in a hall of mirrors, in a world that intimately reflected unfiltered thought so quickly. The speed of technological progress was far outrunning their headlights, a scary phenomenon she'd observed during her single college date, years ago, with a Chicago guy who drove too fast down dark twisty roads. The next curve might end in a cliff.

A crashing chord startled her. She laughed.

Well, then, she would experiment.

She danced out on the floor to test the system, pulling Jack with both arms, putting her hands on his hips, and started a Congo snake.

In five minutes, most of the people in the bar danced in a line behind her to a syncopated beat, and the music pulsed accordingly. Maybe, she thought, it's kinesthetic somehow, monitoring movement rather than, or in addition to, pheromones. She broke free, swirled outward, and a lone melody fought and loosened the tight rhythm. The line fractured and new rhythms emerged. Kita imagined a jazz ensemble, improvising madly, knowledgeable enough to control their own feedback, professional enough to be real musicians, cooperative enough to weave the result to new levels.

She leaned against the wall, breathing hard. She felt better now, her sense of doom somewhat dispelled. At least the tedious rock beat was gone.

Her date touched her arm. He had to yell to be heard. "Ready for dinner?"

"Quite ready," she shouted.

Half an hour later, they were in an overpriced Western-oriented hotel restaurant. The menu was in English, German, French, and Japanese. Jack hadn't bothered to ask her advice about where to go. Well, he was the one who was getting ripped off, but she wasn't exactly sure why she was here anyway. She found him irritatingly flirtatious. Maybe all Americans were like this. She hadn't paid much attention to men when she was an undergraduate in Chicago years earlier. Her father had just vanished—maybe to start a new life with a woman who didn't know he had a family, or maybe he had just jumped off a bridge and not bothered to leave a note—and she was grieving and angry and singlemindedly devoting herself to study. Her sister had married an American and kept pressing her to move to Portland. But Kita turned out to be a homebody, after all her travels and international job stints at various research facilities. Her English was excellent; that wasn't the problem. She just found it wearing to be constantly immersed in a world of foreigners. Her sister found it exhilarating, but their personalities were different.

Jack had longish straight brown hair that kept falling across his blue eyes. He wore a dark, rich-looking tie. She didn't have any idea whether an American woman would consider him attractive. He made her uneasy. Maybe it was just the loudness of his voice after a few drinks—which would not have disturbed her, had he been Japanese. A few tables away a group of Japanese businessmen, entertaining a German, were completely overwhelming the music. But Jack kept staring straight into her eyes and she just didn't like it.

Their orders came. Jack was on his third vial of sake. She politely sipped her first cup. The service was quiet and included more bows than was strictly necessary.

"Do you like to travel?" he asked.

"Who doesn't?" It was all she had done her first thirty years.

"I mean, would you like to travel a lot? On business?"

"I suppose it would depend on the business."

"On how much you were paid?"

"What are we talking about?"

He coughed and rice fell from his chopsticks onto the table. "Sorry. Nothing, really. Do you live alone?"

"No," she lied quickly. "I live with my sister." In fact, she lived in a teeny apartment—a small kitchen/living area and a tiny bedroom. She had a sliver of the ocean for a view. She loved her little place. She was beginning to find Jack incredibly rude.

"What does your sister do?"

"She's a teacher." In Portland, Oregon. "Mr. Erickson, what in particular do you want to know about us? We are not a large company, but we are considered to be very good at what we do."

"I know," he said, looking at her thoughtfully, as if he were suddenly not drunk. "I told you three times; call me Jack."

"And your company—is it very large?"

"No," he said. "Our company too is small."

"And what does your company do?"

"We make stainless-steel containers. We bid on providing Dento with a custom-made stainless-steel piping system with permeable membranes where specified. 'Permeable' means that certain types of molecules can pass through it."

"Oh. I will have to add that word—'permeable'—to my vocabulary." She did her best to giggle.

Now she knew what was going on. Quite well, in fact. She had instructed one of the work groups under her to design such a system. She'd briefly reviewed it two months ago. Apparently the project had been put out to bid. She suddenly wondered if they had generated a genuine bid and if Jack's company was even real. Jack struck her as being somehow off. Yet if there was something not right about him, why was he being so obvious about it? Surely he didn't consider her an idiot. Of course, he did seem to have the impression that she was a secretary, and she'd said nothing to disillusion him.

"I can make you an offer—" he began.

"For what?"

"We can discuss that later. It depends on if you might be able to access some information at your job—I'm sorry, did I say something funny?"

Kita squelched her smile. He obviously had no idea of what she did at Dento, Inc. She had access indeed. "Mr. Erickson, you've been very kind to take me out tonight, but I'm afraid you have been misled. I really have no idea what is going on at Dento. My clearance is very low, you see. I am just a secretary." She paused. "But you will still pay for my dinner? I'm not sure that I could afford it."

She truly enjoyed seeing Jack scowl down at his plate and say, "Of course."

BREAK WITH FOUR SECTIONS

i

Biogenic Magnetite and EMF Effects

Magnetite biomineralization is a genetically-controlled biochemical process through which organisms make perfect ferromagnetic crystals, usually of single magnetic domain size. This process is an ancient one, having evolved about 2 billion years ago in the magnetotactic bacteria, and presumably was incorporated in the genome of higher organisms, including humans. During this time, DNA replication, protein synthesis, and many other biochemical processes have functioned in the presence of strong static fields of up to 400 mT adjacent to these magnetosomes without any obvious deleterious effects. Recent behavioral experiments using short but strong magnetic pulses in transduction of geomagnetic field information to the nervous system, and both behavioral and direct electrophysiological experiments indicate sensitivity thresholds to DC magnetic fields down to a few nT. However, far more biogenic magnetite is present in animal tissues than is needed for magnetoreception, and the biological function of this extra material is unknown. The presence of ferromagnetic materials in biological systems could provide physical transduction mechanisms for ELF magnetic fields, as well for microwave radiation in the .5 to 10 Ghz band where magnetite has its peak ferromagnetic resonance.

—Joseph L. Kirschvink, Cal Tech,
http://epswww.epfl.ch/aps/BAPSMAR96/abs/S2781002.html

ii

Iron Biomineralization in Dugong Brains and Livers

Dugongs have very high concentrations of iron in their livers. They also migrate in the open ocean and therefore likely have some sort of navigation device built into their physiology. This project will examine the brain of the dugong using magnetic methods to determine whether there is magnetic material in the brains which may aid in navigation by geomagnetic field sensing. If magnetic material is found to be present, examination of the brain tissue with transmission electron microscopy will be employed to determine whether or not it is similar to other known organisms which navigate using biogenic magnetite and the Earth's magnetic field.

http://www.biophysics.pd.uwa.edu.au/dugong.html

iii

Structure and Function of the Vertebrate Magnetic Sense

Three Excerpts

We have identified single neurons in the superficial ophthalmic ramus (ros V) of the trigeminal nerve that respond to changes in the intensity but not the direction of an imposed magnetic field, and used a combination of new imaging and microscopic techniques to identify candidate magnetite-based magnetoreceptor cells in the nose of the trout.

We suggest that vertebrates detect magnetic fields using magnetite-based magnetoreceptors located in the lamina propria of the olfactory epithelium and linked to the brain via the ros V.

Our results suggest that a magnetite-based magnetic sense makes an important contribution to long-distance orientation by animals. Responses to changes in magnetic intensity have been implicated in the formation of a "magnetic map."

—Michael M. Walker, Carol E. Diebel, Cordula V. Haugh, Paricia M. Pankhurst, John C. Montgomery, & Colin R. Green, *Nature*, Vol. 390

iv

Homing in on Vertebrates

A huge range of organisms can sense magnetic fields. Do humans remain an exception? We certainly have a trigeminal nerve, with an ophthalmic branch, and we can also make biogenic magnetite . . . the final word on the existence of human magnetoreception has certainly not been written.

—Joseph L. Kirschvink, *Nature*, Vol. 390

THIRD SOLO
Dissonant Swing

Jason | Sedona | 2018

Spring in Sedona was just a softening of the air, and a season of floods as high snow melt swelled rivers. For Jason, the spring of his fifth year was a season of screaming fits and seizures, a season of doing things like smashing the drywall of the small cabin his parents were building, so they could move out of their trailer, with a drywall ax.

The day afterward he lay spent and occasionally sobbing because of his headache on a foam mat, watching his mother and father unroll fiberglass webbing and slather gobs of patch on the walls. He was in what would be the kitchen, and they were in the living room, next to the big stone fireplace. It was chillier up here than in the valley. They had bit into the red rocks with a pointed metal bar and set six by six posts. The view was one of sloping, intersecting lines washed with slashes of green pine and shadows. His mother claimed that it was a holy spot, an unfound vortex. They had bought the land before he was born.

Jason curled up on his side and put his thumb in his mouth. He hardly ever sucked his thumb except at times like this, when everything hurt so bad. He began to replay last night, when they sat by the fire, sparks shooting upward into the vast dark. It soothed him, this story his mother told, and he was able to see it and hear it quite clearly. Remembering his Story kept away the pain.

"My name used to be Julia," she always began. "But now it is Cassiopeia." Speaking in the low gentle voice she used on her hypnosis clients, Cassie leaned forward on her camp stool and clasped her hands; her blond hair fell forward in a curtain made bright by the light of their campfire so he could not see her face.

Jason was snuggled in his sleeping bag and rested against his father's knees.

"Why did you change your name?" he asked on cue.

"Good question," interjected his father. "My name has always been Mike. Never thought of changing it."

"The story unfolds on its own." Jason could tell that his mother was smiling by the sound of her voice. "It was Thanksgiving eve, and I was at the Airport Vortex, giving a tour. There was supposed to be a meteor shower."

Jason was impatient. "But really it was the night of the first Silence! And now you have to say why the vortexes are important."

"And don't forget to tell us why there are male and female vortexes," added Mike. They both knew he was teasing, as usual, and ignored him.

Cassie continued, "There are certain places of power on the Earth. Some people say that they have something to do with what they call magnetic lines of force. I really don't know. But here in Sedona, there seems to be a lot of places like that. Holy places. Where you can *feel* the power. The Anasazi, the people who are gone, lived here for centuries and knew about these holy sites."

Jason liked it when she kind of started to chant. He had gone on one of her vortex tours once. She used a microphone on the bus and her voice was even more powerful. One woman that she used to counsel when she worked for the Psychic Network, before the phones got so bad, still called her whenever phone service was available and talked for hours. "Did you tell Nervous Nellie when it was auspicious to use the bathroom?" his dad would tease when Mom hung up. "And for free? Gosh, Cassie, you had such a good racket going. A hundred and twenty an hour after taxes!" Sometimes Mom laughed, but usually she said something like, "You'll believe it too, when you're ready. Each soul awakens in its own time."

"What happens at a vortex, Mom?"

She stared into the fire, a slight smile on her face. "Your father will just make fun of me."

"*I* won't! Tell me about the infinite, and the word—what is it? Yeah, the word—less—ness. What about that night at the Airport Vortex?"

She picked up the story. "It was an auspicious night. The stars were out, just like tonight. But Heather Crystal, the movie star, lived in Sedona then. Vortex Tours had an agreement with the airport that they would try to allow very few flight plans to be filed whenever we had a special night event. Because the owner of the tour company had a friend on the airport board—or something like that. Most everybody respected that, since most people who live in Sedona—"

"Are kind of nutty," Mike interjected.

Cassie continued calmly, "—believe in the sanctity of the vortex experience. But Heather never cared. She flew in and out whenever she pleased. So her private jet was revving up and I was really irritated. It's hard to be soothing when you feel that way. All the people on the tour were standing around a medicine circle, holding the sacred rocks that they had chosen."

"Say it, Mom."

"All right. 'Feel the power coming up through the earth, through the soles of your shoes, into your feet. That's right. Just feel it. It is like an arrow of warm, loving light. See the light coming into your solar plexus. Now the light is blossoming in the center of your chest. Some of you might see it as a flower, a golden lotus. Feel the energy, the love. You are part of the earth. You were born of the earth. You evolved from the earth. The earth is your mother' "—here she bent down and pressed her hand against the ground—" 'the sky is your father. Feel the energy shoot up your spine. The top of your head is like a blue light.' "

"Like the damned airport lights!" said Jason. "That's what you were thinking, because of the jet being so loud—"

His mother pretended she hadn't heard him say "damn." It was so hard to make her mad that it wasn't any fun. "Then you had everybody lie down on their backs and watch the sky."

"Yes." His mother was sitting straight now, her eyes closed, as if she was feeling the vortex right now.

Jason snuggled more deeply into his sleeping bag and stared into the fire. "And just when you were in the vortex—"

"Just when I had completely merged with earth and sky, become wholly one with Gaia, and thinking in the back of my mind that I wished Gaia would make Heather's jet stop—"

"It stopped!" Jason shouted. He loved this part.

"Just a coincidence," Mike said as usual.

"But everything stopped. The Internet, and telephones, and a lot of cars—it was the first Silence. And Mom knew that I was inside her, for the first time. Growing."

"She did do a test before she went out that night," Mike always pointed out, as if that made a big difference.

"Yes," Mom said. Her voice was firm and happy. "Yes, that was when I knew that you were there and that you were very special.

I was in a trance. I didn't wake up until your father came up and found me."

"He was mad."

"I was worried. Irritated that the driver just left your mother up there alone when he couldn't shake her awake and took the tour back down to town. All that idiot could say was 'I respected her trance. She's a holy woman.' "

"Are you, Mom?"

Cassie laughed. He saw by the firelight that her eyes were serious, though. "We all are holy in our own way. And that was your special night, Jason. It was a special conjunction. A message from the stars."

" 'A message from the stars,' " Jason whispered, just to himself, pulling his thumb from his mouth to say it, then sticking it back in. He felt a little better. And it was good that there was a vortex here, though he had never felt it. His dad hadn't either, but he really liked the view. Because of the radio problem, Dad couldn't make as much money as he used to, so they'd had to build slowly. Sometimes Dad went away for weeks at a time for something he called "projects," and when he came back they would build some more. Sometimes Mom talked about completing a master's degree, whatever that was—something to help her make more money.

When he was a baby, Jason had spent more time than most babies screaming. When he could talk enough to say that his head hurt, many inconclusive scans were done. Things had only gradually come into kilter for him, vision-wise. He was not kinetically sophisticated. He fell, he crashed, he bumped—much more, they said, than he ought to.

He turned over and looked east, where an eagle etched the brilliant blue sky. At least when he was lying down, he wouldn't fall down. A few years ago, he had smashed the television; luckily, he had not punctured the tube but only battered the control buttons with a hammer. His mother said, "We won't get another one. They're hardly useful now, anyway." He almost felt as if it made her happy that the television was gone, although his father made it abundantly clear that such acts were not to be repeated.

He thought he was too old for that kind of thing. That's what his parents told him about the incident yesterday.

But lying on the floor, looking at the spaces and colors arranged by horizontal and vertical lines, he knew that he was not. He wanted to smash the radio.

He would—right now. Only it hurt his head to move. Everything seemed so much worse than ever before. His stomach hurt too. He was feeling very bad and he had used up his story. The radio was playing what his dad called "silly space stuff" from the Sedona station.

Midsong, it stopped playing. That wasn't unusual. His parents paid no attention.

Jason's headache vanished.

He sat up cautiously. The throbbing in his head did not resume. He blew his nose on a tissue.

His mother turned around. "Lie down, Jason. Rest."

She turned back to her plastering. His father continued his steady pace. Jason remembered being locked within his strong arms yesterday, his legs pinioned between his father's, as he screamed and screamed and screamed. That was after he had ruined the wall in a frenzy of pain.

He scooted backward until he was leaning against a post. The french doors salvaged from a remodeled house in town stood open. He felt around for his sunglasses, then realized that he didn't need them today. The sunlight wasn't causing him pain.

Instead, it was causing music.

Not really music, he supposed, but something like it. Broad low tones that filled him as if he were air. Laced through those tones were high thin sounds, vibrating against one another in varying counterpoint; merging, diverging, rapturously, he thought, his vocabulary quite large enough to encompass such a word. He had heard his parents talk about having him "tested" and they always decided not to. They seemed afraid of something. They wouldn't tell him what it was.

"Mom?" he said.

"Hmmm?" She didn't turn around, but bent and scooped patch onto her broad knife, stood and swooped it onto the wall, where it gleamed wet and blue-white. He wanted to help them fix it, but they wouldn't let him get up.

"I can hear it."

"Hear what, honey?"

"The vortex. I can hear it."

She turned and he wondered why there were tears in her eyes. "Rest now, all right?"

He sat absorbed in the music, sometimes dozing off. Now that the pain in his head had receded, he realized that his whole body ached. He really was tired. It was a lot of work to smash a house. He wished it hadn't happened.

The sounds calmed at sunset, but the moon was a single high pure note as his father scooped him up to carry him back to the trailer, and even though the path was lit by the Coleman lantern his mother carried, he could still hear the stars, their distant songs bursts of color inside his eyelids when he closed them, lulled by his father's long, steady stride.

He hoped the music would last.

"We've got to have him tested."

Jason opened his eyes. He was in his small bunk, which folded down out of the ceiling of the trailer and had its own tiny window that was cranked open, letting in the scent of pine and earth damp from spring melt. A model space station dangled near his feet, black. A few luminous stick-on stars and planets shone from the ceiling, inches from his eyes.

"You know how I feel about that." His mother's voice.

"It's not fair to him. You can see that, Cassie. It might be curable. And it's dangerous. I think we should take him to Flagstaff tomorrow."

"But Ed—"

"Ed is not a real *doctor,* Cassie."

"He has his MD," said Cassie, a stubborn tone in her voice.

"But he's veered off into the stratosphere since then. He didn't pass his boards. Herbal medicine, crystals . . . Didn't he say that he thought that aliens had implanted crystals in his body? And he has some kind of hocus-pocus theory about why they don't show up on X rays? Because they're made of *alien* materials—pretty convenient. Anyway, you can see that his treatments aren't helping at all."

"He found out that Jason was mineral-deficient and needs a lot more minerals than most people, didn't he? Maybe he'd be worse without the treatments."

"Maybe he could get *better*. Cassie, there's a world of science. This is your child. How can you deny him the opportunity to get better? Can't you see how he suffers? If you won't come with me, I'll just have to take him by myself. First we'll have to find a doctor in Flagstaff and see what kind of referrals we can get. The last time I went to Los Angeles we had an Internet pulse and I downloaded a ton of stuff. I don't think that he's an isolated case. There are kids his exact age all over the world with the same cluster of symptoms. Not many. But some."

Symptoms. Jason lay on his back, watching his stars. That's what all these headaches and rages were. Symptoms. But symptoms of what?

He was afraid.

"I know," said his mother, her voice weary. "You told me all this when you got home."

"That was a month ago. We've waited far too long. We need to go. Tomorrow morning. You don't have to go if you don't want to."

"The doctors didn't help my brother any."

"Cassie, he had a very serious cancer. And that was years ago. We have to try all we can. Look at organized medicine as a kind of theory, just like all your organic theories. It's a Western theory, that's all. Next time he could hurt himself. Or others."

A sigh. "All right. I always wonder if it might have something to do with that virus I had. That bad cold. There are a lot of viruses that affect the fetus. They can even be something the mother got when *she* was a child—"

His father's voice, gentle. "Don't be silly."

"I'm just at my wit's end."

"I know, honey, I am too."

The sliver of light in the open doorway vanished, and Jason drifted into sleep.

The next afternoon his parents were filling out forms in a clinic. His mother's face was drawn, her eyes worried. Jason was looking at some of the children's books in the waiting room, but they all seemed a little silly. At home he was reading *Kidnapped*. "Put your father's address," she whispered to his dad.

"How will they get in touch with us?" he asked.

"He can forward things to us," she said. "It won't take much longer."

"Cassie," his father said in an exasperated tone of voice, but he shrugged and Jason could tell that Dad would do it. Jason liked this, it was kind of like being in a spy book. They stayed in a motel that night. Jason watched his dad pay the man with cash. They never used credit cards like other parents. The next morning Jason had a lot of tests done. He had to drink thick liquids that tasted bad. He had to lie still in a white tunnel while they did brain scans. They took blood out of him with a needle. They took him to McDonald's, which his mother usually didn't allow. They stayed another day. After that they went into an office and the doctor said that although they hadn't found anything wrong so far, it had been necessary to send some of the information away. The results wouldn't be back for a few days, so Jason and his family could leave. They'd be in touch.

"Are you happy now?" asked Cassie as they got on the interstate and headed south.

"Not really," Mike said, "but I feel a little more comfortable."

As they climbed gravel roads and nosed along the ridge that led to their house, the view reminded him of the grand snow-covered peaks they'd visited last summer. Simultaneously, he thought about something else he'd been learning about with his educational programs.

"Prime numbers are important because they're the only real numbers," he said with excitement, leaning forward and sticking his head between his parents'.

"Why do you say that?" asked Cassie.

"Because you can destroy all the other ones. You can reduce them. They're not really themselves. They're made up of other numbers. Prime numbers. And prime numbers can only be . . . um . . ."

"Factored?" suggested Cassie.

"Yeah. Factored by one and themselves. So they're the only real numbers. You can take all the other numbers apart. You can't take primes apart. You can't make them any smaller. They're real solid. They're themselves. Say you look out over all the numbers in existence. The primes stand taller. They're like mountain peaks. If you could look at them in a different way—like from an airplane or something—they'd form some kind of pattern."

"Nice," said Cassie. "I'd never thought of it in that way." She reached back and ruffled his hair. "I'm glad you're feeling better, honey."

In a week, a forwarded letter arrived in their box. Jason ran into the post office and got the mail, as he usually did, and pointed it out to his dad when he got in the car. "It says it's from the U.S. government."

His dad opened it carefully with his pocket knife.

"What does it say?" asked Jason after a few moments of silence.

"It says that we're to report to a special clinic in Denver for further testing," he said. "But it doesn't say why."

"It doesn't say what's wrong with me?"

"No. I expected to get the test results. If we wanted to, we could just take them to someone here. And we'd have them for your records. But this doesn't say a damned thing about them."

Jason was surprised. His father didn't swear often.

Ascending Triplet

Zeb | Washington, D.C. | 2018

Ellie Pio sat in her small office in the Naval Observatory, contemplating very tall stacks of papers. They were interspersed with very tall stacks of books. She did not want to do anything with these stacks. Looking at them made her feel very tired. One should not have to deal with tall stacks on a bright midmorning in May.

The knock at the door behind her was a welcome relief. She rotated her chair. There he was, the bum in his shabby designer overcoat. His long gray hair was pulled back into a ponytail, and unlike so many bums who went around stubbled, he had a thick white beard trimmed neatly between short and long. His fingernails were always clean and he never smelled of alcohol. She liked his eyes—brown, restful to look into, filled with an intelligence that belied his appearance. "Come in," she said. "Sit down."

He settled into the wooden chair in front of her desk.

"I was just getting ready for my lunch," she said.

"Kind of early for lunch, isn't it?" His voice was quite lovely. A bit of a Southern accent. At times he said "y'all."

But it was his obvious intelligence that was most at odds with his appearance. He came about once a week. He talked about interstellar physics, the radio problem, general astronomy. He'd read an article of hers in *Physical Review* and looked her up; he said he was just an interested layperson, but she did not believe him for a second. She'd had him cleared in permanently after his first visit, when a secretary had buzzed her doubtfully. He seemed half-familiar to her, as if she'd seen him somewhere before. A favorite uncle of hers had disappeared into the streets—an alcoholic—many years ago, leaving a family and an executive position. It broke her heart when her mother had disowned her brother and refused to see or help him. She sensed that this man's grasp on reality was tenuous. She was glad he kept returning.

She unwrapped her peanut butter and jelly sandwich and handed him half. He accepted with a nod. "Coffee?" she said. She rose and poured them both some syrupy stuff into cups of doubtful cleanliness.

"Thanks."

He visited often, and their friendship grew.

A year after he met Ellie Pio, Zeb made his way up a narrow debris-strewn stairway in a poorly kept Anacostia apartment building. When he reached the fourth floor and walked down the hallway, a door opened. Someone peered past the chain suspiciously, then slammed the door.

Zeb pulled a matchbook from his pocket and opened it; turned it so that he could read the number by the dim ceiling bulb. He continued down the hallway until he reached the end and knocked on the door of #423.

Again, the door was opened cautiously, but this time the chain was unhooked and he was pulled into the room. The door was shut quietly behind him.

"Hey, it's the old guy," said a young man with a roll-up keyboard in his lap. "Nice to see you again." About ten people were in the room, sitting on the floor or on the bed.

"Let me take your coat," said Dr. Pio, the door guard. "You've missed several meetings. We've been worried about you."

"That's okay," said Zeb, responding to the coat question by putting his hands in his coat pockets possessively. The room smelled of stale carpet, burned coffee, and cigarette smoke. The windows had aluminum foil taped over them. A large cable snaked through one of them, though, attached to abandoned satellite dishes or other antennae on the roof. All their rooms were the same; they moved every month or so. "I mean, sorry I missed the meetings. I didn't know." Someone at P Street Beach, where he'd been sleeping under the bridge, had given him some money today, offered him a cigarette, lit it with a match from the book, and pressed the matchbook into his hand. Maybe it was the same bum who sat and chatted with him every month or so late at night, and maybe it was the same bum who liked to look at his notebooks every once in a while. He didn't know. Zeb had a dim memory of a heavy beard, sunglasses, a stocking cap pulled down to the eyebrows even in summer, and a voice roughened by cigarette smoke or a perpetual cold.

"Look," said Pio, dressed as usual in drab greens and browns, "I apologize for last time."

"Last time?" he asked, puzzled.

She sighed. "Exactly."

"She took you to a clinic, Zeb," said one of the women. "You ran away."

"Oh," he said and tried to grin. "No wonder I didn't come back."

"You pushed one of the techs down before she could even get you checked in," said Pio in a disapproving tone. "She didn't seem very upset, though. She said it looked as if you were having a panic attack."

"Oh, that's right," he said. "And then—somehow I blamed the whole thing on the shelter, Pio. That's why I didn't go back. Didn't you tell me we were just going out for a cup of coffee? I must have blanked the rest out."

Pio threw up her hands. "Like I said, I apologize. You can return to the shelter with complete impunity." The shelter gave everyone an evening meal and one of many cots in a large room. The shelter did not ask for names. If someone left, driven, say, by an urge for drugs or alcohol, they were not readmitted that night. Zeb never left. But ever since that incident, he'd been wary of the building, turning back when a couple of hundred yards away, even when his buddies yelled at him, "Come on, Star Man! We miss you!"

"We're moving this week," said a young woman sitting in front of a flatscreen hung from a nail.

"Well," said Pio briskly, "let's get started." She went around the room and distributed papers to everyone. She wore white gloves. "The Very Large Array had all of its fused chips replaced for the umpteenth time and is operating. But the atmospheric blackout is complete about 90 percent of the time, as you can see, and the chips need to be replaced so often that it's hard to get a decent baseline. The military takeover of every kind of telescope, radio or otherwise, is complete. I've heard rumors that the military has also taken over all three space hotels, the moon base, and the private Mars colony. As always, I need to emphasize that if any of you ever tell where you got this, I'll be in deep shit."

"The United States military?" asked one of the women.

"Yes," said Pio, "although they're working out information and responsibility sharing protocol via treaties."

"But . . . the Mars colony was tiny. And multinational. Wouldn't all those other countries protest? Or at least the stockholders or something?"

Pio shrugged. "What good would it do them? Besides, our news of them is quite limited. They are very far away and essentially incommunicado much of the time now. They're sitting ducks. Not much we can do about it. Who knows, the U.S. military might even now be waging a battle against aliens in the tunnels of Mars."

A young woman laughed nervously.

Zeb sat hunched over on an old bureau. He tilted the shade of the lamp next to him and studied the papers one by one, setting each one aside after perusal. He had not removed his coat. He hoped the water was turned on. Sometimes the rooms were paid for, but most often the club just squatted during the hours they used the rooms. In this part of town, people weren't very nosy. They just wanted to be left alone. He planned to take a shower after everyone left; it was his habit to do so after each meeting in each temporary room—if possible.

He wasn't exactly sure how to take these people. Enthusiastic SETI members, they were convinced, like him, that some sort of intelligence lay behind the silences. But unlike him, they had concocted a veritable encyclopedia of probable traits of the perpetrators. Zeb had no idea what they might look like and didn't care. He was much more interested in how they thought. He was pretty sure that he couldn't possibly comprehend it.

"Well?" asked the young man in glasses. "What do you think, Star Man?" No one used their real names here.

Zeb finished with the last paper and shrugged. "Not enough information. I do think this is a deliberate and planned effect not necessarily aimed at us. We could just be in the way. It has resulted in a huge backsliding in our ability to communicate with one another. But that may be just a flukish side effect."

"You mean you think that these beings might not have intended this."

"It may well not have been their primary goal. Why assume that it was? Why assume that they share anything about our mind-set, including the idea of war? Maybe we just happen to be in the path of some communication they're sending."

"But see?" said the woman, jumping up with excitement. "Just the fact that they probably exist is so stunning!"

"I agree," said Zeb.

"We're not alone!"

"Perhaps not. But they could well be so far away that it makes no real difference to us. It could be that this is some side effect of what they're doing and it's all we'll ever know of them."

"But wouldn't you like to—like to travel out? Meet them?"

Zeb laughed. "That seems rather far-fetched."

"It's not!" said the woman fervently. "With nanotechnology we'll be able to grow near-light-speed ships and power them. And we'll be able to use various technologies to keep ourselves viable until then—"

"Yeah. Maybe even upload our minds into the ships."

"Ah yes," said Zeb, sliding down from the bureau, half-wishing they would leave so that he could take his shower. "I'm afraid that I'm too old for that."

And suddenly he thought of Annie. Annie, Sal's daughter, getting her degree in nanotechnology. That last Thanksgiving dinner . . . how long ago? A few years? And his self-exile.

It was like this sometimes. Things kept coming back. Those diamonds he kept in his coat. Maybe Ellie would know what to do with them. He didn't know why he hadn't thought of asking her before. But maybe he had.

And with that he remembered that Craig was dead. Dead because of all this.

"Hey, Star Man." The woman patted his back. "Don't cry. What did I say? I'm sorry. Ellie . . ."

"All of you clear out now," Ellie said amid grumbles that the meeting had hardly begun. "And remember that by next week this place has to be vacated. We've been meeting here for too long." Zeb heard murmured goodbyes and a bit of chatter about how they would get the night's information to the national and international SETI network.

Ellie sat on the battered couch with Zeb and held his hand for a long time as he stared straight ahead. Finally she rose, put on her coat, and pulled him up. "You're coming home with me," she said.

"No, I can't." Panic rose in him.

"Nonsense. Let's go down and get a cab. I promise I won't try any funny stuff."

"No clinics."

"No. But why not? I'm telling you, Zeb, it's really upsetting to see the way you get sometimes."

"Because . . ." They were walking down the dark hallway now, and he tried to put it into words. "Because that puts out the lights. The medicine. I'm so normal that I can't think."

Ellie sighed.

Everything looked so strong to him. The faded Victorian women on the wallpaper, the snaking pattern of the carpet, the machined carvings on the wooden frame of the cracked mirror at the end of the hall. They would overwhelm him if he let them. It was better if things were distant and weak. These details pressing into his vision filled the field of thought with too much information. He reached into the right pocket of his coat, thrust his thumb and fingers through the hole in the bottom, used his left hand to bring the coat's hem upward. His fingers grasped the envelope that rode with him everywhere, safe in the coat's silk lining. He worked it out through the hole.

"I have something to show you. You might know what it is."

He opened the packet within the envelope. The money was long gone. He unfolded the translucent brown paper and revealed the diamonds.

"Where did you get them?"

"From a friend of mine. I think he had something to do with intelligence. I remembered him tonight. I don't always remember. He said that they were important. I think that they might contain classified astronomical information. But how would you read them?"

Pio held one up to the dim bulb hanging from the ceiling. She put it back in the paper. "You may be right. I don't know of any machine that would read this. Is it all right if I keep one?"

Zeb shrugged. "I have a feeling that if I showed them to a jeweler, he might be instructed to call the police. They might have some kind of identifying marks. It might not even look like a diamond, close up. I want to know what's in it. I don't think my friend would have just handed me some diamonds for no reason. If they're real, they're probably not worth much. They grow them by the ton now and you can't tell the difference."

Ellie dropped one into her coin purse. As Zeb descended the stairs behind her, he said, "So information is still coming in during the silences, right? That's what those readouts show. But very high-frequency."

"What do you think about that?"

"It means something, of course, to someone. But it would take a lot more recordings of it to figure out what that might be. To break the code. If it's not too complex for human brains."

"Zeb, do you really think—"

"Although as a human I must say I can't help but admire our abilities, I also can't help but realize that they might be somewhat limited."

They reached the ground floor and stepped into the lobby, floored with a cracked, dirty pattern of black and white porcelain tiles. A fanlight and glass doors admitted light from the street, but the overhead light was burnt out.

They walked out onto the concrete stoop. Cars passed occasionally. Most of the streetlights were out, and both sides of the street were lined with town houses, many of them completely dark. Downtown, traffic cops directed traffic most of the time now, but in Anacostia drivers were on their own.

Ellie waved her arm for a cab.

It was a month later. The weather was lousy; it was raining ice.
But Zeb walked through a rain of perfection.

Perfection, like the sleet of buildings crowding toward Zeb; like the sleet of trees all heading toward him like arrows of truth. He was perfection's target, its organizer, its conscious and delighted focusing eye. He trod a favorite path through a park, soaked, the precious packet from Ellie sealed in plastic, and approached the gorgeous Episcopal National Cathedral on the hill. The surrounding oaks, huge and black and leafless against the dark midmorning sky, were slashed like him by truth, a truth like sleet that melted into his intellect sharp and wakening. He turned toward the Cathedral, not having intended to go there but thinking now there was no better place to unwrap the dangerous wonder.

He pulled open a heavy door and was welcomed by candles and incense; High Episcopal. A boy's choir sent practice echoes beating back from a hundred feet above. A tour group scuffled past, listening to their guide's talk diffuse into tones of varying pitches. He walked an aisle and came to a cross, turned left, ducked into a tiny chapel with four pews and an altar decked with cloth, unlit candles, and flowers.

He reached into a pocket and took out a scratched, recycled Ziploc bag, picturing, with an instant's tenderness, Ellie rinsing it at her kitchen sink and setting it to dry on the drainboard. She had given it to him, then whispered that he should leave and never return to the Observatory. Her face was pale. She showed him out a back door.

Inside was a thin object resembling a book, which he opened.

Ellie had gotten it through a friend of a friend of a friend. Apparently, this procurement could be interpreted as a treasonous act. One of the "friends" might well trace the diamond. Zeb wished Ellie had told him all this earlier, but maybe she hadn't known the danger until too late; at any rate, this thought darkened Zeb for a moment. Then he explored.

Inside the left leaf, he saw that the diamond was sealed within a shallow well, which probably read the information.

He touched the ON pad of the right leaf, which was a screen.

Warnings of top secrecy flashed in bright red. He bypassed them and continued to the menu. A screen asked for a code word, but it was automatically supplied when Zeb tried ENTER, thanks to Ellie's friends.

He took a deep breath and dipped into the information. . . . A Y-

SHAPED NEUTRAL SHEET REGION WAS IDENTIFIED WHEN THE THIRD (AXIAL) COM-
PONENT OF THE MERGING FIELD WAS ZERO (NULL HELIOCITY MERGING) OR VERY
SMALL . . . AN IMPORTANT RELATIONSHIP WAS DISCOVERED FOR DELTA, THE
THICKNESS OF THE Y-SHAPED SHEET . . .

Zeb sat with the boys' voices sleeting into him, along with the
light-figures on the screen; they blended and infused him with increasing joy. Made of matter, he also comprehended matter, and matter's
motion, and what it might mean, glimmering down a path he could
only see the beginnings of. They all stood only on the first step of the
path, and it stretched infinitely far. Matter could modify matter again
and again and consciousness and understanding could grow
boundlessly.

Or it could be shut down forever.

He pushed that thought away. It was not one he wanted to enter-
tain at this moment.

It was worth it. The losses, the blackened streaks of time, the
weeks of stumbling stupidity. If the darkness was payment for this
light.

THE SECOND MOVEMENT

The Times, London,
Evening Edition
July 10, 2019

At a press conference this afternoon, the Prime Minister denied reports that there exists an agreement among the members of the North Atlantic Nanotech Organization to fund research focussed on producing the feared, theoretically possible Universal Assembler.

"That would be against international law," she replied. "We have, in conjunction with our treaty members, authorized the release of certain molecular manufacturing machines which will relieve some of the perennial problems of humankind. These machines only have the capacity of replicating in a strictly controlled fashion for serious, and not frivolous, ends. I repeat, there is no move among member nations to open the door to nanotech research that would be as dangerous, reckless, and irresponsible as a Universal Assembler might prove to be."

The Prime Minister did not point out that the United States has not signed this treaty; some speculated that such a reminder might seem accusatory.

When asked if there had been any reports lately from Tranquillity Base on the moon, which has been feared lost to a nanotech cataclysm, the Prime Minister responded that it was too early to know anything for sure. "The Silence will lift, as it always does" was her reply. "Moscow has launched a reconnaissance flight, but as you know, France's similar flight last month was tragically lost when a sudden pulse caused it to plunge into the North Atlantic. We must exercise caution and restraint. However, I must observe that the moon was not governed by our laws regarding nanotechnology and may have suffered serious consequences because of that."

FOURTH SOLO
Tamchu and the Girl

Kathmandu, Nepal | 2020

The tourists watched indulgently, charitably, at first. They always did. As if stopping at Tamchu's little patch of territory was an obligation, a sort of penance for having money, while, presumably, he did not. Else why would he be begging on the street? He barely glanced at them, a trio perfect for this particular act—impatient father, smiling mother, wide-eyed boy.

With a theatrical flourish, Tamchu pulled from one pocket of his loose pants a small green rectangular prism that looked waxy and pliable. From his other pocket, he took a pinch of the golden powder ho kept in a plastic bag and rolled the green prism in the stuff. Then he cupped his hands tightly around it and felt it warm. He smiled guilelessly at the tourists, making sure to catch the eye of the mother. He winked at the boy and the boy looked startled, then winked back. He bowed his head and muttered some utterly meaningless words in Hindi over his hands. His tiny portable radio poured forth music vaguely oriental.

"Come on, let's go," said the father. "We've got a lot of stuff to see. And I want to get back to the Hilton for lunch. No telling what kind of diseases we could get eating around here."

Tamchu felt the fluttering within his hands. He nodded to his sister, sitting on the blanket, and she reached behind herself and picked up one of the small delicate cages she had assembled from toothpicks and glue. She worked on them here by the temple. He could have bought suitable cages for the same price in lots of a hundred, but this made a better show, brought in more money. Besides, hers were complex and interesting, small works of art.

The man turned away, but the boy stood still and the woman said, "Wait, honey. I think he's done."

Tamchu uncupped his hands at the door of the tiny cage and an emerald-winged butterfly staggered into the cage, with barely room to flutter its stiffening wings. His sister shut the door and secured it with another toothpick.

The boy stared. "How did you do that?"

"Magic," said Tamchu.

"Mom," said the boy in a pleading voice.

The father was irritated, but Tamchu bargained smoothly and efficiently for euros and admonished the boy that he had to release the butterfly at the end of the day because it contained a reborn soul. He said that thus would the boy gain good karma. "You will make sure he does this?" Tamchu entreated the mother. He'd had more than one irate tourist return the next day with the butterfly dead in the cage.

She nodded. They moved down the street and turned the corner.

"I'm tired," said his sister. She was not really his sister, which anyone could tell. He had high Tibetan cheekbones and coppery skin, while she was pale and willowy. Like him, she had lost her family. But while he still had distant relatives, members of the well-entrenched Tibetan refugee community here in Kathmandu who had promised to help himself and his sister once they arrived, she seemed to have no one in the world. He thought of her as his sister because she was the same age as the real sister he had lost to fever during the long trek from Tibet to Nepal. Fever, while above them flew some sort of new kind of Chinese helicopter that could morph into a jet, and which fluttered down notices that because they had broken the law, they would not drop the new, cheap antidote. If they would turn around . . .

But the group had refused.

Tamchu knelt next to her. He had known her for eight months. "I know, Illian." It was an odd name. "Here, let me fix your pillow so that you can rest. In the shade?"

"No, in the sun," she said with a little shiver. He moved the pillow and helped her lie down, covered her with a blanket.

"Here's someone else," she said, struggling to rise, her eyes full of pain.

"I'll handle them," he said. "You rest." He turned to the tourists, hating them and their money, the money that could purchase a cure for her.

They had told him about it at the free clinic, where he took Illian when she first had her symptoms. They did all the usual things—a DNA scan and immunizations. The nurse practitioner told him that Illian had a rare virus and gave him a printout that described it. It supposedly worsened steadily and ended in death at an early age. There was a cure that was administered only at a clinic in Germany, courtesy of the government. The cure was experimental and a waiver had to be signed. The bulletin listed only an e-mail address, which was odd, since the Internet functioned so rarely and because it cost so much to use.

But that night after Tamchu put Illian to bed he went to the Web café, where the perfume of hashish was strong and where the cousin he and his sister had been planning to live with let him use the Web for free, because the café's profit came from hashish, coffee, and tea, and because he owed Tamchu a favor.

Tamchu was tired. He ate little so as to save money. It was always a strain dealing with tourists and worrying about Illian. He was probably being robbed by the man who sold him the butterflies. Everyone had them now anyway. He would have to think of something new.

He waved away the hashish pipe that his cousin offered him when he entered. He liked it well enough. Maybe after Illian was cured he could afford to lose himself in hallucinatory visions. His cousin told him that the Internet had been working for two days, but that he should hurry. They never knew when it might quit.

He pulled from his papers the letter he had composed in English, which he spoke well because of India's influence in Nepal. He hoped they would understand it in Germany. He typed in the address and stared at it for a moment, hoping that his letter would be persuasive enough.

Dear Dr. Lenoir:

My sister is suffering from a rare virus. It is the kind that you cure at your clinic. They say that she might die soon without help. We live in Kathmandu, Nepal. I have saved 428 euros for her travel. We have no insurance. I would like to send her to your clinic for a treatment. I hope this is enough. Could arrangements be made to send her alone? I would like to be with her but there is not enough money for that. I am appending a copy of her medical records from the free clinic here.

Tamchu took out the optical sphere holding Illian's sketchy medical history, DNA scan, and test results and seated it into the indentation on the corner of the keyboard. His cousin had taught him how to do all this; he had caught on pretty quickly. And at least the Chinese school he had attended in Tibet had been good.

Illian had dropped into his lap, more or less, and he'd come to love her. She had unusual talents, strange but somehow beautiful ways of doing things that seemed to spring from her soul. She also spoke several languages; they seemed easy for her to learn. He knew she was a unique being. It was so hard to see her wasting away and suffering. He would do whatever he could to help her, but the technician at the clinic had told him that this was a very long shot and that she needed real doctors. Their most recent volunteer had not shown up, so they had been without a doctor for several months.

He thought of Illian, took a deep breath, then pressed the SEND key.

DRIVING RHYTHM
Tamchu Goes Traveling

2021

To ease his nervousness, Tamchu paced up and down the trains he rode, from one end to the other, smoking cigarettes on the vibrating platforms. But now they were in central India, rattling across vast plains, and the aisles were full of the children and belongings of the poor. He wished he could jump off and run alongside the train to expend his anxiety. Tamchu had always thought himself poor. But after spending days with these destitute, ragged bundles, he felt lucky, if not rich. His seatmate, an old man with few teeth, glanced at him in annoyance as he twitched about. Late-afternoon sun glared in the window, blinding him, gilding a lone dusty tree far out on the plain.

He'd heard from Illlian only once since he'd sent her to the Munich clinic. His aunt, a travel agent, had gotten an international charity organization to defray most of her airfare, but it had taken him a long time to get together enough money to follow, and there was no way that he could afford to fly. Planes were extremely expensive, since they now flew only during daylight and in very good weather. There was no telling when the Silence might cause instrument failure—and perhaps engine failure—so most new planes now were small, of ultralight materials, coated with a skin that maximized absorption of solar energy to stretch travel capability to emergency limits should a pulselike incident occur. He'd seen several of the new zeppelins in their stately progress across the sky, but in order to travel in them, you had to have more money than to fly on jets, and storm-free weather. Most commercial airlines were out of business, crying foul, intimating that somewhere there was some sort of secret information about the nature of the radio interference that would have allowed them to continue to safely operate. Another conspiracy theory.

Tamchu's seatmate bent over and extracted a foil packet from his bag beneath the seat. Rice, probably. Tamchu's mouth watered. The man fluffed the pleated bag and pulled the strip that began the heating process, insulated from the foil. The foil was yellow; when it turned color, the rice would be done.

Tamchu was trying to save as much as possible. He rose, squeezed through the aisle amid what were probably a flurry of Indian curses, and emerged in the hot wind of the platform. He lit a cigarette in lieu of supper.

The brakes wailed, and Tamchu grabbed the door lever as he was hurled forward. Above the din of the train he heard gunshots. Against his better judgment, he stuck his head out from the side of the train. The door to the car slid open and the platform filled with shouting people. Though he had a translation card his kind aunt had pressed upon him, filled with thirty-seven languages, their fear needed no translation.

He'd been lucky so far. This part of the world, at least, was plagued by bandits, and governments were not strong enough to protect against them. In many instances, government guards might work in collusion with bandits. He looked out again and, with some amazement, saw that these bandits rode horses. A woman with streaming black hair rode past on a golden horse, wearing blue jeans and some kind of red band binding her breasts. Evidently, his stare had caught her attention, for she wheeled her horse from the band, which was headed for the first-class cars in the rear. She pulled her horse up in front of him and shouted at him in a language he did not understand.

He shrugged as she repeated herself. "I am Tibetan," he said in Hindi and was surprised when she rather unfortunately turned out to comprehend.

"Come with us and change the world!" she said, her Hindi halting but her voice forceful.

"I am a Buddhist," he said, hoping she would understand what he meant.

She did. She spat as her horse pranced restlessly and fought her tight rein. "This is your only life, brother. Use it to make a change. We are building a city from which to fight the scientists who have ruined the world."

"I am looking for my sister. She's in Germany," said Tamchu, thinking how useless it probably was to argue with such a woman.

"Bring her too," said the woman and galloped off.

His fellow passengers glared at him suspiciously. Tamchu could only shrug. He fought his way back inside, went to his seat. His seat-mate, apparently unperturbed, was just opening his packet of cooked rice. Steam burst from it, carrying the rich scent of curry powder. Tamchu saw that it was pocked with raisins. His mouth watered.

To his surprise, his companion smiled and offered him some. Tamchu put his hands together, bowed slightly, saying, *"Namasté."* He plucked a small wad out with his fingers, rolled it into a ball, and popped it into his mouth. "Good," he said. The bandits thundered past, whooping. A dilapidated truck followed them, its open bed piled high with trunks, jouncing over the open uneven ground. The train started up again slowly. The bandits vanished in the distance. The old man pulled out a deck of cards, smiling, and indicated an interest in Tamchu's cigarettes.

A block from the train station in Munich was a clock tower. It looked very old. Within a perimeter of shining glass towers reflecting the dully opalescent sunset, the old city appeared intact, though Tamchu would not have known if it was a recent fantasy construction like many of the Western cities he'd heard about. They were starting some of that in Kathmandu. Disney had torn down an ancient Hindu temple, first removing all of the sacred monkeys who littered the place with their feces. Now strange monkeylike creatures roamed the temple, and no one knew if they were robots or artificially created organic creatures with only a few rote responses programmed into them. The mournful deep thrum of the horns and chanting were programmed on the hour, the monks having been displaced to a housing project.

So Tamchu surveyed the quaint street with some distrust. He brushed snow from a bench and sat and looked at the square, his hands in his pockets. It was not really very cold. He was in Munich at last. He was very tired.

The clock said that it was only three in the afternoon. There were many cafés about. He longed for a cup of hot tea. He'd shared a third-class sleeping compartment with a Turkish family the night before and their baby had cried all night. His stomach was a knot of hunger. His head ached.

But Illian was not far away. He pulled out a map his aunt had printed for him and oriented it. He had planned this part well. The clinic was about a mile away. Down this grand promenade for five blocks, then a right turn. The thought of seeing Illian filled Tamchu with joy and dread. Joy at possibly seeing her. Dread at possibly hearing that she was dead.

He picked up his pack and walked quickly, passing a small glass booth with men crowded inside, drinking beer. It seemed too cold for that. He began to run. Illian was just minutes away. He dared not think of her face, so thin and drawn when she'd left.

He took the third left. The buildings looked much older here, even shabby. His heart sank. He'd expected a state-of-the-art clinic, white and gleaming and filled with the things that would heal his dear friend. The street was narrow and the dull afternoon light touched only the tops of the buildings. Maybe there was some mistake. Or maybe in a block or two things would change. He knew nothing about cities. He'd never been in one before, not this large.

He stopped before 44–27. It was just a plain wooden door. He rechecked the address.

Dr. Lenoir had sent an ambulance to the airport to pick up Illian. He knew this was true because it had been verified by his aunt, in whatever way she did so. Illian had been taken somewhere—by someone.

He climbed the concrete steps and knocked on the door.

In the center of the door was some sort of smooth plate, and upon it a glowing hand. Though he'd never seen such a thing before, Tamchu recognized it as some sort of admittance device. They had them, for instance, on the doors of the Hilton Kathmandu where his brother-in-law worked. His heart rose. This at least seemed high-tech. He brought his own hand up and fit it inside the glowing outline. The hand seemed to demand this action. He was astonished to see his own name appear on the screen above the hand, but realized that it had somehow extracted the information from his passport.

He waited a minute or two, shivering, but nothing happened. He pounded on the door. Then he started kicking it, yelling, and finally, exhausted, fell silent. He could wait.

He walked down the steps and cut a long straight branch from the bare bush next to the porch, the top of which was at eye level. He leaned back against the cold bricks and pulled half a bar of chocolate he'd been saving from his jacket pocket and ate it. The sky grew dark. He wasn't sure how long he would wait. Perhaps he should find a place to stay and return in the morning. Maybe he should call the police, though he doubted that they would care. He got out his translation card and fed it a few phrases and gave each German phrase a number.

The door opened and a man in an overcoat hurried out and down the steps, looking neither left nor right. As Tamchu had hoped, the door closed slowly; he put his stick between the bars of the railing and stopped it; in a second, he was up the steps and inside.

This was better. The inside of the clinic belied the outside. As white and sterile as could be wished, the walls gleamed with a faintly bluish light.

The reception area was empty; he saw a low white counter, an office chair, a computer, and a few waiting chairs arranged around a gray rug. The computer was many generations removed from those he'd used in Kathmandu. He wished he had time to look at it more closely, as it appeared to be one of the DNA-based computers he'd seen advertisements for in the English edition of the German newspaper he'd found on the train. But some sounds caught his attention. Children's voices!

He ran down a corridor lined with paintings hung low so that children could see them easily; another happy touch. Surely Illian would be cured in a place like this. He looked round a corner and stopped.

He counted seven children in beds in a darkened room with a glass window. They were hooked up to various machines. All were sleeping. He found this odd. All asleep at the same time? Or in some near-death coma? Many small screens throughout the room registered information he did not understand. In a clear glass cupboard with condensation on the outside, he saw vials of blood and other fluids. Of course these needed to be tested; why did they disturb him? Then he saw a thin pale sliver of meatlike substance sealed within plastic. BRAIN SECTION #437. SHIP STAT TO CENTRAL LAB was scribbled on its label. He pressed his lips together. Certainly, this sample could not be human.

On the wall was a map of the world on which many pin-sized blue lights glowed. As he watched, two more lit, one in North America and one in Australia. He saw all this in an instant and then, in fear, he quickly inspected all their faces; none of them was Illian. He left the room and followed the voices once more.

At the end of the corridor was a large room and more children were there. Heart beating hard, he stood outside a window, obviously a two-way mirror since no one noticed him, and watched.

As in the other room, the children appeared to be of the same age, more or less. No toddlers, no teenagers. Perhaps the disease was like that. Perhaps it did not surface until a certain age. Perhaps they all died before they got very old.

They were involved in activities he found curious. One appeared to be building a holographic structure. She walked back and forth between two stations and each time she adjusted something and the structure changed. She was concentrating deeply. Another danced to music Tamchu could not hear, which was not so odd, but the boy's eyes were glazed and he appeared deranged, his eyes glittering as if with fever. Suddenly a radio blared on. They all stopped what they were doing. The girl screamed, a high but rather soft sound. More like keening. Another girl started to pull things off the shelves and fling them to the floor. The boy's red face crumpled as he began to sob. Tamchu thought, shouldn't the feverish boy be resting? This loud music was idiotic. He suddenly realized how pleasant it was in Kathmandu because this constant noise was not around—its only radio and television stations broadcast sporadically. Not because of the Silence, which of course heightened that effect, but because few people owned radios and television sets and because not much advertising was sold. The only stations that tried to reach Nepal were Chinese propaganda stations with news everyone knew was fake and subtitled soap operas of impossibly rich Chinese.

Illian was not here. But where were the nurses, the doctors? Then he saw that all within was being recorded by cameras rotating from the ceiling.

As if to answer his question about adults, a heavy hand clasped him by the shoulder and he was whirled around to face a man with a small round face. He was wearing a white coat.

"Who are you?" he demanded in the British-tinged accent of India. "What are you doing here? How did you get in?"

Tamchu shook off the man's hand, anger rising. "My name is Tamchu. Two months ago, I sent Illian here. Dr. Lenoir picked her up at the airport. Where was she taken? I don't see her here."

The man's mouth tightened briefly, then he appeared to relax. He glanced nervously at the children and took Tamchu's arm. "Come," he said.

He led Tamchu back to the reception area. "Sit down, please," he said.

"Where is she?" Tamchu asked. Just then a young woman with a long blond braid entered the room carrying a sandwich and a cup of coffee. She stopped dead on seeing Tamchu and the doctor. The doctor glared at her.

"Where have you been?" he demanded. "Where is Hans?"

"Hans became sick, Dr. Lenoir," she said in a defensive tone of voice. "He called Peter to take his place. He should have been here by now."

"How did he—" Lenoir began, then apparently thinking better of his harsh tone, he turned to Tamchu. "I am sorry. Please forgive me." He bowed his head. The woman, taking this as a dismissal, sat in the office chair at the computer and began doing something with her control sphere, a slight frown creasing her forehead.

Tamchu was sorry he'd sent Illian to this place. And what could she do about it, so young and defenseless?

Lenoir lifted his head. "I am sorry to have to tell you this, but Illian died."

Within Tamchu sprang up the blue glow in his chest that he had visualized since a child in times of stress, taught by his mother, who had also taught him calmness. He stared directly into Lenoir's eyes. The man blinked and cleared his throat.

Because of his own calmness, Tamchu noticed that the woman had stopped whatever she had been doing and was staring at the back of the doctor's head with something like amazement and disgust on her face.

Tamchu thought, It is not true. But if this man wanted to tell him this lie, what could it mean?

He was suddenly, deeply on his guard. The entire aspect of the place troubled him, not only for Illian, but for all the children here.

"When did she die?" he asked gently, willing his voice free of suspicion.

The doctor cleared his throat and sat back in his chair. "Two weeks ago," he said after a pause. "It was quite sudden. She seemed to have improved greatly. And then—" He shrugged. "We sent word, of course. I guess you left before it arrived."

Good guess, thought Tamchu. It had taken him three weeks to get here.

"Where is she buried?"

"She was cremated," said Lenoir quickly.

"Without my permission," Tamchu said, allowing his voice to rise, though he would have preferred cremation to burial.

"You signed permission," said Lenoir, looking relieved to be talking about something tangible.

Tamchu shook his head and said more loudly, "I did not."

"Let me show you." The doctor turned and said, "Karen, please get out the file of this girl. Illian . . . ?"

"She had no last name," said Tamchu. This was not uncommon in Kathmandu and he had not thought to give her one.

Karen opened a file drawer and after a moment's search pulled out a file. She walked over and handed it to Lenoir. He riffled through it, pulled out a paper, and showed it to Tamchu, pointing to his signature.

"That is in German," said Tamchu.

"If you didn't understand it, you shouldn't have signed it," said Lenoir. "I can arrange for you to have her ashes, of course," he said.

"Can I look around for a moment?" asked Tamchu. "Is there anyone here I can talk to, someone who took care of her?" Very real tears rose in his eyes. "You see, this is hard for me. I've come such a long way. I had such hope . . ." He was almost certain that Illian was here—somewhere. The doctor was lying about something. If he really was a doctor. He might be a doctor of something, thought Tamchu, but he was certainly not a doctor who took care of patients.

"I am sorry," said the man. He closed up the file and handed it back to the waiting secretary standing behind him. He did not look at her. Her eyes caught Tamchu's and he saw that they were troubled. She shook her head, once, at Tamchu. She mouthed something at him. Wait? She pointed at the door. She turned to walk away just as the doctor looked behind himself at her. She walked back to the station, tossed the file into a basket on the counter, and set to work.

Lenoir rose and took Tamchu's arm, pulling him up. "There are so many children, and we are working so hard to find a cure. I wish we had been in time for your—for—"

"Illian," finished Tamchu for him. "Don't you have any facilities for the parents who are visiting?" asked Tamchu. "Maybe I can stay and help. Volunteer."

"Thank you, but I'm afraid that is not possible," said Lenoir.

"Just someone to . . . to change bedpans," said Tamchu. "Things like that. I only want to help to relieve the suffering. Illian was very sick. Sometimes I had to—"

"Let me help you to the door," Lenoir said. "Working around here would only prolong your sorrow, I assure you." Tamchu thought to struggle, to run back and grab the file, but just then another man walked in the front door. He was clearly a guard, with a holster and gun.

"Peter," said the doctor. "I am so glad you are here. Please escort Mr.—ah, our guest to the door."

In a moment, Tamchu was on the dark porch. He paused briefly, then, feeling watched, walked back toward the main promenade. He turned a corner, waited a few moments, then slipped back out and crouched behind another concrete porch. It was very cold and he began to shiver. He was sorry he'd eaten his entire chocolate bar. He wondered how long he should wait. No matter. He would wait all night if necessary. And then he would go to the police and the consulate. He stomped his feet to warm them.

He was lightly dozing when someone passed by. The woman! Her long blond braid gleamed in the lamplight. He grabbed her arm and she jumped in fear.

"I'm sorry," he said. "It's me."

"Not here," she said. "Come. Hurry." She glanced behind her and then there was a shout. "They noticed it missing. I hate them." She thrust the file into his hand. "Run."

She darted down the alley and he followed. He heard running feet behind them. Then shots. She fell. He stopped. "Run," she cried. "They'll kill you too. You must do something about them—"

Too? He bent and pulled her up. Peter passed through a streetlight. Someone opened a door and shouted something in German. Tamchu heard the wail of a police siren. Peter was gone. All was confusion. By the time the ambulance arrived, she was dead.

Tamchu sat in the police station, drinking cold coffee. He had told his story to detectives via a translator and they had merely eyed him suspiciously. He'd left out the part about the file, slipped into his pack. He demanded to speak to the Nepalese consulate. The man had come, checked his passport, then scolded him. "You are a Tibetan refugee. You have a lot of nerve getting me out of bed." He left. Tamchu was being held for questioning, but they assured him they didn't think he had killed the girl.

The detective sat at a desk, smoking a cigarette. Tamchu wished he had one, not to mention something to eat. The phone beeped, a low, cool tone, and the detective picked it up. Tamchu heard him speak Lenoir's name, then he glanced over at Tamchu. He nodded once, put down the phone, and rose. "It seems you have stolen some property of the clinic," he said as he approached.

Tamchu jumped up, ran out the door. It was gray morning. He turned down a corner and sprinted. They did not catch him. Perhaps they did not chase him.

Tamchu had never imagined that he might some day be a fugitive from the law. They apparently did not believe his story. Why should they? Or perhaps they did. Perhaps they did and they, like Lenoir, had something to hide.

He bitterly recalled the hope in his heart when he had put Illian on the plane. He had betrayed her.

He slept in a dingy, cheap room for more than a day. Before he slept, he hid the file. But they did not come for him. Whatever was worth the life of a young woman was apparently not worth turning the city upside down for.

He woke and took a long hot shower. After he dressed, he ventured down to the street. It was midday and crowded. He bought some bread and cheese from a bakery and hot coffee and hurried back to his room. He ate and then got out the file, spreading out the papers.

He saw an image of long thin lines of colors—red, blue, green, and yellow intermixed on each line. Number 768. Orphan. Weight, age, vital signs. A stapled copy of some paper about magnetic sensitive properties of fish, bird, and mammal brains, wrinkled as if it had been jammed into the file later. There was the form he'd signed, so eager to get help for her. That was all. Probably they kept most of their information in their database. Tears formed in his eyes. Such a gentle child. They had loved each other. The papers slid to the floor.

He must have been mistaken in believing her alive. It was just his strong wish that had made him believe that the man was lying. If she was alive, wouldn't that Lenoir man want to tell him—if only to keep him happy?

But why had the woman run after him? Particularly if it was so dangerous. Perhaps she had not known the risk she took. Perhaps Illian was dead, but the woman had believed that he could somehow help the other children there. Maybe by getting the papers to the proper authorities?

Tamchu was presently inclined to stay out of the way of any kind of authority.

After a while, he sat up and looked at the papers again. The colored lines looked like genetic information to him. He'd seen something like that in a newspaper.

Why all this secrecy surrounding a child who had had a new rare virus? Why were the children hidden away? Contamination? That was nonsense. If true, the adults would have been protecting themselves somehow. If that were true, he and his relatives would have this terrible virus. It had not been a virus after all. But what was it?

These papers held the key to something important, he felt. But there was no one in Munich who could help him. He was a fugitive.

He considered breaking into the clinic again. That was his only recourse. It had not been too difficult before. Perhaps he could even formulate a plan to free the children inside.

In a club that reminded him of his cousin's hashish club, Tamchu met a man who changed his passport for him. He did not charge. He said it was his hobby. He said he did it to free the world from tyranny. He gave Tamchu a job in the café, weighing out hashish, washing coffee cups. With his money, Tamchu rented a room in the building across the street from the clinic.

But he did not keep it long. After a few days, he was sure that the clinic was deserted. No one had gone in or out. They had fled.

Tamchu learned Munich well. He sought out every hospital, every orphanage, every school, adoption agency, runaway shelter, juvenile detention center. His German improved. He had a photograph of Illian. Everyone shook his head gravely when he saw it.

Tamchu spent months hanging out at the club. He felt safe there. These people were filled with the anger he felt. So much was wrong with the world. Things were changing so fast. Evil governments and more evil scientists were hiding something—something about the pulses. Something about nanotechnology. Something. At the very least, they grumbled, it was a return to the values of the early Industrial Revolution, when the wealthy invested in factories and enslaved the poor; when the poor were sent to the mines to dig the fuel for the factories and died coughing out their slimed lungs. A few owned the patents; a few owned the processes; the few were not about to release these riches to the rest of the world. Much money had been invested in the development of nanotechnology. Stockholders had to be paid and profits had to be shown.

A few of his fellows, Tamchu learned after he had earned their trust, were tapped into elaborate spy rings. One of the young men was a medical school dropout. Tamchu showed him the printouts regarding Illian, which were in German. Tamchu had used a scanner on them that translated the summary into spoken English, but still it was mostly terms that Tamchu did not understand.

"This is wild," the young man said. A slow tattoo, a new layer of skin capable of supporting images, sent a tiny green square careening across his cheekbone as he spoke. "This girl, Illian, has a mutated form of DNA that is showing up worldwide. All the children with this mutation are exactly the same age. Exactly. The theory is that they were all conceived at the same moment." He frowned. "Apparently they require unusual amounts of magnesium in their diets in order to avoid unpleasant symptoms, perhaps even death." He handed the sheets back to Tamchu. "No doubt some sort of illegal government operation caused this mutation, eh? And now they are trying to collect these children, eliminate the evidence. Or use them somehow. Who knows?"

"What government?" asked Tamchu. "I believe that she was born in Afghanistan."

The other man said, "It does not matter. All governments are linked together in their illegal endeavors. There is an illusion perpetuated for the common man that different governments exist, that is all."

Tamchu did not find this answer very satisfactory, but all the man wanted to talk about was governments, not DNA, and Tamchu put his file away.

One day there was great excitement in the club. One of the women brought in a small vial. To demonstrate the powers of the liquid within, an emulsion, she said, which contained molecular manipulators, they rigged up a local telephone system with two phones, a battery, and a cable. The woman lay bare the fiber-optic wires and dropped a bit of the liquid on them. The splay of fibers turned a uniform brilliant green. The phones went dead.

"So what?" said one of the men. "You shorted it out."

The woman shook her head. "Nope," she said. "This stuff eats glass. Fiber-optic cable."

"Big deal," said another. "They'll find a cure for it soon."

"But what fun until they do," said the woman.

Tamchu's anger by now was great. Fiber-optic cable had carried to him the lie of Illian's salvation. He finally accepted that she was probably dead. Dead at the hands of Dr. Lenoir, who was part of some kind of government-backed conspiracy.

He was part of the team that put out the telephones of Munich one night.

The next day he was heading east, hidden in a compartment in the ceiling of a box car carrying stinking pigs. He did not emerge until his watch showed that he should be in Turkey. And then he continued to head east. He carried the file with him. But he rarely looked at it anymore. He thought, once, of the harm he might have done to innocent people by putting out the phones. There was no possible connection to helping Illian in doing that. His friends at the club had changed his way of thinking radically, he realized. It seemed wrong somehow . . . yet it also seemed right to draw attention to all that was bad with the world.

Still . . .

He did not meet the bandit band when crossing India and was mildly disappointed. He ran out of money in Bangkok and went to work for a vendor pulling bobbing coconuts from a tub of iced water, slicing their stem ends with a machete, and sticking a straw in them. He sweated day and night, living in a cheap room with one small window above a whorehouse. The girls were terribly young, about Illian's age. He was always kind to them. They often wept. They were terrified and he saw several die of disease and some of brutality. He spent time wondering what to do to help them. But he was afraid of doing something wrong. Whatever he thought of, he saw a thousand flaws.

Then one day a woman wearing black cotton pants and shirt strode in carrying a machine gun. She and two women with her walked through the whorehouse, killing the owner and several clients while the girls screamed. Tamchu ran downstairs to see what was the matter and found the muzzle of the gun pointed at his face. Several of the girls shouted, "No, no, he is our friend!" and the woman said, "Come, then" and waved him into the truck waiting in the alley. In less than five minutes, the truck roared down another alley and backed into a warehouse. The girls under cover of bougainvillea thickets were loaded into three long-tail boats waiting in the klong behind the warehouse and told to lie in the bottom. They were covered with canvas, then baskets of fruits and fish. The woman donned a turquoise sari, tied a wide conical hat over her head, put on dark glasses, and lit a cigar. "Get in," she said to Tamchu. "Now."

He got in.

They putted slowly up the klong. Tamchu was sure that if police boats appeared, the engines would show themselves to be capable of much speed. From beneath the canvas he heard sniffling and sobbing. "Shut up," said the woman.

By dark they were out of the city. By lantern light they made many turns and though Tamchu tried to keep track of them he was soon confused. The woman did not talk. She smoked a lot. Tamchu wanted a cigar, but did not dare ask for one. She told the girls to pee on themselves if they had to. Finally, after midnight, they pulled up to some docks. By the light of the crescent moon, Tamchu saw a small village of stilted houses.

She made the girls throw their clothing in a pile and bathe in the river. When they emerged, shivering, some women from the houses brought towels and set fire to the flimsy dresses. "Whore's clothing," she said. "Warm yourself by it."

They were given clean shifts and led into the houses. There were other girls there, but they were sleeping in long dormitory rows. The girls were fed a dinner of rice and steamed fish and put to bed. They were quiet and docile, all of them.

The woman brought Tamchu to the kitchen and sat him down. She got out a bottle of whisky and offered him some.

"I don't drink," he said.

"How odd," she said.

"I am a Buddhist," he explained.

She snorted. "Who isn't? All the men I killed today, they were Buddhists. I'm a Buddhist."

"I don't think so," said Tamchu.

Her eyes were long; exotic and dark. Her eyebrows were like wings on her smooth, pale face. Her shining black hair fell down her back to her narrow waist. "Who are you?" he asked.

"You don't need to know my name. I am building an army to rid the country of the scourge of selling girls. These girls said you were their friend. Is it true?"

"It is," said Tamchu.

She lit two thin cigars and handed him one. "I believe you," she said, "and you are lucky that I do. Tell me about yourself."

He did.

Mid-beat Phrase on the Tonic

Jason | At the Fair | 2025

Jason could not contain his excitement. He pounded on the back of the seat with his fists and let out a whoop. Even though, at twelve, he was a little old for this.

"Sit still," said Dad, who was driving. "We're almost there." Jason could see his grin in the mirror, though. They'd put up with just about anything from him since the hospital.

They drove through a golden land, sharp with escarpments and mesas. Black shadows backfilled cliffs, and Jason saw a row of thin, distant pines clinging to a short ridge. The sky was a blue that stunned him with the mere quality of blueness. Just the colors—the gold and blue—were enough to drive him nuts. Colors did that. Especially since he'd been in the hospital. He was so in love with the very fact of color.

But he was also in love with electronics, game theory, and formulas calculating materials stress. The last had given him an odd reputation among his friends, and he'd decided that such things were best kept to himself. But he hadn't seen his friends in a while. He missed them. He wasn't allowed to call or write.

To distract himself, he pulled out the flatscreen from the back of his father's seat. It was hinged at the top, and he unfolded the plastic bar at the bottom and hooked it into the latch on the seatback that would keep it from swaying back and forth. He pawed among the piles of stuff squished next to him on the seat and finally found his control sphere. His fingers fit comfortably into its indentations; he operated it through a complex combination of fleeting pressures similar to those used when playing musical instruments, a skill that had long since become intuitive.

The gps was off today. It didn't matter. He always seemed to know where he was, what direction he faced, even the elevation, once he grasped the concepts of miles and of altitude, and had some feedback. This came in handy, for the gps was usually off now. He guessed they were only about fifty miles from the New Worlds Fair. Mike was driving at a hundred miles an hour, more or less. They were almost there. This road led literally from nowhere or else there would be more traffic. They'd hiked down from a lake eleven thousand feet high yesterday and had seen no one else while there. They'd been keeping to themselves lately. His mom had even taken care to park beneath some trees to shield them from satellite surveillance.

It was rumored that ten thousand people might attend. Almost twice as many as last year's fair. It was getting some kind of reputation among the kind of people his mom hung out with.

He glanced at his mother's profile—her long, straight nose, determined chin. She stared ahead almost tensely, with hunger for what she'd find ahead. Feeling his stare, she turned and grinned at him, blue eyes alight with merriment, blond hair pulled back into one long braid but escaping in wisps around her face. She reached between the seats and squeezed his knee; turned back to stare at the road.

The fair was everything Jason hoped it would be. Sound and sight formed rich currents of energy with him at their nexus. After a lot of begging and not a little discussion between them, he was allowed to explore by himself, as long as he returned to a checkpoint every hour. He was made to know that if he did not, he would be embarrassed by his parents, who would turn the fair upside down to find him. "And just stay in this section," said Mike sternly, staring down at Jason with deep-set dark blue eyes that brooked no discussion.

At first he wandered with no clear direction. He had a few dollars but decided not to spend them until he'd seen everything. He stayed away from the virtual booths—he'd long ago decided that spending time in them was like eating too much cotton candy. Afterward he felt sick and empty.

The air was so clear that the mountains surrounding them were sharply defined. He saw an eagle take flight from a cliff several miles away.

But the New Worlds were waiting. He pulled his attention back. First he went to the Gaian Arena. VOICE OF THE EARTH CHOIR REHEARSAL read a sign with an arrow. A group of people mingled down near the creekbed. He chose an information station but learned nothing new.

The Gaian philosophy had been firmly set for decades. He rather liked it. Sometimes it seemed as if he could feel the oneness of which his mother spoke; feel the living earth pulsing beneath him, joining with the sun in a celebration of specific forms and energies. Since humans were a part of Gaia, though, and their thoughts, inventions, and follies, he did not exactly understand the Gaians' hatred of humanity, indeed, of themselves—at least it seemed so, at times, to him.

When he played solitaire, he thought of how one combination of cards, the initial condition the computer dealt, started out with very little possibility of solution, which would be, perhaps, the occasional creation of life in one-billionth of all the constantly forming and dissolving universes. The elements—the suits, the numbers—were all there, but the building sequence had to happen as the game progressed. Often there was complete failure, game over. Sometimes as he played, Jason tried to envision a universe in which a Goddess, such as his mother seemed to believe in, existed. Surely in all possible universes there must be a fair percentage in which Goddess did exist. Why not this one? Then again, he had also been struck by the realization that the next card turned up could spell the end of the game. And that his own situation—and all of humanity's—might be at the next to the last play just before the cards were all swept together, whisked from the screen, reshuffled, redealt. He wasn't sure how the Gaian philosophy fit into all of this. Something about taking charge, maybe. His mother said that there were terrorists among them, fanatics who wanted to destroy civilization. "They're not the real Gaians," she said. "They're like wolves in sheep's clothing."

He saw, through gaps in the milling crowd, his parents strolling hand in hand, stopping at the Millennialist Arena. They stepped beneath a shading pavilion, one of those things that grew on a filament net from raw material siphoned from buckets placed around the perimeter. When you were finished with it, you just rolled it up and put it back in the buckets and poured some chemical over it. Jason thought they were a lot more trouble than they were worth. As he stood looking at it, he thought that there must be more efficient, easier ways to produce a canopy. Its main virtue was that you could design its shape on a computer quite easily. Then the design was transmitted to each molecule of the polymer in the buckets—the latest generation of computers had a port from which issued the DNA, as it were, of your design, made from an ampoule of all-purpose molecular soup you inserted. That was what was programmed. Then your custom-made pavilion would grow in a matter of hours. This would be handy, Jason thought, if you were setting up in venues where you were constantly assigned different types of spaces.

It didn't really matter here, where there was plenty of space. But on the other hand, it was perfect for this kind of setting, where technology itself was the point.

Jason thought he might as well check in now. He walked over and stopped behind his parents, listening. In front of them, a model of a white hivelike city floated on a shimmering holographic ocean. Tiny waves swept past. His mother bent to restart its evolution. She had loosened her hair and it was swept behind her by the breeze, shining and golden. They were absorbed in the city and did not see him.

He could hear, faintly, a woman's voice describing the process. "First, electrostatically charged nets ionize, collect, and organize matter from sea water."

"You could have a country free of old styles of government," said Cassie as the island grew and formed steppes containing gardens, apartments, fields of produce, sea farming basins. Tiny people boarded elevated trains.

"It could be run by the Gaians," said Mike in a teasing tone of voice. He pulled Cassie close with an arm around her shoulder. Jason had noticed that his parents seemed much happier together than the parents of his friends.

"Don't laugh," said Cassie quietly. "You never know."

"That's for sure," said Mike soberly.

"Have you been to the space colony?" asked Jason. Mike looked over his shoulder and pulled Jason close with his free arm. "No," he said. "Let's try it."

By evening, when they popped up their tent, with a screened sky view for a roof that sealed itself at the first drop of rain, they had seen at least ten types of utopian communities, each suggested by some new flavor of technology. The rapidly dropping temperature activated biomolecular warming filaments in Jason's clothing. He pulled out a hat and gloves. He and his parents sat on low folding chairs, eating self-heated dinners. His parents shared a bottle of wine. As the sharp band of gold on the horizon faded to deep blue, then black, the stars became a brilliant wash across the sky.

"Sometimes I think that it's good that things are changing," said Cassie. She absently swirled wine in a plastic cup. "I'm sure the night sky wasn't this clear anywhere when I was a kid."

"The good new days," said Mike, pulling his blanket tighter.

"Oh, stop," she said.

"Let's have a fire," said Jason. "I'll go get some wood."

"Against the rules," said Cassie. "What if everyone here started their own fire?"

A woman walking past their tent paused. "I didn't mean to eavesdrop, but we have a fire," she said. Her voice was low and husky. She carried a biolantern in one hand and raised it. Thick white hair lay loose down her back. "I'm on my way back from choir rehearsal. Come on over and share it with us."

"I don't—" began Cassie.

"Thanks," said Jason, jumping up. He knew that his parents would follow. "Want me to help collect wood? I saw some driftwood down by the creekbed."

"Brought our own," said the woman. "A pickup truck load. I like a good fire in the evening. Takes the chill off. We're pretty far off from the pack, though. Half a mile away."

Cassie stood and picked up the bottle of wine.

They followed the woman across rough ground and around house-sized boulders. Their bobbing lightsticks caused sharp shadows to dance in all directions across the rock-littered terrain. A burst of laughter rang out in the night before she turned a sharp corner down a cliff face, and faint singing came from the groups scattered throughout the canyon. "Careful here," she said. Though the trail was fairly wide, emptiness yawned at their right, lit somewhat ahead by the fire, now visible.

Seven or eight people were seated around a large fire that illuminated an arch about thirty feet high at its apogee and tapered back into the cliff. The crisp air, the smell of wood smoke, the solitude of the place seemed to take Jason back a hundred and fifty years, to the Zane Grey novels he'd lately taken to.

The people all seemed relatively old to Jason. "Hey, Mabel," said one of the men.

"I brought some company."

"The more the merrier."

They got seated and were introduced to the others. They were a party from Colorado. Civil astronauts. People who believed that governments should not provide the only access to space. Since the first Silence, the International Space Hotel had been taken over under the aegis of emergency provisions in international treaties. Besides, it was claimed, the hotel wasn't safe anymore. Various factions of civil astronauts built their own rockets. The destruction of one of their capsules six years ago and the death of the Argentinean construction worker and her husband whose turn had come up after they'd maintained membership for fifteen years had put a damper on such flights. The Koreans had claimed that they thought the capsule was an enemy missile. The more militant among the civil astronauts claimed that it had been a gesture deliberately calculated to intimidate.

Jason pulled off his hat and gloves, unzipped his jacket. The fire felt good. His parents were smiling. This made him glad. They'd been so worried since he'd been in the hospital.

"What do you think of the fair?" Mabel asked them after the others returned to their conversations.

"I think that we might be forced to make some decisions in the near future about which way we're going to go," said Mike. "It's good to have information."

Mabel nodded. The fire snapped; sparks swirled out into the night. She pulled out a bag of marijuana and neatly rolled a joint as she spoke. "There's more than meets the eye, that's for sure. My cousin on the moon colony said—"

"You have a cousin on the moon colony?" asked Jason.

Mabel nodded and lit the joint. Mike and Cassie had some and passed it around the circle and shared their wine. "He's been there for quite some time too. Been planning on going to Mars, but that might not happen now."

"But they told us—"

"I know what they told you," Mabel said. She leaned forward on her stool and clasped her knees. Her hair shone silver in the moonlight. Her face looked strong with its deep crevices. Jason wondered if she was a Native American. He wondered if she believed in vortexes like his mother did. He'd learned that it wasn't polite to ask people. And sometimes it embarrassed his mother. She said that people's religious beliefs were very personal.

Mabel began to speak then in the incantatory tone of a person telling a story. They had to lean forward to hear her. The others paid no attention; Jason figured they knew all this anyway.

"The moon colony has not closed down. They've put this story out, but it is not true. The people there had to sign a pledge of secrecy. This was eleven years ago, around the time of the first Silence. My cousin was an organic chemist. She wasn't in the military. She refused to sign the pledge. They let her stay anyway. Sometimes she sends back messages about what's been happening. About what they know."

"So what do they know?" asked Mike. His voice had the respectful tone he used when talking to some of Cassie's friends and acquaintances. He avoided the least tinge of ridicule or disbelief. Jason knew that he thought the conspiracy theories that were circulating about the nature of the Silence ranged from the ridiculous to the flatly impossible. Still, he said, he was keeping an open mind.

"The only model that fits all the known facts of the Silence points to the interference of some kind of intelligent source. It need not be close."

"But why?" asked Cassie, and her face had an eager look. Jason knew she lived for this kind of stuff.

Mabel shrugged. "They can't tell that. In fact, the source may not even know that they're doing this to us or may not care. Chances are we're nothing to them."

"We're just part of the ecology of the universe," said Cassie.

Mabel looked at her.

"Like, you know, endangered species," said Cassie. "Something others don't even know or care about."

Mabel snorted. "I don't plan to go extinct. I'm not some kind of moss or microbe. I'm intelligent. I don't have to live or die at the mercy of God or fate or aliens or chaos or whatever you want to call it. If God there was, and God told me that I was supposed to acquiesce, I'd go to war with God." She leaned forward and whispered, "We're leaving."

Mike leaned back on his stool and clasped his hands; nodded. "Oh. And what's the price of a ticket?"

"You misunderstand me," said Mabel. "I'm not beating the bushes for money."

"Most of these—organizations," said Cassie delicately, "want everything you own. I mean, look around. Every one of them is like a religion. Worse than a religion. A cult. You have to pledge all. Your property, your life, all your time. Instead of worshipping Goddess, they worship . . . a way out."

"Or a change," said Mabel. "You know, taking humanity to the next level, all that." They all took another toke of the joint as it came around. "To tell the truth, we don't have room for anyone else. And we don't need any more money. But what we do need is people to spread the word about us after we leave. To receive whatever messages we might manage to send. For one thing, we'll be able to get messages from the moon colony, at least for a while, and we can send them back, coded. So that the government won't try and intercept them."

"Where are you going?" asked Jason.

Mabel's eyes were grave. Maybe even a little frightened. She lowered her eyelids, then looked back at Jason.

"To the source of the Signal," she said.

"The signal?"

"That's what's causing the silences," she said.

"But how close do you think this is?" asked Cassie.

"Closer than the government admits," said Mabel.

"But—" began Mike.

"I'm a codebreaker," Mabel said. "A mathematician, to be sure, but there are others who concern themselves with the distance issues.

I concern myself more with the information that comes during the silences."

Jason leaned forward, his heart pounding. "I always—"

"What kind of information?" asked Mike, cutting Jason off with uncharacteristic rudeness. Cassie's face was impassive as she watched Mabel, and that was strange too. Jason would have thought she'd say something to his dad about being impolite.

They didn't want him to mention how he always got well during the silences. And sick again when they stopped. The last time, he guessed, had been pretty bad.

It had been only a month ago. He remembered waking to his mother's face. Her cheeks were hollow, her hair uncombed, her clothing wrinkled as she dozed in the chair next to his bed. The morning sun was inching across the floor and his chest was filled with a brimming happiness he seemed to float on, out over the world, into everything, every cell of every thing, into the very reaches of the universe, all shot with happiness.

But Cassie looked very sad.

"Mom?" He pushed himself up in the bed. He was surprised at how weak he felt; how dizzy when his effort caused light-shot darkness to hover around him for a moment before clearing.

Cassie opened her eyes. They were so blue—and looked even larger now than they had before because her face was so thin—and filled instantly with tears. "Jason!"

And then she was hugging him, careful not to knock out his IV. "It happened again?" he asked, his voice muffled by her golden hair.

In a few minutes, his parents were having a whispered argument in one corner of his room.

"What's wrong?"

They turned from their huddle. "How do you feel?" asked Mike. He looked worried.

"Fine," Jason said. "A little tired maybe. I remember dreams—"

"You were hallucinating," said Cassie. "You had a high fever."

"But I remember a lot of people standing around me."

"Doctors," said Mike a bit grimly.

"What's wrong with doctors?" asked Jason.

"These doctors wanted—" began Mike. Cassie frowned. Mike glanced at her, but continued. "He might as well know this, Cassie. We might not always be around." He pulled the chair close to the bed, sat, leaned forward, talking very quietly.

"These people told us they were from the government. They told us that you had a very unusual viral infection and that they wanted to take you to an institution where they could isolate it and deal with it."

Cassie stood next to Mike. She continued. "Dr. Howe—Nelly—got in touch with an old friend of hers at the Centers for Disease Control. He told her that there was no such thing. Even if it was classified, he would know."

"They were making it up?" Jason was astonished. "Are they real doctors?"

"There are all kinds of doctors," said Mike. "Some of these were not medical doctors. In fact, I'm not sure we even know their real names. They just showed up after Nelly updated your insurance information."

"The friend at the CDC did say something interesting," said Mike.

"Anyway," said Cassie, "your father thinks—we've decided—that it would be best to leave. Kind of—"

"Kind of secretly?" asked Jason, getting excited. "But Mom, you don't think it's a good idea?"

Cassie sighed. "No, I think he's right. It just seems so extreme."

Mike got up. "Let's go. We're going to pretend that we're just taking you for a stroll in the wheelchair. Cassie, go get the car ready. We'll meet you at the side entrance."

The nurses took out his IV and were glad he was feeling well enough to accompany his parents down to the cafeteria. In ten minutes, they were driving north on the interstate. The back of the van was completely full.

"What's all this stuff?" Jason was lying on the backseat, covered with blankets. He did feel tired.

"We're just going on a little vacation." Cassie turned off the interstate, onto a small road that headed north.

They hadn't gone home since. That had been a month ago.

Jason was beginning to realize that they never would.

New World Strut

Marie | New Orleans | 2027

Marie stared at the music on the piano, looked back at her hands on the keys, muttered, and carefully placed each finger on the correct key; pushed forward with her back. Carnival season was in full swing and Marie had all the doors and windows closed against it. Velvet drapes blocked sunlight. The piano, the bench, Marie, and a huge potted fig tree were the only objects in the loft.

A complex chord issued from the Steinway baby grand.

"Bravo, bravo!"

Now the room apparently contained Hugo as well. He clapped vigorously; Marie thought it a tribute to the genius of sarcasm that his very claps mocked her efforts. She made ready to create the next chord. It took about a minute to place her fingers correctly.

"Moving right along, I see," said Hugo, putting his hand on her shoulder.

She shrugged it off. "There is no need to make fun of me," she said, pushing her way into the next chord.

"Oh, but it's lovely. I could tell from the doorway that it was 'Solitude.'"

Marie believed him. That's all it took for him. A hint of a voice, less than a measure; a note suspended in air, and it was Ella Fitzgerald; more than that, it was recorded in a particular studio on a particular day with such and such musicians—

Marie turned on the bench and faced him, rested her back against the piano. "I need to be doing it. It's a learning thing. I used to be pretty good. At classical stuff anyway."

"Fair," said Hugo and pretended to duck.

"Anyway, that's all lost. And I'm not learning very quickly. Something's slowed down." There had been more falls, glasses slipping from her fingers, dizziness. A shadow passed through Hugo's eyes. Maybe. It was gone swiftly. She hadn't told him about those things, so she was probably imagining it. Anyway, it was only to be expected. These transformations were new and far from perfect.

She had been putting off seeing a doctor. Since returning to New Orleans, Marie had been inundated in the process of implementing a flood of improvements and with sorting out all kinds of political and educational problems. There had been much opposition from the old guard, which had retrenched in her absence, and for months she experienced keen joy stealing back power. A kind of cult sprang up around her seemingly miraculous reincarnation, which she did not discourage.

She also wasted no time in setting up a system of free bionan clinics and staffing them with doctors trained in the latest molecular engineering techniques. Though the kind of resurrection she had engineered for herself was still far too expensive to give away and still fraught with perils which her doctor cautioned her could manifest at any time, there were still major cheap benefits she was able to offer. A cure for some cancers, based on stem cell regeneration. A cure for cystic fibrosis. A cure for heart disease. Dighton had to hire a huge staff to fend off lawsuits based on the similarity of such cures to exceedingly expensive procedures owned by large research corporations. He was happy.

Despite her industry, Zion's vision of a new era haunted Marie. She had sent a lot of money to his school and received lovely letters from his orphans. For a long time, he urged her to visit Freestate, for he feared something had gone wrong. Then there was a long, heartbroken letter bearing the news that it had been destroyed by a hurricane. However, he told her in the same letter, almost everyone had survived, and many of those people hoped to begin to build a new floating island, using what they had learned. They were looking for an investor.

Marie had been ignoring his not-so-subtle hint for some time now.

Increasingly frustrated by the effect *El Silencio* was having on just about everything, she was looking into various alternatives to the new BioCities that were being proposed by the government. So far there were none. Communications were shot, transportation was switching over to the maglev NAMS system as gasoline engines became increasingly difficult to fuel due to shortages, and international news and mail was sporadic. Small towns became survivalist cults and middle-sized cities were nightmares. Marie had police on every corner and all kinds of supply systems in place—not to mention one of the first NAMS stations in the country. But it was still hard. Everyone's energy was spent on surviving, on trying to keep various systems running without the aid of computers, though new DNA computers as well as computers with tiny molecular-sized vacuum tubes were starting to pick up the slack. The retreat to the nineteenth century was not easy.

A week earlier, a shipment of nanotech masters had arrived. Resembling microwave ovens, they ostensibly converted material into new clothing, or metal into new configuration, or grew wooden objects. The clothing aspect was fun. Marie had put them about in schools, shelters, and charity organizations and people were experimenting with the design programs. The three biggest department stores in the city were filing a suit against her. The machining and wood processors were helpful, but the size of the things they could manufacture was limited. Marie had a committee working on proposals on how best to use them.

She had ordered larger tanks but was not allowed to receive them until some kind of government approval came through.

Despite all her activity, her own life felt hollow. She was often quite tired, and she tried very hard to remain interested in things.

"Well." Hugo's look was unusually entreating. "Got your things packed?"

Marie stared across the room, past Hugo, toward nothing. "I'm sorry. You go by yourself. I just can't help it. Maybe when she's older."

Hugo frowned. "She's growing up without you, Marie. You've hardly seen her since she was an infant."

It was true. Marie left every detail to Hugo and Missy, and the place of birth, like everything else, was their choice. She did not consider the child her own. She did not intend to. The memory of her first glimpse of the baby was still painful.

"Kalina." Hugo's expression was silly; joyous, as he held the brown swaddled infant in his arms. Missy too stood beaming, tears in her eyes, looking down at the child. "Kalina Marie Laveau."

The living room of the wretched Pink House shouted out Marie's loss from every corner. Evidently Hugo did not share her acumen. He continued, oblivious to the fact that she had seen this infant before, and that this infant had died because of her mother's penchant for buying unusual stocks.

"Kalina was the original title of Ellington's Ko Ko. He planned it as an opera that would tell the story of the race." He looked at Marie anxiously. "Do you like it? As a name, I mean?"

He held out the baby to Marie.

Marie took one long dreadful look at the beautiful face of Petite Marie and fled the room.

Hugo was disappointed that Marie did not take more interest in Kalina, but he visited often and was giddy with joy whenever he returned. Neither of them mentioned moving Missy and Kalina to New Orleans; even if Missy had wanted to move, both feared—but did not speak of—the possibility of new enemies.

She forced herself to go several times a year, but never stayed more than a day. Even that was torture and she was sure that Kalina could tell. She was sure that Kalina would blame it on herself.

Is there a good time to tell someone that she is a clone? Is there a good time to mention what happened to the original girl?

Marie made her voice firm. "Better for her. Besides, you go and see her every month. She's happy, isn't she?"

"Sure." Hugo rattled on. Marie could tell he was trying to mask his disappointment. "Missy's great. I was kind of hoping she might marry this Chuck she's been seeing, but she doesn't seem to be in any hurry. I checked him out, though. He's a good guy. Furthermore, Kalina seemed even smarter than ever this time and will probably be ready for college math courses when she's twelve. According to her tutor."

"She seemed even smarter than the last time you saw her? How is that possible? She was already the most intelligent child in several galaxies." Marie tried to put a light tone into her voice. Hugo would probably never be able to understand how much it hurt to even listen to distant talk of her. Petite Marie wouldn't ever go to college. "And how is she doing in school? I mean with her classmates?" She attended the local school, even though her tutor did most of the teaching. But Marie had seen to it that her school and the others on Tortola as well had many more resources and better-trained teachers than ever before, and she had set up a college scholarship fund for the islanders.

"She has plenty of friends. One close one, Andrea. She's Joe Alingua's granddaughter. Nice kid. They go fishing a lot."

"See, Hugo? If she lived here, she couldn't go fishing with her friends. And I can't go see her. Who knows who might be following me?"

"Cut Face and Shorty took care of all those connections, Marie. I really don't think that you're going to have trouble from that quarter again. How are they doing anyway? Found out how to reverse that stuff they took?"

"Not yet."

"I gather it's not one of your priorities."

"They seem pretty happy."

"So do dogs."

"Maybe I should tell them to go out and find it."

"That would be one approach."

"Well." Marie crossed her arms. "You'll be back in a month or so?"

"A week's sail there, a week's sail back. Time to play in between. See to things."

"Thank you, Hugo."

Again, the maddening shrug. He turned to go, then turned back. "So you're really not going."

"I'm *sorry*, Hugo! Really, I am!"

"I am too. I really thought . . . that you'd change, I guess. I couldn't have believed . . . I know that if you'd just see her . . ."

"Maybe I'll try to go next time."

Hugo smiled broadly. "That would be great. She'll be so excited to see you. She doesn't understand how you can be too busy."

"I said I'd go. I'm tired now." Her voice was sharper than she'd intended.

"Right." Hugo patted her hand and left.

Marie flopped into the hammock on her balcony and did not cry. She did not cry for a very long time. Then she fell asleep.

Marie was unhungry for several days. She slept around the clock after Hugo left, keeping to her upper rooms, locking out the sounds of Carnival.

On the night of Fat Tuesday, the climax of Mardi Gras, she woke around midnight, dry-mouthed and fuzzy-headed. She rolled out of the hammock, sat in a wicker chair on the balcony, and sipped a glass of former ice water in which floated a spent slice of lime.

Below, the tones of steel drums tangled with a strident cornet and the whine of electric guitars from a nearby bar. Marie observed it from a tired distance, wondering why she did not feel beckoned.

She was convinced that she remembered her first Carnival, when she was but days old. Her mother rose from her bed in gauzy splendor on hearing the Carnival, snatched up her baby, and danced them both through the streets for a good long while before summoning a horse taxi to take them home to a furious Grandmère. In Marie's memory, her infant eyes took in blurred bright colors; her new brain absorbed the counterpoint of a somber funereal dirge followed by a wild bouquet of assonant horns that jolted her nervous system into awareness as she was offered up for blessings to manbos and priests. It was one of her favorite stories and she'd implored Grandmère to tell it over and over as she grew up. But after her mother's death, Grandmère told it no more. Her mouth would grow tight and she would turn away.

Now Marie understood.

She had thought that she was mostly over the deaths of Petite Marie and Al. She could not imagine ever again marrying. But she did have another child, who, according to Hugo's plan, should now be filling her life with joy.

Instead, she felt nothing.

There must, she thought, be something wrong with her. Something that her resurrection had not restored. The emotional imperative to live fully was missing.

She rather wished that some clowns would come along—and this time kill her truly.

Since tourism had withered due to the lack of transportation—which promised to change once the North American Maglev System was completed years hence—Mardi Gras had become much more concentrated, more thoroughly Caribbean. Something else drove this transformation as well—a rekindling of mystery, perhaps. It was more intense than the millennium, this folk-fed feeling, this powerful intimation, that something was happening out in space, in the darkness from which they might soon awake. They were in a pregnant pause between technologies. The old was wrecked and ruined. The new was just barely glimpsed and fearful.

What could one do but dance?

Crowds still seethed out on Bourbon Street, and she glimpsed them from her balcony. The spillover on her side street was more demure. Here, midnight could be construed as being just past the dinner hour. Couples were still capable of perusing antiques and art in the shops below with some attention. The customary line for the latest hot restaurant—Ducks, she thought it was called—snaked around the corner.

Then Marie sat up straighter; tried to see through the shadows.

She jumped up and leaned over the railing. "Grandmère!"

The woman with the stern face, elegant French twist, and even the long black lace-trimmed dress of her grandmother turned the corner and vanished.

Marie was surprised to find that her hand trembled as she held tight to the railing.

She slipped into her sandals and ran out of her apartment, down the stairs, and slammed open the front door. One or another of her bodyguards might be following her; she didn't know and didn't care.

As she passed through pounding skirls of Celtic rock, she thought she heard someone call out her name; she did not stop. The air seemed full of ancient pagan ritual as green-eyed, red-haired, brown-skinned men and women, descendants of Africans and forty thousand Irish slaves Cromwell sent to the Caribbean, moved with pale white Americans of Irish descent wreathed in the sweet perfume of heavy ale.

Marie stopped, jumped up and down, and thought she saw the woman again, turning toward St. Anne Street. Some aunt, some cousin, her rational brain told her as she jogged along. Not Grandmère, stern, loving, tough Grandmère, whom she so desperately missed, even after all these years. Grandmère always had a way of helping her make sense of things. Maybe she could help now. Life was so strange. Time fractured when she saw Kalina and it took her weeks to get over it, to forget the beauty of the months after Petite Marie's birth, which were terribly gone and which could not be replayed. That beauty, those memories, were a curtain between herself and Kalina that she could not tear aside.

She didn't want to.

Past St. Anne, Dumain, St. Philip. Short blocks learned through infant eyes. Following the naked feet of Petite Marie, running, tossing clothes behind her. There—Grandmère! Erect in the lightpool, passing the corner grocery where she bought her French cigarettes. The crowd dwindling, rougher, three skinny white men drinking giving her the eye from across the street, one stepping out, then halting after a sharp glance from Marie.

Out of the Quarter onto Esplanade, she knows now where the old lady's going. It was this way, yes, so long ago, they took the same trolley clanking north on Esplanade, now approaching her like dream or doom, kind bowed front and uniformed driver. She climbs on. Grandmère took the one before, no doubt. She sits across from a man her exact color wearing white shorts gold Saints tank shirt and a shiny new top hat. One leg crossed loosely over the other, leaving that v-space like Adele being Ghede, Death God of the *voudoun* pantheon. Marie nods. He nods. She sits tall. The Queen. Open windows and night scents cool eddy through the car, passing beneath dark inter-states and now crossing Elysian Fields, Athis Street, didn't an aunt live here? Old mansions recede in shadows.

End of the line, Pontchartrain Beach Amusement Park. Dead now, but look—is not the roller coaster lit, are not the carousel horses flying stiff in their calliopied circle hooting its steam notes as she walks the old asphalt paths with others, and Ghede follows too, his long stride pacing her a little to the left, a bit behind.

And then the lakeshore, distant western lights painted on dark water by the low longest bridge. Drums and a tree. Sand and mangrove and light waves lapping.

Drums and a peristyle.

A fire and people dancing.

Ghede holds her hand now, rough dry skin and a French cigarette dangling from his mouth. They fall back seeing her, the drums fail, someone calls her name. A chant is raised.

Marie Laveau! Marie Laveau!
The hootchie-kootchie Voodoo Queen of New Orleans!

Like the old jazz song.

But too there is the draped long altar, crisp white cloth dishes of food bottles of wine candles and flowers. Cut forced magnolias from somewhere scent sweet and heavy, white orchids, pink freesia sprays.

Before the tree an old man stoops, dribbling flour from fingers, forming Agwe's boat on beaten ground. A thin black man the oungan; chief. Right side gilded by fire. A phalanx of five: three bearing swords, flanked by two bearing flags, approach. The oungan kisses the tips of the swords, the tips of the flags. The bearers retreat. From large to small: *manman, segon, boula*, three drums tattoo the damp night air. The oungan raises a bowl of water, shakes anson rattle above and below, calling for Agwe, God of the Sea.

All chant:

Signaling, I'm signaling,
Agwe Taroyo.
Can't you see I'm signaling?
Signaling, I'm signaling,
Danbala wédo.
Can't you see I'm signaling?

—repeating, repeating the signaling, entreating Agwe to appear—

She kicks off her sandals. Mud sand cool beneath her feet, she walks through the vévé verge around the tree. A breeze lifts lake smell toward her, a boating day with Mother, laughing, laughing, splashed by cool waves. She wonders how to find them, Mother, Grandmère, Petite Marie. Only she is here in the world. Only she sifts matter through her. She is too alone to be.

The universe a shell of stars a pulse of drums she moves.

She does not move the stars, but they move her. Their light is strong as hands as strong as hunger. They move her like drums; light and low and fast, the *segon* move her arms; deep and running through the ground, the *manman* move her legs; wide circling sounds from the *boula* move her head.

And then she moves the seas if not the stars.

She watches from where she has been for a long time, watches her body walk toward the shore, watches her Agwe legs through her Agwe eyes approach the rowboat transformed to fit vehicle for a god, sees him nod, her rider Agwe; feels him step with masculine grace into the finely painted barque, painted with eyes, vévé, decked with small white Corning Ware containers of fried oysters, jambalaya, red beans and rice set carefully among flowers and bottles of rich red wine on the flat prow of the boat.

Agwe nods; accepts; helps Ghede into the boat. To the west where the long bridge flows, the golden city shines, a city in the clouds, a new Jerusalem, an African homeland, a city where all are free and strong, and lovers stroll the streets, and their children play without fear.

Without fear of death.

It is not one's own death that is to be feared. It is instead the death of those one loves.

Marie for an instant swallows hard, but Agwe hears the drums, returns and waves, standing as the boat rocks and Ghede holds the pole for a moment when they are ten feet from shore as chanting multitudes push them out, fumbles in his pocket, sticks another cigarette in his mouth and lights it with the third match, poles away and away from them.

But going *for* them. Preparing the way.

Opening the pathway to a new golden city.

Leading them across the sea.

Ghede poles them all the way down to the abandoned Navy dock as the dancing fires grow smaller and the drumming fades. In the darkness, lake noise lapping, they sit opposite now. He gives her a strange look and runs his hand up her leg, up the inside of her thigh, and she is not Agwe now, though he may well be Ghede. She leans well forward to find his mouth and they kiss, grabbing one another's shoulders, then drawing closer still, and though it seems impossible that there is room between the hard seats, they fuck. Marie cries out again and again in the night. But she is also Agwe, taking humanity to the golden city in painted boats filled with po' boys, Hurricanes in frosty glasses, and vials of immortality, equality, and intelligence. Ghede chips open the cork with his pocket knife. They drink the wine and eat the oysters and fuck some more.

Marie Laveau walks the whole way back to her house, barefoot, feet eventually bleeding from rough concrete, eyes fastening on every house she passes, on the streets of her childhood, streets that seem like her own body, streets and houses and people of her city waking as she approaches her corner through litter and booze stench and the occasional drunk asleep on the sidewalk.

She walks wet muddy bleeding tired and smiling through the green door, nods to astonished Shorty, goes upstairs, and falls into bed.

That evening she sent a message to Hugo: BRING KALINA AND MISSY HOME. If they want to come. The message may get there before he turns the *Erzulie* around.

The next day Marie gets to work. Real work, soul-feeding work.

Is it just sex, she wonders? Did beautiful Ghede set up new chemical pathways? Did consorting with Death release the light of life?

No matter. She is changed. Not the original Marie, and not the ghost Marie trying to inhabit a life long gone.

She sees a curious boat of lashed bark and colorful silk sails, two feet in length and almost as tall in an antique shop.

She buys it.

Ad in 437 national and international newspapers, *IEEE Journal, The Journal of Nanotechnology, Science, Nature, New Architectural Times, Pheromone Research, Physical Review* . . .

All professional and scientific disciplines including Engineers, Scientists, Architects, Horticulturists, Technicians wanted for project in New Orleans. Excellent pay and benefits. Send CV to Post Office Box 3847, Main Facility, New Orleans LA.

Kalina is petulant. Clearly impressed, though trying to pretend she is not. "It's nice here," she says coolly, touching things. "When can I go home?"

Marie glances at Hugo, at Missy. "This is your new home, Kalina. New Orleans. This is your house."

"And you are my new mother?" She has Missy's British accent, so cultured.

"No. Missy is your mother."

"She says you are my mother." A long measuring look from deep brown eyes that Marie forces herself to meet.

"It's complicated."

"I know. I'm a clone." Her voice airy, unconcerned. "So what?"

"Yes, you're right. It makes no difference."

"So when can I go home? I miss my friends."

Marie kneels in front of her. "Soon, Kalina. Stay for a week. Please? Hugo and I will show you around. Missy wants to go shopping. Then you can go home. All right?"

A shrug. Marie hugs the girl to her. *It will take time.*

Hugo's voice alerted Marie to his presence in the room. "Well, my dear. You called? You're doing better. That arrangement of 'Caravan' is pretty complicated."

Marie pushed back the piano bench and walked over to the tall, open windows that opened onto Bourbon Street. A hot breeze stirred the leaves of her ficus. Kalina and Missy had returned to Roadtown, but a visiting schedule had been established. Marie was filled with energy and resolve.

She said, "Have you heard about the new pheromone-based city plans that the government is financing?"

Hugo perched on the piano bench and teased out a melody with one twisted hand. "What I read in the news. Sounds pretty far-fetched."

"It is, and it isn't. Since the Silence started, they've been busting their butts to come up with some viable ways of doing business. There's a Japanese company that developed a kind of pheromone alphabet—metapheromones, they're calling them. They're already in pretty heavy use in Asia in various applications. They're going to be the basis for communication in this system."

"How?"

"Well, that's the next thing. People have to get what they're calling receptors. We already have pheromone receptors in our noses. Pheromones go directly into the brain through the nasal passage, like all smells. None of this nerve conduction. No mistakes. It's been in use, experimentally, in Asia already. It's a lot easier over there, apparently. More of a free-market atmosphere, at least in significant patches of the landscape."

"But aren't pheromones for, say, mindless armies of ants and bees?"

"Actually, just about all living creatures use them for communication to some extent. We use them for more information about others than we probably know, though in the public's mind they're associated with sex. Even with ants and bees, the messages that are transmitted are quite complex. They communicate alarms, acceptance, distance to food, and things like that. We like to consider ourselves as being more complicated than insects—and we are—so who knows how much pheromones contribute to what we do and who we are?" She laughed. "And who knows what we'd lose if it were possible to upload minds to a less degradable storage medium than the brain, like so many people are talking about. Pheromones, hormones—probably a lot of things that contribute to our sense of who we are and our sense of community."

"But it would be pure," said Hugo.

"Pure nonsense, maybe. Unrecognizable as human, certainly. Anyway, the technology is way, way beyond basic insect pheromone communication now. It's kind of like—for instance, now we can easily manipulate images and convey information that way, whereas for centuries we were stuck with flat paintings that were not easily reproducible and copying books by hand. We use images—print—to communicate in an extremely precise manner now and literacy is sky-high, relatively speaking. It will be like having a whole new sense; it opens up a whole new world of information and possibilities. We can manipulate this other type of information and install new senses—they're calling them 'receptors'—in the human body in order to process the information. This won't be influenced by whatever is causing the Silence. It's biological. A BioCity. Used by humans who will be different than we are now."

"Sounds like a damned scary setup. Not to mention expensive."

"It is. Scary and expensive. But the government will finance the conversion for any city that wants to try it. The alternative is to turn into the analog of a Rust Belt city, isolated, out of the loop, unable to communicate. It will be like not having any telephones in a city when everybody else in the world has three lines in their house. There's a reason they're financing things. Unlimited government access is a part of this package. In other words, they retain the capacity to be able to worm their way into any transaction, any communication. It's their property. And whomever or whatever comes after the government would have the same access. That's the scary part of it, in my opinion."

"Does everyone here want a BioCity, Marie? Seems that sentiment has been running rather high against it, from what I've read in the *Times-Picayune*."

"Well, after seeing this, I don't blame them." She sighed. "The potential is there for greatness. For learning. For fulfilling human potential. For enabling us to grow. For solving this communication problem. For . . ."

"I get the picture," said Hugo. "So what's the solution?"

"I think we've got to do it."

"Go into hock with the government and let them spy on us?"

"Yes—and let them pay while we change the specs."

"In what way?" Hugo slid off the bench and began pacing, hands clasped behind his back.

"In whatever way we please."

"Translation: In whatever way *you* please. But anyway, I'm sure this would be pretty easy. The government is going to allow all kinds of weirdnesses to be inflicted on United States citizens by Marie Laveau and her counterparts elsewhere."

"*They* are the ones that wish to inflict weirdness on everyone. I just want information to be free."

"What a charming catchphrase. It sounds kind of familiar."

"It's from that old Santa Fe Institute—a kind of slogan for chaos. Remember? I was reading it to you a few months ago. It's what got me thinking."

"My dear, when you get to thinking, it's just grand." He raised his arms in a magisterial fashion. "Hey, let's put on a play!"

Marie glared at him. "You're on thin ice, buddy. Besides, that's my idea exactly. We're going to put on a play. We're going to trick the government into thinking we're going along with their plan, but we're going to subvert it at the last minute."

"Good idea! I'll just run down to the bookstore and buy one of those new BioCity subversion manuals. We'll work our way through the handbook."

"I'm afraid it might be a little more difficult than that. In fact, I've been looking into the concept of Zion's floating city. It would be *created*, not discovered. No one to displace, the way people are always displaced when countries are conquered. We can start our own country or noncountry from—"

"The ground up?" suggested Hugo.

"You are just too funny. From scratch. But I'm hoping that this works out. I think that we need to get off of this continent. Off of any continent. I think that we need a place for volunteers, people dedicated to figuring out what's going on with the Silence. I've been in contact with some Space Pioneers too. There are all kinds of astoundingly bright people who really want an opportunity to use what they know. From what I can tell, no government in the world is giving them a chance. If anything is happening, it is top secret. In fact, I've heard some very strange things."

"Like what?"

"Well . . . listen to this. Six months before the first Silence—now, this is not firsthand information—some kind of virus appeared here. It spread around the world pretty quickly. There were hardly any symptoms at all, except maybe sniffles."

"And?"

"Okay. Some children—again, not many—born nine months after the first Silence have a very distinctive DNA anomaly. The common vector may be this virus that the mothers had. Governments all over the world have joined forces to round these kids up and figure out if there is any connection to the Silence. Seems like a real long shot, right? Well, it seems like there's not much to be derived from these kids so far. Many seem to be astoundingly bright, although a relatively high percentage are mildly to profoundly autistic. All of them go berserk when broadcasting is working."

"And?"

"And that's all I know. It's just one example of how weird everything really is and how little us common folks know about it. I'm sure there's all kinds of information out there that a conglomeration of standard-issue geniuses could use to try and dope it all out. Why should all this be secret?"

"I get your drift. As in, you know, a city drifting along on the . . ."

"Oh, stop. You know I'm right. And it needs to be a secret. No government would like this kind of country. All those people paying no taxes. Thinking as they pleased."

"Yeah. What a mess. Let me get this straight. You'd be willing to let them think as they pleased?"

"Oh, stop. I know that it would be hard. But I just have to have faith. Faith like Zion. He believes in something. He has vision. Ellington had vision. Every piece of his I master, I gain a little more capacity for vision too."

"Hmm," said Hugo.

"That's right," she said. "That's what I'm trying to get. Those vision synapses. And he had faith in the abilities of his musicians. He let them have their own voices. That was the power of his work. His genius. Didn't you tell me that?"

"I didn't mean for it to be a blueprint for a political movement."

"Well, there you go. That's the creative part of me, see? Making that leap."

"Flying off into space, more like."

Hugo dodged the copy of *Elementary Ellington* that Marie grabbed from the piano and threw at him. It flew past him with a rustle of pages and bounced off the wall.

"Sacrilege!" shouted Hugo and picked the splayed book off the floor, tenderly flattening its pages. As he worked on this, he said, "Marie, who is this 'we' you're talking about, when you refer to, say, subverting an entire complex city structure?"

"I have a plan."

"I was afraid of that."

"There are people you have to find, bring together. Recruit. Experts or people that have something we need. You need to convince them to come. I've located all kinds of fragments of information around the world."

" 'Around the world.' That sounds exciting. Travel is so fun and easy these days. Let's see, there's steamship, zeppelin, bicycle—"

"Are you going to help?"

"With a capital S, as in Strayhorn."

"Oh, yeah. He wrote a lot of Ellington's stuff, right?"

"I believe the word is 'collaboration,' although you're probably right about Strayhorn sharing credit when he shouldn't have had to. He was a quiet genius. Apparently pretty frustrated at times because he operated under the Ellington umbrella and maybe didn't get the credit he deserved."

"Is that a hint? I'll give you double billing in my memoirs."

"I salivate."

"I take that as a yes. I'll tell you who and what I think we need."

"Let's just cut out this *we* crap, all right?"

"Okay. We're—*I'm*—planning to convert New Orleans into a non-FDA-approved city in the interim. Dighton said that this could possibly be interpreted as an act of war. He looked over the contract that the city council and the mayor and whoever else they can round up has to sign."

" 'Act of war'? What can they do, besides cut the funding? Blow a major American city to smithereens?"

"Well, that's the thing, Hugo. Whatever happens from here on out is going to be in an arena where nanotech weapons will probably be used. My best information is that a Japanese firm among others has developed a lot of weapons along that line. Substances that, for instance, can reprogram thought and behavior in a large population. No mark on the body—at least externally. Everyone going about their business. A mental neutron bomb."

Hugo nodded. "Kind of like your pet thugs."

"Yes."

"So—this is what we need?"

"No. We need someone who knows something about it so that we can defend ourselves."

"Do you have someone in mind?"

"Of course. And then there's the matter of the Signal."

"What signal? You mean the Pulses?"

"Not exactly. There's something about them that I really didn't know."

Hugo smacked his forehead. "No! Impossible!"

"I know it's hard to believe, but yes. A man showed up two days ago in response to my ad. You know, the one I circulated when you were in Tortola. He won't give me his name. Or—he did give me one, but I'm sure it's not real. He wouldn't stay for more than a day either and I don't know where he went. He intimated—wouldn't say flat out—that he's a former intelligence agent. He was quite agitated and had a lot of strange beliefs about aliens. But he told me that there's a bum living in D.C. that knows a lot about the phenomenon that happens every once in awhile after a Pulse."

"You mean the . . . the radio activity—if you'll excuse me."

"You'll be disappointed to hear that you don't have a first on that."

"Fine. Let's see now." Hugo ticked off points with his fingers. "One, a transformed New Orleans. Which may put us at odds with the Feds. Two, a new floating city. Hell, a whole new country. Or noncountry."

"A new Jerusalem," added Marie.

"Oh, of course. Three—what was three?"

"Three was that I have a lot for you to do. All over the world, beginning, I think, in D.C. Japan eventually. Asia, Europe, Africa . . . it's actually harder to think of a place I *don't* need you to go . . ."

"So—there's a new world a'comin', right? I seem to remember . . ." Hugo picked up *Elementary Ellington* and paged through it. "Here it is. '*New World A-Comin'.*' Abridged for piano, of course. I read you a quote from Ellington's autobiography, *Music is my Mistress*." Hugo cleared his throat. " 'The title refers to a future place, on earth, at sea, or in the air, where there will be no war, no greed, no categorization, and where love is unconditional, and where there is no pronoun good enough for God.' " He closed the book and put it back on the piano.

Mare gave him a few slow claps. "Perfect, Hugo! I'll have that inscribed on the city gate."

"Whatever you're taking, Marie, I'm happy." Hugo shot his wrists from his sleeves, laced the fingers of his hands together, cracked them backward. "I hope it improves your piano playing too." He feinted to one side.

She laughed.

After he left, she made an appointment to see her doctor.

Shorty sat in one of the easy chairs in Marie's office; Cut Face stood, his hands in his pockets. Marie leaned her butt against a long mahogany table and folded her arms.

"How are you doing?" she asked Shorty.

"I be fine."

"Our jobs," said Cut Face anxiously. "We be taking care of things as pleases you?"

"Oh yes!" said Marie. They relaxed. "I am just concerned that you still seem to—to be controlled by me. Because of what I gave you."

"It is of no matter," said Shorty.

"What else we be doing?" asked Cut Face. "Now we be doing good. Doing things for you."

Like killing people, thought Marie. Keeping the vestiges of the old guard from regrouping. "But you need to be thinking for yourselves. Deciding whether or not things are right. Not necessarily be doing things just because I tell you to."

Shorty looked puzzled. "There always be a boss. Usually lots meaner than you. Here peoples treat us nice. We gots plenty to eat."

Cut Face said, "I think I know what you be saying, Miss Laveau. But there be another reason for this. This be our penance. We did— many bad things. Many more than you know. Probably more than we be remembering." His face was grave. "Shorty and I talk about this. Maybe this be how we are making up for them. With Jah."

Marie suppressed a sigh. She did not fancy being seen as an agent of God's will, particularly when the results were twisted about by the victims in this fashion.

"You're Terence, right?" she asked Shorty. "And you, Cut Face— you are Robert?"

"Yes," said Shorty. "But Shorty be a good name for me. Everybody call me Shorty now. I like it."

Cut Face nodded in agreement. "Miss Laveau, do not worry about us. When Jah decides that we have paid our debt, He will release us." He spoke quietly, with dignity.

"As Jah's chosen agent," Marie said dryly, "I'll be searching for that which would restore you. I'm sorry that I did this."

Shorty grinned. "Better this than you be killing us, Miss Laveau."

"Thank you for coming," said Marie. "You may go now."

Marie stood in Jackson Square. It was evening. The birds and the wind were still, but soon the black cloud upriver would push wind and torrents of rain across the city.

Marie felt the contentment, the stasis, of early summer fill her. Something like joy spread around her, as if the centuries-old buildings—the cafés, the museum, the cannon, all the ghosts she'd known since childhood—were really herself. And, as if she were a bird, her mind's eye rose and encompassed all of it—the music, the scoundrels, the fevers, the quadrille balls, the slave dances in Congo Square, the river culture that spanned centuries.

The first breath of wind brought strains of jazz from a nearby café. She smelled oysters frying, coffee brewing, wine being poured, pecan pies coming out of ovens. The leaves of the trees turned up silver. Her city, *hers*. The rhapsody of cities filled her—entities complete as a single person, informed by their histories, forever changing, their fortunes ebbing and flowing. A consilience, a blending of culture, science, emotion, labor, the dailiness of lives, a web of families and friends.

And then as thunder boomed and the first splats of rain fell fat on the sidewalk, hissing, she raised her arms as if the rising wind could take her, hurl her like a leaf. She danced, shouted, threw back her head and sang, the *voudoun* chant of the old woman rising in her, and all was golden, and the veins of the city were filled with the luminous fluid which was knowledge—knowledge of that one poem that would illuminate a dark moment or explain an entire century; knowledge of the antibiotic that would save a young one's fevered brain; knowledge of what the stars were made of, how space warped and folded; the truth about the place from whence the Signal came . . .

She barely noticed Hugo grabbing her hand, dragging her through the golden lightning-veined glory, for her mind once again rose.

But this time she looked down on a new island, a country of truth and vision, a place where things were whole, integrated, not fragmented, where humans at last reached their pinnacle, leaped from it into the unknown, and rose, rhapsodic, into space . . .

"Marie," Hugo panted as he pulled her beneath the museum's colonnade, where they rested against a Civil War caisson. "Marie, are you all right? Why the hell were you standing out in the rain?"

"Rhapsody, Hugo," she said, laughing, as the golden pouring rain sluiced off the roof in sheets, and the gray river was beat full of holes, and a lost umbrella tumbled ownerless through the park and lodged against a magnolia tree whose branches flailed in the wind. "Rhapsody."

Left-Hand Voicings

Zeb | Washington, D.C. | 2028

Zeb stirred on his park bench, moved his arm from his eyes, and saw a small brown man staring down at him.

No. Well. Actually, he was a short man, though he wasn't that small. He was pretty husky. Looked strong.

"Nice suit," said Zeb, sitting up and swinging his legs around. "Want a seat?"

The dwarf hoisted himself up beside Zeb. "Beautiful afternoon."

He had an odd accent that Zeb couldn't place. The dwarf sat quietly and finally Zeb agreed. It was late April. The park, near the National Zoo on Connecticut, was filled with flowers, and trees had lately fattened with unfurled leaves into clouds of grasshopper green. Zeb had been up all night—or, rather, lying flat on his back all night—staring at what stars he could scry in the light-ruined sky.

"How about some coffee? On me?"

"Sure," Zeb said.

They strolled down Wisconsin until they reached a block of small bistros. Hugo indicated one with tables set up outside, behind a sheltering glass wall. They seated themselves. There was no one else there.

"This place looks pretty pricey," said Zeb. The dwarf hadn't said much, and neither had he. Zeb didn't mind. Their silence was companionable.

"It is." A formally dressed waiter came and the dwarf asked, "What's good today, sir?"

The waiter glanced sideways at Zeb. "Steamed mussels with ginger for starters. But we won't be open for another hour."

"That sounds good. Tell Andre that Hugo is here. Tell him to knock himself out. Have your sommelier choose the wines."

The waiter looked doubtful, but said, "Very good, sir," and turned to leave.

Zeb said, "You forgot the coffee."

Hugo called the waiter back and ordered two coffees.

"I don't drink. Your name's Hugo?"

"Never?" asked Hugo, raising his eyebrows. "Yes, I'm sorry. My name is Hugo. And yours is—"

"Zeb.

Hugo nodded thoughtfully when Zeb gave his name. "I think you'll want to make an exception today." The waiter brought a wine. "Excellent choice," said Hugo. The waiter poured and left.

Zeb's stomach tightened. "What do you want?"

"Ah, you like to cut to the chase. You're wanted in New Orleans."

"Me? Why? Who wants me?"

"A woman named Marie. She's setting up a project having to do with certain radio wave anomalies."

Zeb almost choked on his coffee. He pushed his chair back, ready to run.

"Great pay," said Hugo. "Probably better than you're making here."

This Hugo had a great sense of humor. Zeb noticed that his face was slightly flattened; his hands a bit twisted. But there was nothing wrong with his mind.

"Look," Hugo continued, "If I wanted to do you in, would I take you out to dinner first?"

"I can't leave." Zeb was filled with panic at the very thought. His beloved streets. Each one had a meaning. Ellie. His SETI group. His friends in the park.

"Pity," said Hugo. "Mmm. Here are the mussels. Outstanding presentation. Tell Andre, please." The waiter nodded and left. Hugo pried a mussel from a shell, chewed, and swallowed. He tore off a chunk of bread, soaked it in the broth, and ate with a running commentary proclaiming culinary ecstasy.

Zeb realized that he was starving. He looked at Hugo warily. The man couldn't pull things out of his head, could he? But the diamonds. The diamonds were in his inner pocket, sealed in the little pocket. Drop one in, read out the data. He still hadn't exhausted it.

Maybe that's what this guy was after.

"You don't have to decide now. I thought it might be good to hang around some first. Answer your questions. We have a concert to attend." Hugo sipped his wine.

"Oh?"

"Duke Ellington at the Howard, doing *Black, Brown and Beige*."

Zeb decided that Hugo's smile was one of pure bliss. "It's gotten good reviews in the *Post*."

"Ah. You read the paper."

"Religiously, as they say." Zeb reached into a pocket and unfolded a white rectangle of sleek thin material. "Found this e-paper about a year ago. Whoever lost it had a heck of a subscription. Been downloading since then. Whenever the system is up. Maybe once a month. I think they keep trying just because they're stubborn. But when it's not up free papers aren't hard to find. And now that we've got the *Evening Star* back in addition to the *Post* and all those peripheral papers, it's hard to get through all of it." He put his *e-Post* away, buttered a slice of bread, and found it up to Hugo's blissful proclamations. "I don't understand how folks like this Ellington person can do that to themselves."

"Oh, I can," said Hugo. "I think that it would be utterly fascinating to be able to do what others of genius have done. We don't have *new* works of genius coming out of these folks, it's true. This guy—what was his name?"

"Ed? Something," said Zeb, trying to recall.

"Yeah, that's right. Ed Street. Apparently, he was an adequate musician. He didn't go into it from a standing start. He attended Juilliard, Howard, did a stint at Monk. Then he went to Mexico and got the Ellington implant. Even had his appearance changed. The Duke at age, say, fifty-five. Put together an orchestra. I gather most of the guys he picked up were strays—musically adept, but just bumming around, picking up jobs here and there. He convinced them of the beauty of his scheme and financed their implants too. I don't think many of them had their appearance done over. Maybe they will now that they're in the money, but I imagine Street has a lot of debt to pay off. Anyway, I'm really looking forward to it. It's the closest thing to being at some of history's hot moments that we've got. No creative frisson, perhaps. But the faint echoes of it."

After dinner, Hugo suggested that they walk crosstown toward the Howard. "If you're up to it. It would clear my head."

"I like to walk," said Zeb. "It helps me think." Quietly tony Georgetown town houses lined the cross-streets here, interspersed with businesses.

"What do you think about?"

Zeb stopped walking. "What do you really want?"

Hugo stopped too. "Marie is trying to put together a place that will—how can I put this without sounding melodramatic? I can't. She

174

wants to create a place that will pull us back from the brink of disaster. Which is where we are now. There is no free flow of information. Those who know certain things are once again isolated from those in another discipline or even their own, who might be able to spark some synergy. My job is to gather up the people who can help us do that. People who know something. People who are at the top of their field."

"I'm not at the top of my field," said Zeb flatly, starting to walk again. "I'm pretty much in the gutter. As I'm sure you can see."

"But why?" asked Hugo.

"Because . . ." began Zeb, then stopped. Why tell this man anything? He felt torn. Part of him felt deeply uneasy; wanted to careen into the next alley. Another part of him wanted to trust this man with his life. Something about him seemed so solid. How do you know? Zeb asked himself, growing angry. How can you tell who seems solid and who doesn't?

"Look," said Hugo. "If this is how you like to live, you'd be free to live this way in New Orleans. But you'd be *there*. You could check in. You could share what you know, what you think. You can talk to like-minded people."

"How did you know how to find me?" asked Zeb.

"It wasn't easy," said Hugo. "Sometimes I feel as if I'm a character in a fairy tale. You know, the brother who has to find the needle in the haystack, outwit the wicked giant, and find the golden apples of the sun all in one night. It's getting kind of late. Maybe we should catch a cab."

The crosstown ride took only minutes, through small elite neighborhoods, each with its own character. "My aunt used to live there," said Hugo as they passed a small garden apartment of red brick. "We used to visit her every fall."

Zeb allowed himself to fall into the cadence of the ride, lulled by the wine and the good meal. He tried to wonder why anyone would find him valuable in any way and failed. He figured this guy didn't know about the diamonds; otherwise, why this song and dance? He would have tried to take them by now. The kids who gathered around him and called him Star Man were just that—naïve kids, looking for someone to believe in. They didn't really know much. He could have told them anything and they'd believe. For all he knew, he *had* told them anything.

The Howard was a stunning Victorian gem, its previous plain façade restored to its original majesty. The blocks surrounding it were filled with small shops—grocers, florists, gourmet food stores, pre-theater restaurants. Snazzily dressed people, some with skin the color of milk, some with skin the color of ebony, and all shades between, strolled toward the theater through pools of streetlight.

Zeb was perused with distaste—if not disgust—by the doorman. As Hugo slipped the doorman some money, Zeb read a sign about the Howard's restoration, the result of nanotech advances and much trust funding.

They settled into a private balcony; Zeb was relieved because no one would complain about him. The show was just beginning.

Street came on and joked about how the world was evolving toward beigedom. "Ladies and Gentlemen . . . in our travels in Asia . . ."

Hugo stood at the railing. "Amazing," he murmured. "He seems perfect." He turned and sat down. "I am in heaven."

Zeb listened clinically. Music still held little fascination for him, but he'd never had much exposure to jazz and he found himself fascinated by the tonal relationships and rhythmic structures that filled the air. It was a lot different than the classical music that . . .

That who?

He realized that he rarely remembered that he had at one time had a wife, much less her name.

Agitated, he rose to go, but Hugo pulled his arm down with surprising force for such a short man. "The part we just heard was never recorded by Ellington and I've never heard it. It was a tonal description of how the main character, Boola, was abducted from Africa and came here on a slave ship in the fifteen hundreds. This is an archetypal black who lives through centuries of black history in the United States. I am in complete awe."

"It was interesting," conceded Zeb.

"You'll really enjoy the next part."

Despite himself, Zeb did become immersed in the performance. He'd never bothered to seek out live music because it seemed artificial compared to natural random sound. Perhaps because of the wine, he relaxed; let the music rearrange his thoughts.

After the second standing ovation, Hugo led him out a fire exit corridor. "Should we be going this way?" Zeb asked nervously.

"Only if we want to avoid getting crushed." Hugo turned down a branching hallway and yanked open a door that Zeb had not even seen in the dimly lit hall. They were backstage, he saw.

Hugo sought out Street and launched into a complex appreciation of the performance. Street looked pleased. Then Hugo talked about some project this Marie wanted Street to undertake. He handed Street a card and what looked like a tape cassette. Street looked nervous and kept glancing around; finally he said, "I'm sorry, I'm due at a party," and Hugo let him go. They wandered out into the alley behind the theater. The night was cool now.

"I thought we'd stay at the Sheraton tonight. I've booked us seats on the new magrail for tomorrow morning."

"I never said I'd go," said Zeb.

"That's true, you didn't. But we'd appreciate it quite deeply if you would come."

"What if I don't want to?"

"Tell me why and we can discuss it."

"You never told me how you found me."

"We advertised for those with a particular background. Very quickly, a man showed up in New Orleans and told us that you knew things about the astronomical aspects of our current situation that very few people know. He recommended that we get in touch with you. Maybe help you out. Get you away from Washington. He said that you knew him under another name, but he wouldn't give us his name. I've been looking for you for about two weeks. I talked to you last week when you were in that park at Sixteenth and K, but you were raving about aliens and didn't seem to hear me. This man said that he once gave you an overcoat—"

"Why didn't you kill me?" he said to Hugo in a low voice, backing away. This man was pretending to know Craig. And Craig was dead. He just wanted the classified information he'd been working with. Damn. Someone must have seen him using it in the library. He tried to keep the little book out of sight, but sometimes he had to consult it as he worked. "I don't have anything! I don't! Why didn't you just kill me right away! I'm nuts. I'm unstable. I don't know a goddamned thing. Stop following me." His running seemed as slow to him as if he were caught in a nightmare.

Hugo followed, yelling, "Wait!"

Fear pumped Zeb's arms and legs: that tiny vision of Craig on the television motivating him, along with the probable shot from the gun Zeb suddenly knew Hugo carried; tell them nothing, nothing, because after that they might as well kill you. Panting, he entered dark welcoming shadows and heard a small voice yelling from half a block away, "He's not dead!"

The dwarf was trying to make him stop, trying to lure him back. He ran down an alley, cut through some yards, jumped on a passing bus and rode, transferred, rode some more. He rode until he fell asleep. The driver woke him and threw him off, and Zeb wondered if perhaps he had dreamed of the brown dwarf.

BREAK

A boy plays in a park. He is five years old. His father sits on a bench with other parents not far away.

The boy scuffs his feet on the dirt patch below his swing; slows; slips from the plastic sling and stumbles forward a few steps. He reaches down to touch a yellow toy helicopter someone has left on the worn grass next to a crumpled paper cup.

He picks it up; spins the propeller. He looks up to see a woman with long dark hair standing not far from him, watching him with a look as strong as a teacher's look. He wonders if he is doing something wrong. Maybe the helicopter belongs to her little boy. He has an impulse to run away with it and keep it for himself. He notices his father watching him now, so he takes a few steps toward the woman. He should give it back to her. He isn't supposed to keep things that don't belong to him.

Suddenly his hand tingles as if asleep. He drops the helicopter and shakes his hand, but it gets worse. His hand feels stiff and numb. He tries to scream, looking around for his father, and sees the woman smile and walk away. He hears his father's wild shout, but he is very stiff now, and it is hard to breathe. He barely feels his father's arms as he grabs him up, and his eyes stare upward at the blue reeling sky.

The New York Times

MASSES FLEE CITY IN WAKE OF THE DEATHS
OF CHILDREN IN THE PARK

A panicked exodus clogged major arteries yesterday afternoon as word of the deaths of twenty-three children in Central Park spread. Two other children afflicted with the mysterious paralysis remain in serious condition in the intensive care unit of Children's Hospital, according to an anonymous source. A hospital spokesperson denied that the children were there.

PRESIDENT INVOKES WAR POWERS ACT

In an unprecedented move, President McPerry today invoked the War Powers Act to justify his signing of the controversial North Atlantic Nanotechnology Organization Treaty. This treaty gives broad powers to the Federation, an international organization set up on the model of the United Nations, to concentrate solely on nanotechnology proliferation and use issues.

Both houses of Congress are expected to support McPerry's action. Congresswoman Benetti of the newly formed New York Boroughs District cited "that unspeakable tragic act that took place in Central Park" last week as her motivation, saying that she had strong support from her district to take steps to avert other terrorist acts.

Extended Riff in Past and Future Minor

Annie | Washington, D.C. | 2029

It was amazing, observed Annie, just before the Metro slid beneath the Potomac through one of the several new tunnels facilitated by recent molecular manipulation breakthroughs, how spring in Washington still had the power to fill her with the joy of nature's rebirth. She closed her eyes to hold within the image of pink cherry blossoms on trees that always reminded her of pirouetting dancers held in exquisite pause. She'd strolled among them yesterday, trying to mentally prepare for the ordeal she imagined today would be.

Too soon the second stop came and she had to debark and rise into the politic-stained world of science she now inhabited. She fought her way to the escalator.

She was not looking forward to this morning's meeting. She was to be an expert witness before Congress regarding the development of a master plan for the implementation of the new communication system based on metapheromones, and in an hour would be deposed. She'd just spent a predawn briefing hour at the Pentagon. Now she would stop by her office, pick up a few things, and wait for the limo.

Sunlight as she emerged into the upper world was pale, the air chill despite the presage of cherry blossoms. As she waited to cross I Street, a parade of variously shaped vehicles, depending on their fueling system, met in their daily homage to the god of gridlock, and she quickly wove through them against the signal. In less than a year it would be illegal to drive anything in the United States except solar-powered vehicles. Or bicycles. And she had a feeling that anything except public transportation would be outlawed in most cities, anyway.

She stopped by her regular coffee stall and Feng handed her her customary cup of near-viscous Vietnamese coffee. As she sipped, she cut through a greening park. A statue of some general on a horse loomed over her. She went over her objections to this particular proposal. The main one being that it could all get out of control so easily. But how to make that stand up against panic? They would just respond that the world was in a state of emergency. Radio and wire communications were all but shot. Cables were limited as to the amount of information they could carry, and only two weeks ago a key cable to Japan had been ruined by nanotech sabotage. There were a lot of angry people in the world now. Some were just mad, and some wanted the whole world to revert to some kind of bucolic Gaian vision, which meant a radically reduced population and very little technology. Terrorist attacks from various quarters were on the rise. Conversion to BioCity mode would give a greater measure of detection and immunity—at least, this is what the developers claimed. She planned to heartily dispute this idea.

She was not looking forward to her day in committee. Who was she, they would say, to try and derail these excellent proposals from some of the most prestigious international nanotech firms presently operating? For weeks her head had been spinning as she tried to set down precisely the problems she foresaw, and then tried to cast the problems into scenarios that would be easy to understand. She'd spent nights of cold fear. She shivered now as she passed through the general's blue shadow. The sun disappeared. A gust of cold wind rattled the bare branches above her.

Suddenly a face was in front of hers, bearded and pale. The man wore an ancient overcoat. His eyes were sharp, not rheumy like those of many bums. She opened her mouth to say she had no change, then closed it.

They stared at one another for a long moment. It had been years. How many? Fifteen? And how heartbroken her mother had been. Annie believed that the sorrow had led to her cancer and her death. Could it really be him?

"Uncle Zeb?" she said gently, for he looked frail and as if he might bolt.

He stood as if dazed.

"It's Annie," she said. "Remember? Sal's girl?"

He blinked. "I thought so. I've seen you. Walking through the park. You come this way every day."

Annie frowned. She had been coming this way for about three

months, ever since she got a cryptic note, sealed inside a battered letter with a Tokyo postmark, saying that she might find her uncle here. She'd considered it a baffling prank, but concern won out. At first she looked for him, then stopped, but the route became a superstitious ritual.

Zeb lifted his hand, pushed back her hair as he had done when she was little. "How's Sally?"

The deep sadness she had for the most part conquered resurfaced and made her nose sting. "She's dead, Uncle Zeb. She looked for you everywhere, you know? She spent three years searching. Dad thought she was crazy."

" 'Dead.' " His hand dropped to his side. His mouth sagged. He looked back up at her. "I'm—so sorry, Annie. You see, I haven't been . . . well, I guess. This is . . . a good time. I mean, for me. For thinking."

Annie brushed tears away. A fine way to greet the committee. "I have to be somewhere in ten minutes. Come with me. You can wait outside. Afterward we'll have something to eat. Damn, the hearings will probably take all day. Look—"

"It's all right, Annie," he said gently. "You're busy." He turned to walk away.

She followed him. "Zeb, are you crazy?" She could have bitten her tongue, but continued on. "You need to come home with me. I have an apartment on Kalorama. You know, up by the zoo. What have you been doing all this time?"

He stopped and asked, looking straight ahead, "How are Pleiades and Zephyr?"

She felt like strangling him. She took a deep breath. "They both died years ago. Brad was devastated. But they had three litters and he kept several puppies. He breeds collies now and raises sheep." She looked at her watch. "I've really got to go. My office is on the next block. You can wait there. Come on." She took his arm, but he didn't move.

"I like it better outside."

"I wish I had more time. Here's my card." Exasperated, she scribbled on the back. "This is my address. I'll tell the security man to expect you. I'll see you at my condo tonight, all right, Uncle Zeb?" She tried to sound as firm as possible. Then she ran to make the light. Damn. She'd be late. And her thoughts were all scattered. She looked back from across the street. He was gone.

She splurged and took a cab home that night. What the hell. What was she saving for anyway? Her old age? Judging from her experience today, she wouldn't have one and neither would all the shortsighted assholes she'd tried to be so straight with. They'd be washed away in some sort of nanotech surge. Her mind danced with horrific images. What was she doing here? She should be with Brad, raising sheep down in the valley. She might as well be weaving blankets for all the good she was doing here. There was no way logic could cut through all the money that was flowing under every table in Washington these days. Not to mention the exciting ways in which these international corporations could present their expensive and dangerous visions of the future. Maybe they all deserved to go back to the Middle Ages. In her opinion, that was where they were heading, more quickly than most people seemed to realize.

Sure, she was a curmudgeon—and pretty young to be one too. She was proud of it. And now was the time to go for broke. Desperate measures were called for. Her day had convinced her of that if nothing else.

It was dark and she jolted from side to side in the tiny backseat. The driver didn't speak English; she'd punched her address in and the cab's map told him where to turn.

She felt as if she'd spent a day breaking rocks. She'd had a quick glass of wine while waiting for the Vietnamese carryout meal that was in the large bag next to her. She relaxed into a mental state where thoughts flowed freely.

These were strange times. Humanity had been powerfully jolted in the past few centuries, always, before this, by the truth. The Enlightenment had been the first great change. A flowering of thought directly due to the availability of books printed with movable type. Then, in the midst of the Industrial Revolution, Darwin's assertion that everything in existence was not designed by God but was the result of natural forces. In her opinion, that powerfully revolutionary thought had never been entirely assimilated by humankind as a whole, mired as it was in some sort of hardwired attachment to religion and mysticism. Then physics had spawned the atomic bomb and the cold war that, true to its name, froze political enmities for fifty years. But just as now, the threat had accelerated scientific progress. The Internet, with its lack of rules and hierarchy, had been designed so that people (read: Americans) could communicate with one another after the world was flattened and begin to rebuild it. In their own image, of course.

Now the advent of nanotechnology, coupled with the Silence, had brought humanity face-to-face with all kinds of truths it seemed to be choosing to ignore.

The Earth was part of a larger galactic ecology, which was now affecting them in powerful ways. They were on the cusp of being able to manipulate matter in all kinds of subtle fashions, and this included the matter of the mind. A huge room, a cracked door, a sliver of light admitted—

Would they slam the door or traverse the enormous room and fling it open?

Well, unlike Brad, she couldn't help caring about them all. She opened her eyes and watched the lights reel past. They were new biolights and cast a cold greenish glow. The cab sped past a corner where a gang of girls sat on the sidewalk, smoking and checking out their weapons for whatever spree they had in mind tonight. She was nuts to live here. She ought to get a condo across the river in Virginia. It was safer there. Or so the ads implied.

She thought of the opening line of one of her favorite poems, Blake's "The Tyger": "Tyger! Tyger! burning bright." If all their intelligence was the tyger, how long would they last, how would they be able to fare into this coming forest of the night? No immortal hand or eye had framed this fearful symmetry. At least not in this universe. Symmetry was just a part of the basic package, on a very deep level. And now it was up to them, the mortals, to frame whatever would come next.

She unlocked the cab door with her credit squirt, and it flashed the total as she opened the door. She grabbed her dinner. Their dinner. She hoped to see Uncle Zeb. The taxi door slid shut and the guard came out to escort her the ten feet to the door.

She'd had no time to think about Zeb. She didn't want to think about him because it would just remind her of those dreadful years when her mother wasted away and all the time since. Fifteen hard, strange years, with two near-misses at marriage.

"You've got a visitor," said Harry as he walked her to the door. Another guard watched from inside the glass doors and several more were on call about the building.

"Sorry they made you wait down here, Uncle Zeb. Hi." She hugged him. He did not smell like a bum. She remembered his smell from her childhood—woodsmoke and outdoors. Now it was just like plain soap.

He hugged her—hard. He stepped back and seemed to be struggling to speak.

"This is nice," Zeb said finally, as they stepped into the apartment. A narrow hallway led to the living room, dining room, and kitchen on one side and to two bedrooms on the other side. She used one of the bedrooms as a study. The apartment was furnished with some of her mother's furniture and old art deco pieces picked up at estate sales. Unmatching, faded oriental rugs covered the wooden floors. Zeb stood in the living room, not speaking. He looked uncomfortable, as if he was a wild being unused to walls. "Sit down while I heat this up," she said.

"That was your mother's dining room set, wasn't it?" he asked, standing in the dining room. "It was your grandmother's."

"Yes," she said. She wondered if Zeb was an alcoholic. He didn't look it. He just looked weathered. "Can I take your coat?" she asked, but he shook his head.

She went into the kitchen. Zeb followed. She got the stuff out of the bag and set the cardboard boxes on the induction plate. It was old-fashioned but came with the apartment. "Only problem with this is that you have to stir it," she said. She opened a drawer and handed him a spoon for each box.

There were noodles, some kind of beef dish, spring rolls, vegetables. She poured herself a glass of wine. "Want some?" she asked hesitantly.

"Sure," he said, but left it sitting on the counter after a sip. She got out plates and bowls and he poured steaming food into them.

"How long have you been in Washington, Zeb?" she asked, trying to keep her voice steady.

"Oh." He was quiet for a minute. "For a long time." He piled silverware onto some plates and she took the food and they went into the dining room. They pulled out chairs and seated themselves. Outside of Annie's tall old-fashioned windows, the lights of the city twinkled. Annie helped herself to some spring rolls, thinking how pleasant it was that there had been no gunfire yet.

"It smells sweet in here," said Zeb. "Kind of like your mother's house." He bent his head down and sniffed at the table. "Old wood does that. Exudes a fragrance." He looked up at Annie and said, "Some people think that scent can be the strongest trigger of memory."

She filled Zeb's plate. "Eat. You're too thin."

Zeb didn't feel like eating. I only want to remember, he thought. He gazed at Annie, his vision filled with not only her face, but the dear face of her mother. Annie looked so capable, so much in charge. He was very glad that she seemed to have crossed the developmental shoals in which he'd foundered.

She stood and lit candles in crystal holders that also were Sally's and smiled at him. "A special occasion," she said. Or at least he thought it was something like that from the look on her face. She turned back to Craig and they were talking about something. He wondered when Craig had come. He hadn't seen Craig in . . . so long. When was it last? Craig pushed the plate toward him again, nodding.

Their words—Craig's and Annie's—were like shots of sound that blurred into the air. Pleasant tones, though a bit like sparring. Annie looked at him anxiously and he smiled back. It was all so lovely. It was as if, in the dimness of the room, they floated in a sea of stars, just the table and chairs and the old family buffet behind Annie, ornate and holding the glow of years. If he walked over and opened the drawers, what memories might he pull from them and shake out like napkins long folded . . . the archetype of the day, perhaps, when he and Sally had gone swimming down at the creek, dogs barking from their sentinel stones, blue mountains visible between the trees, and then Dad setting the table with this same china in the summer evening . . .

Then Annie was hugging him, and Craig looked on worriedly. He heard Annie quite clearly. "Zeb, *Zeb,* it's all right, oh, honey, it wasn't your fault, really." He realized he was sobbing. He sucked in great gasps of air and made keening animal sounds. "So much gone," he heard himself say.

"I've never seen him like this," Craig said.

"He's just found out that his sister died," said Annie, her words tight and angry. "Not that it makes any difference to you. Come on, Zeb. Give me that damned coat. That's right. I've got heat here. Now come on over and lie down on the couch for a minute. You just rest."

Zeb felt his protective shell being peeled off, heard Craig murmur "I've tried to give him a new coat, but he likes that one." Well, of course he did. It had been a present from Craig.

"I'm not always like this," he protested as they got him onto the couch. Craig wiped his face with a napkin and he realized that he was sweating profusely. "I wish," he said. "I wish." And then he fell asleep. From time to time, he opened his eyes and saw Craig and Annie across from him, talking and sometimes arguing, but he always lapsed back into sleep again—safe, protected sleep. He felt Sally hovering around him. He was sure he did. She'd gone where dimensions undid themselves, a place where he often dwelt, while the world flowed past around him.

Annie collapsed onto an overstuffed chair of vaguely thirtyish mode, upholstered in forest green with lime green piping. She drew her legs up beneath her. She held tight to her newly poured whisky and water. The food sat uneaten on the table. Zeb lay on the couch across from her. It had been a very long day. She wondered who Craig was. Zeb had clearly been hallucinating.

She decided that she would take the morning off. They could have a quiet breakfast. Maybe coffee would help him. She tried to remember what her mother had said about Zeb's condition. She sat back in her chair, sipped her whisky, and watched him sleep.

He was very thin. Probably malnourished. But alive. "Oh, Mom," she murmured, and tears came to her eyes and this time she let them fall.

She'd been in her sophomore year of college. Sally had been worried about her, of course. It was a distant, steely sort of worry. *Will you crack up like my brother?*

No danger, Mom. Levelheaded. Dependable. Good old Annie, that's me. Brad had suffered one or two scary episodes, but now seemed . . . almost all right, with his collie-herded cloned sheep and his little wool factory down in the valley. All the latest stuff. The wool practically fell off the sheep and made itself into smooth cashmere sweaters. But still All-Natural, of course. All-Natural was a great selling point. There was a nice picture on his package of sheep and collies. Very natural, indeed. And on Zeb's land. It had been hard as the devil to wrest that place from legal limbo, seeing as how there had never been a body.

Annie took a sip of whisky and let it warm her throat and chest. She tipped her head back, closed her eyes, and remembered.

It was a blustery day in January, about ten degrees. The sky was pure blue and cloudless, but the wind kicked up great gusts of powdery snow and whisked it across Route 460 as Sally fought the wind's grip on the truck.

"Didn't even take his pills with him," Sally said again. She said that often. Annie said nothing. Sally had been able to wangle the truck from impoundment in D.C. with a sizable donation. "Now where is that turn? Do you remember, Annie?"

"No," said Annie. She'd quit school for a semester to try and help her mom. She was worried about how it might affect her standing and hated herself for it. But she couldn't help it if she was a perfectionist. Nanotech was such a hot discipline now that it wasn't easy to get into the best grad schools. "Wait. There, I think. Between those fence posts. I remember that old barn." Zeb had brought them up the previous summer.

Sally turned the truck so it went beneath the posts. "Tire tracks. Sand. Somebody's been up here, haven't they?"

Annie tried not to think about who that might be. Since the blackout, there had been a government clampdown on an amazing amount of activities. She'd had to go through a security check in order to continue a completely mundane astronomy class she was taking just for the credits. "Are you sure we should do this, Mom?" she asked.

"He was up here the night it happened," she said. "He found out something up here."

"And now he's gone," said Annie. "Doesn't that tell you something, Mom?"

"I won't have you talking like that!" Sally said.

"I didn't mean it that way—oh, never mind," said Annie. "He's still alive. I know it."

"He might have wandered in front of a truck," said Sally grimly, but they both knew that wasn't true. They'd seen him on SNN. The whole world had. Saying something about a government cover-up.

"I've got a better idea," said Annie. "The antenna wasn't far from the Appalachian Trail. Why don't we get some winter hiking gear and go in that way?"

Sally fought for the steering wheel as they jounced over a big rock. "I've thought of that."

Annie stared at her mother. "You have?"

"Sure. But if they're guarding the place, they'll have thought of that. It seems a lot more dangerous in a way. If we seemed to be sneaking up on them, we could get killed. This way—" She shrugged.

"Be careful," said Annie as they crawled along a narrow road next to a cliff. Sally didn't reply.

There were guards, of course. From the Army. Annie was vaguely surprised. Wasn't this a National Guard sort of thing? They were just to maintain the perimeter. Despite the fact that she and Sally were in Zeb's truck, these guards just believed that they were driving up for the view or to check on cattle or something.

They had spent two weeks in Washington. Of course, all was in an uproar; the city was packed and it was like a pilgrimage. Washington had to know what to do!

When Annie returned to school, she was not penalized. Far from it. Because of her scores, she was put into an accelerated program. When she told them that she couldn't attend through the summer because she had to work, the government put her in one of the new scholarship programs. Suddenly science was important. A new grim atmosphere pervaded not only the country, but the entire world. Alternatives to so many kinds of technologies had to be found.

Annie woke because someone was talking and because it was cold. She was sitting in the living room, but it was dark. The windows were open. Freezing wind had scattered a stack of her papers around the room.

Zeb had his coat on again. He was smoking, using one of Sal's china cups as an ashtray. She quelled the impulse to jump up, grab it, and wash it.

His face was lit by the light of the kitchen. He was talking very fast. He jerked his cigarette to his mouth, jerked it away after a quick puff.

"I didn't mean to do it, you know, but I had no choice, Annie. There was something I knew." He laughed—loudly. "Did you see me in the newspaper, *The Washington Post*? Not long ago."

"No," she said. Though she tried to read the paper religiously, some days she was just too tired. The news was pretty much back to print medium now, since radio was so sporadic. "You know, pretty soon you'll be able to get the news just by touch. Kind of like in a Kurt Vonnegut novel. Of course you'll have to change yourself to do that—somewhat." She realized with a start that she was rambling as much as he was. It was all so dreamlike. "Why were you in the paper, Zeb?"

"Apparently, I gathered a huge crowd around me. I was hollering about aliens. Nothing new, you know, just the same old stuff. Same old stuff people have been ranting about for years."

A chill went down the back of Annie's neck. "Does this have anything to do with the antenna? Remember what you talked about that Thanksgiving—"

Zeb's face underwent a powerful transformation. He looked dazed for a few seconds, losing the manic energy that had tightened the skin around his eyes. He swallowed. He took a deep breath. He looked around and switched on a light. Then he closed the window. He took the china cup into the kitchen and Annie heard water running. Annie couldn't get up to save her life. She felt as if she were being held underwater by a powerful force. It was all so strange.

He came back into the room and took off the coat, hung it next to Annie's. He sat down on the couch, leaning his elbows on his knees, clasping his hands. "You remember. But you were so little."

"No, I wasn't," she laughed. "I was nineteen."

He looked around. "This is a very nice apartment. What do you do?"

"I work for the government. This antenna stuff is driving you crazy, isn't it? I mean, it has." She tried to be distant, clinical with him. It wasn't that difficult. She was an adult now.

He looked alarmed. "The government!"

"Don't worry. I'm a lowly nanotechnologist. I work on developing codes—legal definitions and limits—for the implementation of nano-tech." She laughed. "After today, I can't think of anything more ridiculous."

He nodded. "I'm not surprised. I mean, that you're doing important work. You were always pretty focused. Look, I'm sorry. I don't know how long I'll be like this. I can never tell."

"I guess you don't take your medicine," Annie said. "I'm sure they have much better stuff now. We can go see—have you checked out—"

"No!"

"Okay, then," she said. "We won't. But why not?"

"You think I'm crazy."

"You are."

"In some ways. But not in others. I mean, I guess I'm not always in control of myself. I'm manic. I know that. I realize it. But Annie, when I'm that way, I can *think*."

"What good does it do you to *think* when you're sitting on a steam grate?"

He looked surprised. "It doesn't matter where I am. Really. You work for the government."

"It doesn't matter what you tell me, Zeb. It will be a secret. I won't tell anyone."

"But that's the problem," he said. "Everyone needs to know. I have proof."

Annie laughed despite herself. "Uncle Zeb," she said hopelessly. "Proof. Hey, what we wouldn't give for proof. I know what you *think*. At least vaguely. But people who think that aliens are causing this are totally ridiculed. Batted down."

"Kicked around," said Zeb without rancor. "But I know what I know. That makes it bearable."

"Kind of like . . . Copernicus, right?" she asked.

"Exactly," said Zeb seriously. "You want everyone to know. You really do. But I guess . . ." He shrugged. "Maybe it would be good to—to get into better shape. Get some kind of credibility. But how? *They* aren't going to hand some kind of podium to me. I've tried that approach. Really. I went to Tech and tried to get my job back a few years ago. I had tenure. They told me to wait in an office. Within half an hour, some men in suits showed up. I managed to get away from them. I knew about some old steam tunnels that nobody remembers now—under the physics building." He turned to the side of the couch and picked up a remote control that was sitting there. "Television working?"

"Zeb!" she said, bolting from her chair. "You can't see that!" It activated her hv platform and a copy of what she'd been working on to show to Congress.

He laughed, kneeling in front of the platform. Laughed like a child, delightedly. "And they think *I'm* crazy. How the hell is this supposed to work?"

Some city was there, the tallest building about a foot high. Chicago, remembered Annie blearily. They'd been afraid to show this happening on their home ground, the District. Somewhere pleasantly removed from their everyday experience was deemed best. As far as she could tell, no one was prepared to risk a changeover—a "conversion," as the process was being called, in Washington. Because a conversion carried risk of a *surge,* among other complications—a disaster wherein the molecular process mutated and began to change everything around it in an uncontrolled fashion.

"This is prototype number three, it says." Zeb sat back on his heels, his weathered face bathed eerily in patches of multicolored light.

The buildings were topped with what looked like swimming pools. Lines streaked down the sides of the buildings. "They conveniently left out the buildings without flat roofs," mused Zeb. "Guess they'll have to cut the tops off."

"No," said Annie quietly. "They're just going to *enliven* them. Change their molecular structure and then regrow them to suit. Make them more—plastic, I guess, is a good word."

"Hmm," said Zeb. "What a thought."

Tiny spheres, like Ping-Pong balls, bounced between the building tops, touching down in the pools and darting to those on other rooftops.

"What if it rains?" asked Zeb. "What if the wind blows?"

"Try number . . . seven," she suggested.

A wonderland of huge flowers blossomed atop the buildings. Large bees took the place of the spheres. Zeb stared at it for a moment, then burst out laughing. He switched to number five. "Anyone thought of infrared?" he asked.

She sighed. "People are leery of depending on anything having to do with frequencies. They're thinking more and more along biological lines. The bees and the flowers—that's phcromone-based. The bees will be fairly large, capable of transporting information packets that are analogs of pollen. Wind won't be a problem for them unless it's quite extreme."

"Pheromones?" he said. "You mean like sex?"

"Kind of," she said. "Except that the idea is to use that basic form of communication like an alphabet. There are thousands of naturally occurring pheromones and all kinds of creatures use them for very precise communication. Say that we develop more pheromones. Combine them into words. Metapheromones. Grow receptors for these metapheromones in humans, so they can know things by touch. Or by smell."

"The smell of the Bible," mused Zeb, rising and settling back onto the couch. "The smell of Newton's laws. The smell of *The Origin of Species*. The smell of 'I Love Lucy.' "

"The smell of facism," said Annie. "That's why I'm at least trying to steer this toward touch. That's a little more controllable. Not that I have a whole lot to say about it."

"Here," said Zeb, raising his arm as if in a toast. "Have a sip of *Das Kapital*!"

"You're getting the picture," said Annie.

"But wouldn't bike couriers and vacuum tubes be just as fast?"

Annie laughed. "*Hell* no! Information is ferried constantly, by air. Pickup and delivery almost as fast as a phone call or fax. No street traffic. And couriers would have to haul a truckload of paper to transport the amount of information we can put in a milligram of the pollen analog. 'Information at the speed of consciousness'—that's one motto I've heard. This concept was developed by a collaboration between an American and a Japanese company. Their stock is sky-high right now. But the plan for American cities is a little bit different."

"How so?"

"Encryption. Or lack thereof. It will be illegal, and they're trying to make it basically impossible to change anything about the system. Particularly the part of it that makes government access to absolutely any exchange of information crystal clear. And no other plan is to be approved for use in the United States."

Zeb frowned. "Is that constitutional?"

"Well . . . you see, we're not officially at war, because there is no visible enemy. There are signs of a possible enemy, of course, but they really don't want people thinking about the Silence in those terms, because they're afraid that the result would be anarchy. But the War Powers Act has been invoked rather indiscriminately. I think that it's an index of how helpless we feel."

"Despite that, I read a lot of conjecture in the paper about the Silence. In the legitimate press."

"Yeah, and it's kind of on a par with 'Did Oswald act alone?' So they've demeaned the whole idea of possible intelligence out there, at least publicly. If anyone's got any clear proof that aliens are causing the pulses, instead of some natural galactic event, they're not speaking up. Still, with so much terrorism and the possibility of their spies being here on Earth—"

"*Their* spies?"

"Sure, Uncle Zeb. Alien spies."

"Wouldn't they—whoever *they* are—be trying to find these alien spies? I mean," he added wryly, "I've certainly had a taste of the invisible 'theys.' "

"Oh, they are." She laughed. "Trying to. There's talk of some mutation having occurred that night—remember that Thanksgiving Eve?"

"How could I forget?"

"Well, I don't have a thing to do with that project. In fact, I'm not entirely sure that it even exists. I've only heard rumors. Something about increased levels of magnetite in their brains." She laughed. Then she looked at Zeb's face. "What?"

"Magnetite. Annie . . ." Zeb tried to remember. "About twenty years ago, we found a new form of neutron star. It revolves two hundred times per second. It creates a powerful magnetic wave and messed up some satellites from time to time. If . . . such a field was generated by something closer, it could even affect the iron atoms in your blood." He looked up. "It seems to me that magnetic forces would also be affecting magnetite, right?"

"Why, sure. In fact, not that I know a lot about it, but magnetite in the brains of birds has been connected with their migrational abilities. Apparently, they're tuned in to the magnetic fields. And there's been a lot of bird die-offs since the pulses started. Erroneous migrations. Really a tragedy. One more tragedy. No one knows how that's going to affect world ecology." Annie slumped back in her chair.

Zeb sighed. "It so frustrating to be stuck here when *somewhere* something astounding is happening. Somewhere out there." He smiled faintly. "I've heard rumors too. I've heard rumors that despite the blackout, NASA is still sending out satellites and even ships. That people on the moon, on Mars, know what is happening."

"That may be true. But I don't have access to that kind of information. If it is true, I suspect that very few people do."

Zeb said, "It's the very opposite of the way we grew up. We grew up with a spirit of scientific enterprise. We were all in this together, together in the world, together in trying to get to the heart of the great mysteries. We shared information. This is terribly wrong. The world is like a police state now. This is the biggest mystery that has ever occurred and anyone who wants to do something about it is persecuted. Who put these people in charge, anyway?"

"Well, let me see if I can spell it out for you. Not that I've got the clearest picture. Because it isn't clear. The military, of course, has a whole lot of power and jurisdiction over matters like this, and they've used that to the hilt. For instance, I was not allowed by the Defense Department to talk about certain nanotech weapons that have been developed or that are in the pipeline today when I was deposed by the Congressional Committee on Communication. Various agencies always had overlapping turf and that's gotten more confusing. People out in the rest of the country seem to think that their elected officials have a lot of power. They don't. They come and they go. They can fund or defund an agency or a program, but that's about it. There's a lot of inertia here—as in moving objects that won't stop until an equal and opposite force is applied. Even the National Institutes of Health are doing a lot of classified research. So it's not at all far-fetched to think that this or that government agency-slash-cabal is doing what they please. Top that off with all the economic chaos . . . whew!"

"Isn't there anyone that's trying to . . . to rebalance things? To find the truth? To set things right? To go *out* there?"

Annie thought back to the letter with the Tokyo postmark. The postmark had been nine months old. The letter mentioned a certain Marie Laveau and New Orleans. It suggested that Annie's expertise would be useful there. She had thought of it as some kind of prank.

But it had been right about Zeb hanging out in that park.

"Why did you vanish that day?"

Zeb opened his mouth as if to speak. Then he closed it.

"What?"

"I really don't want to say."

"Why the hell not? I mean, we looked all over creation for you, Mom and I. You can at least tell me what happened."

"It might be dangerous for you."

" 'Dangerous'! That's kind of a fascinating assertion."

"I was told that I had to . . . to cooperate concerning some information that I had. And I didn't want to."

Annie leaned forward and put her elbows on her knees, cupped her chin in her hands. She narrowed her eyes.

"Zeb. Who told you this?"

He looked away.

"Are you afraid?"

"I've been afraid for many years, Annie."

"I'm very, very sorry about that. But I can keep you safe, I'm sure."

He shook his head. "I don't think so." He pushed himself up off the floor. "In fact, I'd better go now. I've probably put you in danger."

"No, Zeb!" Annie jumped up and grabbed his arm. "No, please don't go."

"I have my work. Annie, I'm doing some very important work. I'm thinking."

"Yes, yes, I'm sure you are." She was frantic. He couldn't just walk out now. "Stay the rest of the night. Look. In here." She dragged him down the hallway. "See? Mom's walnut bed. All made up! Look." The headboard was intricately carved with a running motif of flowers and leaves. She pulled back the covers. "With Mom's sheets, remember these? The little red tulips. She would want you to stay. Please. And we can talk tomorrow."

Zeb stopped resisting. "All right, Annie. But just until tomorrow."

She turned down the covers. She brought him some chamomile tea and set it steaming on the doily next to the night table lamp. She brought him towels and showed him the bathtub. She told him to leave his clothes out and she'd wash them in the morning. The window was covered with wide venetian blinds and she pulled them up a bit and opened the window a crack. The stream of cold air felt good. "There. Now promise you'll be here in the morning."

Then she remembered something. She went into her bedroom and opened the closet, climbed up on a chair, and pulled things down from the top shelf and dumped them behind her. She had to go get a flashlight and then she had to find batteries for it. She wondered if she had forgotten where this thing really was. Then she saw it, squeezed in the corner.

The Virginia Tech tote bag held the printouts from Zeb's truck, along with a tape on which he raved about all kinds of mathematical relationships. Once again she was suffused by a wave of sadness as she pulled it out and wondered if she ought to give it to him. It might upset him too much. It certainly upset her. It brought back the last years of her mother's life with a rush.

But it was his. She dragged it toward her, sneezing from dust, and let it drop to the floor with a dull thud. He said he was thinking. Einstein hung around the Institute for Advanced Thought for thirty years, thinking. Why not Uncle Zeb?

She peered in the bedroom door. "Zeb?"

He was sprawled on the bed, snoring. Wearing his clothes and his shoes. But he opened his eyes. "What?"

"I'm sorry. Here." She set the tote bag next to the bed. "I kept this from your truck."

He sat up and leaned over, pulled out the tape and the first unfolding sheets. His face worked. He looked up. "Annie! I had no idea! This is incredibly valuable. Thank you so much!" He stood and gave her a rough hug and sat down again, shaking his head in what seemed like wonder. "This will be such a help! You know—what I'm really working on is a Theory of Everything. I really believe that whoever is sending this must know the answer, whatever they might call it and however they might be using it. They must have long ago found the link between quantum and Newtonian physics. I think they're trying to tell us what it is."

Annie was quiet for a moment. It seemed hilarious and absurd and touching. But . . .

She remembered what her mother had said about Zeb's early intellectual powers. Maybe it wasn't all that silly.

"Kind of picking up where Einstein left off?" she asked in a gentle voice.

"Sounds preposterous, doesn't it?"

Annie's chest felt tight for a moment. "Not so much, Uncle Zeb. If anyone can figure it out, you can. I really have to sleep now. But don't you dare leave. You just plan on staying here and doing your work, all right?"

She slept on the couch to make sure she'd catch him in the morning. But of course, when she woke up, the covers were turned back on an empty bed. The printouts were gone. She felt keen disappointment.

And yet, as she stood in the tiny day-bright bedroom filled with her mother's things, elation filled her like sunlight. His work. At least he thought he was doing something important. Most people didn't even have that. He was alive. She couldn't cage him. And evidently he had some paranoid belief that he was a danger to her. But she could at least keep an eye out for him, without being obvious.

It was a small redemption, but somehow it made all the difference.

THE THIRD MOVEMENT

ARGENTINIAN INTERLUDE

2029

Angelina hardly minded that radio and all that was going bad, except that she couldn't call Oliveira very often. She therefore had to fall back on writing letters, which she hated because she was not very good at it and it was embarrassing. His letters were filled with close observations of not only his own thoughts and feelings but telling and intelligent interpretations of the actions of those around him, eloquent descriptions of moods, of which he had more than she'd ever suspected, and lovely, detailed word pictures of streets, shops, days, nights, strewn with phrases that shone like pearls. Her own letters were terse, abrupt things pulled out of her by guilt.

"Weather fine. Rode out to the east pasture today. I'm trying to figure out how we are going to power the electric fences." Well, she was damned tired. She didn't have time for all these prettinesses, like him. Still she managed her weekly letter, one page exactly, not one word more. "Soon I'll be sending these by carrier pigeon," she wrote him. "They are trying to restore the old steam engine from the museum. But it's the wrong gauge for the bullet tracks."

She stared out the window. Her pen stopped moving. It was raining. Cold rain from the south. Right time of year, of course. Usually by now she was all snugged in for the winter, the warehouses full of hay and feed, vast larder full of supplies for herself and the occasional visitor. Any day now it would change to snow and and the feed wasn't here yet.

How had Grandfather Paulo done it, so long ago? Well, he hadn't been fool enough to come before the tracks had been well laid. And now the train had stopped running. For a while they said tomorrow and then they said next week and soon they'd stop saying and the station would be empty. For all she knew, they'd come for her cows and claim them for the state, for an emergency.

Even if she had bought that system to grow beef in stainless-steel containers—revolting thought!—how would she have shipped it from here?

When she looked out the window again, it was snowing.

Prelude to a Somewhat Distant Kiss

Artaud and Illian | Prague | 2030

Artaud watched Illian soak up the admiration as he sipped red wine at an opening. He'd managed to procure a huge loft in Prague; it went for gutbucket prices because of the last year's surge scare. Now only the avant-garde wanted to spent time in Prague.

Illian had elected to wear a shimmering purple bodysuit draped with sheer red fabric, sarilike. It set off her exotic looks well. She'd rimmed her wide dark eyes with kohl. Her pale skin glowed, putting him in mind of a silvery moon.

No one, looking at her, would know how sick she was.

"It's the end of an era," murmured the woman next to him. She was heavy, dressed severely in black, with the exception of a yellow scarf around her neck. Her white doughy face was made more lively by the patches of pink she'd applied to her cheeks. Perdita reviewed for an international art bundle.

"End of an era—you mean because of locality," replied Artaud. And indeed the theme of medievality—glossed and romanticized— seemed a major attention-getter lately, though it certainly didn't figure in Illian's work, which was wide and sweeping and connected one somehow instead of isolating. But most everything else in the world seemed to be moving backward in time. It was now more possible to produce what one needed within a small community. Certainly the models he'd seen of some of the first fully designed nanotech cities were self-sufficient. London, Paris, and Beijing were on the verge of major changeovers, and the world was watching nervously.

"I mean because of everything," Perdita said crossly. "And this work of your protégée reminds me of it too much." She set an empty glass on a table and set to work on her third—if Artaud's count was good.

"I guess you could call her my protégée," he said doubtfully.

"You've obviously taught her everything you know," said Perdita.

Artaud choked on his swallow of wine and tried to make it come out a chuckle. He shook his head while Perdita pounded him on his back. Another swain—Artaud could only think of them as swains—joined the group around Illian. They were too suave by half, all of them. "It's just her," he gasped. He didn't add that all he'd done was try to keep her alive and try to keep his awe under heavy wraps. He didn't want to limit her with history. Yet he wanted her to have a strong foundation to fall back on. It was a fine line. She absorbed things quickly, though. Often with frightening speed.

He had found her several years ago, selling paintings on the sidewalks of Amsterdam, a girl so young that at first he did not believe that she could be the artist. He was a bitter old man, dying of cancer and uninterested in cures, staying alive only so that his insurance would pay off his granddaughter when he died. A respected art critic for most of his life, Artaud had been stunned by Illian's work. He took her in. He held on to her, and decided to hold on to life, because she showed him something utterly new, something interesting enough to make living through pain worthwhile.

She made him want to see what would happen next.

"What is this stuff anyway?" Perdita continued, sweeping her glass-holding arm in a one-hundred-and-eighty-degree arc so that wine sloshed wildly. "It moves me on some deep level and yet I can't really be articulate about it. It irritates the hell out of me—if you really want to know. 'Moves me on some deep level.' Right. That oughtta fly. With people her age, anyway."

"Now, now," said Artaud. "Let's not hold her age against her. Despite the fact that it makes me burn with envy."

Perdita had come to Prague decades ago, an expatriate American eventually holding fast to art's hem, as had Artaud, rather than creating its fabric, ungracefully coming to terms with her own lack of talent. "Though you could have talent easily enough now, my dear," said Artaud, horrified to hear himself replying aloud to his own thoughts. Was it the music—loose, and loosening stuff that Illian insisted on, despite his insistence that the visual arts should remain unsullied?

"What?" asked Perdita.

"Nothing," he lied. "Too much wine. I'm immensely proud, of course, but it's nothing to do with me, I assure you. You see her age.

Do you think she'd follow a word of my advice even if she secretly agreed?"

"Well, I can see that it's a lot more than mere Hogwash," said Perdita. Prague was awash with nanotech snifters of talent. Or "Hogwash," as it was called.

Artaud had long puzzled about talent's hidden origins. Basic skills were necessary, of course, and could be learned. You had to know the scales, had to train your voice or fingers or eye, had to absorb the basics. But some took flight, their eye on a goal out there in the infrared. Not seen at all until they unraveled its edges and set it concrete into the world, embedded it in matter, filtered it through notes or color or film and left its record as unfinished as they dared. Artaud was a fan of not muddying the colors. First thought best thought. He'd tried to keep Illian always on the breaking cusp. Apparently, he'd succeeded.

What did Hogwash do? It was closely related to endorphins and required biofeedback to induce a certain brain wave pattern. Application exercises washed through the hopefuls in the community constantly. Mostly it had to do with imitating the masters and hoping to train your own brain cells in this fashion.

Artaud could only hope that it would improve the world. It seemed to him that it might make people happier. Some expression of oneself in the arts seemed essential to every human.

But nothing could improve on his happiness, on his pride, at this moment. Not even wishing, as he'd caught himself far too often, that he was younger and Illian older.

But even removing the manifestations of age was possible now. He didn't really think it was right.

Still, he was doing it. Or having it done.

He was startled and even afraid for an instant when Perdita brushed his cheek and said, "You look younger every day, dear." Could she read his mind? Were the preparatory treatments showing? They merely helped ready the body for its ordeal. The real work would take months, and he would have to go to Mexico.

"Perdita," he said, "I was wondering if you would mind looking after Illian for a few months or so. I have to go to New York and you know how long it takes nowadays."

Perdita looked at him with eyes make-believe wide. "Why, of course, dear. Though I might wonder why you're not taking Little Miss Genius with you to unleash upon the art world there . . ."

"She's not ready," he said abruptly.

"Of course not," said Perdita and pinched his cheek rather too painfully. "She needs to stay here in the boonies. You go . . . arrange some shows. All this is collapsible, of course?" She meant that the pieces were on a sphere which, inserted into a gallery wall-system supplied with the right stuff, reproduced the entire show overnight.

He shook his head. "Every last one of them is simply itself. They weren't grown. She painted them with oils and turpentine. They have to be hung and set up. She welds too," he said proudly.

Perdita wrinkled her nose. "Oils! Oh, how smelly. That ghastly solvent stuff. Excuse me, Artaud, but how healthy is that for a young woman?"

Artaud recalled seeing Illian in bleary 3 A.M. darkness, opening his eyes as he lay in bed. In his stubbornly separate bed in their studio; she'd gone through her oedipal stage of wanting him and it had passed quickly and stormily. Her hair tied up in a scarf of silken paint-smeared butterflies, she leaned against a stool, gazing at a painting for a good half hour as he fought sleep. The bar downstairs provided the scene with a dull roaring accompaniment of drunken singing. Tears tracked her face and she attacked the canvas with a flurry of brush-strokes hard as blows. The easel fell backward. The music from down-stairs was suddenly overwhelmed as a radio somewhere in the loft blared on. Illian collapsed to the floor. He jumped from bed, saying, "Shit!" And it was two days before she woke.

Her ascension to celebrity had been too swift for him to control. He would have preferred her talent to be tamped and richened by experience. But she did harbor unexpected depths. She had suffered— somehow, somewhere—beyond words, before he had found her, and her bouts of sickness were unbearable for him; frightening. The first time, years ago in Amsterdam, he had taken her to a doctor by ambu-lance, but she slipped out of the examining room and he found her after hours of frantic search, fevered, in a nearby alley. But not too fevered to fight, frenzied, drawing blood from attendants when he car-ried her back and she awoke on an examining table. When she recov-ered at home, she told him simply that she would run away and disappear completely if he ever took her to a doctor again. In a way, he understood. At least, he felt the same way about doctors. After that, he hired private nurses to care for her. He came to dread the times when radio worked. For he quickly realized that those were the times when she was unable to function. Yet afterward it seemed as if she'd moved to new levels; it was as if she only knew the alphabet before her spells, but woke up knowing how to read.

With fame, it seemed that her personality was transformed. At first he was worried, then gratified. She was happy at last. He knew that she was not at her peak, not at all. But she might not live to reach it, so—let her have her day. There was no way he could have prevented it, at any rate, not after he'd promoted her so tirelessly.

"I *said*, Artaud," Perdita said crossly. "How healthy?"

"Not very healthy, I suppose," he said. "But she's stubborn." He regretted his decision to leave Illian in Perdita's hands for a moment. He didn't want Perdita to know too much, but he was handing her too much on a silver platter.

He knew he was in over his head. How delicious it was, after all these years. His granddaughter hated him for not dropping dead after all, despite his giving her five of his most valuable paintings outright, more than enough to set her up for life if she moved fast. Everyone had to move fast these days. Sell out, cash in. What good were diamonds, for instance, when replication flooded the market with as much precisely arranged hard carbon as was desired? Where would value lie when all was available to kings and paupers alike, spread across a smorgasbord? His patrician background asserted itself when he thought about this. Without an appreciation of beauty, whether created by humans or found in nature, what good was the gift of consciousness?

Perhaps new forms of appreciation were waiting in the wings.

Illian strolled over to one of her pieces, a three-dimensional wire thing that reminded Artaud of a cage. She built cages of toothpicks. They all contained the same odd conjunction of angles, like some kind of giant molecule from one of his childhood chemistry classes gone awry. She left them all around the studio. She fashioned them when she was sick and filled them with butterflies created from all kinds of mediums—metal, tissue paper, clay. They clearly meant something to her, but she could not or would not tell Artaud what that might be.

Illian bent from the waist and tweaked the large cage gently. Its loose center part, a mobile of copper butterflies hanging from a ball bearing joint, swayed and as it did the tempo of the music did so as well, enveloping them in a sweeping rhythm. Artaud feared she would raise her pointed chin and dance, eyes shut, face blissful, as she was wont to do when enveloped in such music. Oh well, they would just think it was part of the work, but not only was it distracting, it was far too private . . .

But they would probably never see her broken down, in tears, as he so often did. They would never hold her, her thin, long, limbs awkward as those of a fawn, as she sobbed uncontrollably.

Was it just hormones?

She looked up and smiled at him directly, her wide enchanting smile. Without breaking their locked gaze, she straightened and walked toward him and, to his surprise and near-embarrassment, hugged him tightly.

"I am so happy," she whispered in his ear.

He hugged her briefly, then released her. "Me too. Go talk to your public."

Afterward, it was hard to shake them. He knew she was tired but she refused to allow him to drive them off, first at the café, where she devoured a huge plate of egg noodles, and afterward as she bought a pink felt hat at a hat stand and they fed the processor an old black fedora from a bin of hats shielded from the rain by a sheet of plastic. "A coat too," Artaud said, but the young man didn't even remove the cigarette from his teeth, just jerked his head toward the stand next to him. As Illian sported in her hat, balancing on a brick wall behind some benches and leaping down in a plié, which brought applause, Artaud let them suck 4.7 euros from his card and wrapped a black velvet cape around her shoulders. She looked into his eyes with sudden apology.

"You're tired," she said. She was quite as solicitous of him as he was of her, though it was no longer necessary. The seventh or eighth cancer cure had been successful. It had taken four years to work through them and she had nursed him as much as he'd allowed, though he hired people to do things technical or heavy. It had been interesting to observe how irritated this made his granddaughter.

"No," he said. "It's you I'm worried about."

"Well, then," she said and smiled. "I supposed we might have some ice cream." She looked over her shoulder and back at him. "Shoo!" she said, waving her arm at them. A few of them looked surprised, some of them annoyed. "What, you've never seen a woman change her mind? I'm tired now. Thank you for coming. I enjoyed your company. Now GO!"

Muttering among themselves, the half-dozen of them trooped down the rainy, gilded street toward the St. Charles Bridge.

West Coast Cutting Contest

Jason | Arizona | 2031

Jason always felt naked when he went down into town, as if layers of himself peeled away with every downturning switchback of the narrow dusty road. As if, when he got down there, everyone would be able to see how different he was. As if those who were after him would be able to find him and take him . . . wherever they wanted to take him. Some top-secret facility somewhere. The faceless place of his nightmares.

Up on the plateau at nine thousand feet, the three of them had built what could only be called a bunker, backed into a rise in the land, huge south-facing windows made nonreflective, his mom and dad constantly arguing about whether or not they should have an arsenal, more weapons than the three rifles they used for hunting. So far she'd won. When each new crop came in, they'd truck a load back from the farmers' market; can or dry it. Herbs, chilies, and garlic braids hung from the heavy beams of the kitchen—beams from no forest, beams that had never known roots nor leaves. This distressed his mother, though she could never say exactly why. "It's never known the joy of life," she said. "That's right, and it never knew the pain of death," his dad would invariably rejoin. "It never felt the saw bite into it."

The brilliant sun burned him through the roll bars of the Jeep he'd found in a junkyard when he was fifteen and converted to solar. That was one good thing about being out West. It was more sensible to go solar. The majestic roar of the sun, which he sometimes likened to an orchestra or to musics previously unthought of, unheard, was the background of his consciousness now. He'd gotten used to it.

207

In the East, there was a lot of talk about some new kind of BioCities; apparently Beijing had already converted to some bizarre system using pheromones, and plans were afoot to convert several U.S. cities. They still got newspapers in Dog Leg, tossed off of the shiny new maglev every afternoon. The pheromone plan was to imbed the DNA of a special strain of *E. coli* with news, pack that in tamperproof pouches, and ship it on the system of magrails that even now was being constructed—NAMS, the North American Maglev System. Nanotech developments made tunnelling swift and danger-free; rails were grown just as swiftly. The news would then be released into the citywide system to be downloaded at will.

The Dog Leg maglev stop, one of the first because it was a primary east–west route, was one reason they'd chosen to set up their factory here. People could come in by train and pick up the cars they'd manufactured for them, drive them away. They offered a "free" train ticket from anywhere in their ad. Minerals was the other draw. The raw materials they needed to grow things were plentiful hereabouts. His dad had found the optimal place by downloading old sonar maps, locating pockets of minerals for mining corporations back around 2010. Things were cheaper at the source.

In addition to growing the special kind of car Jason had designed and which he had patented, they grew the regular kinds of prefab houses, which they shipped out on train cars, and feng shui houses designed by his mother, complete with furnishings and an initial visit from her to determine the orientation of the house on the site. These clients were incredibly picky, as far as Jason could tell, and often paid for many consultations before they were satisfied. It was by far the most lucrative part of their business.

Jason swerved to avoid a boulder that had fallen in the road, leaving inches to spare on the cliff side. This didn't bother him in the least, but he figured he ought to come back when he had more time and rig up something to get rid of it. Maybe blast it. His mother would probably get out and walk this stretch till then and she certainly wouldn't drive it except on a moped.

He reached the blacktop, and then it was another ten miles to Dog Leg. In anticipation of new cheap roads that constantly maintained themselves, most secondary roads were not maintained at all. Despite the rumpled, potholed surface, Jason shifted into fifth and cruised fast, enjoying the tumbleweeds of the flats, the line of mountains to the north, the wind in his hair. Dog Leg, a cluster of low scattered buildings, grew larger.

He drove down the alley in back of their factory and parked, as was his habit, two doors down. He climbed the rusted fire escape of the building next door and looked down into the parking lot, which was empty. He climbed down and unlocked the back door and stepped inside, touched on the bank of biolights in the ceiling.

He walked over and checked the first of his three tanks, where a neon-green car grew. He opened the hood of the control panel and touched a few pads; readouts echoed back in bright crisp colors on his screen. He lost himself in creation. It was not a job to him— not yet.

The Long Neck Saloon was crowded on Thursday night; not only was it a game night but TV was working. A rare coincidence nowadays.

Jason was rooting for the Astros, for no particular reason. It was just more interesting when he rooted for someone. He was on his third Bud, hunkered at the end of the bar, the physics textbook he'd brought to pass the time lying open, forgotten. He stayed over in town once or twice a week and generally ate at the Long Neck and had a few beers; read or studied, following a curriculum set up by his parents years ago, to the twangs of country music on the jukebox. The game was an unexpected bonus.

Although the times when broadcasting worked still sometimes made him nauseous, headachy, cranky, or just plain caused him to fall to the ground gripped in a cold sweat while the world whirled around him, he'd learned that if a television was in the room and if he focused on the picture, he could sometimes stay steady. And tonight he wanted to. He cheered with the rest of the room and pounded on the bar with a fist. Drinking seemed to help too. He signaled for another Bud.

The screen went black. A general groan arose, spiked by deep curses and the sound of a bottle smashing. The room went silent for a remarkable moment as everyone stared at the screen, hoping the picture would return.

Then most everyone rose and started shuffling out of the bar. There were a lot of general good nights. Jason put his money on the bar and moved to a booth. The generator had kicked in, but Brenda went around lighting the kerosene lanterns at each table. Jason thanked her, ordered some soup, and opened his book to the place he had been. But for a long time, he did not look at the book.

This was his sacred time.

He did not always hear tones now. At times the things he saw became sharper; became more deeply tinged with hue; displayed geometric relationships he'd never before noticed, held together with spaces and lines and depth of field. At times like these, he understood how one might be called to be an artist. His field of vision seemed to demand replication in one way or another and he tended to sketch at these times on whatever might be available. A line of mountains; a table scattered with dinner's debris of dirty dishes and half-devoured foodstuffs; the folds of fabric heaped on an unmade bed; a Western highway stretching to infinity. He rarely kept the results, although his mother always did if she found them. For him, the satisfaction—the compulsion—lay in the act of sketching, not in the finished product.

At other times, sounds seemed to be precisely organized. The soughing of wind in the high pines; the pitch and hum of traffic in a big city; the rustle of pages as his father read the newspaper. Music was an unbearable delight, especially Bach, where relationships leaped out like crystal into the air.

Tonight it was needling tones and a wide swath of low warm sounds suggesting to Jason the aurora borealis, which he'd never actually seen. The beer blur vanished and he leaned over his book, relaxing into the satisfaction of hard information.

He was on a page of problems. He got out a notebook and prepared to do some figuring.

But to his amazement, his mind leaped to the answer of the first problem immediately. He held it in his mind for a moment, doubting and not doubting, then turned to the back of the book.

He was correct.

He turned back and looked at the problems.

These were not simple challenges. He had fully expected to solve perhaps one in the next hour. Perhaps none. Yet he worked his way down the page with as much ease as if the problems were asking his age or his hair color. There was an odd, insistent clarity about the workings of the universe. The laws of physics were bare and visible, with his steadily accumulated background of quantum mechanics and all of its bizarre spinoffs. The matter of his surroundings—the scarred wooden tables and floor, the plastic napkin holder, the aluminum spoon Brenda plunked down next to the steaming mug of soup—fairly screamed with obvious relationships and revelations so powerfully that he caught his breath and stared, as perplexed as if he were William Blake suddenly observing the divine lineaments of London.

He stood, pulled on his jacket and hat, and stepped outside. His breath puffed in the cold desert air.

The two-lane road widened into a short comb of parking spaces as it passed through Dog Leg. No one thought it important to provide backup power for the single streetlight, so the luxury of total darkness was his.

The heavens were as ordered as the interior of the Long Arm Saloon. He was ordered thusly within and connected with them. He had been created from the dust of the universe. It was all so simple. Pathways to infinity were everywhere—within each atom, and outward forever, clear as a map that he might sketch.

He remembered, now, feeling like this as a child, as if he could extend his arms like ever-popular Superman and fly like an arrow into the heart of it all.

The music he heard, and *saw,* was so sweet, so compelling, that it brought tears to his eyes. If Gregorian chants ordered the soul, this universe chant was ordering his mind so that it meshed with and understood everything. The cold asphalt road beneath his feet led to Los Angeles. The star road that signaled from afar led to . . .

Where?

Then the sounds vanished. The sky was just the sky, rich with stars. The Long Arm Saloon and Myer's Kwik-Mart and his own nano-tech manufacturing warehouse across the street, where he was experiencing the first whispers of successfully earning a living, were immutably and dully themselves and nothing more.

He was beckoned nowhere except back inside the Long Arm Saloon, because it was warm, and out here it was freezing cold.

The next day around lunchtime something caught his vision. Through the one-way glass at the front of his factory, he watched a small bland car reverse and back into the parking lot. He knew it was some sort of official car. No one else would drive such a plain vehicle, not in this age of molecular splendor where color was a matter of changing the programming of your car's surface using the control panel on the steering wheel.

A man and a woman stepped out. The man wore a suit, the woman a dress suit and high heels. They looked up at his sign—MUSICAL SUN MANUFACTURING—said something to each other, and walked up to the door.

He could pretend he wasn't here. But they'd be back.

He went over and answered the knock on the door.

The woman said, "Hello. We're from the FBI."

"Got any ID?" Jason asked. They showed him cards and badges. Big deal.

"Are you Jason Peabody?" asked the woman.

"No."

"When will he be in?" asked the man.

"Won't," said Jason.

"But our sources show that he holds the patent on at least one component of the cars you produce."

Shit. But he'd known that was stupid. He was just so proud of it.

And it seemed so obscure. He shrugged. "Could be. I wouldn't know. Your records are out of date. I bought this factory a year and a half ago. Check in Phoenix. The state should have everything in order by now." He frowned. "I think whoever owned it before me might have done a little fancy bookkeeping. So far it's not turning the profit that the real estate agent claimed he got out of it." He held out his hand. "Name's Ned. Ned Holdman."

The woman shook his hand with a doubtful grasp. She narrowed her eyes at him. "Well, Mr. Holdman, any idea where Mr. Peabody might be?"

Jason shook his head. "Couldn't say. I think he was probably kind of shifty, you know? In a hurry to move on. A drifter." He cleared his throat, ready to either burst out laughing or devolve into hysterical shakes; he didn't know which.

"Mind if we take a look around?" asked the man.

Jason shrugged. "Help yourself." He'd gone through everything meticulously, wiped out any trace of his old identity. He hadn't expected them to zero in on him this soon, though.

He pretended to busy himself at his tanks while they poked around, rifled through his computer, pulled open his file drawers. He marveled at his calm hands. That meditation stuff of his mom's really did come in handy sometimes. The agents didn't speak, but their mouths were compressed and they looked angry.

He looked a lot different than his last known picture, taken when he was twelve, a group photo at a school he'd attended for six months. His mom dyed his hair black in that town. Now his hair was carrot-colored and curly, as was his full beard. He wore two small earrings high on his right ear. He was strong and fit; he spent his free time hiking in the mountains. And thinking. Yearning, as he hiked, for something—what? he'd ask himself in exasperation. True love? A calling in life? Freedom? A more typical life? But it seemed as if the whole world was becoming undone now.

He was startled when the woman tapped him on the shoulder. "We're finished," she said. "Sorry to bother you. Here's my card. If you hear from Peabody, please get in touch with us immediately. It's very important."

He put the card in his pocket. "Will do. Sorry I couldn't be of more help. I'd like to get hold of him myself. It's taken me months to straighten out the mess here. What did he do, anyway? Some kind of embezzler?"

"No, he . . ." began the man. The woman quickly said, "That's classified. We have to go now."

After they drove off, he dropped down onto a folding chair and started to shake violently. "Why?" he whispered, head in his hands. "Why?"

It was quite possible that they hadn't swallowed his story and that they'd be back with a warrant for his blood. "Shit," he said, rising and stuffing his hands in his pocket.

He really loved his little factory. He loved inventing. He loved creating a template for something and seeing it grow, ironing out the flaws. It was so damned much fun. And it was so easy. Just dump it back into the vat, change the program, and have another go. There were more sophisticated programs than the ones he used, much more expensive ones. Programs that operated on a different level, which didn't allow the elementary mistakes he made to occur. But he preferred to learn. He wanted to be the one designing the programs. Once he was at that level, he could sell them. Until then, he needed the hands-on aspect of his factory. And it was quite fine to make his own money for a change and help his parents out.

He closed his eyes. He saw a bald head, white hair flaring outward in a wild fringe. He saw a weathered, wrinkled face. His heart pounded.

There were real problems with changing one's appearance so radically. A lot of the problems were as yet unknown. But it was not as if you could backtrack. Was he willing to trade his youthful face for one that was old?

Could he perhaps just shave his head, or strip the color from his hair? Maybe that would work. Maybe. He looked too much the same age as Jason Peabody, fugitive.

But what could he do about his blood? His strange blood. A new type. Type XX.

He couldn't take any chances.

He went around to the stations and started the downloading process. He rummaged around on a shelf and found a box of spheres and loaded one into each station. I'm not running, he told himself. I'm just making backups. He wouldn't run. He was tired of it. He had lived in more towns, attended more schools, and played with more kids than he could remember. Any time a teacher or neighbor showed the slightest interest in him, they ran. Until they got here, which was nowhere. It had seemed safe here. This would really upset his parents. They'd give up the bunker they'd spent years building in a flash and move on. Same old story. But what would those agents think if they came back and he was gone? They'd be hot on the trail again. Maybe he could make this new identity stick.

As he worked, afternoon light fell in golden shafts through high windows. He thought about L.A. He'd heard that there were places there where you could be biologically altered, deeply altered, no questions asked. No records kept.

Could there possibly be some kind of obscuring marker placed in his blood? Would it take away the music of the sun? What price would he have to pay?

Or . . . could there be another alternative?

He began to get excited. He stopped stock-still between stations. The evening chill was setting in.

What if he died? What if they found the body? That would put an end to their pursuit.

He started moving again. He collected the finished backups. He left one set and a coded message for his dad, one of many they'd devised. This one said, basically: I HAD TO CUT OUT. I'M SAFE FOR NOW. WAIT FOR ME. IF YOU HAVE TO LEAVE, WE'LL MEET AT THE APPOINTED RENDEZVOUS. I'LL BE BACK WHEN I CAN. Uncoded, he wrote: HAD TO HEAD UP TO SALT LAKE CITY FOR SOME SUPPLIES. KEEP THE ORDERS ROLLING. BE BACK SOON. He patted his pocket. As always, he carried an astounding amount of cash. You never knew when this sort of thing might happen. He put the other set of backups in his pocket.

He stuck his head out the back door, saw no one, locked up. No one hassled him as he started his Jeep.

He backed out and continued down the alley, past the back of his factory. He turned onto Main Street. To his left, his homeward side, the Long Arm Saloon threw the only lights in town onto the road. The supermarket closed at dusk.

He reached into the back and rummaged around with one hand, pulled out a jacket and put it on. He looked toward home and sighed. Quit stalling, he told himself.

He pulled the wheel to the right and roared west. Out of town quickly, within a minute. Then out across the desert. Toward L.A.

The stars sang as he drove, a wild, whistling, many-voiced composition he heard whenever he held in the clutch and shifted.

He would never see his father again.

He was not prepared for L.A.

For one thing, it was huge. His head throbbed as he wondered exactly where to begin. He'd popped up his tent just off a logging road about 2 A.M. after he was well into the mountains and slept fitfully. He really should have had something to eat. He promised himself he'd stop at the next place, but he just kept driving. Toward the high towers on the narrow littoral plain at the foot of the mountains. He finally stopped, unlocked his storage bin, and got out his navigation system. It was just maps; the gps was out today. It usually was. So he had to travel in the old-fashioned way, without voice promptings, stealing glances at the map to try and figure out where he was and where to turn.

When he got into the city's edge, he was overwhelmed by the brilliance and constant shifting visage of signage, more aggressive than he'd ever seen. He was in a seedy strip-joint section of town. Near-naked women effervesced, seemingly out of thin air, for a second or two of lewd dance before he moved through the beam's foci. He crossed some border and was in a neighborhood of coffee shops. He parked and retraced his route and walked into the Anatomy Club. He stood in the doorway to let his eyes adjust to the darkness. A few men lounged on stools at the bar. A spotlight shone on a woman sliding up and down a pole, varying her motions by languidly swaying every once in awhile.

Jason sat at the bar. "Whatever you got on draft," he said to the bartender. "And a cheese sandwich."

"Alls we got is egg salad." The bartender jerked a thumb at a clear refrigerator door. Inside huddled a few sorry-looking cellophane-wrapped specimens.

"Fine," said Jason. He slid a rather large bill onto the bar. "Keep it open." He'd spent more than one night in the Long Arm Saloon in the past few months, drinking beer and dodging the occasional knife fight. Alcohol balanced nicely with his mother's hallucinogenic mushroom regime; the peyote made him so damned sick that he'd eased off in the past year or two.

As he sipped his second beer, he asked the bartender, "She real?"

The guy snorted. "You kidding? It was kind of a tossup between fighting the union or buying her. Both were expensive. But she don't whine and she don't ask for raises and we can change her any which way we want. Anatomically correct too—if you know what I mean." He winked at Jason. Jason's stomach turned. He grinned back, hoping it looked authentic. His only girlfriend had been left behind three moves back. Jason thought of her often. He hoped she didn't hate him.

"Where you get her?" She's not real, he told himself. These constructs had no history, no consciousness, no brain. They were grown to resemble humans right down to the last cell, but they never woke up. They were part of a new—and horrible—slave trade, the crux of an ongoing legal battle, and were a completely underground creation.

The man frowned at him. "Why you want to know? You some kind of snitch?"

Jason tried his grin again, hoping it was convincing. "I just—you know." He lowered his voice and beckoned the guy closer. "My brother runs a prostitute ring in San Diego. He sent me up here to try and dodge the heat. You know, they keep a close eye out down there." Jason hoped that years of watching miles of videos was giving him a boost here. He felt wildly improvisational. He hoped he didn't sound that way.

"What's in it for me, I recommend someone?" asked the bartender.

"Two hundred."

The man slapped the bar in disgust. "Excuse me, I got work to do."

"Well, then, you name a price. We're not made of money. You're the first place I've stopped in. I might get a better deal down the strip. Who knows?"

The man shrugged. "Six."

"Four," said Jason, fanning the money out on the bar.

The man shrugged, reached under the bar, flipped a card out, and grabbed the money. "Keep the card," he said.

Jason drove over to the beach. It was sunset, and the sun looked as if it were dissolving into the ocean. He found a spot, parked his car, and walked along the concrete, watching smooth sets of orange-tipped waves roll in. Out in the surf, people in jetsuits frolicked, body-surfing. Jason zipped his jacket. It was early spring; still cool. He missed his parents.

As he strolled north, the streetlights came on and the surf turned to a white surging line defining a dark sea. The jetsurfers became iridescent; they surfed by ear, by sensing the surge, by being familiar with local conditions. It was dangerous. Their cometlike lights, though, were part of the local attraction. People sat on the balconies of the low-rise hotels facing the boardwalk, bundled up, drinking and laughing. Loud music issued from bars and gradually the strip became seedier. Jason started checking street signs. Finally he turned up a side street and from that onto another.

He was on a block of small apartment buildings mixed with motel signs. He found his address and rang the bell. A light came on, blinding him; he threw up his arm. A voice boomed from the intercom: "What you want?"

He reached into his pocket, found the card, and held it up for the camera.

"Ernie sent me."

"Ernie who?"

"Ernie at the Anatomy Club under the five."

A woman's voice came on. "So?"

"So I have some business."

"What else you got?"

"Money."

"Cash?"

Jason nodded.

The door opened.

He stepped into a world at odds with the street. The door swung shut behind him and in the gentle glow of whole-wall aquariums, curving in free-form, two burly men stepped up and frisked him. He had expected this; in fact, he was surprised at being let in so easily.

"You have a sweet face," said the woman, who came around a curve. She was tiny, perhaps five feet tall, and severely thin. She looked like a child. Her long black hair was curly. She wore jeans and a plaid shirt. "Come in," she said. "You want some girls? Going into competition with Ernie?"

Next to him black mollies drifted upward; a small shark glided with a jerk of his tail into a cave; lionfish sported their manes of poison, all amid an undersea jungle of plants and waving fan coral. "This must cost a fortune," he said.

She beckoned. "Come to my conference room."

He followed her through an arch into a small plain room with cushions on the floor. The entire bland room was layered with sound-absorbing foam. Several cameras ostentatiously rotated, making sure he knew he was being watched.

"Sit." She tossed a cushion toward him and sat on the floor. "Now," she said, "tell me. I hope it's interesting. I'm really tired of those girls." The foam swallowed her words instantly, creating an eerie muffling effect. Jason noticed that he couldn't even hear the stars and was disturbed, almost panicked, for an instant. He couldn't remember such silence . . .

He took a deep breath, sat on the cushion, and crossed his legs. His mouth went dry. "I . . . I want me," he said.

"Oho!" The woman chuckled. Her face was pale and freckled. "Yes, certainly, that would come in handy. The mind leaps at the possibilities. I've been waiting for this." She crossed her legs Indian-style, her motions lithe. A curtain of hair fell across one eye and she looped it behind her ear, leaned forward, grinning with almost unholy glee. "Yeah. I love it."

"But it has to be identical to me," he said. "Cellularly identical."

"Ah. I see." She nodded many times, almost as if she were in some sort of hypnotic state.

"Can you do it?" he asked.

Her eyes, blue, fringed heavily with long black eyelashes, opened wide for a moment, as if she'd been awakened from sleep. "Sorry," she said. "Sure. I trained at Trans-Bio Corporation. You know, the

217

beef people. You gotta get the cells just right. For the flavor. It'll cost, though." She smiled. "I'll have to order some new equipment."

"And I watch the whole process," he continued, "and we destroy all the records—templates, samples, everything."

"Hmmm," she said. "Sure. You're the customer. We aim to please."

"And no questions asked."

"Absolutely," she said. He thought he saw a gleam of interest in her eyes.

"What . . . what do those women at Ernie's *think*?" he blurted out. "What do they *feel*?"

"Ah!" Her grin returned. "A man with a conscience!"

"Really," he said.

"Think? Feel? Well . . . what is your name—no, excuse me, what am I to call you?" she asked.

"Jason." It would be easiest.

"Jason, their brains are an amalgam of mammal characteristics. They have a bit of loyalty. They have good motor control, as you may have noticed. They know to eat when hungry; they have, of course, fine brain stem function. Their memories are rudimentary. I provide Ernie with a training template to teach them their moves. That's what he gets to play with. He sits in a VR booth downtown for a few hours and drools over his ladies and what he's going to make them do, perfects their dances. They are highly visual and imitative. When they're new, they go into skinsuits of material that flexes and hardens according to directions from the program. It's cool stuff. The motions organize their brains."

"Don't they ever get smart?" asked Jason.

"Not so far," she said seriously, "but of course they're all pretty young. Their chromosomes are not normal either. Nothing about them is normal, Jason. Every avenue to intelligence has been foiled. They are limited flesh. Very limited. As for emotion—no. They have no fear, no love, no happiness. They have"—she paused, and he hoped he heard bleakness as she finished in a rush—"no *spirit*."

Jason heard the echo of his mother's voice, deeply sad that the beams of their ceiling had never felt spirit. He bumbled to his feet, blinking back tears. "I don't know—" *Someone* will die, he was thinking, and I can't do this after all, not such a bright idea . . .

She grabbed his hand. "Come with me. Let me show you something." After all she had just said, the sheer cynicism of it, Jason was amazed at how young her face looked, like the face of his ten-year-old playmate in some town whose name he couldn't remember. "Here," she said, so gently that the sound of it was almost swallowed by the foam, pulled him upright, and pressed a part of the wall.

A door slid open, revealing a spiral of narrow metal stairs.

He followed her upward three stories, he judged, though the stairs were never interrupted by a landing. The cylinder through which they climbed was also foamed, and their footsteps made no sound.

They emerged into a huge room with a vaulted ceiling. There was clear glass all around. Suddenly his mind filled with sound again, and he felt tremendously comforted.

"Don't worry," she said.

He stared down across two blocks of rooftops to the ocean, where the white path of the moon heaved with the waves. Whirring machinery pulled part of the roof back.

"No one can see in. I don't know why I'm showing you this." She bustled around, clapping on lights. A futon, its covers in disarray, had been pulled onto a balcony. The walls were crammed with books and about five computers—or at least a dozen screens—connected to who knows what, with a welter of wires running between various gobs of intelligent plastic. Oriental rugs lay over tile. Vines and a profusion of orchids hung from the beams; huge cacti grew in pots. He counted five cats, saw another dart across a low cluttered table, and stopped counting.

"Come on, come over here," she said with something like glee in her boylike voice. She unbuttoned her plaid shirt. She wore a neon pink tank top under it, and her shirt billowed out behind her like the cape of some comic book madwoman. Jason, tired and homesick, felt completely disoriented now. He wished he'd eaten. But he followed her over to the darkest corner of the room, and after she clapped a few times, a dome lit.

It was a hemisphere about six feet in diameter. He recognized it at once. It was one of the very latest luminous computers. "Come closer," she whispered. "Wow. You never know." She sat on a low stool, rested her chin in both hands, and stared.

He did too. For lying in golden state was a beautiful perfect woman, her eyelids shut, a pleasant smile on her face. "Is she—" he began, but quicker than he could see, the woman reached out and touched the side of the dome and the body changed to many small bodies, a hundred, five hundred, and then a city began to grow within the dome.

He watched, astonished. "Is it a hologram?"

"Kind of," she said.

It was like looking down from the air at . . . there was the ocean . . . "L.A.?" he asked.

She nodded and tapped on the shell again, evidently in some kind of code, for the woman appeared again.

Jason's heart beat hard as the dome woman opened her eyes and stared straight into his. Her mouth moved. The dome said, "What?"

Then she lazily smiled, closed her eyes again, turned on her side, pillowed her head on her hands, and pulled her legs up. Her breasts receded, her pubic hair disappeared, and then she was clothed in a white nightgown and lay on a maple bed. In a bedroom. Jason saw it from the side, as if a wall was cut away, and the scene became smaller, part of a house, and a woman walked down a hallway and opened the door and peered in and her face was just large enough for Jason to see a smile on it before she was absorbed again into a subdivision and the subdivision into the surrounding countryside on one side, the city on the other, and then with another tap a man walked through pools of light in the evening . . .

"You try it now," said the woman at his side.

"What?"

"Tap, hug . . . it responds to touch."

He flicked it with a finger and a new scene jumped to life. A girl smiled out at him, straight into his eyes. She twirled, her dress standing out, and laughed, and a boy walked into the room and they picked up some crayons and started drawing on the walls, laughing. They were writing some kind of complex mathematical formula, but he had no idea whether it made any sense. Like cartoon word balloons, the numbers sprouted blank white spaces and then in each space something appeared . . . a blender, a journey fast through a green yew-smothered lane, an Arab marketplace . . .

She whispered in his ear.

He was startled; he'd forgotten all about her. He nodded and they watched for hours. At least it seemed like hours. Finally she touched his face. "I'm tired. Want to go to sleep?" She walked out to the futon, pulling off her jeans, her underwear. She was so tiny. Her black hair covered her entire back. He followed her as if sleepwalking and lay down next to her on the futon fully dressed, closed his eyes, and fell into wild, restless visions, half-nightmare, half-dream.

He woke to her face next to his at dawn. She was staring right into his eyes. He saw a tiny black spot in one blue iris.

"Who are you?" she asked.

"I—" he said, trying to get his bearings, "I—no questions—"

"I have a million," she said, reaching down to unbuckle his belt. "And you're damned well going to answer every one."

Abbie opened her mail over coffee at a low wooden table at which she sat on the floor. "There's hourly mail delivery service in L.A.," she told Jason as she slit open the first envelope. "You and I will take care of our business after I see if there are any priority items here." She grinned slightly and pushed an intercom button. "Do we have a James Dean on file?"

"I think so" came the answer.

"When you find it, Ace needs one." She went through the rest of her mail quickly and stacked it neatly in a box marked PENDING and weighted it with one of the many rocks sitting on the table. This was a smooth river rock, gray strata revealed edge-on in striated swirls.

"There," she said. "Nothing else that can't wait." She closed her eyes for several seconds; Jason noticed that her eyelashes were long and that her skin was smooth and pale beneath the freckles, with faint pink coloring over her cheeks. He had not seen her breasts, only felt them this morning as she pressed against him urgently; he remembered her body in a flash: well muscled and lithe, her mouth warm and open against his.

She opened her eyes. She looked at him with no expression for a moment.

"Now," she said. "You." She reached across a table and pulled a small erg toward her. The screen lit when she touched it. "Let me show you something," she said. "This is you."

Screens of data appeared on the screen in bewildering succession. After the fifth or sixth, Jason said, his voice shaking, "How did you get all this?"

"From you."

"How—"

"A mosquito?" she said. "A few skin cells? Semen? It doesn't matter." She looped her hair behind her ears with an impatience he was beginning to recognize was habitual. "Stop running your paranoid programs. I'm not after you, kid. This is strictly my information. If we were going to do business, I wanted to get started. I have a lot cooking and not all that many burners. Although you never did mention how you were going to pay me."

"I—" Jason's hand went to his pants pocket.

"No, stop," she said with a wave of her hand. Her fingers, he noticed, were beautifully long and graceful as they moved on her small keyboard. She brought up a DNA helix. "There's something very unusual here," she said.

Jason's heart thudded in his chest. He wanted to get up and run out the door, up the beach, jump into his Jeep, and drive it into the ground to get back to his parents. Back to their safe haven in the mountains. He hadn't counted on this kind of intense analysis, though he wasn't sure why. He thought he could just go, order up this . . . this Frankensteinian *thing*, and be done with it. It would never know anything. It would only be meat, shaped like him down to the final iota. But . . . she knew. The whole world knew he was a freak. He could never escape. He could only submit, turn himself in . . .

"Calm *down*!" she ordered, her reedy voice irritated. "Let's cut to the chase here. I know exactly who and what you are. And I know this because *I'm the same*!"

Her last three words stunned Jason. "What do you mean?"

"Are you an idiot? I mean that my DNA has this same anomaly. The same one yours shows. The one that makes the men in black track you. I don't know how I can be any damned clearer." She glared at him and tears stood in her eyes.

The sky was intensely blue, Jason noticed, in a dizzy, distant way. There was not a cloud in it. The sea was kind of a navy blue, a dark blue. He'd been up and down the coast before; his nomadic life had ensured a lot of traveling. But he'd never seen the crystal clarity of a sky, a sea, like this. Gulls' raucous laughs mixed with the roar of surf, the shrieks of children, the bass beat of music playing somewhere. The salt air filled his nose and bathed his brain with something so deep he'd always reckoned it ancestral memory.

"So," he finally managed, his voice husky, "how can you stay here? Don't they want to take you—" Despite himself, his mind was flooded with the ideas she'd practically commanded him to forsake. Instead— *Trust me*. Such an idea was alien to his very core. Somehow he'd ended up in the very place he'd been trying to avoid—

"JASON!" She was standing, shouting at him. "Stop it! You're safe here. No one can find you. No one can find me."

"Why not? What's your secret?" He was standing too and shouting. "I'm so sick and tired of it!"

Then she was holding him and he was shaking, horribly embarrassed but unable to stop, and her arms were tight around him. So tight. "Relax," she said. "Just relax." She walked him back to her futon and drew a curtain around it and, incredibly, in a moment he was making love again for the second time that morning, lost in a barrage of sensations that merged into an overwhelming emotion of feeling at home. Feeling at home. He'd never felt this way, he realized. She would protect him. It sounded ridiculous that a skinny young woman could protect him, but he felt that it was true. She knew him. She really knew him.

He was alone no more. He could stop running.

So why didn't he believe it?

Jason discovered immediately that one of Abbie's affectations was tableware. She had a small portable manufacturer dedicated to dishes.

Naked, she crouched at a screen she kept on the floor for no reason he could discern other than sheer lack of organization and sketched a teapot and small round teacups, which took about fifteen minutes to assemble. Light fell softly through skylights, making her pale skin luminescent. Water was boiling on a gas burner installed in a long low marble countertop when she took her creations from the assembler, holding them in a towel as they were hot. She looked at the pot critically. "I don't think I'll save this one. The spout's too long."

"I like the color," he felt obliged to add, feeling awkward. He had pulled on his shorts.

"No need to be polite," she said. She whisked in powdered green tea. "Um, sorry. I'm sure you're hungry. I am. I have some . . ." She opened a small gas refrigerator and frowned. "Well, I have some cold rice cakes. And some miso dipping sauce. Not too old. I mean, I could heat them up if you wanted—"

"No, that's fine," he said, clumsily opening cupboards until he found some plates, and pulled four chopsticks from a vase on the counter.

She brought along the sauce; tired slices of ginger and garlic floated in a cold broth of soy sauce, vinegar, and sugar.

"Do you feel settled down now?" she asked, smiling into his eyes. Hers held a hint of irony.

"Oh. Yes," he said, still flustered. His sexual experience was rather limited. Hers, apparently, was not.

"Then," she said, dipping a chunk of rice cake into the sauce and chewing it, "I'll get started here. I'm sorry I startled you so badly. I was just very excited. This has never, ever happened before."

"What?" The wonder in her eyes warmed him. He realized that he wanted to hear that she had never felt so terrific about a man, that she was falling in love for the first time.

But no.

"I've never met anyone like myself before. I knew there were more. But without this kind of corroboration it begins to seem like a fairy tale after a while."

It took a moment to sink in. Jason had imagined that he was quite unique, even though one of his mother's friends had inflamed them with talk of a virus from space and altered DNA, things that seemed as far removed from reality as talk of vortexes and psychic powers. He felt a pang of disappointment. He dreaded what she might say.

But he had to ask.

"How are we different?"

"You don't know."

"I really have no idea."

She looked surprised. "Well, for starters, we have a very high concentration of biogenic magnetite in all of our cells and especially in our brain and in our magnetoreceptors." She touched her nose. "Here."

"What makes you think we have magnetoreceptors at all?"

"Oh, come on. That was proven years ago. All vertebrates have them. Even a lot of bacteria orient to magnetic information. Anyway, the nerve that takes the information back to the brain is very, very thick. At least fifty times the normal size as most humans. The resulting sensitivity to magnetic stimuli is what causes the frequent nausea, but as we have grown, we have adapted. Some people theorize that this has some relationship to the process that triggers seizures in epileptics. You've read about Dostoevski, for example, right? How he experienced moments of powerful clarity just before a seizure? Well, I think that this is what happens to us and it has to do with electromagnetism. But it's more controlled. More manipulated."

"How do you know all this?"

"Well, I've heard—"

"No," Jason said. "I mean evidence. Someone like you wouldn't believe this stuff unless there was evidence."

She looked pensive. "It's only fourth-hand. Fifth-hand. Stories that people smuggled out of the facilities—about the research—"

"Gossip. It doesn't matter to me anyway. I don't want to be part of some group. I'm just myself. I want to be normal. I want to be useful. I want to be accepted by society, not hunted by society." It sounded childish as it came out, but he realized that it was how he had felt for years and that he wanted quite badly to stop his ears against anything Abbie might say.

She seemed amused by his outburst. "It isn't society that's hunting us, Jason. It's what they used to call a black op in the government. I believe that they split off from any semblance of sanctioned operation years ago—but that might not be entirely true. Someone is paying their salary. They're fanatics. Twisted. And powerful. Power feeds on itself. They have places around the world where they stick probes in the brains of people like us. Section our brains, even."

"So how are you safe?"

"I have the dope on them. I threatened to make it public. I told them—one of their operants—that if I die or if anything happens to me, others have this information and they will make it public. Simple blackmail." Her eyes were disingenuous; her grin contrastingly wicked.

He learned that Abbie had grown up a pampered only child—much like himself, except that her parents were quite wealthy and had access to more information because of government ties. Abbie thought that the car crash they died in when she was sixteen was no accident, and she had found all the information they had gathered—the type of hearsay evidence that Abbie was handing him—in their safety deposit box after they died. Jason gathered that Abbie was a lot more savvy than he had been at that age, and with the help of a trusted uncle, she had continued her parents' plan, the plan that had protected her all these years.

But when he proposed that he use the same umbrella, she demurred, saying that it would put her in danger anew.

Only much later did he realize that simple hubris had been her reason.

He was running along a beach, heart pounding. His feet slipped in the soft sand. They were after him. It was dark. There was a bonfire ahead. It was very far away. A small flicker of light. His only goal. There was no moon. He was so alone.

The man who looked like him was after him. And the woman. They were shouting. They thought he was stupid. Maybe he was. But he knew certain things.

His foot struck a sharp stick and he stumbled for a moment. He wanted to stop crying, but he couldn't. They wanted to kill him. He knew that. He wasn't very old. He knew that. And now he was supposed to die. He had never done anything wrong. He had only wandered out the door one day and stumbled down the street and onto the beach. He wandered through the mobs of people there, amazed. He sat next to families and learned to talk. He repeated everything he heard. He ate garbage. He was very happy. The world was very big. He swam in the ocean. He loved the taste of the salt water. He loved the smell of the salt air. He played with children. He tried to find children, small children, who would talk to him. They helped him and corrected him and never treated him as if he was stupid. He liked playing with them a lot. Sometimes parents shouted at him and took their children away. But he didn't mind being alone.

And then they found him. The man who looked like him and the woman. They pretended they liked him and took him home and fed him and gave him a bed, even though he said he liked sleeping on the beach better. They had looked surprised when he said that. They looked surprised every time he said or did anything. Then he heard them arguing about him. They were easy to hear because they shouted. They thought he didn't understand. Or maybe they didn't care. The woman said they had to kill him. The man said no.

That was when he had run down those winding stairs, pounded on the locked door, then picked up a metal chair and smashed out

a window. He'd run down to the beach. He hoped to find a police-
man. One little girl had told him that if he was ever in trouble he
should tell a policeman. But he saw none. It was getting dark and
the beach was empty. He looked behind him and there they were on
the boardwalk, and then they were running down the stairs, and so
he started running too and he had not thought too much about which
way to run and now there was nothing but ocean and sand and
no people.

His breath was ragged and short. He didn't think the man could
catch him because they both ran just as fast as each other. He
thought the woman couldn't catch him but maybe she was faster.
He didn't know.

He did not want to die. He had to run—faster, faster. He heard
a pop behind him. That was the gun. He heard another. The woman,
the man, shouting. He had to get to the light. The people there would
save him.

There were more pops behind him and more shouting, but it
sounded farther away than before.

He ran on into the night. Maybe that wasn't a fire up ahead. But
it was something.

Jason's legs were on automatic, pushing into the soft sand, and
the air he gulped seemed as hot as fire. He was almost there. He
pushed harder, and leaped, praying he wouldn't miss.

He caught the running figure ahead of him around the waist. They
both went down with a hard thump. She rolled to one side and hit
him on his temple with the gun. The blow stunned and angered him
and he managed to wrench the gun from her hand and toss it away
into the darkness.

"It's not too late," she gasped. "It's not too late, Jason. He's up
ahead there. If you won't do it, I will." She wiggled out from under
him and started running around, patting the sand for the gun. "Damn,
it's dark."

Jason rolled onto his back and lay spread-eagle on the cold sand.
He let the roar of the surf drown her curses. He had found that it
blessedly drowned all other sounds too. A fog had rolled in and all
seemed muffled. The light that, presumably, his double had been running to had vanished.

Abbie returned after some minutes and squatted next to him. "I
hope you're happy," she said.

"He's not me," said Jason. "He's a person. He's a baby."

"He's going to go to a clinic at some point or the police will pick him up and then they'll come and get him and know that he's not you. Furthermore, it's possible that he may have an awful life."

"Maybe," said Jason. "I don't care. I don't want to kill someone else to protect myself. It's that simple."

"You knew what you were doing," said Abbie.

"Wrong," said Jason, sitting up and hugging himself. It got cold fast on the beach after the sun went down. "By the time you explained to me what these people—"

"They're not people," said Abbie.

"What these creations of yours really *are*—which is *people,* Abbie, you've got to face it—he was already started."

"He could have been aborted. I told you. I do it all the time. Somebody cancels an order, I keep their deposit, but do you think I want to create another mouth to feed?"

"I suppose," said Jason. "You're right. It's my fault. Maybe I was curious. I thought you said that these people were unable to learn. He seemed to be learning pretty fast."

"For one thing," said Abbie, "he's you. And for another thing, when I create, say, a stripper or an ex-President who's going to be somebody's house servant, I only create the exterior. They're all the same inside."

"How?" asked Jason. "How do you know they're all the same inside?"

She didn't answer.

"How do you know, Abbie?" asked Jason, starting to get angry. It was curious, this anger stuff. He'd seen his parents disagree, even argue, but he seemed to have been utterly protected from the emotion up to now. But with Abbie he felt powerless. She did what she did, she thought what she thought, and he seemed to have no effect on her at all.

"Abbie!" he shouted, leaning toward her as she sat crosslegged on the sand, taking her shoulders tightly in his hands. For a few seconds, she seemed curiously limp. Then she shook free, jumped to her feet, and stood over him.

"Because I make sure that their brains don't have the biochemistry for learning, idiot!" she yelled at him. Then to his amazement, she started screaming into the night, flapping her arms. "This is the first time I've made an exact copy. It was stupid of me. But it was what you wanted. They're not clones. They're *creations.* Like mice! Like squirrels! Like dogs, maybe. But *not like people!* Do you understand now? My clients don't want to raise children. My clients want slaves. That's what I give them. Like draft horses. Like sled dogs. Except with hands, a Michaelangelo ass, a famous face. That last is where the real art comes in. And they have to be preassembly; everybody now has his or her face copyrighted or trademarked. But you know what? I never get an order to replicate a lost loved one. Never. Except once, and I talked her out of it. It wouldn't work. I just make replicants. Shells. They're assembled quickly. That's not how real growth occurs." She had gradually calmed. Her voice was low and hoarse. "You act as though I have no conscience. It's not true."

"But they feel, Abbie," said Jason, close to tears. "They feel. Dogs feel. These people do too. It's the first thing humans do."

"Not these creatures," she said. "They're dull as posts."

"Oh, Abbie," said Jason finally. "I'm so sorry."

They were both silent. He stood and dusted off his jeans. He walked back the way they had come—slowly.

He didn't ask Abbie to come. She didn't follow.

Two Intervals of Overwhelming Distance

Zeb | Bridge of Lions, Washington, D.C. | 2034

There had been so many days, Zeb thought, during his anguished meander away from S Street—*anywhere* away from S Street. He did not know or care where he walked. Because he had spent so many pleasant mornings in Ellie Pio's small venerable apartment on S Street, hashing over his ideas, giving her his notebooks for safekeeping. Though it was nestled among embassies, Ellie did not seem to notice that her place was slightly shabby compared with the façades of her neighbors. And she was too busy to care about housekeeping details. The small red and white can of McCormicks cinnamon was usually sticky when Zeb picked it up from the white-painted kitchen table to sprinkle cinnamon on the instant oatmeal she always forced on him, as if it were some kind of tonic. Inside the kitchen cabinets was an unorganized maze of crockery, much of it cracked and dating back to Ellie's grandmother, the original owner of the apartment, and Ellie herself was sixty. But she always had fresh flowers in the kitchen window; they gave forth light on even the dimmest of Washington winter mornings.

Compared to the kitchen, her front room was startlingly stately, rich with mahogany antiques and a grand piano, papered with art deco wallpaper up to the foot-wide cornices. Ellie inhabited that room with easy grace and kept it beautifully in memory of her partner, a literature professor at Catholic University who had died fifteen years earlier, a woman whose vast library still occupied one room.

This morning he had gone to her apartment to find it locked. He

229

went next door to ask what day it was, fearing he must have forgotten. "Ellie asked me for coffee—"

The neighbor, a heavy sallow man who talked to Zeb through the crack in his chained door, blinked. "I'm sorry to have to tell you this, but she died last week." He explained that the police had come—and some other people too—asking him questions. He hadn't liked this much. "My parents came here from the Soviet Union in the 1970s. It seemed a lot like what they had to put up with. That's why I'm telling you—they were asking about someone that seems a lot like you. And also about that other man who used to come see her all the time."

"What man?"

"How should I know? Not special-looking. If I were you, I'd get out of town."

"How did she die?"

The man shrugged. "They didn't say. Heart attack, they implied. With people like that, who knows? Now go before somebody else who likes the police more than I do sees you." He shut the door. Zeb heard the lock turn.

Zeb didn't believe him. He didn't believe that anyone killed Ellie. That was ridiculous.

But she was still dead. He stumbled down the stairs and turned right.

It was drizzling. Zeb trudged along, his head gradually collecting moisture until it ran in rivulets down his neck. He was heading toward Georgetown in general. Town houses gave way to a block of tony shops and restaurants, then a short greensward curving around toward an impressive bridge, flanked by stone lions.

Zeb stopped and stared up at the lions. What public sensibility had produced them? They were magnificent, a statement of power and pride. He supposed that lions were extinct now. But maybe not. He'd also heard, dimly and distantly, that vast changes were taking place in the world because of the work of the Gaians, an underground terrorist movement that used nanotech in many illegal ways to restore wilderness. They could dissolve the infrastructure with metal-corroding nanotech. Cut down on the human population by putting sterility drugs in the water. So that the Earth could breathe again.

Yes, the Earth. Possibly a part of an interstellar community only now evolved enough to forge links. Except that there were some people here—powerful people, apparently—who wanted no part of it. Zeb's grief over Ellie was joined by frustration. He might as well be trying to teach evolution in Tennessee in the 1920s, or in Mississippi in the 1980s. Information was being held in thrall—but by whom? Perhaps it would have been best to join Craig's shadowy group on that winter's day so long ago. Maybe everything would have gone differently. Some days were clear for him. He could see across the demented valleys he had mistaken for illumination. Perhaps there never had been a right path, a right decision, for him. He had thought this way would prove more honest, more useful. Instead, it had only caused heartache. His work was vast but unfinished—and impossible to keep in his head all at once. He had left many notebooks at Ellie's, he remembered suddenly, and his printouts. He wondered if someone had them now. It was not entirely lost; he had condensed many of his speculations after arriving at them and transferred them to new notebooks and he had one thick bound book, blank, into which he transcribed what he felt was the beginnings of a new school of intergalactic physics and the possible basis for a form of alien intelligence.

He had that, but he might as well be a radio signal flashing through space—abstract and utterly alone.

He walked onto the bridge and looked down into the river as an astounding variety of vehicles steamed, cranked, combusted, and cycled behind him.

He was quickly mesmerized by the flow and swirl of Rock Creek about thirty feet below. At how the water followed inevitable paths which, at its present speed, it had no power to change. A stick rushed downriver, kayaking over slick rocks, and was caught in an eddy just below him. It slowly gyrated and each time almost escaped into the stream again, but at the apex of each swirl, it was drawn back into the slow pointless circle.

He watched the stick, his anxiety growing. The stick was like humanity, crippled by politics, by governments. It was time for all of them to join the current. To venture out. To see what was really there. Again he thought of the technological power of the visitors. How much they must know! How much they could share! So far they had not blasted the world to cinders nor filled it with aliens, at least not visibly.

Zeb trudged back to the greensward and found three rocks about the size of bread loaves, all he could carry in one trip. He made a few such trips and created a small cairn of rocks on the sidewalk next to the concrete wall of the bridge.

He lifted one over his head and heaved it over the wall. A sizable splash arose, so distant that he could not hear it. But he missed. The stick still eddied, stuck in its cycle. He tried again, working up a good sweat.

He had worked his way down to the last few rocks when he felt a tap on his shoulder. Without lowering the rock, he turned his head and saw a park policeman.

"What do you think you're doing?"

"That stick. See that stick down there? It's stuck." Zeb threw the rock he was holding down into the creek. It smashed off some other rocks and sank into the main current. He bent to pick up one of the last rocks. "I have to get it free. It has to be able to go down the river."

"I can't let you do that," said the officer.

"I have to," panted Zeb and let fly his next to last rock. Missed again. He bent to pick up another one.

"Then I'm going to have to give you a ticket," said the officer. Zeb didn't reply. The officer grabbed at his arm and Zeb shrugged him off, lifted the final rock to his shoulder.

"Didn't you hear me? I'm going to arrest you if you don't stop."

They engaged in a scuffle, the officer grunting, Zeb fiercely holding on to his rock. He managed to give it an unaimed heave.

Zeb's stone hit a large flat rock, skidded across it, and splashed into the eddy where the stick was trapped. A wave washed the stick from the eddy. It was free.

Zeb leaned over the bridge, watching his stick slip and swirl over rocks. Without heeding traffic, he shook loose from the officer's grip and crossed four lanes, barely hearing the screech of brakes. "Look!" he yelled. "Look! I did it!" He watched till it was out of sight, rounding a bend beneath a canopy of bare trees.

He was poised to run when he saw a woman walking toward him with two collies on leashes. One was a tricolor, black gold and white, like Zephyr. Another was a merle, silvery blue, like Pleiades.

As they approached, he was washed by memories. Sally. His old life, so distant, so lost, so settled. Why had he given it up? And Annie. Yes, Annie. He hadn't dared risk seeing her again. Ruin her life like he'd ruined Sally's.

He leaned against the pedestal of one of the lions, overcome, as the dogs approached. He knelt and pulled their heads toward him, and they happily accepted his embrace, nudging forward even as their owner tried to pull them away. "Hey, you scumbag! Leave my dogs alone!"

The officer pounded up behind Zeb. "Come on, fella. You need help."

Zeb disagreed violently.

All the way to the hospital, in the cold steel of handcuffs, he exulted. I will vindicate you, Ellie. I will.

He emerged from the hospital the next morning unsullied by their drugs. As always, he'd managed to convince them he was rational and sane and cited his constitutional rights. They'd had no choice but to release him.

As he stepped out into the street, the rush of pale gray sky and traffic confused him. Loud people passed him on the sidewalk, talking to one another, laughing, and an ambulance pulled away from the hospital entrance. For an instant, he wondered why he had been taken to the hospital this time.

Then he remembered Ellie.

And then he remembered his work.

It was all he had.

Kyoto Sandman

Kita | Japan | 2037

Kita splashed through slush on Tokyo's streets at dawn. The sky was like fine old pewter, heavy, with a slight sheen, infusing the air with the hollow hush of snow poised for the imperceptible shift of release. Her heels were not made for messy weather, but she'd felt she'd had to wear them. And the long train ride from Kyoto! Why so necessary? Why not meet Hugo there? But she did appreciate the danger. And the difference. Kyoto was the opposite of brash new Tokyo in spirit as well as kanji order. Tokyo/Kyoto; braced against each other, material vs. spiritual.

This was reflected by the fact that the BioCity conversion of Tokyo was progressing in cautious stages, while the same conversion was outlawed in Kyoto, city of ancient temples. Much of Tokyo had been infiltrated by a vast information web with extensive hypertext capabilities, analogous to that of the now-dysfunctional World Wide Web, except that it was local. Kita admired the glow of the soft permeable surface of a sign she passed, accomplished by the use of genetically engineered bacteria. The sign gave the reader the location of several nearby receptor booths wherein they could gain the biological sense necessary to access the deep information banks Tokyo was even now compiling. The charge cited on-screen, more than a year's salary for her, helped pay her salary. Dento, Inc., in conjunction with the Japanese government and their various nanotechnology research foundations, had helped develop the setup. When she had returned to Japan to work for Dento, she hadn't had an inkling of where her work might lead. This accomplishment—the design of a wholly new communication system in a very short time—demonstrated how much people could accomplish when information was shared. It also showed how much such endeavors had been damaged by the interruption of broadcasting. Without a dependable Internet, telephone system, transportation, and broadcasting, all available when the disparate elements of this project had been researched and developed, it was doubtful if such a feat could be re-created. Which had been the point—get it done before complete darkness falls. Assemble it. Make it work. Fill in the blanks. They had all been living under great stress; Kita had taken no holidays in several years.

Not that this promised to be one. Her jitters increased with each step. Why was she doing this?

As a favor to an old school friend—a favor spiked with curiosity as to why she had been remembered. And irritation too, because of the sense of secrecy pervading the atmosphere at Dento. She felt that her contribution to the project entitled her to a wider range of information concerning its broad applications.

Fat snowflakes drifted downward. Across the street were windows full of plastic examples of what the nanotech programs they sold inside could build. Retro neon flickered in an approximation of a molecular robot arm enlarged a million times. She jammed her hands deeper into her pockets; wished she'd worn thick tights instead of sheer panty hose. A few salarygirls on bikes whizzed past as a signal changed, wearing zipsuits over their office clothes.

What did she remember about Marie? A slight residue of admiration was the extent of it. They had shared several virtual classes, although they hadn't known it until they were brought together for a seminar, along with other university students actually living in Chicago.

The wind gusted and wet snow stung her face. Kita spotted her destination, a twenty-four-hour okinomiyake grill. Plastic piles of noodles topped with various fish, meats, or vegetables were displayed in the window. No neon, no holograms. This must be a district that lost power during the shutdowns that often took place during a Pulse. Tokyo, like most cities now, depended on solar photoelectric alternatives that didn't draw juice from far-off turbines that might be destroyed during a Pulse; networked systems in which each node functioned independently, yet could loan power to another node if necessary.

But it would only be a few more months until Tokyo converted completely to a BioCity system. The last stages would happen within hours. It just took time to set things up. And there were possible avenues of nanotech application that could change matter in a frighteningly swift manner; these were being explored, Kita vaguely knew, in venues designed to convert entire cities in a matter of days. The key would be a protein-folding breakthrough, coupled with enzyme advances that would allow DNA inserted within emptied *E. coli* cells to rapidly transform anything they came in contact with. The problem was to control these transformations very finely.

For all she knew, such systems were all ready to go. That was part of what irritated her about Dento. It seemed that everything was being decided by a smaller and smaller cadre of people, often political appointees who knew nothing about possible ramifications, who only cared about seeming to be in control of that which might prove to be as uncontrollable as an earthquake or the effects of a nuclear meltdown.

She opened the door to the café. Each booth held a low table with a griddle, and gas-flame sconces lined the walls. A young woman gestured toward the tables, all empty. Kita checked her watch. She was ten minutes late, and he was later. She didn't like this.

She'd read somewhere a long time ago that you had to have a screw loose to be a spy. She had thought that she might, but maybe she didn't. Maybe she would leave. Soon she could be back in Kyoto. Or maybe she could spend the day at the Ueno while her mental and physical borders sublimed into the slow mists and mountains of past centuries . . .

"Ms. Narasake?"

She turned and looked down at a man with a large head and brown skin.

He was impeccably dressed. A wonderful homburg perched on his head, and he removed it with a flourish and bowed. "Sorry I'm late." His green eyes were sincere and worried. "I had to ask directions and the man smiled and pointed the wrong way."

Kita smiled. "You are—"

"Hugo," he said. "Sorry." And he did have an odd accent, though it didn't seem exactly French. As she followed him to a table, she warned herself not to let down her guard. Any friend of Marie's had to be pretty damned sharp. Now she remembered seeing him in Chicago, tagging along.

The middle of the table was a gas griddle. "So what is this stuff?" Hugo held his hands over the griddle to warm them.

"Okinomiyake. Noodles and cabbage cooked on the grill with eggs broken over them. You add whatever you want and put sauce on the top." She was actually surprised by how handsome he was. His head was too large for his body, certainly, but within itself it had a sort of harmony and integrity. She liked and trusted him and thought herself stupid.

He slipped off his overcoat and let it lie behind him on the cushion. He wore a dark suit and a tie with a string of subtle jeweled threads woven into the silk. There were diamonds—a large diamond ring on one hand and a diamond stickpin in his tie, both in ornate gold settings. Kita was sure they were old, not the cheap new diamonds available everywhere now. She was glad she'd worn her heels. He unbuttoned his jacket and was wearing a vest beneath it. He seemed utterly relaxed.

The waitress turned some music on, ancient American rock 'n' roll. A young man came in and brushed snow off his hair, took off a black leather jacket. His T-shirt read ELEPHANT COKE WANDERS. He slid into a booth, signaled for tea, and lit a cigarette. Just the type of kid she'd have fallen for when she was a teenager. She frowned. Why was she thinking this way?

In five minutes, she had hot, strong coffee, and the waitress had brought bowls of eggs, vegetables, and black cod for them to grill with the cabbage and noodles sizzling in a big pile between them. Using her chopsticks, Kita deftly pushed the foods around for the minute or so it took them to cook, then divided the hot food into two portions. "You eat it off the griddle," she said and saw that he handled chopsticks as if born to them.

It was snowing in earnest now. More people had come in. The music and conversation around them were sufficient mask for what they said—if anyone understood spoken English.

Hugo laid out Marie's thoughts in a low precise voice and with each sip of coffee, Kita had the increasing sense that she was speeding away from the past, toward a crevasse that would break cleanly and finally into a future strikingly different from all that had come before.

"We believe that the company you work for has developed something that is unique and somewhat dangerous. And that you understand some of its key points and have access to the rest."

Kita was disconcerted. "How in the world would Marie know what Dento has developed?"

"You don't trust me."

"I don't even know what you want."

He leaned back, rearranging his legs beneath the table. His lopsided grin was that of a small boy. "Many years ago, Marie developed various data-viewing programs. They organized information. They framed it; they interpreted data the way our brains interpret the raw information of the cosmos. Even with the Silence, she has ways of collecting such information. But the velocity of collection has slowed down in the past few years. Anyway, she followed your progress closely for quite a few years."

The raw information of the cosmos? It sounded like bad poetry, yet when he said it, Marie became aware of the materials in which she was clothed, the way her skin interpreted them, furnished words like "rough," "silky," "tight"—and with that wanted to loosen her belt. She was here, somewhere in space. Surrounded by matter, made of matter, yet able to think about things distant, abstract, in another time, or even impossible. That was all, really. It was all a matter of organization and of first having a nexus, a point of view, a lens.

"So Marie discovered something about my company that I don't know?"

"If that's how you want to put it, yes."

She cleared her throat. "Does she know what's happening to broadcasting?"

Hugo looked at her in the same direct, unemotional manner. "Possibly."

She blinked. "That's preposterous,"

"Do you always believe what you're told?" Hugo's smile was mocking.

"Hardly ever."

"Yet you believe that the broadcasting problem—the Silence, everything—is all a great mystery to everyone, including governments, right?"

"Well . . ."

"We're digressing, though. I really can't tell you any more at this point. But I haven't told you enough to convince you to trust us." He regarded her thoughtfully. "Maybe we shouldn't get you involved. Maybe there's another way."

"Another way to do what?" Kita heard her own voice—sharp, quick, just like her mother's—and wished she wasn't so jittery, so quick to go into nervous overdrive. "You are going to have to make yourself more clear. What are these tremendous plans? I took a day off work, came all the way here from Kyoto—"

"I'm sorry. I don't want to alienate you. Maybe I'm not the best person to do this. I'm—" He gestured at himself.

"What does that matter? I mean—" She took in his physical details more carefully. His hands were small and twisted. His thumbs jutted out at an unusual angle. His head seemed ponderous; oddly large. "It's true that you're different. But it's something you could change if you wanted to. Surely you could afford it."

"Maybe I chose this." He smiled. "Maybe I used to be tall and thin. I have this theory. I think that one's consciousness, one's being, is intimately connected with one's physical body. And I'm used to my own way of feeling like myself."

An introspective man. "How did you meet Marie?" Let him talk. It would diffuse her nervousness and allow her to think more clearly.

"At school. One day a couple of the older boys took me out back and were letting me know how they felt about little people in a rather physical way. Marie came around the corner and they said something like 'Go away, little girl,' only not as politely. Instead, she joined in. Started kicking their butts. I guess it surprised them as much as anything; she was only ten, but of course she'd had a lot of martial arts training by then. Her grandmère was a tough old bird. She wanted Marie to be ready for anything. We both had black eyes the next day. From then on, we were buddies. Her grandmère took her out of that school and Marie insisted that I come with her. Nobody objected. I'd lived in foster homes all my life."

"She bought you," said Kita.

"She loved me. Instantly. She's like that. Everything sudden. Intense. Now she plans to save the world."

"From what?" asked Kita.

"From itself." He stood, clapped on his hat, and pulled on his overcoat. "Want to help?"

Kita looked around at the café. Just an ordinary day. She wondered how many customers were quite as aware of the fragility of their world as she was. Most people seemed content to let those "in charge" take up the slack—ration the electricity, think about what to do. Maybe there was a deep frozen fear at the core of everyone, a controlled hysteria.

And Hugo frightened her in the way the pheromone bar had a few years back. A way that made it seem necessary to pay close attention.

Maybe it took a shock or a new conjunction of events to realize that one ought to be frightened.

Maybe she couldn't afford to hide in her lab any longer.

"Would you like to see more of Tokyo?" she asked.

Hugo looked down at her heels. "In those shoes?"

She ordered some warm boots at a stall set up beneath the massive legs of an earthquake-proof high-rise. Snow swirled in wind-driven forays beneath the thirty-foot-high platform. The stalls huddled in the middle behind a shared barrier of wind-bowed plastic did a brisk business in hot drinks, and as usual there were several nan carts, all plugged into the same loose junction box. Stealing electricity, no doubt. The vendors had loaded programs for scarves, hats, boots, and the like; on a rainy day, they'd be churning out umbrellas. The sign on one stall said SWIFT AND PRECISE MANUFACTURE OF ARTIFICIAL THINGS in English.

Kita agreed to sacrifice her shoes in exchange, since she didn't want to carry them. The vendor quickly weighed them and handed them back for her to wear until the boots were ready. She had to pay a hefty fee for the convenience, and if there had been a shoe store somewhere in the next few blocks, she would have gone there instead. These product franchises were extremely expensive. The much-vaunted nanotech promise of "Free goods for everyone" had so far not materialized. Those who developed such programs owned them, had put a lot of money into research and development, and were not about to give them away for free. But once the city converted, these vendors would be competing with booths contained in the very architecture of the city and owned by the owners of the buildings. Each city had to work out its own business arrangements. Some leaned toward capitalism, some toward socialism. Unfortunately, despotism was a pretty clear option too.

Hugo hunched on a concrete bench next to Kita as they waited for her boots to grow. "Damned cold," he growled.

Kita shrugged. "No worse than Chicago."

"Chicago was no picnic either."

"Is this a good time to tell me what Marie wants?"

Hugo's voice was close to her ear, low and a bit rough. Flakes melted onto his shoulders, releasing a woolly scent that mingled with his own rather interesting smell. She did not realize that what he was going to say would change her world in the time it took for him to say a few stunning words: "Marie believes that the company you work for has developed a Universal Assembler."

Beyond Hugo's face, so close to hers that she saw the deeply etched lines that surrounded his mouth; saw that his eyelids tended to fall at half-mast; saw his breath puff in steaming coils—beyond all that were stubby concrete towers that receded into shadow, poised on the verge of change, veiled by sifting snow that seemed to glow with a radiance suggesting a light source other than the sun; bright, but cold.

"No." She looked away from him.

"I'm afraid so."

She had only heard rumors about the development of the Universal Assembler. Theoretically, it was a tiny lab, easily contained in a space taken up by an old-fashioned computer diskette. Within this lab were directions for assembling any form of matter via the interface of a computer.

Or, by the same token, using the same information, disassembling anything.

Earliest speculation about the creation of such a device generally included powerful self-destructing mechanisms should anyone attempt to open it and thus liberate the destructive protein processes contained therein. For with such a device, one could quickly unmake a square block, a city.

Or the world. Stuff—and more than stuff—might wash through the world unstoppable, a wild growth would probably evolve in completely unexpected and possibly dangerous ways, unlimited even by human imagination. There would be strange weapons, mind plagues, bizarrely transformed humans, and perhaps even the terminal gray goo Drexler had warned about decades ago, wherein the world would be turned to one undifferentiated soup of matter in short order.

After a minute, she spoke. "This is what you want me to get? I don't think it's possible."

Hugo shook his head. "We don't think so either. The Universal Assembler is military. Tightly guarded. It has been developed under the auspices of a defense treaty negotiated about ten years ago. Ostensibly so that when terrorists developed such an assembler, governments would have experts who understood how they worked and how to possibly stop their spread. Actually, we want something more innocuous, more positive. But I wanted you to know why we have this sense of urgency."

"So—what is it? Why am I sitting here on a cold concrete bench in Tokyo?"

Hugo's slight grin was maddening. "We understand that you've done extensive work on the prototype for the new BioCities, like the system presently coming to fruition in Tokyo. We think that you have developed many of the processes yourself and that you know as much about BioCities as anyone else in the world."

"Really!"

"No reason to be modest. You know it's true. A lot of money from governments and private investors has gone into Dento the past two decades. Dento has a lot of labs around the world, and not all of them even know that they're connected with Dento. All of that research information has been fed back into Dento and into what you have been working on. It's still classified, of course—if only for economic reasons. But most of the security effort at Dento has gone into protecting the Universal Assembler. All we want is the entire unabridged prototype."

"Oh, is *that* all!" She laughed.

"What's so funny?"

"You must think I'm an idiot! Why would I do this for anyone? I'd probably be killed." Kita jumped up and briskly marched toward the vendor, who was signaling her. Her right heel caught in a crack and she slipped and fell. Hugo braced his short legs apart and reached down a hand. She glared at him, took his hand, and allowed him to boost her up. Her silly stockings were torn. One knee and both palms were bleeding.

"Doma," she muttered. "Thank you."

His eyes glinted with irritating merriment. "Any time."

Kita didn't want to accept his offer of a supporting arm, but she'd loosened the heel of her shoe and couldn't walk without leaning on Hugo. She reached the cart, practically threw the shoes at the poor vendor, and slid her legs into the warm comforting boots while holding to the cart. Her palms stung and she jammed her hands into her pockets. "Now what?"

They walked a short distance from the cart. Hugo said, "I realize that I need to convince you of the importance of this endeavor. The BioCity program is being sold to U.S. cities, but it is modified so that the government has complete access at all times—"

"What?"

"Yes, they claim that it's for national security reasons. They say that they have the right to eavesdrop on anyone at any time because of the possible extraterrestrial threat. Or whatever. Marie doesn't think that's right. Neither do I. It's just a license to snoop, which is a license to control people. More important, she doesn't think that in the long run the natural goals of humanity have an opportunity to be well served in such a politically charged atmosphere. People need to be free to disclose information in their own way, in their own time, or to be able to choose not to. She is creating a floating city in the Caribbean—Crescent City—that she envisions as a model environment for creative and scientific work. Very important scientific work. We might be able to solve the mystery of the Pulses rather than be at their mercy. We might be able to use nanotech to its fullest advantage without destroying the world."

"Imagine! That's what I thought I was doing already. But what do you mean about the Pulses?" Caught up for so many years in the rush to create new systems of communicating, Kita had become isolated, inured to speculation and rumor. The Silence was like weather—something that affected her but was beyond her control.

"We can talk about that later. Do you have complete freedom to access information about what others at Dento are working on?"

"No."

"And you are not allowed to let others know what you are doing either."

"That's right. But I've been so busy—there really hasn't been anyone or any party that I wished to share with anyway. It seemed to be enough to be working on this team. It was fine with me to let Dento decide what to do with it. Until lately."

"And now?"

"I need time to think about this."

"Can we go somewhere in the meantime?" Hugo fished a small flat from his inside shirt pocket and looked at it. From the darting of his eyes, Kita saw that he had the implants that allowed him to give commands to computer screens through eye movements. Apparently, he felt sufficiently comfortable with some bodily modifications. She wondered if he had an expensive universal, which could be constantly upgraded to include any new access patterns so that he could read anyone's records, or just a local, which initialized him for one operating system. The first would certainly be handy for a spy.

"Here," he said and handed it to her. "Where is this?"

It was in Japanese. Now it was her turn to smile.

She walked over to a map vendor, purchased a Tokyo map for the price of an apple, entered the address on Hugo's screen, and told the map to search. Years ago, it would have included a global positioning chip, but those were useful so rarely that they were no longer a part of such maps. Instead, she entered their location and the map displayed three alternative routes.

"I could have done that," he complained when she handed it back to him.

"You thought I might just know where it is? In a city with millions of people? We're lucky. It's only about five stops away."

She was relieved to find sitting room on the train. "What kind of shop is this?"

"A toy store." He didn't offer any more information.

When they emerged from the underground, the wind struck her full in the face, whipping her hair around, and she pulled up her collar.

Could she believe Hugo?

She followed him while he read the map, trying to concentrate on the stunning information he'd dropped on her. If it was true, what was her responsibility? The concept of a single personality, the concept of dependable matter, the framework of the world as everyone knew it might end tomorrow. If Hugo was to be believed.

If Hugo was being honest with her and if there actually was something she could do, did she have a choice? What did she really know about Dento—their morals, their values, their goals? Who was Dento, really? She was chagrined at how little she'd examined such things over the years. The joy of working fully on her ideas had sated her completely. Funny how time could slip past when one was working hard. Funny how so many things could be ignored. And it had begun in college, she realized. Right after her father disappeared, she embraced work, as if, by doing something that might be pleasing to him with intense fervor, she might call him back from his alternate life. Or from death . . .

"Here it is," Hugo said, startling her.

The storefront display was colorful and intense. Constantly changing shapes were lit from within, using some very recent sugar breakthrough that caused photons to be released as certain cells divided. The colors were spellbinding in their intensity as they mutated. A cat, looking almost alive, coalesced in one corner. It stepped carefully through the mayhem, sat and licked one paw, then dissolved. A small forest grew, the trees about two feet high, and beneath them Japanese knights in medieval armor battled. In the background was Himage Castle, small but precisely detailed, and Kita shivered, fascinated, recalling a childhood visit when she'd seen the slots for pouring boiling oil onto the enemy. Castles had appeared almost spontaneously worldwide, it seemed, at one point in history, one point in economic time.

Now they were on the threshold of another such breakpoint.

"It's a foam shop," Hugo said.

The interior was dark, so that each bright display shone like diamonds on black velvet. The atmosphere was hushed, though foams had sound capability.

They gazed at a foam of planets; within a clear cube, the solar system went through its cycles.

"Go on, try it," urged Hugo, seeing her gazing raptly at the display.

"Oh, I'm too old for this," she said.

"I'm not."

He opened the small lacquered box labeled CELESTIAL WONDERS. "Something simple. The Milky Way, and keep the cube shape."

He picked up a small pink wafer with those words on it and stuck it on the side of the foam.

The planets began to dissolve. Gradually the gel cube filled with tiny brilliant stars.

Kita squatted and touched one. A voice named the star. She noticed that the information was hypertexted, and that by touching the screen, she could access other screens. She pinched the foam with both hands and pulled it so that it flattened and the surface enlarged, and the latest information about Venus appeared.

"May I help you?" she heard in Japanese.

Kita twisted around and saw a man in a lovely kimono standing in the dim light, his face in the shadow. He bowed.

Hugo said, "I don't see any price tags."

Kita began to translate, but the man replied in English.

"Just ask."

"How 'bout this baby?"

It was two weeks' salary for Kita. "Rather a lot for a toy, isn't it?"

"I'll take it," Hugo told the clerk. "Do you gift-wrap? Green paper?"

"Of course, sir. Are you sure you don't want to look at others?" He looked at Hugo intently, as if suddenly remembering something.

"No. I'm in a hurry. This'll do."

The man bowed, took the foam, and left them.

Hugo said, "Marie has a daughter. She asked me to bring her a present from this shop. She could have ordered it sent, but it's so much nicer to bring it personally, don't you think? And maybe faster."

"How old is she?"

"Nineteen, maybe?"

"Isn't she a little old for this?"

"There's a lot of information in this. She's kind of an amateur astronomer. Think I can smoke in here?"

"I don't think anyone would ask you to stop."

He lit a cigarette and she watched his profile, lit by foamlight, as he completed the transaction. She got the impression that Marie's child was also Hugo's. But he hadn't spoken of her in that way. No, she was *Marie's* girl.

His eyes were thoughtful, faraway, as the clerk did the quick retina scan, then looked at Hugo appraisingly. Must be some unusual information there. But . . . people always looked thoughtful, unfocused, during a scan. Kita decided that "thoughtful" might be some kind of unfounded characteristic she was attributing to him. Some kind of tragic history that didn't exist. Still, she found herself wondering if he was married.

This shocked, surprised, and then rather pleased her, all in quick succession. Except—she was completely uninterested in men. Had been for most of her adult life. Particularly men who were interested in her work. Not that she cared for women either. Not that she even thought about such things anymore, for the most part, she realized grumpily. She stared out the window while the foam was prepared for travel.

Hugo touched her shoulder gently and she jumped. Despite her coat, his touch seemed to flow into her body. Amazing. But he was rather like Jack, those many years ago, wasn't he? Interested in what she knew. Interested in what she could do for him. And for Marie. She steeled herself and stood. His green eyes reminded her of the sea at Okinawa. Tropical; intense.

So what?

"Sorry that took so long," he said.

"What's this really about?"

Hugo looked back at the clerk, who was watching them from the shadows. "It would be best if we discuss it later. What can we do today? While you're thinking."

She looked out at the snow. Memories from a happy childhood interval flooded her. "I'd like to go to a ryokan" popped out. She stopped, a little embarrassed.

"A hotel?" asked Hugo, his eyes amused and interested—but not, she thought, in a personal way. Just interested.

"Not really. It's just that snow always reminds me of when we were kids. We spent a month in the mountains every winter, either at my grandmother's cabin or at a little lodge, living the traditional Japanese way." She pretended to shiver. "You know, no heat. The way it is now, again." She laughed. She'd worked hard to teach herself to laugh instead of giggle.

"It sounds like something only very rich people could do." He opened the door for her and they stepped outside.

The cold wind took her breath away for a second. "We weren't very rich," she said. "My parents arranged their work so that they could do that. We lived all over the world. They were travel writers."

"Unusual," said Hugo. They hurried toward the underground entrance and down the wet concrete stairs.

"They were artists," she said. "Really. My mother is an internationally known poet, and my father was a photographer. They did travel work to make money."

They had retraced their steps to the train station. "You know, I'd like to visit the Ueno. It's the national museum." She couldn't remember when she had last been there, but it seemed so soothing and familiar to her at this point. Visions of Japan that spanned centuries. Mountains and rivers without end. "It too is at its best on snowy days. A lot of pictures of snowy mountains."

"You're very enthusiastic about snow," said Hugo. "I remember it only as a rotten inconvenience. I've done my best to stay out of the way of snow for most of my life."

"You're a barbarian, then," she said.

"I live to be educated."

"I'll bet you do. Here's our train." She wondered, during the brief ride, why she was even considering this. The train rumbled forward and plunged into a tunnel.

"For the good of humanity," said Hugo, watching her intently from his facing seat.

"What?" She looked up, startled, and saw her own reflection in the dark glass.

"You look as though you're wondering why you're doing this."

"I'm Japanese. You can't figure out what I'm thinking by looking at *my* face."

He smiled. "You're not as inscrutable as you think, Kita. While you're thinking about it, let me add that this is extremely dangerous. It's even possible that you might be killed. Although I believe that the odds are well against it. I just want you to know."

"But how would I do it?"

Hugo tapped the pocket in which he carried the gift-wrapped foam. "Maybe these kinds of things seem more important when you have a child."

Kita threw politeness to the wind. "So she *is* your child."

"Not genetically. But I created her. I'm completely responsible for her."

And that afternoon, while looking at masterpieces of snowy mountains, icy streams, cloud mountains and real mountains, Hugo told her the story.

Kita felt some edge in him crumbling as he spoke. Some edge, some wall, she didn't know how to say it in English. But he was upset about this. He had been for years, she saw. It was a strange story. She felt that he'd told this story to no one. That Marie knew all of it, and yet she held the same amount of pain, the same amount of joy, as he did, and that none of the joy or pain could empty out of one and into the other. "Marie's child is her floating city," he said. "I didn't realize that it would turn out that way. It upsets her that she doesn't love Kalina as she thinks she ought to."

Kita was not entirely happy that she seemed to be the one, so suddenly, that he thought could absorb these strong feelings of his. It made her feel rather like a counselor or even a tissue he might blow his nose on. He might as well be talking to anyone, she thought, as he rattled on into the afternoon while they sat drinking green tea in the Ueno cafeteria and then as they boarded the shinkansen to Kyoto.

For somehow, during the afternoon, she'd agreed to help, as Hugo so melodramatically put it, "save the world."

At least, she hoped it would turn out that way. It seemed only marginally possible. The future had always seemed a bit farther down the road, a little closer to the horizon than where she stood.

Until today.

That evening, while they hurtled toward Kyoto in plush first-class seats paid for by Marie, the air suddenly became rich with sound, and the screens on their seatbacks lit, overriding the OFF command. For a moment, the screens flickered with images constantly broadcast so that whenever it was possible information would be exchanged. The programming local to the train, which many were watching, was submerged. The train filled with polite, muffled exclamations.

The Japanese rail system was the most advanced in the world. Many countries could not afford new systems and the old fell into disrepair as economies spiraled downward. The trains of most countries did not have windows made of materials that would manifest images, as Hugo's did now, of a bar of radio frequencies. Hugo tapped INS ENGLISH and the speaker said, ". . . the International News Service reports that the famine in Kenya has worsened. Since . . ."

Then their screens were dark once more.

They were dark the rest of the trip.

Kita and Hugo, sated with train-purchased bentos and overpriced sake, did not speak much after disembarking in Kyoto. They walked up the narrow, twisting streets through falling snow. Old-fashioned, dependable gas lights illuminated centuries-old eel shops and the smooth, unrevealing gates of hidden temples. There was nothing slick and modern about Kyoto. Kita loved the city, for its age balanced the work of her mind, where she lived in realms powerfully new. Before settling here, she'd traveled quite a bit, doing graduate work in Paris, trekking around Europe and Asia. The fear in the back of her mind was the same as everyone else's fear—*This may soon vanish*. Until now it had been hard to know exactly in what way or why the world would vanish, since there were so many unknowns: the parameters of the Silence, whether or not the race to develop a functioning nanotech would make it under the wire of some unseen finish line, whether or not what some pundits were calling the Information War would escalate. Whether it was not, perhaps, too late for the planet to survive at all beneath its weight of rapacious humans.

Kita was unsettled by the fact that she now had a better handle on the problem and the possible time frame.

Her apartment was on the fourth floor of a small elegant building. "There was never an elevator here," Kita said as they climbed a broad stairway. "Just as well. I'd probably have to move out if this was a more sophisticated building. Keeping the power running for elevators and alarm and security systems makes them so expensive that a lot of skyscrapers in Osaka are going bankrupt."

They stepped inside Kita's apartment.

"Cozy," observed Hugo.

"Adequate," she countered.

"A bit warmer than the street."

"It's the floor. Steam heat piped through. Leave your shoes here." She gladly dropped her heavy bag, took off her newly manufactured boots, and set them neatly in the alcove. "Here are some slippers for you. I think they'll fit. Want something to drink?"

Hugo was examining a wall of framed photographs, her father's. "Tea? These are interesting. I like the one of clouds. It reminds me of his Number 47. In the *Himalayan Folio*."

"The picture of my sister is my favorite," Kita said, putting water on to boil and dropping a handful of green leaves into a brown teapot with a stylized running horse etched into the side. "It's in the center."

"She doesn't look like you."

"No, she's much prettier." Kita brought the teapot and two cups to the low table. Next to them, a window overlooked a spare courtyard garden, its single stone sculpture snow-covered and faintly washed with lamplight through which large flakes swirled.

"I don't think so," said Hugo. They settled onto the cushions. "This is quite comfortable."

"I hope so. It's where you're sleeping tonight."

"Wonderful view," said Hugo, smiling and pouring the tea. It steamed, releasing a delicate fragrance. He reached into his pocket and pulled out a small packet, which he put on the table.

It was brightly wrapped in sleek green paper.

Hugo's face was very grave. Kita restrained an impulse to reach over and touch his hand.

"My nephew will love it." She got up and slipped it into the briefcase she would take to work in the morning. "There are towels in the bathroom. Make yourself at home. There's a nice place to eat breakfast on the corner—we passed it when we came in. I'll try and get off work early tomorrow and we'll do some sight-seeing." She picked up her tea and went into the only other room in the apartment and shut the rice paper door.

The room was small, only two mats, with barely room for her wardrobe, her futon, and a low black table holding a small battery lamp, a pile of books as well as a universal book, rolled into a scroll, and a half-full bottle of water. The universal contained just about everything in print and could be updated at a local shop a few blocks away. In New Tokyo, it would be possible to update it practically anywhere.

She bent and switched on the lamp and undressed, carefully hanging her clothing in a wardrobe of sweet-smelling wood from the mountains of New Zealand, one of her few possessions. She didn't care much for owning things, unlike her sister, who'd filled a sprawling house in the American way. Kita lived as her parents had lived. Ready to enter the world without looking back—if need be. Or leave it, on a sudden whim . . .

She hesitated for a moment, standing nude in the center of the room, the chill air defining her. She heard Hugo get up in the next room and—what? Was he pouring more tea? She stood for a moment, indecisive, then laughed at herself silently. What made her think he would want her, anyway? He had some sort of complicated relationship with Marie. She still wasn't sure what it was. But she wasn't going to get mixed up in it. She liked her life as it was. Simple. Direct.

"Cowardly" was the next word that popped into her mind and then "dull," but she decided to ignore them.

She snuggled beneath her comforter and switched off the lamp; opened the shade. Light from the other room still spilled into the snowy courtyard. She lay awake for a long time, watching snow fall. She had done so, alone, on many nights, watching the world created by humans become magically transformed by nature.

And waking to find that cold rain had washed it away.

She rose and opened the door.

He was still sitting at the table, wearing his coat, sipping tea, and writing on a slate, absorbed.

"Hugo?"

He looked up and smiled. He didn't seem the least bit surprised to see her standing in the doorway, wearing nothing. That comforted her. Then it irritated her.

He carefully set the cup on the table and rose, a helpless look on his face.

She went to him then and embraced him. He was only about four inches shorter than she, and she leaned over as he tilted his head back. His kiss was deep and strong. "Kita?" he whispered as she pulled him into the bedroom, as she pulled off his coat, his tie, unbuttoned his shirt. "Are you sure?"

She laughed. "Don't I seem sure?"

Omato, the young guard at Dento, Inc., pulled the brightly wrapped package from her briefcase the next morning when she arrived at work. She sipped a can of hot coffee, willing her hand not to shake.

He looked up at her. "What is this?"

She took a big swig of coffee. "Oh. I thought I took that out. It's a foam. A present for my nephew."

"The oldest?" asked Omato, putting it back.

250

"Well, they'll probably end up sharing it. I should have gotten two, but they're so expensive."

Omato beeped her in.

She had a meeting first thing. They were doing a design package for some officials from the Export Ministry and she had a demonstration prepared.

As she spoke, she marveled at how cool her voice sounded. No one would have imagined that she was preparing to betray her Japanese family.

"This is a computer-generated holographic model of how a human-analogous limbic system is implanted in the bee analogs of the BioCities," she said. "This creates motivation for them to carry out the tasks assigned to them. A BioCity is a complex biological entity—yes, a question?"

"What is to prevent the entire contents of a human mind or personality from being implanted in such a bee analog?"

"Actually, nothing," Kita replied. "In fact, some models show that it is entirely feasible, given the architecture of the bee analog. Groundbreaking cryonics work in the past several decades has illuminated crucial aspects of the cellular basis of memory and personality." She did not say that such a model had actually been created. That was one of the many secrets that she always took for granted—secrets that now hedged her thoughts like an unwanted fortress. It was quite probable that some militant group would attempt to destroy a lab that had done such work. One theory was that embedding human emotional imperatives within the beelike creatures would make them easier to control.

She finished, bowed, and during the other presentations, she considered Hugo's sparely rendered visions of what the rest of the world was like, news that was filtered here in Japan and everywhere; news she'd been too lazy or too preoccupied to seek out.

The lights came on. She found that she was looking at a man with a strangely familiar profile. She tried to think, despite her nervousness. It seemed important.

Jack? Yes, it was the man from several years back, who had tried to get her to spy for him . . .

He turned as he stood and she saw his face for an instant before the others in the room obscured him from her view. It was him, though his hair was short and blond now, rather than brown. His company was doing business with Dento. There was nothing to be nervous about.

She jumped up, left the room, hurried to her cubicle, and realized that she was drenched in sweat. She patted her forehead with a tissue and took a few deep breaths. "Marie believes that information should be free," Hugo had told her. No, that wasn't it exactly, was it? "Information *wants* to be free." As if information was an animal in the zoo, captured from wild savannas of human thought and imprisoned within the bars of industry. Rather than industry generating it all in the first place, providing the all-important capital.

She did little nothing things, fiddling around. She went to look at her bees. People would think something was wrong if she didn't look at them. She pretended to closely examine some bees they had been feeding with a special mix of hormones and examined her assistant's training plan. The bees were trained before they were pulverized. This had something to do with hivewide recognition of a new visual pattern and the evaluation of their pheromonal pattern compared to that of the control group. She added voiceprint approval to the notepad waved in front of her.

Then it was lunchtime. The lab she needed to get into would be deserted. She reached into her briefcase and palmed Hugo's package, stood, and slipped it into her pocket in one motion. She picked up a box of bentos she'd bought at the corner, as usual. But with extra, for her friend in the lab.

As she walked, balancing the bento box in her left hand, she reached into her pocket and pulled back the self-sealing flaps of Hugo's package with her right hand and eased the foam from its colorful wrap. She walked through a clear tunnel that crossed over the street. The snow had ceased during the night, but the sky was still cloudy, and the sea, half a mile away, was steel-gray. Her badge opened the door. She looked around. "Nisawa? You here? I brought you lunch. I should have called . . ."

She pretended to look through the cubbies and shrugged. "Oh well." She settled on a stool at the lab table Hugo had specified. She took off her jacket and pushed it up next to the interface mode used to transfer biological information—casually, she hoped. Her hand still under the jacket, she slipped the rectangular foam from the pocket and pressed it into the slot that automatically activated the transfer.

It fit perfectly. Hugo had said it would take fifty-seven seconds to transfer the information. He claimed that someone had it all set up.

Lucky for him that she was so predictable. But there was no time for regrets now. There was no going back.

With an eye on her watch, she fished out a bento and took a bite. She pretended to choke and coughed loudly when fifty-three seconds passed, muffling the ping with which the transaction was acknowledged.

Still coughing, she used her fingertips to release the foam, squeezed it in her hand as if, she thought wildly, she wanted to choke it to death, swept her jacket toward her, and put the flattened foam in her pants pocket. Sniffing, her eyes watering, she grabbed the box of bentos and hurried from the lab, carefully shutting the door behind her.

Anika, the guard for this wing, was hurrying down the hall toward her. Kita rushed to the water fountain and started to drink, deliberately inhaling some water, which set off a quite genuine round of coughing.

"Are you all right?" asked Anika, pounding Kita on the back. She pulled some tissues from her pocket.

Kita blew her nose. "Sorry," she said, gasping. She pointed at the box of rice rolls. "Went down the wrong way."

"What were you doing in there?" asked Anika, frowning. "This was just upgraded to top clearance. They're changing the locks this afternoon."

Kita had a second to feel astounded. Hugo had cut things pretty close. "I'm sorry. I thought Nisawa and I had a lunch date. I must have gotten the day wrong. Tell her I dropped by, okay? She'll be sorry. I brought her favorite. Smoked eel and avocado. Well, I'd better get back."

Kita hurried back across the glass bridge, heart thumping. Information wants to be free, hell. This was her last experiment in espionage. She wasn't cut out for this at all. On her way back, she slipped the foam back into the packet and folded the edges back together. In her cubicle, she blew her nose loudly and shrugged into her coat; bent over and put the package back into her briefcase. She buttoned her coat, put on her hat.

At the front checkthrough, Omato went through her briefcase and pockets so slowly that Kita was sure he could hear her heart pound. "Leaving early?"

"I think I'm getting sick," she said. She resisted looking behind her. She prayed that his console wouldn't beep with a message to apprehend her. This was probably espionage. After all, the government was involved. Damn Hugo!

"You do look like it," he said. "Rest, then."

A quiet solar tram was just passing; she caught it and perched on the edge of a seat next to the door. She was trembling. The driver looked at her in the mirror. No, of course he wasn't. She was imagining things.

She made herself walk casually up the street to her building. She unlocked the door. Hugo, as precisely dressed as yesterday, sat at the table writing in little boxes with a pencil. Ah yes. Acrostics. How soothing for him, while she—

He looked up. She opened her mouth; he shook his head briefly. She just stared at him, enraged.

"Hello," he said. "I haven't eaten yet. Want to go out to lunch? I didn't know how to work that thingamabob on the counter."

"That's a rice steamer. Very high-tech. You need certification to use it. Come on, then."

She put on tall, scarred leather boots she'd had made in London years ago. They were much more comforting than her new ones. She was breathing deeply, regularly, deliberately. She transferred the foam to a tote bag and snapped the top shut. The plan was that she was to give it to someone at some point. Hugo had not been clear about that. She was just supposed to trust him. Like an idiot. Maybe, she thought, I should just take it back, confess . . .

"You'll hyperventilate," Hugo told her as they descended to the streets. "Are you all right?"

"No," she said. "Go left. This is Teapot Lane."

They climbed the steep street on foot. Kita's legs soon ached, but she did not stop. "Where are we going to eat?" asked Hugo more than once, puffing along behind her. Was it cruel to make him climb so quickly? She hoped so. They passed through the gate of a large temple. She took a sip of cold water from the dipper just past the gate and Hugo imitated her, lifting his eyebrows in a question she didn't want to acknowledge. People milled around on the cobblestones. A wide wooden platform extended over a broad tree-filled valley in which small scattered temples could be glimpsed.

"Did you get it?" Hugo asked, an edge of desperation in his voice.

"This is Kiyomizu-Dara Temple," said Kita, holding on to the railing and staring out over the valley. The scene was very dear to her. "I come up here about once a month. They say that when someone has an important decision to make, it is like jumping off this balcony."

"It's beautiful," said Hugo in a quiet voice. "Is there any particular reason you came up here just now?"

She said nothing.

He put his arm around her waist. "Did something go wrong?"

"I'm not sure," she said. "I've never done anything like this before."

He looked down, across the sweep of the trees. "Maybe you've already jumped."

"Maybe. Come on. Let's eat."

"But—"

"I thought you wanted to eat."

In a small steamy café, she ordered miso soup and black cod for them both. She felt his eyes on her face as she ate slowly and carefully. She sighed and looked up. "I'm sorry—"

"No need to apologize," he said, his face concerned. "I'm the one who should be sorry."

"No doubt Marie is not quite so sensitive," she said.

Hugo smiled. "Good guess."

Kita pushed back her half-eaten meal. "I'm full."

"Kita—"

"I have it," she said sharply.

"Relax, then," he said.

"I can't."

Hugo glanced at his watch. "How about a visit to the Temple of the Golden Pavilion."

"Then what?"

"Then we meet someone. Is the temple close?"

"About five minutes by cab." The Kiyomizu-Dara Temple had not helped. Maybe this one would. Maybe nothing would.

She felt as terrible as she had the day her father disappeared.

Multicolored koi swam slowly in the frigid water of the kinkakuji, the mirror-pond, as they crossed the bridge to the low classic pavilion. Even though the sun did not shine, the temple still seemed to glow. She began to talk, her words coming in nervous spurts, as if she just had to talk about something, anything except what she had just done.

"Everything in Japan is like an idea." She kept her voice level, analytical. As if she was safe in a hall, giving a lecture. "An idea clothed in matter. Replaced many, many times. This was completely burned in the 1950s and was completely restored. The temple we were at before—it's been there a thousand years. I sometimes imagine that nanotech will be that way. An idea constantly restored by repair nanotech. Or an idea living within a small piece of matter for years, maybe centuries, and then finding the ideal situation for reproducing itself. But what will we reproduce? Temples or weapons?"

Hugo faced her on the bridge. He put his hands on her shoulders and squeezed them gently. "You've done a very good thing today, Kita."

"How do I know? For all I know, *you're* making weapons like that."

"You're upset."

"Absolutely."

"And you're worried about what might happen now. Talk to me, Kita. Did something go wrong?"

She shrugged and he dropped his hands. "A guard saw me coming out of the lab."

"Oh," he said and looked thoughtful. "But that's not unusual, is it?" He met her glare easily. "I told you we know a lot."

"No, but the security clearance has changed."

"But the locks don't change until tomorrow," he said gently.

She shook her head. "This afternoon."

He frowned. "You should have told me sooner."

Kita tried to control her tears but failed. She felt like screaming at him but couldn't. That would be rude.

He held her tightly. Like a lover. His quiet energy flowed into her most strangely. She'd never felt like this before. Not really. Of course, he probably did all the time. She lowered her face and began to kiss him. I'm mad, she thought.

"I'm sorry," he whispered. "It's best that you don't go home. In fact, maybe it's best if we leave Kyoto. Now. I was waiting for a contact, but . . ."

She sighed. She stepped back from him. He wouldn't let go of her hand, though she tried to tug it from his grasp. "Why am I not surprised?"

"I am," said Hugo. "I thought I had everything taken care of. The guard should not have been there. I'm sorry. There's a good deal of money in your account now."

She stared at him. "But I didn't—"

"I know you didn't do it for the money. That would have been the first question most people asked. You did it just because an old friend asked and because you remember things about her."

"And because of you. I trust you. It's very strange, isn't it?"

"Cause for celebration, I think." He looked past her. "Two women are walking up the path toward us. They look very determined. I think something has gone wrong with my contact situation. Is there a back door to this temple?"

Kita could never remember what happened next very well. Hugo turned and pulled a gun, but the women had theirs out already. Hugo fired a shot that made Kita's ears ring, pushing her aside at the same time so that she sprawled into some bushes. One of the women fell and the other crouched behind a rock. Hugo yanked Kita back by the arm toward a path that snaked off through a formal garden. Then he crumpled forward. Blood blossomed on the shoulder of his coat. His gun fell from his hand.

Kita picked up the gun—the first one she had ever held—and aimed its unfamiliar weight vaguely in the direction of the rock where the other woman hid.

Then someone grabbed her wrist and wrenched the gun from her hand; she turned and saw a bald monk wearing heavy black glasses and a black robe. He quickly ejected the automatic's cartridge, which clattered onto the concrete and bounced into the mirror-pond with a tiny splash, startling the koi so that they darted away. He motioned to Kita to follow him into the garden. Kita looked back and saw a group of a dozen monks converging on the woman behind the rock, shouting. Some wielded heavy-looking sticks.

Kita followed the three monks who were carrying Hugo. They ran awkwardly downhill through the winter garden until they crashed through a hedge to a crowded road lined with small shops; pedestrians turned in surprise. One of the monks ran into the road in front of a taxi, which screeched to a halt. "Get out," he yelled at the driver. "Now!"

The driver argued, but the monk pulled him out and flung him onto the street, where he sprawled with a look of amazement on his face. "Get in," one monk told Kita, holding open the driver's door.

"But—" She realized that she had dropped the bag with the foam in it somewhere.

"Get in!"

The other monks pushed Hugo into the backseat, leaning in one door and pulling from the other, grunting and ripping his coat collar. Then they slammed the doors. The one next to Kita yelled, "Go!"

Kita looked in the mirror and saw Hugo, the front of his coat bloody. He caught her eyes and his lips moved slightly. "Drive," he whispered hoarsely.

"I have to—"

Hugo hoisted himself up and hollered, "Now! Now get the hell out of Kyoto!"

Kita stepped on the gas. The crowd fell back. She was soon careening through the streets, down this alley, up this street, always heading outward. Hugo held on to the seat back for a few blocks, swaying, then slumped back onto the seat.

It was evening and then it was dark. She was driving through a pine forest on an old bumpy road at wild speed. She had been driving for over an hour. She didn't remember how she had gotten out of Kyoto. Hugo was still breathing.

The road passed into farm country and entered the foothills. The land steepened to mountains. It was snowing again—hard. She slid around corners on snowy roads lined with pines. She did not slow down. She coasted, shifted, fishtailed, held to the road by her grandmother's ghost. She almost missed the turnoff. There was no sign. The narrow driveway cut through thick hemlocks heavy with snow as in some ancient print and continued for almost a mile until she began to fear that she'd taken the wrong turn.

By the headlights, she saw the old cottage. She almost skidded into it, but the taxi slowly crushed its right headlight against a huge rock and came to a halt.

She opened the car door and smelled snow, breathed in silence pattered by dry flakes sifting like crystal through the woods, heard the roar of the falls in the gorge below the house.

She clumped onto the wooden porch, half-hidden by drifting snow, kicked open the door, found the matches on the wall with her fingers, lit the candle that always stood in the center of the table. Yes. She knew it all from memory. She knew it blind.

The fire was laid. Her grandmother, then her father, had always kept it ready. And someone was doing so now. One of many cousins. Her fingers were steady as she held the match to the paper.

The fire caught and flared, playing off of jars of beans, rice, noodles, pickles, and whisky bottles lined up like soldiers on wooden shelves on the other side of the firepit. She went outside, rolled Hugo out of the car, dragged him in by his armpits, and lay him in front of the fire. She was trembling when she was finished. Though she regularly worked out in the Dento gym, she'd never actually felt very strong. She sank to the floor and started laughing. She stood and started priming the pump in the sink. It creaked. It needed oil. But muddy water spewed forth, and it gradually cleared. She laughed harder.

"What's so funny?" whispered Hugo.

"I dropped my bag. The bag with the foam in it."

"You'll just have to come to New Orleans and do it all again," he gasped, his words nearly incoherent. He said something in French that she didn't understand.

"Shut up." She collected water in a jug and poured it into the cauldron hanging over the fire. Most likely full of dead bugs. "Isn't that what Americans say? So rude. Shut up while I undress you." She knelt next to Hugo.

"Mmm."

"You might die!" she said, and it came out more irritated than sad.

"I sincerely hope not," he said. "Kita—"

Then he passed out.

The next morning Kita slipped out the door into a world in which she always saw the stylized beauty of classical Japanese painting. Pine trees laden with snow, their long branches perfect curves, tilted on the edge of a steep drop-off. Below, in a gully, a series of waterfalls sounded, distant and soothing, the music of her childhood. If she squinted, she might be able to think herself back in time and see a wide-coated solitary fisherman crossing a narrow wooden bridge high in a gorge surrounded by round-topped cliffs. If she really tried, she could be that fisherman, and her mind would fill with telegraphic poems.

But now the incongruous taxi, its nose crushed against a massive rock, kept her firmly in the present.

She was frightened. Hugo was seriously injured. He had tossed and mumbled all night, dripping wet with fever. The bullet had gone in at his shoulder and out at his back. She had no idea what this might mean. The cabin had but rudimentary first aid, which she had administered. Antibiotic powder on the wound. Opiates for pain. But what about lost blood? What about fluids? What about the delicate balances monitored so carefully in hospitals? He'd had a brief seizure during the night; she had been surprised at her ability to seem so calm and soothing when within she was screaming hysterically.

He awakened briefly in the morning and she gave him miso soup thickened with dried vegetables and dried shrimp from jars on the shelf and heaped him with blankets. This seemed to give him enough energy to forbid her to take him anywhere and to impress upon her the danger of letting anyone know where they were. Anyone. If he did die, a concept he seemed to find irritatingly amusing, she was to head for New Orleans. He mumbled something about a backup Hugo, laughed, coughed, and grimaced. "Ridiculous," he said, his eyes shut.

Now he was sleeping. Sleeping and clammy. His lips were blue. She did not know much about the coloring of other races, but she was sure his lips should not be blue. She left a note. No doubt they were looking for the taxi—and for her.

But she had to go. If she could just get to a pharmacy, she could buy a range of nanotech products that would encourage quick healing and simple monitoring devices that came in the form of patches. She couldn't help him at all by staying.

She got into the taxi and flipped the ON switch. The charge readout lit. If she was lucky, the owner had complied with the law and this vehicle was sprayed with the expensive fuel cells that used a form of photosynthesis to get power from the sun. Unfortunately, sunlight was in short supply during Japanese winters. The readout showed that she had only fifteen miles of charge.

That might get her to the nearest train station. She put the car into reverse. The tires slipped, then slowly caught on the debris beneath the snow. She turned onto the long driveway and stopped for a moment, looked for the control for the hologram generator that covered the seats in a doily pattern. The latest thing in taxis. Real doilies, pressed beneath sheets of heavy clear plastic as in the olden days, were passé. She found the switch, turned it off, and registered an extra two miles. She did not turn on the heat. She was warmly dressed in the heat-generating clothes that were kept at the cabin. They were rather old-fashioned-looking, much thicker than newer generations, but they worked.

The icy drive down the ridge did not bother her. She was expert in driving in such conditions. She watched the long sloping lines of the ridges descend around her, the wash of dark leafless trees in a curve within a nearby hollow, passed an ice waterfall that clung to a cliff. She drove through a small farming village and hoped no one would mark her; smoke rose from chimneys and she imagined rosy-cheeked children inside eating chunky stews thick with homemade noodles, as she had done so often when a child.

She hesitated before turning onto the main road, but it was eerily free of traffic. Probably the storm; the roads were icy. She drove as fast as she dared. She passed a few strip malls and then hushed Kyoto asserted its power and extinguished them; all had to be old within a certain perimeter. Though to the west and north, the towers of the massive Osaka metropolis flourished, steel-gray, the buildings gradually diminished as they neared Kyoto. Kita rubbed her eyes to get the black specks out of the coastal sky; they appeared to be bouncing in the air. She'd gotten little sleep.

She lost power only about two miles from the maglev's last stop. The taxi coasted to a halt as she pulled it to the side of the road. Though she was within ten miles of the city, there was still no traffic, which was very unsettling.

She pulled open the neck of her thermal suit as she hiked. She finally got to the turnoff to the train terminal and thankfully felt the coins in her pocket; she intended to get some noodles and a can of coffee from a machine.

When she looked up and really saw the terminal, she stopped suddenly, her heart pounding hard.

Narrow lines of neonlike light coursed round the bulbous entrance node. There were many vehicles in the lot; that seemed normal. But no one was going in or out.

A surge.

It had to be.

She looked again at the black specks. They were Bees.

Nanotech Bees.

Immature, of course. But in Osaka, she recalled, they had been cold-stored at the ready against the time when the decision to convert was made. Except that as of yesterday afternoon there had been no decision, for she would have known about it. After a decision was made, the projected conversion time, taken in very gradual steps, was six months.

This was an accident.

For the past ten years, the possibility of a surge had hovered beneath the conscious level of all of those working on this project. Many thought it impossible. But she didn't. Nanotechnology had the potential to be the atomic bomb of the new millennium.

Standing on the rise, beginning to feel the chill of her sudden inactivity, she was the lone witness to a change so vast that it left her without emotional touchstones. It had come with the suddenness of a snowstorm, apparently; had precipitated out of particular and precise conditions.

She squinted once again at the specks on the horizon. She wished for binoculars. With a sudden sense of urgency, she dashed for the train station escalator and ran down stairs still moving, though they serviced no one. The schedule lights were on and counting down. At the appointed time, a hundred and thirty-two seconds later, the train arrived. The doors opened. Kita looked inside at the lighted, empty seats. For a second, she wondered if she ought to go. But only for a second.

This was her life's work. She squeezed through the doors as they slid shut.

The train welcomed her in words some Apiary Project committee had developed, people she had never seen but who had been part of the interlocking circles she'd moved among for even longer than she'd been in Kyoto, since back in Copenhagen. She bent over, hugging herself, her chest squeezed so tightly that it was painful. Her raw, hoarse sobs echoed in the empty car.

"It's all wrong," she shouted. She pounded an indifferent window with a fist, feeling distant pain from yesterday's scrapes. Then she sat—quiet, afraid, and utterly alone—as the train silkily accelerated.

The main Kyoto station was crowded; for a heartbreaking moment, Kita was able to think that she'd been imagining things.

But she knew that one of many alternative programs had apparently been put into effect, accidentally or on purpose. She did not even know the protocol that was to be used to decide whether or not to convert a city to the nanotech metapheromone communications system she'd been working on for so long. She worked on technical rather than social problems.

She was dizzy with fear as she stepped off the train. In one version of the city, one of thousands that they had been blending and balancing for what seemed ages, she might be attacked as a foreigner. That had been a very easy element to include; identification and attack of outsiders was one of the basic pheromone functions of bees. Yet the statistical possibility that Kyoto was now that type of city was exceedingly small, and as two business-suited men passed her without a glance or a move toward her, she regained her ability to breathe. She leaned against a post, wondering what to do. She ought not to have come at all, of course. She saw one of the businessmen sink onto a bench and hold his head in his hands. A movie poster on the wall near the exit escalator began to slowly morph into an information terminal. She walked toward it. She could not touch it; she didn't even want to be near it. But perhaps it might give her a clue.

A woman in a black dress stood in front of it, staring.

"Kanitchiwa," said Kita. The woman appeared not to hear her. This proved nothing. "Touch the green bar at the top," Kita suggested. The woman reached out her hand without hesitation and touched it. This was a powerful clue in and of itself, apparent lack of volition, if Kita was not imagining it. "Now touch the blue dot where it says 'Access Functions.' "

A group of people was now crowded around the poster. After two more directions, the specification screen scrolled past slowly. Kita did not have to look at it for more than a few seconds. She knew that this was a tragedy of untold proportions and that she was fairly safe.

She took the escalator to the street. As she walked, she searched for and saw clues that confirmed her fears.

Brightly colored lines were inching their way up buildings like plants in a fast-growing jungle. She moved briskly, but her heart was lifeless. She was looking at her past and seeing a future that she was not a part of.

People sat leaning against buildings here and there, which was the hardest to see. They were not begging. Their brains were changing.

They were adapting to the new city.

That which had changed them was a molecular metaprogram, a weapon that was designed to be used to take over an enemy's city and program the inhabitants to accept whatever ideology might be convenient. The window during which it was initially virulent was tiny; once it entered the matter of a city and the populace, it operated quickly and became self-contained so that the conquerors could enter without fear of falling prey to their own weapons. But perhaps if there had been no perpetrator, there would be no such effect. After all, she didn't think that they had gotten to the stage of developing a menu of ideologies. That would be incredibly complex.

She passed what had been the window of a large store, unusually large for Kyoto. Instead of minimalist furniture, the window was now full of . . .

Hexagons. The end of the system that had apparently chosen this place in which to manifest, butting up against the window. Within the hexagons were shimmering membranes, nothing more.

Kita was completely aghast. The membranes were cryogenic sheets, capable of transforming humans into Bees. Bees were necessary to the Kyoto system. And they had not been stored.

They had to be created. Out of available bodies.

She must have run for a mile without seeing where she was going, flowing through crowds that parted with complete docility for her passage. She had to help them. She had to help them. Only she was left to help them . . .

She stopped in front of Dento's main entrance.

She was soaked in sweat. She peered through the tasteful glass doors with their kanji-etched name. She punched in her code and the door slid open.

What was she doing here? She barely knew. What could she do to help?

She walked briskly through the empty corridors. The event must have begun yesterday evening. Or maybe . . .

Yesterday afternoon? Perhaps the foam she'd stolen . . .

For a moment, her heart filled with dark heavy anger. It was her fault. She had probably downloaded prototypes that contained the seeds of events that were unimaginable.

But no. No. Calm yourself, Kita. She leaned against a cool wall, jumped back despite knowing that it could not infiltrate her, else her very boots could be a conduit . . .

No, the foam had not done this. It hadn't contained the seeds itself, only the information leading to them. But the timing could not be a coincidence. Perhaps whoever had done this had hoped to catch *her* in this surge. And prevent the contents of the foam from leaving Kyoto. If that was so, she would have to take everything she possibly could with her.

She hurried toward the central laboratory. But as she walked, she thought she heard footsteps.

She turned and saw no one. Heard nothing.

She continued and thought she heard another sound.

Jumpy. Whoever was here was as affected as those in the streets.

She hurried onward. Just another turn. There. She punched in her code with trembling fingers, thinking, Of course, that's how they would know.

She leaned against the closed door, considering.

A maze of counters filled the huge room, and cabinets hung from the ceiling above. Desk-level surfaces were interspersed among the higher counters, and the latest generation of DNA computers was linked throughout the lab.

Kita kicked some stools aside on her way to her cabinet and punched in her code. The door slid open.

The refrigerated interior had small fans that whirred away condensation. She saw what she was looking for. A sheet of RNA medium. One square inch could hold the information of an entire library. She removed it and the door slid shut.

Again she thought she heard a sound but again saw no one. She stepped to a cool flat surface different from the rest of the countertop, about a foot wide, and at her touch it began to glow green. Once again she punched in her code on a keypad that manifested at the table's edge, which sensed her presence. It then gave her a circle of symbols and she did not hesitate. She entered ALPHA through OMEGA. APIARY. CONFIGURE TO #38.

It was a backup emergency system, a prototype for possible eventual marketing. They'd never tested it on humans, only on computer-generated models of humans.

The foam idea had been good. If it had worked, she would have been able to come back to her job with no one the wiser. And surely this was suicidal.

But in a way it appealed to her. Step into the future you've created, Kita. It's the least you can do. All these people have and they didn't even have a choice. Her colleagues at Dento, the woman who had served them yesterday on Teapot Lane, the taxi driver pulled roughly from his vehicle. All were wiped clean.

A blue light glowed at her elbow; the matter of the table had reformed and was ready to transfer. She carefully laid the sheet in a slight glowing indentation about half an inch square. The RNA sheet immediately turned green. The process was working.

She looked around for the crystal console, which would save the same information in laser-accessible form. It would probably take at least an hour to do so, however. But she might have time. If she did have time, it would be infinitely better. Crystals, however, were made by techs and she wasn't as familiar with their storage location as she was with the RNA system, which she'd been working on. She wandered through a few rows of lab tables.

There it was—a row of semicircular indentations. She knelt and opened the cupboard below. She pulled out a box of blanks, set one in the indentation, and once again called up a keypad.

"Ms.—Narasake?"

She whirled. It was Anika, the guard.

"*Kanitchiwa,*" Kita said, forcing the welcome through a tight throat.

Anika nodded slightly. "*Kanitchiwa.*"

Relieved when Anika just stood there, Kita pushed on the button that would start saving the information. The crystal sphere glowed as it whirled. She walked back over to the RNA sheet. It was brilliant gold. Almost finished. Once she swallowed it, all the information she'd developed related to BioCities presently lodged in the Dento databanks would transfer to her junk DNA.

She just wasn't entirely sure how she would get it back out again.

If Hugo had proposed this to her, she wouldn't have listened for a second. Now here she was, doing it of her own free will. She looked back at Anika, who was standing straight, her straight black hair covered by her guard cap, just watching her. Perhaps she would not know that Kita had not been changed. Why should she? How could she?

Still, she made Kita nervous.

Kita looked back over at the laser sphere a counter away. There was no way that she could stick around until that was finished. It was time to leave. She peeled the RNA medium from the programming space. It was slippery and gellish, yet solid to her touch. It would not last long; it was very unstable.

"I feel very strange," said Anika suddenly, her voice jerky. "I remember coming to work this morning. I remember not knowing why. No one else was here. My console told me to watch training videos and I did. Something terrible has happened and I am not sure what it is. But I do know that you aren't supposed to come into this lab. You were here yesterday when you were not supposed to be. I remember that too. And I remember"—a fleeting frown creased her forehead—"I remember my console telling me that there was an emergency and that I had to do *something*—" Another frown. "Something I learned to do in training. I'm not . . . I'm not sure why I have forgotten everything." She moved toward Kita, skirting a lab table. Then she stopped. "It would be nice if we could go to the movies, wouldn't it? I haven't been to the movies in a long time." Her face was filled with longing, like the face of a young girl.

Kita thought of her sister. She could not bear this sadness. She couldn't. "Yes," she said. "That really would be nice." She looked closely at Anika's face. She seemed to be developing a rash across her cheeks . . .

Receptors? But they should only be on her hands. She moved toward Anika. "Maybe I can help you."

Anika felt her face with both hands. "It feels funny," she said, her voice choked. "I . . ." Then she looked down at her hands, at the patches of tissue rising up in pink regular ovals on her palms. "What's this?"

She looked up at Kita, black eyes filled with fury. "It's you! You did this! You and everyone in this place. My mother this morning . . . my mother . . . oh!" She struggled to pull out her tranquilizing gun.

Kita took one last longing look at the laser sphere and began to run.

She stuck the gel in her mouth and swallowed as she heard the *pop* of a tranquilizing gun. She dodged wildly and felt nothing; realized she would have to put her code into the door in order to get out, doubled back and ran right at Anika, who stared at her wide-eyed. As she ran, she stretched out her arm and swept an armful of lab glass into the air; it smashed through the air in a wild scattering of light. Kita turned back, put her code into the door, slipped out just before Anika got there. As a guard, Anika automatically overrode the code, but it didn't matter. Kita was through the door and running very fast now.

A block from the office, around a corner, Kita found a row of solar bikes. She jumped on one and while she did not exactly speed away, these being sluggish, at least it was faster and easier than running. Her hands trembled on the control bar; she felt sick and told herself it was just her imagination. She decided that she had to be crazy, then she decided that she wasn't. What else could she have done? She began to pedal to feed the generator; the bike moved a bit more quickly. There were people everywhere, but no one seemed to be disturbed by her presence.

She looked behind her as she gained the more rural roads and thought, You could have stayed and tried to fix it.

She stopped then and turned the bike around, straddling it. She had been to Beijing two years ago and helped set up their conversion. She had seen the system in operation before. But this was different. Without an army or at least a plan, Kita could do nothing. She wouldn't survive long in there. She had panicked, certainly. But she was lucky to have gotten out without being changed herself. It would take months of study by highly adept committees to determine what needed to be done to help Kyoto.

The fact that the entire contents of the Apiary Project system was now being lodged within the junk spaces of her DNA via specially engineered messenger RNA did not make her feel better either.

Then something to the east caught her eye. Her heart began to pound.

A few miles away, against gray afternoon sky, the road was filled with dark advancing shapes. Soldiers. Tanks.

She retreated a quarter mile, turned onto a side road, branched again onto another, hoping that the soldiers were only on the main road. They had to be some kind of international force. She'd heard that some kind of complex treaty arrangement was now allowing forces to enter countries to attempt to contain nanotech accidents. Or to do as their commanders pleased.

She continued on. She had no choice. She had to get back to Hugo. As the minutes passed, she encountered a few vehicles going the other way, but they seemed to be civilian. After half an hour, she relaxed. She was well out in the country. It was late afternoon. She was starving. She would have to ride steadily to get back to the cabin before dark.

That is, if this bike would make it that far. She wasn't sure how long she could pedal uphill if the charge ran out.

As the bike labored up the ridge road, snow began to fall.

Two weeks later, Kita stepped into the Tokyo foam shop. It was evening. She left the door open, looked around cautiously. There were no customers.

Outside, Tokyo's conversion was in disarray. Soldiers from the International Federation of Nanotech Conventions paced the street. Kita stepped back onto the rainy street and opened the car door.

She bent to help Hugo out. His face was ashen and covered with sweat.

Halfway across the sidewalk, the man from whom they had gotten the foam reached them. He helped her get Hugo inside; the man shut and locked the door; opaqued the window.

"What happened?" he asked. "You shouldn't have come here. It's dangerous."

"Hugo said that you have the facilities here to heal him. He has a gunshot wound. He wouldn't let me take him to a hospital. He said that you are part of some . . . organization."

The man frowned. "He should have said nothing about that."

"Oh, I suppose he should just die!" flared Kita.

"Do you have the necessary programs?" the man asked Hugo. He shook Hugo a bit. Hugo groaned.

"Stop!" said Kita. "He has some kind of . . . I don't know, regeneration, resurrection, something like that. A program. It's embedded somewhere in his body. He hasn't been too coherent. He thought you could help."

The man nodded. "Yes. Let's take him into the back. He looks pretty bad. We've not done this many times. But we'll do our best."

Two hours later, two technicians arrived with a truckload of equipment that they carried into the back with many grunts. Hugo lay on a futon set in an alcove in the living quarters at the back of the shop.

As equipment was set up, after some discussion, the shop owner apparently decided to trust Kita. Seeing as how, Kita thought with irritation, she seemed to know so damned much about Kyoto.

He had her sit at a table in the tiny kitchen and offered her a cup of bancha tea. She inhaled the woody scent gratefully and took a sip. Then he handed her a scrolled screen. She shook it sharply with her wrist and it unfurled to the size of a sheet of paper and snapped flat; lit with sharp colors. On it was a picture of the international terrorist suspected of stealing the Universal Assembler from Kyoto and setting off what was now being called the Kyoto Plague in an attempt to divert attention.

"Do you know him?"

"I've seen him before."

It was Jack.

THE FOURTH MOVEMENT

MAJOR TONAL CHANGE
Paris Stop Time

Artaud and Illian | Paris | 2037

Seven years after Illian's Prague exhibition, Artaud waited at the tiny café table, tapping a closed matchbook on the marble circle. Though it was winter and the café owners were apparently depending on the body heat of their customers to take the chill off, Artaud was sweating. He shrugged off his overcoat and let it lie over the back of the chair. He removed his hat, a black formal gentleman's hat, set it on the table, fiddled with the brim, and put it back on. He signaled for another drink.

It was twilight, and the tables of solitary readers were being replaced by noisy crowds of diners. He welcomed the confusion. He would be completely inconspicuous when Illian came in, as she did every evening, for soup and bread and wine. The place was fairly large.

Paris had changed immensely since his last visit. But then everything had. The world had undergone frightening paroxysms of replication surges, thought-viruses called the Information Wars, and the emergence of BioCities.

He had been awakened nine months ago by Brazilian revolutionaries who were freeing relatives being held for ransom by government officials. He had no earthly idea how his rejuvenated body, to which he had closed his eyes in Mexico City years earlier, had become mixed in with this batch of unfortunates in Rio. The complex trail represented by bills of lading an apologetic woman handed him were too complicated to peruse. He was alive. He'd gained a new body. But he'd lost the woman he wished to give it to. A silly thought anyway.

Yet he'd searched what he could find of the art world, taking a ship to Istanbul and attending parties with all his might from the Mediterranean to the Atlantic. And he'd finally gotten word of her.

Now he touched the cool, small glass the waiter set before him with his fingertips and ridiculed his caution. She wouldn't recognize him anyway. Couldn't possibly.

Even so, yesterday he'd imagined that a pensive look had crossed her thin luminous face, that she'd pushed back the long lock of sand-colored hair that fell forward quite self-consciously; that the two pink patches that colored her cheeks suddenly had to do with his quickly averted stare. He could not think that her large deep-set blue eyes betrayed loneliness, no. That would be new.

But something had touched her. In Prague, before he'd left her, before the world had gone through the wild changes that had so delayed him, she had been vivacious. She had dressed in swirls of rich color. Even her hair had been rainbow-striped. Now her clothes were plain, elegant, dark.

Isolated from the world in the Mexico City Clinic, he had not known that Perdita, Illian's ad hoc guardian, had dropped dead several months after he left Illian; otherwise, he would have returned to her immediately. But had he not been heavily sedated as part of his treatment, he would have fled anyway. It was nightmarish, horrible. So much had been replaced; changed. It had been a great struggle, one he would have never undertaken had it not been for Illian, and one which he may well have given up many times without her functioning, unknowingly, as his anchor to the world. And then it amused him to think of the voyage his body had gone on, by ship and by train, according to the paper trail. He supposed he was lucky that it had not been shot into space for some unknown reason.

But now he was well. And young.

But still himself? In the first throes of the drink, he blinked away sentimental tears that seemed to arise so easily now at the slightest provocation. He'd been a hardened old man, philosophical, cynical. Had he ever been this sensitive, really, in his younger days? He could hardly credit the thought. Only the few simple, direct works of art that had survived his purge—and that only because they'd been forgotten in a nephew's attic—betrayed his credulous, childlike, pre-critic nature. He shivered, suddenly chilled again, and pulled on his coat.

She would not recognize him. He had told her that he was going away to track down some obscure artist on the other side of the world. He had thought that she wouldn't even miss him, wrapped up as she was in the swirl of young admirers and acclaim. She seemed not to care, and promised to keep in touch, but her voice-letters—something in her brain twisted reading and writing—were few. Those of a daughter making the effort to keep in touch, but so involved with her own life that it was hard to remember to take the time. As he'd expected. He was not upset.

Why had he not been honest with her? Because he still had the illusion that some parts of his life were still his own? Because he thought she should not be burdened with the thought that he might well die—why that, when he had seemed so often at death's door in the years since he'd taken her under his protection? Perhaps because he was afraid of what her reaction might be knowing that he might live.

And might be young again.

The music was cranked up another notch. It was past dinnertime. Bar patrons filled half of the large room, talking loudly. He sighed, put on his hat, and pushed back his chair. He knew where she lived. Had walked past it, gazing up at her window. Why not just go to her flat?

Why this damned fear?

Because he was in love with her. He was in love with her, and he should leave her and never see her again. He should realize that her life was her own and watch over her from afar. Why? Simply because he'd been a powerful influence on her life. Though not, probably, on her person or on her personality. Probably not nearly as much as he feared.

He blinked again, squeezing between tables as he made his way to the door. Now what was wrong with that, anyway? He had been sick—and old enough to be her grandfather. He was still that old, but didn't look it. His short hair was jet-black once again. Although he had whiskers, his skin was soft and smooth as that of a child. It was frighteningly easy to take his strong, lithe body for granted. He remembered the aches, the recalcitrant joints, the slow-burning pain. But even those memories were fading.

Near the door his coat caught on someone's chair and he turned his head and apologized. When he turned back, she was holding the door open. Two feet away from him. Staring at him, bright pink staining her cheeks. He tried to turn away, but could not, pegged by her eyes. Tears streamed from them. "Close the door, damn it!" yelled someone at a nearby table. But she stood as if frozen.

"Artaud!" she said.

He was deeply shaken. He'd imagined sitting next to her, talking, getting to know her mind, deciding whether to reveal himself. He wanted to deny it. "I—"

She stepped up to him. She had grown even taller, taller than him, and was as lanky as ever. She slapped him, then hugged him, crying out, "How could you do this to me! Why didn't you tell me! I thought you were dead!"

Pinioned in her strong grasp, Artaud heard a roar of applause around them, shouts of "Good for you!" and "Slap him again!" The power went off, as it did so often, and only the table candles lit her face, her deep eyes, as she drew back and grasped his hand tightly.

"You're so beautiful now," she said with a catch in her voice.

"How did you know it was me?" he asked as a waiter jostled past them and lit the gas lamp in the wall sconce. The golden light danced in her eyes, which were puzzled. "How could I not know? You are you. Your essence. Your . . . pattern. Artaud, please never, never leave me again. I simply could not stand it." And she broke down and cried as he held her. He understood that it had something to do with the part of her life she never spoke of, which was all her history before he found her. She had suffered great loss before. Of course. How stupid he'd been.

"I'm so sorry," he whispered, and it seemed so natural to touch her face, to brush that lock of hair aside, when he never had before, when he was older, and she was so young. Now they seemed of an age. He had never played father or grandfather to her—only mentor, guarding and nurturing her talent, trying to see that she had friends of her own age, but they all slipped off her smooth surface, never gaining entrance to her soul. And he had not either, though its existence, like a new sun, had so clearly given him life.

Her eyes were frank, adult. All those thoughts and more, assuredly, passed through her quickly.

"Come," she said. "Let's go home."

The walk through sleety streets was like a dream for Artaud. Gaslight made the falling ice into scintillating dashes. She gripped his waist tightly through his thick overcoat and he was overcome by odd shyness. His older self was being washed away on a flood of hormones and life and joy. He let it go. That self was worn ragged, lemon-sour, world-weary. This new self saw everything anew.

She lived, surprisingly, in a small flat in a building with no elevator. "This was built in the 1600s," she said as she fiddled with the lock. "I think the wallpaper has been there that long too." She swung open the door.

It was dark, but she kept matches in a metal box attached to the wall next to the door and in the dim light from the window, he saw her pull some out with long fingers. She struck one on a strip of roughened metal and lit one candle after another as she walked through the apartment—and finally a kerosene lamp. "Gas heat," she said. "These places are in great demand now."

Unlike himself, she did not seem nervous at all as she bade him sit on a long, low couch with battered cushions. She moved with unhurried grace, spoke perfect French in throaty tones that soothed him, almost as if their roles were reversed now and she was the mentor, the caretaker. The kitchen was a rectangle of flickering light and he heard glasses clink. She emerged with a bottle of Absinth and a liter of water. She smiled and tilted her head as she poured. "Do you disapprove? I have been known to hallucinate with this. It's a different quality than hashish. But not tonight; just a taste, tonight."

His mouth burned with licorish flavor. He coughed. He hadn't had Absinth in—what? Fifty years? He looked around.

"Do you have enough money?" he asked.

She laughed, settling back with her small opaque drink. She pulled a blanket from the back of the couch and wrapped it around her. There were no sounds in the tiny side street, and, through the tall windows, he saw that the sleet had turned to snow.

"I suppose you want me to live in a sleek hotel?" she asked in a teasing tone of voice that was new. The smile left her face. "This reminded me of your—our—place in Amsterdam. It is homey and the neighbors have all lived here for years. They don't know who I am. I am just the somewhat eccentric young woman from whose studio strong smells of oil paint emanate from time to time. I have been fitting in." She leaned forward suddenly, her face serious, her eyes intense. "It is so important to me. Fitting in. Having someone—more than one someone—" Her voice broke and he found himself next to her, taking her in his arms, holding her.

"I'm sorry," he whispered. "I'm so sorry."

"Did you think I wouldn't miss you?" she asked, yearning and anger crowding together in her voice. "Oh, Artaud, maybe I never said anything to you—I know I didn't—I didn't think I'd have to, and you were going to die, and I would have to go on alone, and it seemed better not to—"

"I know," he said, somewhat frightened by this breakdown and more words about feelings than she'd ever uttered in all the time he'd known her, first as a sullen girl prodigy, then as a self-absorbed teenager. But she was different now, so different.

She drew back from him then and took his face between her hands. "You look so *funny,*" she said and burst out laughing. After a second of feeling indignant, he joined her. He knew exactly what she meant. There was a look of comic artificiality about his face. They laughed until he too was weeping and then her mouth was on his and

275

their kiss was long and slow and deep. She loosened his tie and pulled it off, unbuttoned his shirt.

"Don't think this is my first time by any means," she said.

He felt as if it were his, and it was—the first time in his new body and the first time in perhaps twenty years. She pulled him into her bedroom, piled high with clothes, armoire and dresser drawers standing open, the bed unmade.

"Don't say a word!" she said when she saw him taking in the mess.

"It's quite wonderful," he said fervently.

Artaud woke wrapped in a delicious jumble of warm blankets. Golden sun poured through tall windows. At first he thought he was at his grandparents' in Orleans, over the bakery, for he smelled strong coffee and could almost hear the adults laughing in the kitchen, ready to tease him for being such a sleepyhead.

But it was Illian who came through the doorway with a tray of pastries and a pot of coffee, and it was she who laughed at him, her sand-colored hair tousled, wearing a heavy robe, for it was cold.

"I must have worn you out last night. Are you sure you're really younger?"

He rolled out of bed, took the tray from her hands, and, looking around, saw that the dressers and chairs were mounded with clothing, so he placed it on the floor. Illian watched, a bemused look in her eyes. He untied her robe, pushed it back from her shoulders, looked at her for a long moment, and pulled her close.

They went out later in the day, long after the coffee became cold. The day had clouded over. They bought crepes from a street vendor and strolled down toward the Seine, entwined and blissful. From the Pont Neuf, they watched a rowing race pass beneath them. "This is the most extraordinary day of my life," said Artaud.

"I may have to scrap my current projects," replied Illian. "They're all about loss and loneliness." She laughed, throwing back her head as she did so, holding on to the railing of the bridge with both hands and leaning back on her heels like a girl so that her long loose hair swung low behind her.

Artaud wondered if it would ever be safe to ask her about her childhood, even wrapped within this new lovers' intimacy. He decided to wait. Perhaps he would wait forever. It might do her art harm to discharge it in talk. But . . . would it do her good otherwise?

"Were you ever married?" she asked, startling him.

"Twice," he said. "Once happily, once miserably. And I had a seven-year-long relationship with a man. He considered us married. I did not. Eventually it became a problem."

A low rumble filled the air as they continued their stroll toward a flea market on the opposite bank. As Artaud was wondering why the hell he'd waited so long to do this, air raid sirens pierced the air.

The scene before them came alive with people he hadn't really noticed, hurrying this way and that, diving into doors, reaching into their pockets, shouting. Illian pulled on his arm. "Run!" she said.

But he stood for a moment before taking action and saw the dark cloud coming from the east. "What?"

"Bees," she shouted, for it was becoming louder, and he heard the hiss of a missile being launched just blocks away. "Bees from the Free Nations. The so-called Free Nations. They are a Slavic affiliation of old countries."

"What can mere bees do?" he asked, but she just pulled him onward, uncharacteristic panic on her face.

"They can turn us all to fanatics. Oh, how could I have forgotten hoods for us?"

They were running now and Artaud was once more pleased with his new body, at how it moved painlessly, with even a certain joyfulness in motion. At the same time, he recalled seeing posters about keeping a hood close at hand and he also recalled that he had simply paid no attention to them, nor had he even wondered what they were all about. He'd been completely engulfed in his newness, in fear and in anticipation . . .

Illian pulled him into a small bookshop. Most bookshops were kiosk-sized, since book discs took up very little space. But Artaud, for the second time in the day, was yanked back to his youth, when with his fiery grandmother, he made a daily trek to the bookshop in the town square . . .

There was no one inside, and Illian was throwing things out of drawers in a frenzy. "Where are they! They have to have emergency hoods! It's the law!"

"Don't they have a pipe in here?" Artaud started to look around for the object machine, as small nanotech manufacturing devices were called in France.

Illian's laugh was sarcastic. "Of course not. Paris has always voted against such corrupting influences. You can go to the socialist-operated object bank and get whatever you want, for free. As long as it's been approved by the Cultural Committee. This isn't Prague, you know. Wouldn't want to have stuff running rampant here." Artaud heard an edge of hysteria in her voice. She was crouched down in front of an open cabinet. He leaned over, held her shoulders gently, and kissed her on the lips. Her sigh relaxed her shoulders, and she raised her hands to both sides of his head and pushed his hair back, a sad, ironic smile on her face. She rested her head on his chest for a moment and whispered, "What will become of us? Now that we've found each other—"

"We'll always have each other," replied Artaud. "I promise."

He knew she would find such a declaration irritatingly romantic and waited for her to laugh. He bit her ear gently. "I do promise."

"Me too," she said, surprising him, and her eyes were green as summer trees. Through the open door, the street had filled with a mob, shouting at the sky, brandishing sticks. "Their heads look like onions," murmured Illian. "With those hoods."

The roar of the Bees grew louder, and the street grew dark. Gunfire filled the air. A Bee fell down right in front of the window, mangled, legs scrabbling. A woman's legs stuck out from beneath it. Artaud leaped up.

"No!" screamed Illian, but her hands lost their grip. He was in the street instantly. He and a few other people leaned against one side of the Bee. It didn't really look like a bee. Sharpish filaments grew in a pattern of three stars on its side, some sort of emblem, Artaud realized, for whatever they stood for.

As they pushed, the man next to him said, "Get away! You have no hood! Hey, careful of that pollen sack!"

"It's already ruptured," grunted a woman, and by now Illian was next to him and grabbed him by the waist and dragged him away. He couldn't understand a word of what she was screaming; it was in some strange language he'd never heard her speak.

By evening, the buildings were changing. Refugees fled, on foot, in cars, in buses that honked and jerked through the mêlée, past buildings that seemed to be ever so slowly melting, then hardening; melting, then hardening.

The civil defense sirens sounded every ten minutes. Illian and Artaud had been making their way toward the Eiffel Tower for hours, fighting the general flow.

"We are trapped," said Artaud, panicky for the first time. "You must go, Illian. Whatever happened to me when I touched the Bee will not happen to you, right? So—you must go."

"We stay together," she said firmly, pulling him along. "There is a plan," she said. "I read about it in the newspaper. If we'd had hoods, then I'd be for leaving. But without hoods, our best chance is to stay and try and help and see if they can develop an antidote fast enough.

The Ministry of Science has the latest evolution banks. The Tower is supposed to be one of the emergency stations."

Artaud felt a curious mixture of despair and elation as he hiked along matching Illian's long sure stride, clasping her hand. He wondered if she'd had any attacks lately, but now was not the time to ask. There was so much to talk about, so much he'd intended . . .

Yet he was here, in a body that functioned free of pain. He had made love with a strange and beautiful woman . . . how many times? He smiled. He couldn't even remember.

Illian stopped walking abruptly and gazed at him.

"What?"

"That smile. *Your* smile. I don't think I've ever seen it before. It's . . . lovely."

"Then why are you crying?"

It was Illian's idea to enter the Hive, which had grown in a few hours to fill the space at the base of the Eiffel Tower. Artaud's heart sank when he first saw it. Emergency station, indeed! Plan, indeed! As evening fell, Artaud watched in wonder and terror the way Paris lit as if every building were outlined with tubes of neon. "It's too late for you to leave, isn't it?" he said sadly.

"Leave!" Her laugh startled him. "No. *This* is the way we must go. Forward, not back. Into . . . something new. Do you know how hard it is to find something completely, utterly new?" She stared at the Hive, looked up at the glowing Tower with worship in her face as crowds stampeded past and people shrieked in fear. "I have read about these Hives and this whole arrangement, you know, in the fright literature they hand out with the hoods. For instance, those glowing colors—they are interstices, filled with communicative bacteria."

"Oh." Artaud supposed that this final newness would be the end of him. He was dizzy, feverish, hungry.

But there was such joy in Illian's eyes.

"I can *use* this, Artaud. This is a new medium. Maybe . . . a new form of consciousness. Please. Please come with me. *Change* with me . . ."

" 'Change'?" Pervaded by weariness, such a thought was almost beyond him. He had already changed so much . . .

Illian gripped both of his hands tightly. "*Become a Bee.* It is possible. I know from what I have read. It was meant to scare us. But it only excites me."

Her arms went around him. Her kiss electrified him. He thought, I will probably die either way. Why not? In a daze, he allowed her to undress him and he undressed her. They kissed and whirled about as they undressed. There was madness all around in the darkness, and no one seemed to notice as the glow of the Hive illuminated them. "We will share a cell, Artaud. We will make love. To the last. Or to a new beginning."

That, at least, sounded halfway pleasant.

The hexagonal cells were growing against the side of the elevator, the size of, Artuad could not help but notice, coffins. Illian chose one and climbed in; shivering, Artaud squeezed in next to her.

The cell of the Hive was warm; almost unbearably hot. Its golden glow surrounded them.

She opened her mouth and her body to him. The Hive itself smelled sweet and pleasant and clasped them more tightly together. He had a moment of panic but realized that he could still breathe; he met Illian's triumphant gaze and then she closed her eyes in ecstasy. He wondered, as the points of consciousness he considered to be *him* flowed outward, if he was dreaming. Bliss and fear, as one might feel in the presence of angels, swept through him.

Artaud! he heard, and it was Illian's voice, sounding all around him. *It is working . . . you must come too . . .*

He did not give up his new body easily. But there was no escape. It was as if he were dissolving. In the darkness within his closed eyes, unspeakable memories exploded; memories too complex and too wrenching for words; memories of the painful purging of cells, of a deep and endless nausea, of a shifting of mind from all but the most basic shreds of identity, during which he forgot that it would all be restored. But even that was a memory and he felt that there would be no restoration this time, that it was truly death he was undergoing, a transformation beyond the veil of the possible into the wildness of something beyond human . . .

But maybe closer to *her* . . .

Artaud, my love, Artaud . . . I am learning the system! She was in his mind, as he had been within her body. *Please, oh please, do not give up! I am almost ready . . .*

And then a joining past comprehension. *Her* being, *her* mind, so much more complex and at the same time so much more simple than he had ever imagined. Their physical lovemaking had been only the first step, a childish step, compared to what he now experienced via, he realized, this new system of consciousness.

He felt as if he understood the very source of her strangeness, which even she could not comprehend as fully as he now could, just as one never sees one's reflection clearly. Artaud saw Illian clearly at last, not with his physical eyes, but with the core of his being.

And what he saw was powerful.

Illian reveled in receptored consciousness. Her thoughts found unfettered expression at last, direct and pure, without the intervening muffling barriers of time and matter. She was electric, she was photons, she was *light*! Light in patterns, in intersecting planes, in revelatory arrangement, flowed through and from her—light programmed through intervals of pain, nurtured by pure natural stretches of radio ecosystem unsullied by artificial human broadcast confusion, when the delicate magnetic-sensitive cells in her brain tuned and rested, tuned and rested, unfurled new connections and linked without end until she was charged with vast, perfect, wordless understanding.

Understanding of time; understanding of distance, understanding of gravity. Understanding of how to join theories of light and gravity; how to harness energy at its source.

Understanding of how to return to her distant heart.

And yet—

Her body was human, imperfect, too delicate a vessel to hold this understanding for very long.

It needed a wider canvas now, one of more dimensions, one which might express that which she had ached to express for so many years.

It needed Paris.

The City of Light.

And Artaud, transformed once again, was her ally, her vessel, her filament of communication. He—or, now, *she,* since he was no drone but a Queen, because Illian had wrested the power to infuse him with the processes that turned a drone to a Queen—Artaud commanded the city, from the center of . . . *her* . . . transformed being. Artaud translated Illian's thoughts into pure metapheromonal language; tapped into the roots of her own new form with joy and the exhilaration of freedom; allowed Illian's essence to flow into the interstices, into the city's ancient matter, to make of Paris a precisely arranged mapping antenna, mirroring that which was lodged deep within Illian's mutated genes, deep within every cell.

Artaud fought her way free from the Hive, seeing with her faceted eyes the crowd that had gathered during the hours of their transformation scatter and fall back across the wide piazza. The scene was lit by the Hive, and by the moon, and by lines of colored light that emanated from the Tower.

He—*she*—was changed. And Illian . . .

Artaud rose on her new wings and glanced back at the cell from which she had emerged. But she knew that the cell was now empty.

Illian had not been transformed as Artaud had been. But neither did her body lie in the translucent cell.

*   *   *

The stolen program the terrorists dumped on Paris—the program that had found its way to them from Kyoto—was powerful. But it did not function entirely as the terrorists had thought it would.

A stronger will and philosophy than theirs hijacked it. The terrorist-spawned Bees were transformed as well and now ferried the messages of utter newness emerging from Flowers blooming across the rooftops of Paris, a vast garden open to the moon and the stars.

Illian had been subsumed, fully transformed, in the process of understanding the BioCity at its deepest levels. Her brain, her mind, that which had produced such strange and lovely art, flowed through the interstices of the city.

Paris sang with the Signal and its mapping patterning of matter, its revelation too intense, too complex, too *different* for humans, with their limited senses, to comprehend. Only slowly could they grow toward understanding, and Paris would be their school.

And Illian—

Illian was an adult. Finally. Only she among all of those few frantically created decades before had now traversed, through environmental accident and innate fitness, the rough road to a maturity purely imagined by her distant invisible creators. And even they had known not what might come of it. They had only hoped—if such a concept could be ascribed to them. Illian had taken advantage of this new medium as she had taken advantage of every medium before.

And this time she learned and grew in a tremendous leap.

Illian was an adult such as had never before been seen in the universe, lonely and stretching outward, searching for she knew not what. She still knew not what.

But she yearned with all her expanded being toward a light past human seeing. That light, which had long filled her human ears with pain, was now changed to ecstasy as her mind passed through time's doorway.

And took Paris with it.

Legal Jive; Briefly

Marie | New Orleans | 2037

Sharbell Dighton III, when asked "What are you?"—a question he regarded as being one step removed from being asked if he was Jewish, African American, Iranian, Cuban, or Irish—all unfashionable in the United States at one time or another and all part of his background—generally replied in his calm low voice: "Human being."

Dighton was a New Orleans mongrel who had made his fortune and reputation the hard way—on his own. Marie counted the fact that Dighton was willing to play in her court as one of her great blessings. He had an aura of quiet power.

He knew how to get things done.

Except, annoyingly, this thing.

"New Orleans cannot secede from the Union, Marie. That's been tried before." Dighton was casual today. His beige linen jacket was unbuttoned, and it gaped open as he leaned back in the leather couch opposite her desk and draped one arm over the back. He had not unbuttoned his vest. Marie had never seen him unbutton his vest. He wore a yellow bow tie. On anyone else, it would have looked slightly ridiculous. But on Dighton, it merely worked with all of his other attributes—his black hair cut severely short, his dun-colored skin, his short beard and mustache, and his large brown eyes, somewhat magnified by the narrow glasses he wore. These glasses had, compressed within the DNA computers that comprised the frames, vast legal libraries that could be accessed with controlled glances if one had special implants. Many attorneys preferred audio feeds direct to the cochlea, but they were disallowed in many jurisdictions.

"But things are different now," said Marie. "And New Orleans isn't a state. It's a city."

"You just want to be able to lay your changes on downtown without FDA approval, right?"

Marie nodded.

"Well, then, I have several other approaches to suggest."

"Whatever works," said Marie. "And we have to do it soon. I mean, I think we'll just do it. The heck with all that nonsense."

The corners of Dighton's mouth lifted ever so slightly. "Have you ever thought of just establishing your own country?"

"Many times," she said. "I'm not kidding. In fact, that's what I'm doing as we speak."

"Really." He didn't look surprised. He never looked surprised.

In fact, a small band of knowledgeable survivors from Zion's Freestate were now living on the base of a new floating city, which was being grown using the most advanced techniques nanotechnology could offer.

"Really," she replied. "But I need New Orleans as a jumping-off place, so to speak."

"So it's not going to be here."

Marie brightened. "Could it be here?"

Dighton smiled slightly. His smiles were always slight. "It would be infinitely easier if it were not here. For example, the necessity of raising an army from that"—he gestured out the tall arched window next to him, indicating the rest of the city's population, which led lives rather less focused than his—"would never become an issue. I fear their enthusiasms lie elsewhere. As do the enthusiasms of most intelligent people."

"An army would be no problem," said Marie.

"I've heard about your zombie powers, my dear. Let me go on record as saying that I can think of a thousand ways to pursue you to your death in court should you attempt something like that if I ever knew the particulars."

"Well. Maybe you're right." Marie stood and strolled around the room, hands in her pockets. It was so much fun to rattle Dighton.

But this was serious business.

Marie looked out across the city.

Her new BioCity.

It was quite astonishing.

First, every building in the city had been assessed by molecular intelligence, mapped, and infused with sensory cells. Months of city-wide seminars had taken place to instruct the citizens on the nature of these changes, on what they could expect, and the various levels of understanding they could purchase or be eligible to receive free. Marie had subsidized receptors for anyone who was unable to afford them; the government agents had been astonished at the expense that she was willing to incur. Apparently, their idea of BioCity users did not include anyone below a particular economic or educational level. But there was no proscription against such inclusion in their specs; apparently, they had been counting on sheer economics to maintain social stratification.

The wall of her Canal Street glass tower office now harbored a six-inch-wide stripe on the inner wall.

Marie had gone through the receptoring process. It consisted of swallowing a vial of material containing genetic instructions that tailored themselves to her biology. She had to wear gloves for a week to protect the formation of receptors on her palms and fingertips. The receptors themselves were smooth ovals of skin that contained cells similar to those in the nose and brain that interpreted pheromone information in all humans. These cells, however, were not activated by airborne pheromones. They were only activated when they came in contact with the interstice membrane, which was made of highly specialized material.

The most difficult part of becoming receptored had to do with training. Marie spent hundreds of hours of biofeedback training in which she learned the universal Mindscript being used, which resembled pictographs. Envisioning concepts in Mindscript and learning Mindscript grammar gradually became second nature, since it was a very intuitive language, and drugs were administered that caused the brain to mimic certain aspects of early learning conditions. Envisioning Mindscript caused precise electrical activity in the brain. This was endemic to the individual, but feedback produced the precise focus needed in order to communicate fluently.

Marie's thoughts were then converted into metapheromones within the receptors, which was a hormonal process engendered by an implant. The metapheromones were transmitted to the reengineered DNA of the *E. coli* within the interstices, which flowed upward and were transmuted into pollenlike analogs held within large genetically engineered flowers. Creatures that looked a lot like bees, but which were as large as a four-year old child, ferried the information between buildings.

Marie had set up the meeting with Dighton today by using her receptors.

In the future, of course, all of these steps would probably become much more streamlined and require about as much conscious work to learn as breathing.

"Dighton," said Marie, "you know that we're subject to constant FDA monitoring. If we can prove that it's really the FBI that's using this information—"

"I'll have to go over the licensing agreement," he said. "But doesn't the monitoring fall under the auspices of quality control? They have to be able to shut down the programs to protect everyone in case of some kind of imbalance."

"That's just an excuse for them to spy on us. We can hire our own private nanotech engineers to do quality control."

"That's definitely disallowed in the licensing agreement. That's grounds for them pulling the program. And, as I recall—" There was a moment's silence as Dighton stared at his glasses, across which information invisible to Marie flowed. "Yes, here it is. Paragraph twenty-one. New Orleans would still owe them $200 million for the setup. But instead of the city making payments, it would become due in its entirety immediately. I told you that Mayor Ransom shouldn't sign this, despite the enthusiastic support you whipped up."

"Everybody's pretty happy with it," Marie said. "You have to admit. We haven't had reliable telephone service for years. And now we can get the news—warped though it probably is. But the problem is, how do we get rid of the government snoops?"

"You mean, how do we steal the program?"

"You got it, Dighton."

He sighed. "The only thing I have is a headache, Marie." He stood. "Let me do some research, all right? I'll get back to you in a few days. But taking this through the courts will probably take years."

"I'm aware of that, Dighton," she said. "Come over to the window. Don't those old-fashioned lilies and roses set off the French Quarter beautifully?"

They gazed down at a bizarre garden, bounded by the brown curve of the Mississippi on one side and Lake Pontchartrain on the other. "I feel as if we're on the move again. We're alive again. The blackout was horrible."

"Yes," he said. "We're on the move like the Confederacy was on the move."

"But we're on the right side, Dighton."

"Sometimes that doesn't matter."

"It always matters."

She turned her thoughts to Hugo.

He had been gone for years. Recruiting. The highly qualified people flocking to New Orleans were due to his tireless efforts. But something had happened. She hoped desperately that he was all right. Apparently, horrific changes had recently occurred in Japan. And the latest fitful news had it that some kind of terrorist transformation plague was sweeping through central Europe. These were frightful times. She was glad that at least here in New Orleans one or two eminent scientists or city planners arrived every month. She sent many of them on to the fast-growing floating city.

They were calling it Crescent City.

The last she had heard from Hugo was through Kita. A brief message saying that he had been injured, that he was recovering, and that some unforeseeable problems had occurred. And not to wait up for him. He might not be home for many months. The message was delivered by a bike courier and bore the stamps of the six private mail agencies it had passed through during the month it took to get to Marie.

She wished she had never asked him to leave.

Transformative Syncopations

Jason | Los Angeles | 2038

Jason and Abbie danced in golden fields, wheat wind-bent and brushing them as they wove through waist-high grain, information flowering within them, the prepared targets of its broadcast, dictating their every move. No earthly instrument transcribed the precision of the singing in their heads, in their bones, in their blood. Each movement subtly reprogrammed neuronal patterns, and the dance went on and on, long past sundown, and lasted all their lives, as they changed, and changed, and changed again, pulled by light past telling—

Jason sat up and hit his head on the roof of the junkyard trailer in which he slept. The air was thick with the smoke of the smoldering fires that dotted the junkyard and his eyes burned. The dream was always the same. It always woke him with a blaze of light. He always felt tired, hopeless, and discouraged when he opened his eyes. And now his head ached.

He tucked in his shirt, buckled his belt, grabbed his pack, and slipped out of the ruined trailer, leaving the door hanging open. The sky was graying toward dawn as he stumbled through the debris of the junkyard, the flotsam of the previous century, heavily defended against those who tried to reorganize its matter with transformative nan by a fierce—if nonorganized—impromptu army of bums.

Jason had only a few miles to go. He'd been oddly reluctant to venture into the fray of the Festival to End All Festivals and even now wanted to turn back.

But the darkness within drove him on.

Now sunlight colored the haze. A breeze picked up and the sky begin to clear—gradually, at first, and then instantly, fully, as if a light had been switched on. Instead of being swathed in softening oblivion, the crushed, jumbled buildings below, many of them partially submerged in crystalline ocean, were clear in every detail, as if he had hawk's eyes. Blackened ridges ran down to the sea, having shrugged off their burden of strip malls, roads, and houses in fiery paroxysms that came and went for several weeks, transforming the geography of the West Coast the previous year. Since then, Jason had been staying in one of the relatively undamaged pockets. He felt like he'd passed through the eye of a needle into a season of hell. It was a strangely ambient hell, but a hell all the same, one which he'd just realized might never end. It hadn't so far.

The morning was now astonishingly clear. Mornings were often astonishingly clear if the winds were just right, for the carbon-monoxide-eating particles were transparent and some claimed lent a sparkle to things after the transformational snap—a very slightly audible crackle when they did their communal stuff all in the same instance—hence their name. When released, five years ago, Snaps were not FDA-approved, but Los Angeles did not care. No one seemed to care about the government in Washington, D.C., anymore, and the farther one got from it, the less people cared. Anarchy was the rule. Los Angeles had declared itself a sovereign nation with all the rights appertaining thereto, and a grand transnational celebration had ensued, Latin in nature, a Day of the Dead writ large.

Jason topped a rise and glimpsed the infant Dome, a hemisphere of light bulging on the mountain's flank a few miles away. As usual, it seemed to have swelled overnight. He blinked, looking around. He would never get used to the way the air cleared so suddenly—really, an oddly minor detail in the midst of so much change—if he lived a hundred years. He laughed bitterly. Why not? A hundred years of this. He already looked about forty, perhaps, even though he was only twenty-three. After leaving Abbie, he had quickly aged and he did not know if it was something that would have happened to him anyway, given his anomalous biology, or perhaps something Abbie had done to him in those weeks when his doppelgänger had vanished and Jason had audibly and frequently hoped that he would be able to survive on his own, when Abbie had insisted, more and more frantically, that Jason2 had been created to die and must be tracked to his death. And if Abbie had done this thing, had it been in revenge for his withdrawal from their plan or had it been to give him protection? Had she changed something vital within him as well? Did this aging mean that he would die soon? He went back to find her, those two years ago, to demand answers, when his fast aging seemed a certainty, to see if perhaps she was changing too, but her whole neighborhood had transmuted to Victorian houses with large porches and big chrome-laden cars parked out front, the way it had been in the late forties.

Jason walked through an empty thoroughfare that zigzagged down the mountain. Suncars littered the streets as if people had been raptured out of them entire; doorways stood open and he could see inside to well-kept living rooms, some of them with activated holograms playing. He'd overnighted in more than one house but had come to prefer the junkyard to the memories of others' lives that populated each house. They reminded him of his own family—and of his failure to find his mother. This morning would be his last out here. There was no point to it anymore.

This outer ring was relatively empty. Jason could have moved more quickly. He could have gotten into one of the suncars and threaded his way along the road, at least until he came to a serious rumple in the road. The suncars were without value now, at least, right here they were. Just about everything was without value now, at least to looters, since it could be so easily replicated. Those who wanted a lot of stuff had it and lived in heavily guarded enclaves in the hills, preparing for the post-stuff era they believed was coming soon. It seemed to Jason that everyone saw a new age coming soon, all of them spectacularly different. But for most people, the necessity of owning physical things had evolved into an odd mixture of spiritual thirst spiked with the first tang of a variety of available immortalities. Genetic engineering. Which he could probably have—if he cared to bother. On-the-spot gene-repair clinics. Hormonal transformation. And . . . the Dome.

He approached a short strip of storefronts and saw that a café door stood open. The sign outside read NEW SHIPMENT OF BRAZILIAN CHILDHOOD CERTIFIED PURE BY OUR OWN CHEMISTS. An ever-changing sphere of rain forest hanging in the doorway advertised the possible experience that one might have—for several hours or for a dazed lifetime. "Damp," whispered voices, "Cool, Chlorophyll Vision Guaranteed" amid a lacing of Indian flutes as he passed through it. He bought coffee and a donut, turned down the proffered squirt of "Brazilian Childhood Certified Pure," suffered the sphere again, and sat on a bench out front, sipping coffee, next to a teenage girl who had a chatting disorder. At least she looked like a teenage girl. She might have been a banker or a grounded astronaut, willingly or unwillingly transformed. It was hard to tell these days.

"It must have been like this when the pioneers came," she said, her voice breathless. "You know, back in the 1920s. When they started

Hollywood and all. When it was nothing but orange groves. It's hard to believe how primitive it was. Hardly any shopping. Real quiet, like this. Hear those birds? Mmm, smell those orange blossoms!"

Jason nodded, chewed, watched the Dome shimmer, almost invisible as the sun rose higher. The ocean was a brilliant blue. The girl pointed. "My boyfriend is down there. He's a surfer. They shoot the strip. That's what they call it: 'shooting the strip.' The waves are monster."

A middle-aged man progressed down the street, dipping a rag in a bucket, rubbing the posts of streetlights, doors, storefronts—every surface within reach. Jason mildly wondered what he was doing—or what he thought he was doing. Life was a circus, and he was weary of it. Other people, whom he was sure resembled celebrities he'd never heard of, made their way toward the café now that the air had snapped, chatting, laughing.

Insane.

Those interested in this slow primitive life outside the Dome were engaged in restoring many of the old neighborhoods, which generated much rancor when discussions of mood and tone became necessary. It was as if an entire city of writers, directors, and mood generators were given their own studios. Unfortunately, territories often overlapped. A carefully engineered noir neighborhood might be superseded overnight by a surprise attack of "I Love Lucy" followed by bitter reprisals of, say, *What Ever Happened to Baby Jane?* in blocks previously devoted to "Road Runner" cartoons. Everyone was young and beautiful and went around with snifters of early Eastwood, Monroe, Brando, or Dietrich in their bags, spouting bits of dialogue, striking poses.

Jason noticed that some Flowers were opening atop some sunken downtown buildings, but there were only about three, and the buildings they serviced were partially submerged in swirls of shark-infested currents. Los Angeles's BioCity days had been cut short by the quake, coupled with the ongoing melting of the polar ice caps. A flyer skittered along the sidewalk and fluttered upward. The girl grabbed it.

"Haven't you heard that?" Jason asked as her touch generated the embedded audio of Polly Newface's famous "Dome or Doom" speech:

"We—the newly formed Gaian, Extropian, and Psychic Coalition—the PEGS—are willing to move boldly into the new era of complete and instantaneous communication. There will be no death in the Dome. We shall only grow in wisdom and in luminosity. The dome will be self-sustaining, solar-powered, made of light, so that it will not deplete the Earth's bounty

*any longer. Those of you who are Gaians will have the oppor-
tunity to resolve the dilemma of having to sustain your bodies
by killing and, what is worse, by being forced to use technologies which are proving deadly to our Mother Earth. You can
simply leave your body behind, but not by dying. By living
more fully. For those of you who wish to become pure information—that time has now—"*

Jason grabbed the paper from the girl's hand and tore it to shreds
methodically. Polly's speech became stuttering fragments that floated
toward the sidewalk. "Ever." "Med." "Indel." Then the words blew
away on the breeze.

"Why did you do that?" the girl asked with more sadness than
irritation.

More than one psychic turned in his or her union card after that
speech and resigned from the Coalition, claiming that their support
had been betrayed. "If everyone knows everything, what's the point?"
they asked. "This is going to put us out of business." Some of them
just couldn't handle the idea and hove to the hinterlands of Arizona
or Oregon.

It all had to do with the earthquake, of course. The earthquake
had not only changed the physical face of L.A., leveling the downtown
to rubble, shattering the freeways past easy healing, but it had changed
the psychological complexion of the city. With so much death and
destruction in one's face, perhaps the only way to respond was to
retreat to fantasy, dwell in the false, in the past, to yield to the nanotech storytellers, which would restore one's past life or any past life
one might want to have had. After the fires, strange seeds bloomed in
the hearts and minds of the city folk. They were ready for a change.
For those who felt that Los Angeles existed in the confluence of mighty
rivers of positive psychic forces, no other location would do. For those
who had always called it home and wished to re-create it and revisit
its every face again and again, there was no other option. Watts, slums,
racial tension, all that was folded into the mix too, Jason feared, for
it was all human and the Dome would be nothing but human. All
human. Human at its best and at its worst. Wholly artificial. It was a
great wonder that any Gaians at all would want to condone it. Some
said that strange glowing beings from the Silicon Valley had wandered
in overnight and started the baby dome, then infiltrated the Psychics,
the Gaians, and the Extropians, whose neural architecture would be
read into the Dome, become part of its exponentially growing referen-
tial power. So much wisdom, they claimed. As if you had lived every
life in there. Had access to the memories. Yet you could if you wished

retain your node of individuality; maintain the illusion of having a body, a house, any life you might dream of. Every mental experience imaginable was available within, and many more now unimaginable promised. It reminded Jason of nothing so much as the mini-dome he'd seen at Abbie's.

But there was no point in puzzling about why someone would want to give themselves over to the Dome. At least not for Jason; for him, it seemed marginally more interesting than suicide. It was certain, with the vast changes of the past several years, that no one was looking for Jason, or anyone with his blood type, any longer. He often longed for his father and mother, felt deep grief that he had lost them forever that evening he took off in Dog Leg. His feelings about Abbie were mixed. But still strong. Still abiding.

"Sorry," Jason told the girl, still holding a shred of flyer that said VITAMINS. VIGAMINS. VIGATOMS. VIGATACE. "Lost my head." He finished his coffee, rose, and joined the increasing flow of pilgrims.

He'd watched the long lines at the portals, which never shrank, toying with the idea of transformation, wondering what his strange biology might do to the mix. And, he had to admit, half hoping to see his mother there. If she was still alive—and he had some old shreds of evidence that she had come to L.A., long ago, to find him—this was surely where she would come, eventually. But he'd always turned away. Until this morning. He trooped with the rest of them, lemminglike, block after block, turn after turn.

"You gonna do it?" asked a woman who looked like young Judy Garland as she fell in next to him. A little Toto ran along at her feet. Light voices sang, "We're out of the woods, we're out of the dark, we're out of the night—"

Jason wondered vaguely how the sound was generated and nodded.

"It'll be good, won't it. I've been going to the Church of the Transformation. They say that it's like St. Anselm said. You remember St. Anselm?"

Jason nodded, though he had no idea who Anselm was. He would have preferred to be alone with his thoughts, but what did it matter?

"He said that God is that which cannot be conceived of by human thought. Or whatever. Something like that, you know. It's something that you couldn't possibly imagine, no matter how hard you try. 'Cause everything you imagine is not . . . grand enough, because you're human, just one human, and what's in there is so very many humans, how many now?" Her words mingled with a faint "Over the Rainbow."

At every portal, a tally was kept: twenty-foot-high glowing numbers, increasing constantly as people fed into the many portals around the Dome.

"I don't know," said Jason.

"Well, you don't seem very excited," she said, a hurt tone in her voice. "I'm not sure if you're quite ready. You might . . ."

"Pollute things?" suggested Jason.

"Well, I didn't say that."

They were now walking in the midst of a crowd. As they topped a hill, he stopped and let his companion go on.

And then—

A blond ponytail up ahead, among the barkers, the hucksters, the Tribe of the Gladly Impure, who relieved the pilgrims of all things of value and fed them into their transformers in the Old City where the sea lapped against a breakwater of rubble. Jason's heart pounded.

He'd seen other blond ponytails and been fooled by them, combing the city streets. He'd returned to Dog Leg, of course, as soon as he dared, and found their house empty, his father's grave on the mountainside. His mother left an address in Los Angeles for him, but when he got there, she'd been gone for months and the wealthy client barely remembered her. "Oh yes, I let her live in the garden house for a while. She changed my life. What was her name again?"

Jason had posted countless bulletins in the brief BioCity, did whatever he could, but he had never found her.

Still, he ran, pushing through the crowd, calling out, "Mom! Mom!" until he was behind her and she turned—

He stared for an instant into her unmistakable eyes. He said nothing, just hugged her tightly while she said, "Jason?" She pushed him back and stared at him with puzzled eyes, then they both burst out laughing, eyes locked.

"It is you," she said. "But—"

"And you! I never saw you look this young—"

"Ah," she said, "there's no reason to look old now. But you—what happened? Is it—"

"I'm not sure what happened," he said, chattering madly. "Not at all. It really doesn't matter. Oh, Mom, I was going to—I was going to get in line today. But now I'm not going to! I'm so happy! I'm so glad to find you alive. Let's leave. Let's go somewhere. Anywhere. Colorado. Sedona, even . . ."

And then they were both overwhelmed by sadness, sobbing in one another's arms. "How did it happen?" whispered Jason.

"It was just sudden," she said, drawing back. Behind her the Dome arched away like some massive rainbow. "Your father died in his sleep. I don't know why. We looked for you everywhere. He was devastated. I was too, but he took it so hard. No—don't look that way. It wasn't your fault. You did the right thing. You did what you had to do. Your father didn't have anything to fall back on, like I did. I knew you were alive"—her voice was fierce—"but he didn't. He never really believed the same things I did. I think it just wore him out. He didn't care if he lived or died. He kept going over and over everything. He should have gone into town that day with you. We should have moved overseas when you were little. We should have this, we should have that, until it was about to drive me crazy. But I understood."

Jason was quiet, remembering his father. How strong he had been. Infusing his life with meaning. Being there when he was sick—and weak. Teaching him how to survive—

"There's something you need to know, Jason," said Cassie. "I've taken the pledge."

"You what?"

"I'm a PEG. Fully certified. Ready to go. We get priority, you know."

Jason struggled with many reactions. Finally he said, "I was ready to go too an hour ago. That's what I came down here to do."

Her eyes lit. "We'll go together, then! I'm sure I can get you in with me—"

"But now I don't want to go. I only wanted to go because everything seemed so meaningless. So useless. Now that I've found you—"

"Jason," she said gently, "everything has changed for me. This is not something I want to do because I feel hopeless. Quite the opposite. This is all that I've ever wanted—besides you being well and normal. It's transcendence. It will heal the Earth." Her voice became low, anxious. "I had a vision, Jason. It was . . . do you know anything about the Great Famine in Ireland?"

"No."

"Your many-times-great-grandparents were from Ireland, and I read a lot about it when I was young. The land was plucked bare. It was scoured of any possible thing that could serve as food—even grasses. Thistles, nettles, anything. Absolutely bare. And my vision was of the entire Earth like this. Plucked bare. We are part of a galactic ecology, Jason. I know that you don't believe this, but someday you will. This is something I've felt—and seen—since before you were born. And *you're part of it!* You're important in a special way—a way that we don't understand. I'm convinced of it. Don't you see?"

"No. I don't see."

"If all of us go into the Dome, the Earth can be healed. Maybe with everyone's shared knowledge, we'll understand why you're here. And the galaxies will be rebalanced—"

"What the hell good is the Earth without people? Saturn doesn't have people. Venus doesn't have people. So what? People are—are people!" Others were staring at him. He realized that he was shouting. He continued in a lower voice. "We can make a difference out *here*. We have everything to live for—now!"

"Jason, honey, I'm *not dying*! I'll live forever!" Her upturned face was wet with tears.

"How do you know? Has anyone ever come out of there?"

Her face assumed the patient expression he remembered so well. "Those inside can communicate, of course. It's hard to get them to communicate, though, but there have been reports—"

"Just like death, isn't it! Like communicating with the dead! Oh, didn't someone knock? Look, the spirits are spelling *b-u-l-l-s-h-i-t* on the Ouija board—"

"Jason! I won't have you talk about my beliefs in that tone of voice!"

"I'm sorry," he said. "Just—just put it off for a while. A day or two. A week. Please. Give me a little time with you. I've missed you so." He was sobbing like a little boy now, holding her shoulders tightly, wanting to fall to the ground and grab onto her legs. His entire heart was in his plea. *Mommy, please don't go.*

"I . . ." she began, her voice doubtful. She looked over at the Dome.

He saw her face light once again with the look he'd seen since he was tiny. Her mark. If one single visage could illuminate one's hopes and beliefs, one's core, this was it. She was right. This was truly what she had yearned for—always.

Part of Jason dropped away at that moment. His childhood vanished in a flare of sunlight reflected from the Dome. He took his mother's hand and held it within both of his.

"I'm sorry, Cassie," he said. "I love you. I love you with all my heart. Go with my blessing. Thank you for everything you've done for me. Mother."

She blinked. Tears overflowed.

"I love you too, Jason. You know that. With my very life and being. When you were a little boy . . ." She paused for a moment, then wiped her eyes. "I couldn't have asked for anything more. But now—can you forgive me?"

"There's nothing to forgive." His heart quailed within him as he said, "Can I—can I walk you over there?"

He gave his mother over to the portal guards after a long hug. "Stay well," he said foolishly.

She whispered, "Join us if you can, Jason. I love you."

He wasn't sure if they would let him watch, but he didn't want to. He turned abruptly and walked blindly into the crowd.

*　　*　　*

The coast road was still foggy, Jason found as he made his damp way north. The short bitter Snaps War had been fought between the Mid-State Greens and the Los Angelans, limiting by treaty the type of particles Snaps were allowed to transform and their potency. They were designed to disintegrate after forty-eight hours and were pumped from an underground station on the Mexican border. So far, their effects were successfully contained. At any rate, they probably wouldn't have affected fog, yet the Greens were fearful that heavy fogs, crucial to ecosystem balance, might be subtly changed by some side effects of the Snaps.

Sunset colored the Pacific. There was little traffic here. NAMS— or whatever sections of it had survived the earthquake—serviced the L.A. to San Francisco route. It was, apparently, busily rebuilding itself and would soon go right into the Dome. Jason couldn't really imagine what that would be like, any more than he could imagine what manner of being his mother was now. He felt like ashes.

His boots trod wavy pothole-filled asphalt, broken away at the edges. He was in no hurry. He had been walking for two days now. Deer foraged nearby on the steep hillsides. Occasionally, driveways led off into the wilderness. He passed signs for old bed-and-breakfasts. It felt good to walk. In his pack, he carried bread, cheese, wine, and candy bars. Late afternoon on the previous day he had made his precarious way down to an outcropping fifty feet above the ocean, and his mind was cleansed by a night of the surf's thunder.

Now the evening chilled in sunset's afterglow. Jason started looking around for a likely camping spot. He was surprised to hear the sound of a car behind him, far, then closing in. Headlights emerged from the last fold of the highway and they belonged to an old Jeep. It was pulling a trailer full of large metal canisters.

His heart contracted as memories of his Jeep effervesced. Well, it was part of his old life. That life would never return.

The hardtop slowed and stopped next to him. A man of perhaps fifty was driving. "Hop in," he said. Why not? Jason threw his pack in the back and took a seat.

"Going anywhere in particular?" the man asked. He had a white beard and wore a red plaid shirt beneath overalls.

"San Francisco, I guess." Jason leaned back in the seat, feeling the muscles in his legs contract.

"Not going that far, but I can get you close," said the man. "Got some methanol to deliver. Make it myself. Well, actually, my good old chickens do a lot of the work. What's an old guy like you doing hiking to San Francisco?" asked the man.

"Oh," said Jason, as usual at a loss at the assumption that he had a lot more experience than he actually did. "Just want to see it."

"What's left of it, you mean. I guess it's better off than L.A. Functioning. But I'm just not the type of man to want to crowd into a place like that. Give me my farm, my vegetables, my fruit, my chickens. My own little house. A good strong wind to keep away the goddamned Snaps and anything else might blow up from the city. Don't want to get mixed up in that nonsense. Got a daughter who went there. Years ago. Haven't heard from her since. She never was one for keeping in touch. She might still be there. Heck of a thing." He drove in the center of the road, straddling faded double yellow lines.

He dropped Jason off an hour before dawn as he turned off the coast road. "Here's where I drop this stuff off. They got a mill here; I'm going to lay in some flour and corn meal. San Francisco is right over that rise." He laughed. "Can't miss it! Sure you don't need a place to stay?"

"Nah," said Jason. "I got my tent."

"All right, Captain. Stay good." The Jeep jolted down the overgrown road and its taillights vanished.

Jason was tired, cold, and hungry. But there was a glow over the horizon. He continued on.

Maybe his future lay here. He didn't know what his future would be. But he knew that San Franciso had no dome. That was all he cared about right now.

That and learning as much about nanotechnology as he could.

His education had been disrupted since he'd left home. More than the Earth had fractured. A huge fault line divided his life with his parents and his life today, and the whole world seemed to have changed in that time. But it was knowledge, more than anything, that he felt would heal him. He was tired of kicking around on the fringes of things, skulking and hiding, knowing less and less. The motto emblazoned on one of his elementary school notebooks said KNOWLEDGE IS POWER. He did not particularly aspire to any kind of power, but he definitely did not like being powerless.

He topped the rise and stood still while a strong wind rushed upward and assailed him.

The land plunged away beneath him like darkness itself. Spread out on the hills below was a fairy-tale city.

It glimmered against the coming dawn. Jason picked out the vertical lines of the interstices, through which flowed raw information piggybacked on the DNA of a certain pure laboratory-evolved strain of *E. coli*. It could be accessed by touch. The interstices ran like neon pinstripes up the sides of the buildings. Above, huge Flowerlike entities, where the information emerged to be carried from building to building, remained open. They seemed to be moving in the wind. That was one of the limitations of Flower Cities—anything moving between the tops of the buildings was subjected to the vagaries of weather. But in an earthquake-prone area, underground pipes were just as impractical. Not only that, central processing centers were necessary for assembling the information; it had a tendency to degrade if the system was too large. Apparently, there was a lot of work being done on moving beyond the Flower model, but for the time being, this prototype seemed to have taken the world by storm, with minor variations, mainly because old-fashioned computers were casualties of whatever was causing radio silence. And they worked. They worked beyond anyone's wildest dreams.

Jason's receptors were for Los Angeles. He would have to have them modified before he would be able to access the San Francisco system.

He stood for a moment, taking it in. The great bridge had been ruined and lay slanting crazily into the bay. From this distance, it looked like a toy.

He had spent his whole life avoiding people. Avoiding what they might find out about him, avoiding capture. Living with a three-person survival team in the wilderness. He wanted to be a part of something. He wanted to do something, change something. And to do that, you had to know something. This was the nearest place to L.A. where he might be able to do that.

He owed this to his father. And whether she believed it or not, if indeed she was still capable of such things as belief, he owed it to his mother as well.

But mostly he owed it to himself.

He was in Chinatown several weeks later, having tea.

He loved his new receptors. They were small ovals on his fingertips. San Francisco was much more advanced, more complex, than L.A. had been. When he touched an interstice with his receptors, he was flooded with information. At first it had been overwhelming, but then he learned to use his filtering capabilities. He had an address. Anyone could track him, once he touched something. He didn't care. He was tired of running, tired of hiding.

He sat at a small table, reading, having finished the noodles he'd ordered by tapping the table menu, which switched to a table surface proclaiming it to be the Year of the Horse when he completed his decisions. After about thirty seconds, the Year of the Horse was overwhelmed by swarming, flashing ads, which he ignored. Instead, he pulled up a text on lithium interfaces and studied it, using some of the credit he'd amassed by commanding a layer of the table to loosen. He peeled up his text, which was now embedded in a thin light substance, scooted back into the booth, crossed his legs on the seat, and read by the soft internal glow of the stuff. He was slowly training his brain to absorb information in other ways, but if you did that, you still had a sorting process to go through and he liked reading better. Many people did. He found that he was able to retain a lot of information and build on it. It was quite satisfying. He thought that he would enjoy being an engineer.

"Don't you think it's rude to put your feet on the seat?" It was a woman's voice. It was familiar. He looked up, heart pounding. "Abbie?"

It was questionable. But the sound of her voice had caused him to blurt out her name. In fact, she didn't look anything like Abbie. Her eyes were black and her eyelids lacked epicanthic folds. Her hair was straight and black. Her skin was somewhat weathered. "Abbie?" he said again, definitely puzzled.

"Yeah," she said, sliding into the booth opposite him. He set down his text and watched it melt back into the table. Inside he was trembling. Questions seethed.

"What are you doing here?"

"I'd say, 'The same thing as you,' but it wouldn't be true. I'm getting ready to go to China."

"China? Why?"

"I only came when I found you were here because . . ." She looked down at her hands for a moment. "I only came because I thought you might want to go too."

"Why would I want to do that?" Damn her. She generated too many questions. He had a thousand and wanted to shake the answer for each one out of her.

"Because I've heard that we're building a space launch there."

"We?"

"Yeah. People like you and me."

"Right." He swung his feet to the floor and put his elbows on the table. "What am I like anyway, Abbie? How come I've aged so much? Why do I think that you know why?"

She cleared her voice and looked nervously from side to side. She sighed. "You're right," she said. "I . . . I was a lot younger then, I guess. I wanted to disguise you. In case the . . . the other thing didn't work."

He slammed his fist on the table and a bottle of soy sauce jumped.

"You might have asked me. I might have wanted in on the decision." His voice was strangled; it was hard to get the words out. "You have a lot of nerve."

"I always have," she said, her voice steady.

"And you're sure it wasn't to . . . to hurt me for not going along with your plan."

"*My* plan!" Her narrow eyes widened. "Whose idea was it? You came to me!" Tears glittered in her eyes. "I *loved* you, Jason. I wanted to hide you—hide us—keep us safe—" She controlled her face with obvious difficulty and wiped her eyes on her sleeve.

Jason sighed. He reached over and took her hand. "Oh well," he said. "I don't much mind looking like an old fart. You look kind of striking yourself. Having fun?"

She glared at him. "I just thought it would be a good idea to kind of fit in when I got over there. I'm working on my Mandarin."

"It's probably not all that hard for you," he said. He dropped her hand and looked at her keenly.

"No. Actually, it's pretty easy. Just like everything else. Except you." After a short pause, she said, "So, you want to go?"

"Run that by me again."

"People like us—you do accept that there are other people like us, don't you? It's true, those things I told you in L.A. About us having expanded capacity for sensing electromagnetic data. We're kind of like birds in that way. It's what helps them migrate. We still don't understand why."

"It does raise a few questions for me. Where are all the rest of—of 'us'?"

"Not all of us worked out, Jason. That's the truth of it. In fact, most of the kids were flawed somehow. A lot of miscarriages. A lot of cognitive mental handicaps. A lot of biochemical problems and insanity. Deaths. But we're going to take all of us that we can find. Liberate others from government camps. It's our duty. We're like family. We have to stick together."

He didn't know why he was even listening to this nonsense. "How do you know all this?"

"The guy from the government that I blackmailed told me."

He shrugged. "Well, whatever the problem is, it's a problem. Done nothing positive for me."

"We think it might. Eventually. Anyway, there's a pretty dedicated group of people like us in China and they're building a spacecraft. At least that's the plan. It might take decades, considering the state of the world right now. I'm going to be working on the project. In fact, I'm going to have to leave soon."

"And where is this spacecraft going? Assuming it will fly."

"I don't have any doubt about that," she said. "And it's going to the source of the Signal."

"Really."

"Yes, really. Why do you have that tone in your voice?"

"Because I think it's all bullshit."

"I thought so. But it's not."

"I think that you're right about us being unusual. But so what? We have no idea why this has happened. I think it's just some kind of mutation from a cosmic ray that washed across the Earth at some point—if you really want to know. Genetic mutations are not all that unusual, Abbie. Everything's such a mess now. Nobody's looking for us anymore."

"Don't count on it."

"I just want to live a normal human life."

She burst out laughing. "Oh, Jason. You're such an idiot. What's a normal human life anymore?"

"I don't care," he said stubbornly. "Normal is what I make it. I don't want to run away. Everyone's running away. I want to stay."

"What do you mean, 'everyone'?"

He almost told her about his mother. Then he didn't. It was too recent, too personal. He didn't want to talk about it to anyone.

"I'm an American. I'm not Chinese. I've lived all over this country. Mostly in the West. Where have you ever been, Abbie, besides the West Coast? North America is beautiful."

"It's beautiful in China too, I think. And way beautiful in space." Her eyes shone. "And when I get there, I'll *know*."

He didn't bother to ask what she'd know. She'd know what his mother knew. Some kind of nonsensical transcendent otherness. "Well, suit yourself." He slid toward the side of the booth.

She caught his hand. "Please don't run away, Jason. I'll be gone soon enough." Her voice was small and quiet. "I'm sorry." She looked at him imploringly. "I really am."

"All right,"he said, standing. "All right, Abbie."

She rushed into his arms and he embraced her. What now? he thought.

"It was a bad idea, I guess," Abbie said. She sat up, stared out the window at the steel-gray bay.

Jason ran a finger down her spine. "No, it wasn't," he said gently. "I've just been through a lot in the past few years. I'm different. And so are you."

"I always thought we were the same," she said, her voice stubborn.

"We're the same in one small way, I suppose. But that's not enough to base a—"

"A what?"

"A relationship on," he said doggedly. "We want different things. We're two very different people. You want to fly away into space somewhere, and . . ."

"Don't *you*?" she asked, turning around and facing him. She pulled a blanket over her shoulders.

"No," he said, surprised. "It's never crossed my mind."

"It's all I've wanted, since I was little. It's what I was saving for in Los Angeles. I wanted to at least go to the Mars colony."

"I thought that was abandoned."

She laughed sarcastically. "You'll believe whatever they tell you, won't you? No, it's still there. Still triangulating. Still transmitting, whenever the signal gets through."

"What do you mean, 'triangulating'?"

"I mean, between the Earth, the moon, and Mars, they can calculate exactly where the Signal is coming from."

Her voice was excited. She'd talked a lot about the Signal in Los Angeles. He'd kind of believed her then. Now he didn't believe in much of anything or anyone.

"Jason. Don't you remember when the headaches went away?"

He wanted to say no, but he did.

"And don't you remember when the music started?"

He sighed. They'd talked about this a thousand times, so eagerly, so excited. He and she called it "music," automatically. But it was much weirder than anything anyone had the nerve to call "music." "I guess."

"It's all coming from the Signal. That's been established."

"Established by who?"

"Well, the people in China."

"How do you communicate with these people in China?"

"We send news packets back and forth by clipper ship. Also of course radio when it's working." Which was more and more rare. Hardly at all anymore.

Jason pushed himself up and rested against the headboard. "It's all kid stuff," he said. "You've got to grow up some time."

"You grow up," she said, getting out of bed and dressing. "I've got too much to do." She looked at him, sighed, and left the room, closing the door quietly behind her.

*   *   *

He saw her off at the pier a few months later. The *China Queen* was held fast by thick ropes, and supplies were being carried up the gangplank. Huge bare masts held furled sails.

"It's pretty strange, don't you think? Taking a clipper ship so I can fly in a spacecraft?" Abbie held his hand tightly.

"Mm-hmm." Once again someone was leaving him. He was almost sorry he'd spent the last few months with her. He thought what he was doing here was taking a crash course in engineering. All kinds of engineering. And using it as a basis for understanding BioCities so that he could go into them, work in them, as a civil engineer.

Instead, he realized, the chief thing he'd done in the past few months, though he had certainly done all the engineering education he'd planned and more, was that he'd gotten used to Abbie. He'd forgiven her. He'd gone beyond forgiveness. He'd fallen in love with her again.

But she was a fanatic. He wanted to save her from her fanaticism, and she wanted to save him from his inability to accept his true being. It was a parting of the ways that seemed inevitable.

But he pulled her close and hugged her. "Oh, Abbie, don't go," he said.

"Why don't you come with me?"

But they'd been through all that and its infinite variations a thousand times. He just hugged her more tightly.

"Please," she whispered. "Change your mind."

"I can't," he said and was surprised that it seemed as if his heart was breaking.

Jason hitchhiked northeast from San Francisco three months after Abbie left. He spent the time completing basic nanotech engineering courses and becoming certified. The city, which automatically and impersonally awarded him his certificate of completion and lodged it within his DNA in the privacy of his own apartment, most certainly had access to his genome. Yet it did not comment on his genetic orientation; no one sought him out; no one came to take him away, though he was, he realized later, braced for that possibility. Of course, San Francisco had a lot of laws concerning individual freedom. Perhaps he wouldn't be so fortunate elsewhere.

But he had to go elsewhere.

He hitchhiked across rough, dry country in early winter, struck anew by its grandeur and beauty.

The farther he got from the coast, the harder it was to find rides. One day he walked till afternoon. Ten or fifteen vehicles passed him during the day without stopping. Around three in the afternoon, he was jolted by a dopplered honk; a hand holding a pistol emerged from a window of a westbound car and squeezed off several shots directed nowhere in particular. Their reports rang in his ears as Jason watched the car vanish into the distance.

He wasn't sure what to do. The previous night had brought a light dusting of snow and clouds promised more. He carried his tent and sleeping bag in his pack, but wasn't particularly excited about striking out across open country to avoid the road. Yet that might be the safest thing to do.

A sign he'd just passed promised that Haven's Crossing was only six miles ahead; another solar billboard loomed ahead, its battery obviously low, dimly proclaiming the existence of the Western Inn, with restaurant and an all-you-can-eat buffet.

Hyperaware of his surroundings now, Jason half-jogged, his pack snugged close to his back, hoping to get there before dark. He heard a car approaching behind him and veered off toward some rocks. He heard it stop and doubled his speed. A voice called out, "Want a ride?"

He allowed himself a quick glance and saw that it was not the shooter's car. It was a pickup truck. "I ain't got all day," the bearded man yelled. He was wearing overalls.

Jason paused, turned, and walked toward the truck. There was no room in the back of the truck, so he squeezed his pack onto the floor of the cab and climbed in after it.

He saw that his benefactor was perhaps fifty. Jason was starting to look younger. The gray was going out of his hair; his muscles were firming up easily. Abbie. She'd probably done something while he slept. He didn't like to think about it. But he looked an age with this man.

The driver said, "Name's Howitz. Yours?" He put the truck in gear.

"Peabody. How far you going?"

"Salt Lake."

"That'll do." Jason leaned back and found the aroma of pipe tobacco pleasant. They quickly arrived at Haven's Crossing and Jason saw that it was empty too; the windows of the Western Inn were smashed and a small grid of streets seemed to have no sign of life.

"Glad you picked me up," said Jason. "I was planning on spending the night there."

"I might not have if I hadn't seen you run off. If you meant harm, you wouldn't have tried to hide. I reckon you've had a hell of a time getting rides in this part of the country. We've been suffering. Some young woman—a stranger—let go a plague there in Haven's Crossing about six months ago."

"A plague?"

"Plague of some kind of Shambala nonsense. Think that's what it was called. Some guru place in Oregon. Had them all walking and talking guruspeak. Must've been like the 1960s, what I know about them. They all headed out to Oregon and took anything worth taking. Cleaned out the Seed and Feed and Haven Hardware. Probably laid all that stuff at the feet of Guru Shambala and he's got them slaving away for him. That's how we were introduced to the idea of plagues. I tell you it's a strange, strange world nowadays."

It was growing dark. Dry snow sifted down across the headlights, blew in wavy lines across the road.

"You taking something to Salt Lake?" asked Jason, nodding at the full bed behind them, covered with a tarp.

"Biodiversity samples. Government's paying good for them. All kinds of plants and animals and insects, all labeled. Wife and me collect them. Ever since the wheat crop was wiped out last year. We were growing the cloned wheat the government paid us to grow and a virus come along and killed the lot. Every damned plant exactly the same. That's what got us interested in the project. I kind of want to get one of those nanotech manufacturing boxes I've heard about, but the wife, she's not so crazy about the whole idea. We got a son in Salt Lake, though, and I think he's about got her talked into it. He's worried about us living out there so alone with the roads so bad and things getting so dangerous. Wants us to get those receptors and move into the city with him. I don't know. I think I like it out here better. We're not alone. We've got each other and the whole world around us. If I was to wake up in the morning and not see Crane Ridge, I think I'd go nuts. My son, he says that they can fix it up there so it would be just the same." Howitz puffed vigorously on his pipe. "I don't believe him. Where you from?"

"All over."

"A drifter."

"I guess. I'm kind of looking for a job in Salt Lake City. Just came from San Francisco. Been learning about the operating systems and all." He held up his gloved hands. "Finally got receptors in San Francisco. I like them. Seems like a good thing to get into."

Howitz shrugged. "Maybe you're right. Maybe the best defense is knowing what's going on. My wife, she's one of these ham radio nuts. Before the Silence, she had friends all over the world. She still keeps the thing hummin'. Guess it's important, even though it wastes current. Maybe once every other week, she'll get a blip. Sometimes even fifteen minutes of stuff. It's pretty compressed; just some kind of code shorthand these folks thought up because talking's too slow when your time is so limited. Don't know as anyone's got the real scoop anymore.

Just swappin' rumors is all. My son claims to get the news through the train line. I say that the news there is whatever they tell him it is. Can't trust it. I'll tell you who we can trust. Our friends and our family. We got about fifteen households where I live, not too close, but we're there for each other and we get together every Sunday at one of the houses. Rotate the meetings. Trade goods and what we know. It works. It's enough."

Jason pulled a candy bar from his pocket. "Want some?"

"Where'd you get it?"

"Little town about two hundred miles west. Emoryville, I think."

"Sure," he said. "Haven't had a Snickers in years. Didn't know they made them anymore."

"They might not," said Jason. "I think these are pretty old."

He offered to drive after a few hours, but his offer was refused. Tired, he napped until they rumbled to a stop and he jerked awake. "Where are we?"

"NAMS station outside of Salt Lake City," Howitz said. He opened the cab and got out, pissed on some plants next to the truck.

It looked to be almost dawn. There were two inches of snow on the ground. Jason saw lights in the distance.

Bright lights.

Jason helped Howitz's son Ed load the biodiversity samples onto the train. Ed was inclined to chat as they made the twenty-minute trip into town, so Jason felt a sense of sweet frustration about getting to know the train, almost as if it were a person. Not only was it fast, but the state-of-the-art cars pulsed with so much news, entertainment, and educational opportunities that he was astounded; the entire inside surface seethed with access invitations.

"I wish Mom and Dad would move to Salt Lake," said Ed, his feet propped on boxes. On the way out, he'd slagged a few rows of seats down; their matter raised the level of the floor a few inches and that was where they stacked the boxes. "I really worry about them way out there. These plagues are the worst thing, it seems. Back in the 1990s, they had this phenomenon called drive-by shootings. These are about the same. Cook up a belief architecture that can interface with 80 percent of normal brains. Let it loose, sit back, and laugh your head off. Or take charge of your army. Whatever. It's bad, man. Bad shit."

"How would you do that?"

Ed looked at him sharply. "That what you came here for?"

Jason shook his head. "No. I'm an engineer. Level one. I just thought it would be good to earn my different levels in different cities. Be flexible."

"Well, you don't want to get mixed up with anyone that makes that kind of stuff, let me tell you. Not only is it a local, state, federal, and international crime with stiff penalties, you really have to wonder about people who want to take the volition of others away."

Jason thought of his mother. It seemed to him that she'd willingly sacrificed her volition. But of course she'd chosen to do that.

"Yeah," Jason replied. "But don't you think it's important that some of the good guys know how to do this stuff? Otherwise, how can it be stopped?"

"Well, you've got a point," said Ed. "Here's our station. There's my hands. They're going to take this stuff to the lab. I'm going to ride back out and spend some time with Dad. Good luck. Look me up if you need anything."

"Thanks," said Jason. "And tell Howitz thanks again too."

After four months in Salt Lake City, Jason was on the move again, but this time he took NAMS.

In Houston, he became a janitor at NASA. No one knew who he was, nor that he had the expertise to access their systems and read information that was classified. Information about the moon and Mars colonies.

Information about the Signal.

Information about the persecution of those like him.

He copied it all.

He heard that New Orleans might be a place of freedom.

When he was on the verge of being discovered, he hitchhiked east.

Crescendo of Light

Tamchu | Cambodia | 2038

Tamchu and the General sat at a card table on a long roofed porch perched on the edge of a jungled gully. In front of them was the drill field and, down a steep hill, a slow river. The General had imported all manner of parrots and finches, despite Tamchu's pointing out that they might upset the natural ecology of the place. "So much the better," she had said. He realized that "upset" was the wrong word to use as a deterrent. The General lived to upset.

Tamchu was very tired. He'd just returned from one of his routine trips to Bangkok. He was, simply, a spy. He dressed like a businessman and carried expensive businessman accouterments: a Toshiba wristphone with a huge roam zone to gobble signals from far off—if there might be signals anywhere. A nose ring which, were it real, would be capable of sensing the fine gradations of metapheromones now often present in the highest levels of government and of business. His was not. Real nose rings passed information up the nasal passage directly into the brain. Wearers underwent intense feedback training so that their brains translated the metapheromones into a new type of language, based on the learning profile of each individual. The level of precision manifested by adult-level grammar was still difficult for most people to achieve, so many messages were in primitive toddlerspeak. The receiver closed his or her eyes and dreamlike visions arose, the speed of which could be controlled by the user. And unlike dreams, such visions would be remembered. One great advantage was that information could be embedded in tablets which, when put into a cup

309

of steaming hot water, could be inhaled and held in a buffer. The information could be saved for extended periods of time.

But when Tamchu mingled in the downtown clubs, he was taken for a high-rolling foreigner, particularly since his Thai vocabulary retained an accent and because the cast of his face—his high Tibetan cheekbones and burnished skin—heightened this effect.

It was assumed that any businessman in Bangkok was there only peripherally for business. It was mostly for sex that they flocked to this vast city, a city that Tamchu found tragic and exhilarating. The poverty was nothing new. That it was so pervasive and that it existed among people who had fought to defend their independence for so many centuries in a land rich with resources depressed him greatly. Was it simply a given of human existence that almost all people were relegated to subsistence living, that they would, generation after generation, be denied the resources of people like the General? When was all this nanotech stuff going to help them? There was a lot of resistance to the kinds of change that seemed to be sweeping other parts of the world.

He looked across the table at the General. She'd adopted a mannish haircut; her straight black hair fell across her eyes. She hardly ever ate and exercised ferociously every day; her body was a thin athlete's, flat-chested.

Tamchu figured her to be in her early forties. When he had met her, her face was lined and her mouth bracketed by dour creases that had only deepened in the past decade. Her black eyes were quick to see everything, yet introspective, as if they gazed upon atrocities even when the sky was blue and the sun shining. Tamchu suspected that she'd never had an easy moment in her life. She'd worked rice paddies until her parents, a brother, and a sister had died of some unknown plague. The General and her remaining sister had then been sold by their uncle into slavery in the brothels of Bangkok. She stabbed her second client with a knife she hid beneath her pillow—after hiding from the daily injection of calming drugs—and escaped into the streets. It took her a year to find her sister, who had contracted AIDS and was dying of a particularly virulent virus. After her sister died, the teenager went to the airport and walked unseen onto a cargo plane bound for Hong Kong. There she joined the Chinese army, which was taking all comers at that time. They gave her an education that kept extending when they saw what a dedicated pupil she was. She served out her time, fighting in several border skirmishes—perhaps against Tamchu's own family—and returned to Thailand.

It was then that she declared war on brothels. As a result, the Bangkok brothels had metamorphosed into a floating world, constantly moving. The General was not concerned about high-class call girls who had survived long enough to make their own decisions about their livelihood. Her goal was to free the girls, some as young as ten years old, who sat behind a one-way mirror wearing a number and usually perished within a year or two of their enslavement. The General also had spies working on the supply networks, infiltrating the brothel operatives who went around to the villages in big cars with lots of money. Sometimes parents were promised that the girls would get an education. Her troops regularly ambushed the fancy cars on the way back to Bangkok with their cargo. The General also had a traveling video bus that went to villages and showed raw footage of the lives of the sex slaves, including videos from the morgue.

Tamchu had found that there was death in the past of all terrorists, usually the death of some innocent—a mother, a brother, an old father. He found comfort in this at first. This world of pain and anger was his world. But unfocused rage at the hidden controller who had no feeling for the lives of others made terrorists, in a way, like those they hated. Tamchu was beginning to see this. It was not something he wanted to see. He told himself that there were no innocent victims in his form of protest. But he knew that was not true. He did not understand why the General found it necessary to kill brothel clients. Terrify them, yes. It was the owners who wanted killing, argued Tamchu, not the clients. "You have to put fear into them," said the General. "Fear of death is the only thing that will ruin the slave trade." It was all too easy for the General's army of former victims to be trained to kill with no compunction.

One of the girls brought Tamchu his customary green tea and curried soybeans. He thanked her. Her arms hung at her sides. As she turned and walked away, he noticed that her hands were clenched into fists.

"It is difficult for that one to change," observed the General, lighting a cigar, pushing her chair back, and putting her booted feet up on the railing. She pushed aside her sparse breakfast of rice, cold steamed fish, and mango half-eaten, as usual. "I'm not sure what to do about her. Some are more sensitive than others."

"Let her be," suggested Tamchu. "Not everyone is cut out to be a killer."

"Of course they are," replied the General. "In the right circumstances, anyone will kill. And if they won't, they don't deserve the gift of life."

Tamchu thought of Illian. He could not imagine her killing anyone. Ever. "That's not true," he said. "In fact, I think that's a ridiculous statement."

"When the world is changed, I may agree with you," she said. "My sisters did not fight. And they died."

"You're saying that they deserved to die," Tamchu pointed out.

She stubbed out her cigar in what was left of the mango. Her movements were never languid. They were always sharp, economical, decisive. She looked at him directly.

"Believe me, if I could find a cure for this condition, I'd support it with all that's left of my heart. Perhaps it would be better to say, I would support a cure with all my military and organizational skills. That's what I wanted to talk to you about this morning, in fact. I've been in contact with someone in Hong Kong and I'd like you to go and meet him. Find out how much product he can manufacture, how much it will cost. Bargain for it, but get it no matter what. Find out which vectors we must use in order to get the maximum effect."

"What do you mean, 'vectors'?" asked Tamchu.

"As in vectors of infection."

"So this is some sort of sickness."

She hesitated for a second, and looked away from him. She appeared to be thinking. "No. It is some sort of cure. Yes. It is a cure of this sexual sickness that drives men to victimize women."

"Oh," said Tamchu. He was quiet for a minute. "I'm not sure that I want to do this sort of thing anymore." He was surprised at himself. He had not meant to say so. But he realized that that, in truth, was how he felt. He probably ought not to have said it so baldly. He knew that the General depended on him extensively. He was not afraid of her, but she would certainly not let him go too easily. He knew too much.

To anyone else, she would have appeared to have no reaction at all to his statement—mild, yet heretical because she knew that he usually meant what he said. But her slight brief squint and the sudden wildness of her eyes as she studied the glowing end of her cigar said as much to Tamchu about what she felt as another's screaming tantrum.

Of course, she continued speaking as if he had said nothing. "I know you object to the word 'sickness.' Let me put it another way. I've been trying hard to think of this in other ways. Whether or not you believe it, I realize that I have a sickness as well—and that you have the same sickness, but to a lesser degree."

Tamchu was a bit surprised that the General was able to be so objective about herself. "What other way of thinking about it have you found?"

"Every species has mating rituals and reproductive strategies. The male urge for coupling with young women—and as many as possible— is part of this. But we have more than enough people on this planet already. The male reproductive urge must be stemmed. Women would then be able to have more control over whether or not they ought to reproduce—and the methods of reproduction. Men who really do want to raise children could decide to do so in a rational way, based on their resources and their emotional capacity for doing so. Women could decide to pair with a mate based not on sexual urges but on whether they both have the time, money, maturity, and love to raise a child."

"Maybe there would be no more children in such a world," said Tamchu. "Who that is thoughtful would feel capable of raising children?"

The General snorted. She almost never laughed, because she never seemed happy enough or free enough to simply laugh. She snorted, instead, in ridicule. The ridiculous thoughts of others moved her to snort rather often.

"I have my girls; I am raising them," she replied.

"You have an agenda," Tamchu pointed out. "You make them into killers. I'm not sure if this is mature. You are using them."

"Which is exactly what I'm talking about!" she said, as if scoring a point. "Go to Hong Kong and get this substance. We can put it in the water, perhaps. Release it from helicopters."

"What is it?" asked Tamchu. "Dissolvable compassion? You'd better avoid taking it."

She was impossible to rile. It was one of the things Tamchu liked about her. She was honest and direct and, though she usually ignored criticism, it didn't anger her at all.

"You seem to be talking in circles," he added.

"What I'm doing now is primitive. It doesn't work. The people in the villages don't believe my movies. If I paid them enough so that they could afford to keep their girls at home, it wouldn't matter. They'd keep the money and sell them next month when I wasn't around. I think that the devaluation of girls is so great that things will never change without some great jolt. Some enormous change."

"Things aren't this way in Tibet, in Nepal," said Tamchu, thinking of his mother, his aunt.

Another snort. "The literacy rate for men in Nepal is 12 percent. For women, it is 3 percent. If what you say is true, it would be the same."

Tamchu sighed.

"It's always hard for a man to see things in this way," said the General. "You're not bad, for a man."

"I don't think it's the fault of men," he said.

"Men are as much victims of this as women," said the General.

Tamchu sat back in his chair. He was often confused when around the General. He had the feeling that he'd gotten involved in a war that was not his own, even though he felt great pity for the girls the General liberated.

"It's the same system," she said, zeroing in, as usual, on his thoughts. "The whole human system. This is what killed your sister."

"Some . . . strange government policy killed her," said Tamchu, his thoughts surfacing to language slowly, as usual. Over the past years, he'd allowed the General to convince him that Illian was dead. Still, in his heart, he couldn't believe it. At first he'd told himself that he was gaining skills that would aid him in locating her. But the General's corrosive philosophy had a way of extinguishing hope.

"You've been wrapped up in this for ages," said the General, lighting another cigar with a snap of her lighter. "It is a local thing for you. You've gotten involved. But what you want is to see the bigger picture. You want to know what killed your sister. I understand." She took a drag of her cigar and stood. "Go to Hong Kong. Meet this man. Find out about what he has to sell. But ask him other questions. He knows a lot. He knows about things I don't care about. Maybe he can help you."

She patted him on the shoulder and descended the balcony stairs. Cigar smoke lingered, mingled with the scent of flowers. Girls drilled below, shadows shortening as the sun gained midsky. They marched, turned sharply, halted, inspected their weapons. Their faces were as free of emotion as that of the General's. She walked out into the wide green drill field next to the river. They saluted and snapped their heels together. The General saluted them back. Her commands rang out in the languid jungle air. The girls turned. They marched. They scattered to the trees, to begin the guerrilla part of the morning.

Tamchu decided to go to Hong Kong.

Hong Kong gathered Tamchu in with gaudy embracing arms and he tried vainly to remain aloof. It is all a fantasy, he reminded himself, yet he kept forgetting in the thrall of multisensual stimulation and cursed the General for sending him here.

He found that he had to do business via a virtual booth, which did not please him. The booths were 3-D, networked, and ran on some sort of new juice, juice because Hong Kong now operated on information-carrying liquid that was piped throughout the city. This was a tentative step toward converting entirely to BioCity mode.

An hour later, he stumbled, dazed, into the streets of Hong Kong. He had bought whatever it was that the General wanted, described by the code name Black, after a flurry of fierce bidding by unseen parties.

To him it was like any of a hundred transactions he'd facilitated for her, from weapons to trucks to explosives. The only difference was that this was astoundingly expensive. He wondered where the money had come from, wondered if perhaps she was sharing the cost with other groups who would then share this mysterious substance she praised so highly. The object he had bought was zipped inside his money belt. He had gained no information about Illian, but he was not surprised. He had not really expected to.

Two blocks from the parlor, a brown dwarf and a Japanese woman fell in beside him. The dwarf said, "We can't offer you a lot of money for what you have. But we can offer you a chance to do the right thing."

Two mornings later, Tamchu got off the express maglev in Bangkok and decided to stay overnight before catching a local train north, where the fast trains did not run. He was tired and wanted to rest before meeting the General, and he felt safe in this city. Of course you do, he told himself. You hold their life and death in your hands. You are the invisible gnat with power over them all.

He was not happy that this was so. But the dwarf and Japanese woman had told him that he was in possession of something far more dangerous than the General had led him to believe. The woman seemed terribly agitated and Tamchu would not have listened to her for a second. But the dwarf, in contrast to the con men and liars Tamchu was accustomed to dealing with, was calm, certain, embued with a moral energy that reminded Tamchu, rather oddly, of his mother. Besides, the amount of money the dwarf considered not a lot was almost twice as much as he had paid for . . . for whatever he had.

But Tamchu had turned down their strange offer. The General depended on him and he would not betray her. Yet the dwarf's assertions bothered him.

He decided to stay in a hotel in the district he usually frequented. He welcomed the heat as he stepped from the train station and hailed a runner. Noisy polluting tuk tuks had been replaced years ago by bicycle cabs or pedicabs.

A few minutes later, as he waited in his pedicab for a signal to change, he realized that a Buddhist nun in diaphanous orange robes was looking straight at him. She stood at a bus stop only a few feet away, holding a green sun parasol. Her old brown face was drawn into a fine network of wrinkles. She had no hair, and on her forehead spun a moving tattoo, a prayer wheel. She was probably of Tibetan extraction.

315

Their glances mingled. He was too tired to even look away, as one generally would when catching a stranger's eye.

The Buddha sprang forth.

A force resided within her being. He had not encountered this force since leaving Kathmandu, but his memory gave back all the associations built up during a childhood where Buddhism was common as air, and he was flooded with the realization that this force existed as surely as the cab in which he sat.

This energy flowed into him, scoured him, revealed his shabby excuses for what he did and who he was. Shame at having called himself a Buddhist for so many years caught fire and flared, incandescent as a burning magnesium wire. The nun's gaze was calm, deep, certain, and showed no surprise at what was happening. In her eyes, Tamchu saw certainty and understood that she contained and directed this energy, much as the banks of a klong contained and directed the flow of water. She briefly sketched a mudra in the humid air with her free hand, never breaking the current of their gaze.

The runner jolted forward as the signal changed and all that Tamchu saw—the long avenues filled with seething crowds, the occasional tree, the haze at the ends of the streets—seemed filled with this inner cleansing fire. It continued with him, spread through everything, changed everything, much as the dwarf had claimed what he carried in his belt would change things. He saw all this without wonder, without judgment. The universe mutated for him in that moment. He did not know what it meant. He did not know much of anything, except that a light issued from all beings, the pure light of the Buddha.

Arriving at the hotel, he paid the runner and entered a cool dark lobby, rich with intricately carved woods. The clerk apologetically told him that they could have a room ready in half an hour.

He went back out on the street and wandered into an expensive gallery. He glanced around, restlessly eyeing paintings and sculpture. As he turned to leave, he passed a glass shelf containing smaller objects, none larger than a bowl. He was almost out the door when his brain finally processed what he'd seen and shouted at him to go back. He turned on his heel, wondering why.

On the shelf was a small delicate butterfly cage of metal sticks, welded together at crazy angles. The sticks were not safely contained at the ends but extended past one another, giving the piece a bristly quality.

He picked it up and examined it, heart pounding, reminded of the cages Illian had made for him all those years ago. The same size, the same basic construction.

Trapped inside, loose but unable to fit through any of the gaps, was a tiny metal girl.

Tamchu's first thought was that he was so tired that he was dreaming and didn't know it. Or that perhaps he was still trapped within the virtual network of Hong Kong and that the dwarf and the Japanese woman and the long train trip and the nun and the light, which still burned here, were all part of the same manipulations inflicted on him by some unknown dream master.

But no. He was awake, in the flesh, and holding this butterfly cage in hands that trembled.

Eagerly, he turned it around and around, hungry for whatever information it might yield. It was some strange fluke—some bizarre coincidence—that such an object should exist. Surely it could have no connection to Illian.

But there. On one of the metal sticks a small indented Roman numeral I was etched into the metal. Or perhaps . . . it was the letter *i*. i for Illian. Her signature. And PARIS.

His throat tightened and he felt tears. A strange sensation; he had not cried once during all his years with the General.

And he could not buy it. For years, he had depended completely on the General and had no material needs that were not filled. The hotel, the train, the ship, his clothing, everything was paid for with her account.

He did not want to use her account of death to buy this thing. This cage was alive, and the light within all objects now revealed to him that he was not. His life was not his own.

He lived, he realized suddenly, to wreak havoc on anyone the General deemed unfit to live. He lived at her pleasure. He was her tool. He'd given up his own thoughts, his own life.

He'd given up.

Now, suddenly, he wanted to reclaim his life with a fierceness that took him by surprise. The urge to do, the urge to be, the urge to think for himself filled his mind and being, wiping away his fatigue. In fact, perhaps this feeling was joy. Joy such as he had never experienced in his entire life.

Illian lived! He had not sent her to her death!

He looked around. The attendant was occupied with a Japanese man. He wished he could ask her about the artist, but she probably would not know anything.

He walked out the door holding the cage; holding, he felt, his life. Behind him he heard an alarm; imagined that alerted guards pursued him. He made no undue haste. He simply slipped into the crowd. He'd

317

been doing such things for so many years that he didn't even think about it. He returned directly to the train station.

When the train pulled up to the platform in the Cambodian village, it was late afternoon. Tamchu had decided it was best to face the General and tell her he was leaving. They did, after all, have a long relationship. And she had paid for whatever was in his belt. The dwarf said that whoever owned it would have the world at his feet. That he could demand any ransom, for it could unmake the world. But why should he trust a dwarf he did not know over the General?

To his surprise, she was waiting on the concrete platform, next to the small ticketing kiosk. He saw her as the old train—an anomaly in this age of nanotech wonders—squealed to a halt. She looked harried, Tamchu noted with tenderness, as he appraised her through the dirty window, sealed to hold in barely functioning air-conditioning. She must have come every day on the chance that he might arrive, something she had never done before.

She did not look at the windows, but only at the door, as she smoked her cigar with jerky, agitated gestures. She seemed unlike herself; she was usually unperturbed and in control.

She stamped out her cigar and scowled. She tried to light another, but her hand shook so badly that she tossed the match down in disgust and searched her pockets frantically, finally finding a lighter.

Tamchu knew at that instant that all the dwarf had told him must be true. He carried in his belt some terrible substance with which she could wreak untold havoc. She would not be satisfied until all men were dead, including himself, and all women who did not believe as she did. It was, as she said, a sickness. But he did not carry the cure she'd promised. He carried only that which would feed it.

He could not move from his seat.

At the last moment, as the train began to move ponderously, she looked up, scanned the windows, caught his eye.

She tossed down her cigar and ground it out with her boot. Like the Buddhist nun, she held his gaze without blinking.

Her eyes were not filled with light, but with darkness.

She became small in the green afternoon, straight and stiff and dressed in black.

Then the train rounded a curve and she was gone.

A minute later, the brown dwarf came down the aisle. The Japanese woman was behind him.

Tamchu was not surprised to see the dwarf and the Japanese woman. They approached him, holding on to seats as they swayed down the aisle, with the inevitability of dream, replacing the General as the phenomenon requiring his immediate attention. Perhaps, he reflected, the Buddhist nun had wiped surprise from his universe and replaced it with this new sensation of inevitability, coupled with an intimation that his inner stance might possibly make a difference. There was also a sense that it was necessary to put himself at the disposal of the universe, without even hoping that this might bring him redemption.

He wasn't at all positive, however, that the dwarf was his path to implementing his dim memory of the four noble truths.

The dwarf and the Japanese woman sat across from him. Sunset angled down a brilliant green valley and brightened the face of the Japanese woman, as if she were being pierced by a sword of light. The ancient train jolted onward toward the next tiny station, a mere ten miles and twenty minutes away.

Finally the dwarf—whose name, Tamchu recalled, was Hugo—said, "You have made the right choice." His big square face was solemn.

"Maybe," said Tamchu.

"Are you now coming with us to New Orleans?"

"No," said Tamchu. "I am going to Paris."

"That's on the way." Hugo wiggled back into the threadbare seat. The Japanese woman curled up in hers. She looked weary.

"How did you find me in Hong Kong?" asked Tamchu.

"I am a spy," replied Hugo.

This pronouncement struck Tamchu as hilarious, though he gave no sign of this. The eyelids of the self-proclaimed spy were stuck at half-mast in a ridiculously studied fashion.

Hugo continued, "You must be very careful with what you are carrying. I'm not the only person who knows about it."

"I am carrying nothing with me," said Tamchu. "I stored it in Bangkok."

Hugo just looked at him.

He elaborated on his lie. "In the hotel safe."

Kita said, "Do you mind if I smoke?"

Tamchu shook his head and she lit a cigarette.

"We didn't want only what you're carrying or we'd have taken it from you as soon as you got it," said Hugo. "Perhaps even earlier. We wanted to know who intended to buy it. We've been tracking it for months. It was stolen from Kyoto. I was seriously injured there and it took me a while to recover. By then the trail was difficult to pick up. You've heard about Kyoto, haven't you?"

"I don't know," said Tamchu. "Yes, perhaps. Some kind of disaster."

"Some kind," said the Japanese woman, her eyes sad and distant.

Hugo continued, "An agent of the International Federation cartel stole it. We received intelligence that a lone terrorist managed to flee Kyoto with the prototype you carry. He sold other important Kyoto information to an Eastern European group with retro politics. He was holding out for some very high bidding to conclude in Hong Kong. But we were just on the verge of finding his booth in the virtual arcade and he panicked, switched venues to throw us off, and sold it to you, even though I don't suppose you offered anywhere near what it was worth. Had you attempted to give it to that woman back there, we would have intercepted it instantly."

"Why didn't you take it earlier?" asked Tamchu. "It would have saved you a return trip to Bangkok."

"Because we wanted to see where you were taking it. And because what we want more than anything is you. We need you to help change the world."

This drew a reaction from Tamchu in spite of himself—a thin snorting laugh that might have issued from the General herself. "I had something that could destroy the world, but I am more important? There is nothing important about me."

"You have connections to every terrorist organization in Asia," said Hugo. "You have information about their plans, how they could be circumvented. They know and trust you."

"Trust is not something that any of them practice," said Tamchu.

"Your boss paid a huge sum for what you have," said Hugo.

"I am curious," said Tamchu. "Why did this substance not destroy its container?"

Kito stubbed out her cigarette. Her face was not quite as pale as that of most Japanese women, but she had the same fineness of complexion and her cheeks were tinged pale peach. Her black eyebrows made thin perfect arcs above her black serious eyes, and she was tiny and dressed in jeans, boots, a T-shirt, and a dark blue tailored silk jacket. She spoke excellent English in a sharp and nervous voice.

"Inside your belt is a flexible sealed assembler lab containing molecular-scale softwear. When plugged into practically any late-model DNA computer, it is capable of giving directions for molecular assembly of virtually any substance. Including directions for a substance that will progressively change everything it comes in contact with—unstoppably—forever. It is the first and only one in the world. A prototype. Its very creation is against international law. It was being tested at my company's headquarters." Her hands shook as she pried a crushed cigarette package out of her jeans, and pulled another cigarette out.

The train was squealing to a halt. "Better light that later. We need to get off here," Hugo said, as if it were an afterthought.

"That's probably a good idea," conceded Tamchu. He'd allowed himself to be distracted and the General would surely be on his trail. "But then what?"

"Trust me," said Hugo and grinned, his eyes completely open and perhaps even a bit excited. The woman rose a bit unsteadily. She was new at this game. Hugo quickly led the way to the platform between the cars. The station was visible just ahead.

One by one, they jumped from the slow-moving train and stumbled into a narrow verge of dense vegetation. Tamchu pushed through it cautiously and found that it was only about ten feet wide. The concealing shrubbery ended at a narrow gravel road. They were crouched about fifty feet from the tiny station.

Hugo and Kita joined Tamchu. Hugo pulled a candy bar from his pocket. He tore off the bright red wrapper, offered it around silently, and was declined.

Tamchu heard shouted orders. He parted the leaves and saw a dozen empty Jeeps parked helter-skelter down by the station. Hugo bit into his candy bar, dropped the wrapper at the road's edge, and yanked Tamchu into the center of the screening bit of jungle.

Tamchu turned and peered back at the train through a tiny opening.

Thin young girls marched resolutely up and down the aisle of the car next to them. Two of them pulled a trunk from the luggage rack; he could not see more but imagined them breaking it open to see if he might be curled inside. Their faces were fixed in the habitual grim expression mandated by the General. Other girls jogged engineward atop the car, their heavy boots pounding a hollow tattoo. These were the fifteen-year-olds—in Tamchu's opinion, the most terrifying age of the General's troops. Some, when they got older, questioned their mission, but at this age they relished their apparent power and reported any infractions of their fellow soldiers with tremendous dogmatism.

They would find him soon.

Tamchu removed his belt and handed it to Hugo. Hugo nodded, pulled his own belt from the loops, and threaded Tamchu's through. He handed his old belt to Tamchu, who put it on. He took a step toward the road. Hugo grabbed his arm. Very tightly. "I told you the truth," Hugo whispered in his ear. "We need you."

Tamchu was puzzled. He'd given the man what he wanted. For some reason, he believed in Hugo, trusted him. This man truly did want to save the world; Tamchu was certain of it. Not just young Cambodian and Thai women. All people.

There was madness in the world and Tamchu had been a part of it. But perhaps, if Tamchu gave himself up, Hugo could be gone before the General discovered that he did not have her doomsday weapon and killed him out of irritation. He opened his mouth to tell this to Hugo when he heard the crunch of tires on gravel.

A brown delivery van paused at Hugo's candy wrapper, its open door flush against the foliage. Hugo nodded to Kita. She rose and slipped into the truck; Hugo gave Tamchu a little push and he followed. They huddled in the dark interior as the truck continued on. "It's so nice when things work out as planned," Hugo remarked. The bitter shouts of the still-searching General and her officers faded behind them.

It was now dark. Hugo and Kita stretched out on the floor and slept. Tamchu did not understand how they could sleep, but after an unsuccessful attempt to converse with the driver, he too dozed off.

They were delivered at dawn to the Bangkok train station. As they trundled through Bangkok, Hugo disguised Tamchu, much to his consternation, as a monk, draping yards of saffron gauze around him with a practiced air, instructing Kita to fling the end over Tamchu's shoulder. When the truck stopped, they shaved his head. Tamchu was worried about tickets but Hugo apparently had several first-class passes and reservations.

They had to pass through the station to get to the train. Kita went first, Tamchu next, and Hugo brought up the rear; they were seemingly unrelated as they wove through the crowd in the tremendous echoing room.

Tamchu almost faltered when he saw a phalanx of the General's girls halfway across the station. They were scanning the station systematically. He thought he saw one of them point to him, but did not hasten. Before anyone could do anything, if indeed the soldiers suspected him, they climbed onto a westbound bullet train and entered a private suite with drawn shades. Hugo locked the door and tied it shut as well with a piece of thin rope that he pulled from his pocket, then checked every inch of the compartment quickly but with a thoroughness that Tamchu admired. Then they collapsed on deep, comfortable seats.

"Why do you want to go to Paris?" asked Hugo.

Tamchu opened the bag into which Kita had thrust his clothing. He had kept a careful eye on it at all times. He pulled out the sculpture. "To find the girl—the woman—who made this."

Hugo and Kita both looked at it in their turn, Kita murmuring appreciatively. Tamchu noticed that the train was under way only after the speed appeared next to the time and date on a small console.

"Who is she?" asked Hugo.

Tamchu told them the story of his life.

Tamchu watched the plains of India pass by, remembering the bandit he'd seen so many years ago. He'd accepted her invitation, it seemed, to the ruination of his being. He'd thought he was doing the right thing. Or, at least, he had done the thing that had *felt* right. He hadn't realized then that there might be a difference.

He often pulled out the small cage and looked at it.

He imagined that he saw Illian's features on the face of the girl, even though it was so tiny. Trapped like a butterfly in that German cage. Or maybe it was a larger cage now. Everyone was caged in some way. He looked over at Hugo, who was asleep. Take this woman of whom he spoke, Marie Laveau. Laveau seemed to exercise a lot of control over Hugo's life. But perhaps Tamchu wasn't seeing the whole picture. Hugo did not seem the type to be controlled.

Kita devoted a lot of attention to making sure that her cigarette supply was ample. She'd taken a liking to a certain Indian brand that gave off a wretched smell. She didn't say much. She did say that she hadn't smoked until a few months earlier. Apparently, she hadn't known Hugo then either. Tamchu could tell they were lovers, though they'd barely touched one another in his presence.

Gradually, Tamchu learned about Marie's floating city. It seemed to him that he'd heard glimmers of it before. Apparently, it was not finished. It had experienced setbacks and was itself the target of terrorists. Tamchu decided that perhaps this was why he was wanted—to anticipate possible weak points.

They began hearing about Paris as far away as Yugoslavia. Something strange, something transmutational, had occurred after an attack by Bees governed by a terrorist coalition.

But when they finally crossed the French border, one bright early morning, Tamchu fancied he could feel a difference in the air. Fields of yellow flowers sloped down to a deep blue sea, for their train had taken a southern route. They were on a tourist line that hugged the coast, as the direct line northwest into Paris was not open. Tamchu had grown a beard and felt relatively safe. As they breakfasted elegantly on caviar—Tamchu had found that Hugo had extravagant tastes, but then he was one of the exploitative elite Tamchu had devoted a lifetime to destroying—Kita worked in a notebook. Tamchu gradually learned that she was a noted bionanologist. That, in fact, she was responsible for a vital pheromone breakthrough that had made Bio-Cities possible.

Tamchu had been to a few BioCities, but always under duress. Beijing had been most impressive, though he'd felt that his temporary receptors somehow distorted his vision. Life couldn't really be as strange as it seemed in that vast place. And he felt as if nothing was really private there. This was not optimal for the terrorist mode.

He had no idea how to find Illian—if indeed she was in Paris. Hugo had sworn to help, though, which was comforting. He had not relied on anyone in this way since his mother had died. It was as if all his years of suspicion and isolation were but a brittle shell that shattered upon finding Illian's sculpture. Daylight had flooded in—and with it trust.

It seemed that everyone on the train spoke French. Tamchu noticed that as they drew closer to Paris, excitement mounted. Hugo translated for him. "They are like pilgrims. They say it's Paris as it was always meant to be. Everything that makes it Paris is still there— the Arc de Triomphe, the Pompidou, Notre Dame, even medieval neighborhoods that have been restored. But the most exciting thing is that it is now a work of art in and of itself. It is in fact so strange and different that most people cannot stand to be there for very long, its beauty is so intense. Probably some other aspects too."

"Like its concentration of myrcene," said Kita, writing, without looking up. "That would be my suspicion."

"Is that unusual?" asked Tamchu.

Kita looked up, but gazed into the distance, not at him. "All of these new developments are unusual, of course. These new cities are biological organisms. They can mutate, and they can do so fairly rapidly. It is one of the problems that the International Standards are supposed to prevent."

"Why?" asked Tamchu, his throat tight. "What could have changed it?"

"They're saying that it's a woman named Illian," said Hugo. "The Sun Queen."

Tamchu could not remember ever being this excited in his entire life. The glow of Paris, even in daylight, was intense, visible from afar.

Everyone on the train received temporary receptors. Kita, apparently, was already deeply transformed and only required a brief initiation to orient her system. Hugo assented to the temporary receptors, as did Tamchu—grudgingly.

Then the train pulled into the Paris station.

Even as he held on to the escalator railing, Tamchu was flooded with information. Ads for pensions, enticing restaurants, plays.

Kita looked thoughtful as they left the escalator and pushed into the street, which was hot and crowded with people. "There is something very strange about Paris," she said.

"What?" asked Tamchu.

"I am not a mathematician. But it seems, as a whole, to embody certain relationships. To manifest them, even."

"It was laid out mathematically by L'Enfant, during a latter-day transformation," said Hugo. "I imagine that there are certain Pythagorean proportions to everything."

"It's more than that," said Kita. "Deeper. In fact, I wouldn't mind spending a month or so here and acquiring the capacity to really understand it. I didn't know this was possible. It's very exciting."

"*What* is possible?" asked Hugo.

"Well, look. Let's go in here." They entered a café and ordered coffee. As they sat down, Kita wiped her hand across the table, causing its surface to light up. Tamchu removed his cup, but Kita said, "It's okay. It knows that's just a cup. Now let me see if I can give you a taste of *this*." She used her finger to tap through various visuals on the awakened tabletop, her straight black hair spilling in a perfect curtain following the line of her cheekbone. She looked up, her eyes more eager than Tamchu had seen them thus far. "Okay, I want you to touch that picture of the Eiffel Tower. That's where it's coming from." She even smiled. "What a surprise."

Reluctantly, Tamchu touched the picture of the Eiffel Tower.

First it was as if he could feel all his bones, as if his consciousness radiated through them. Then it was the other networks in his body—nerves, hormones, muscles, blood. But this was utterly fleeting, as if it were just being laid down as a foundation.

The grid of the city assumed the same sensation for him, as if it were his own extended body. He expanded upward, into the air, high and low depending on the architecture, slipping through the pheromonal interstices and conduits of Paris. He tasted the immensity of light, the pulse of the thoughts of others, transforming instant by instant to new form.

But there was more. Paris itself seemed to generate spectra previously invisible to him, a sculpture of light. It too pulsed, changed . . . *directed; called.*

Tamchu jumped up and ran from the café. Hugo, behind him, yelled, "Wait!"

He knew which bus to catch; felt each street, imprinted, it seemed, upon his nervous system.

He felt the mind of Illian: bright, strange, powerful.

"She really is alive!" he shouted. "Illian!"

Kita and Hugo panted on a seat next to him. An old woman sitting across from him, carrying a string bag of oranges and two cheeses, nodded and smiled. "Illian," she agreed and filled the air with French words.

"What did she say?" asked Tamchu.

Kita said, "You can get a translation by—"

"*What did she say?*" demanded Tamchu.

"She says that Illian is like the sun. Illian is the new Sun Queen."

They got off the bus at the plaza of the Eiffel Tower. Tamchu looked upward, his arms upraised. "She's there!" he said. "Illian!"

Bees were much more evident here than in other parts of the city. Paris was abloom. A vine of purple deadly nightshade wound around the Eiffel Tower, which seemed to pulse and fill the very air with power. Gazing at the Tower, Tamchu was reminded of Illian's matchstick construction. She had not invented this. But it seemed made for her.

He ran toward the base of the Tower, Hugo and Kita trailing him. "An elevator!" he shouted. Next to it was a bank of what looked like a huge . . . *beehive* . . .

A guard stopped him. "I'm sorry, sir, but you do not have clearance here."

Hugo said, "You must let him in."

The guard looked down at Hugo with a supercilious expression. "You are an American."

"An American with money," said Hugo, pulling some bills from his wallet.

"Your money is worthless here," said the guard.

"Then I'm an American with a gun," said Hugo, pulling it out.

The guard stepped back, clearly surprised.

In that instant, Tamchu rushed onto the elevator.

The door closed behind him.

As it slowly rose through the lacy ironwork, Tamchu felt increasingly as if every facet of his mind and being were drawing together, echoing the inevitability he had felt after seeing the nun. He pulsed with light and joy. He experienced a thrill of vertigo as the ground receded. "Illian!" he whispered, putting his hands to the glass and staring down at her city.

"I'm here," said a voice.

Tamchu spun around. He was alone in the elevator. "Illian! Where are you?"

She was silent for a moment. Then she replied in the Tibetan they'd shared in her childhood, "Everywhere."

This frightened him. The elevator climbed higher.

"What do you mean?"

"I am . . . preparing for something." The elevator reached the top. The door opened. He stepped out onto the platform. The wind was cold. The Tower still glowed.

A woman appeared before him. She seemed to condense at the center of the platform. At first she was translucent, but she gained solidity and finally smiled.

"Tamchu!" She walked toward him and flung her arms around him. He could not feel them. She seemed to be weeping. "I didn't know if you were alive or dead!"

He realized that this tall graceful blond . . . *ghost* . . . must be Illian.

The apparition was dressed in a long, tight yellow gown that hugged . . . her body? . . . but she had no body . . .

But it *was* her. Somehow. His words burst forth. "Illian, where have you been all these years? I followed you to Germany and you were not—you were not at the clinic—they told me you were dead—"

"Let's sit over here." She led him to an empty glass-enclosed café. It seemed as if no one else had been there for a long time, though all the tables were dressed with white linens and a full battalion of plates and silverware. They sat down.

At least, he sat down. She only appeared to sit down, he realized. She gave him the same disorienting sensations as did the holograms of Hong Kong. Perhaps she was one herself and able to manifest wherever she wished.

But her eyes looked directly into his, and her smile transformed her, for a second, to the girl he had loved so dearly.

"I ran away from the clinic. They used all kinds of probes and needles on me and kept me in a room that made me sick and crazy. I tried to get the others to run away with me, but none of them wanted to. They seemed stupid. But maybe they were just drugged, and I wasn't drugged enough yet. I had to fight hard and smashed a chair against that doctor. He told the guard to shoot me, I remember, but the guard refused. I escaped and made my way to Amsterdam eventually. Artaud took me in."

"Artaud?" asked Tamchu, feeling a pang of jealousy.

"Yes. He was an art critic. He's my lover now," she said proudly. "She, actually. He was changed into a Bee."

"Oh." Tamchu tried to understand this bizarre revelation. The years reeled through him. He had done so much killing in her name. How could he tell her?

"Tamchu, why are you crying?" She reached over and rested her light-hand on his. He felt a slight warmth and was surprised.

"Because I am a terrible person." He covered his face with his hands. "I have done terrible things. I—you would not want to know me now."

"I want to know you now, Tamchu. I love you. I have always loved you. You tried your best to help me. You worked very hard for me in Kathmandu. I have always been grateful for that—for knowing that you loved me. At first, when I escaped, I tried to get back to Kathmandu, but I didn't know how. I didn't even know where it was. I was afraid the doctor would find me. A few years ago, I went back briefly and tried to find some of your relatives. I did find a cousin of yours, but he said that you had disappeared. Whatever you have done, Tamchu, whatever you are now, I know the heart of you. You are a good person."

Tamchu picked up a cloth napkin and wiped his face, blew his nose. "Do you really think so?"

"Yes," she said quietly, firmly. "I know it."

He was silent for a moment. Then he said, "But what *are* you? Why are you . . . this ghost thing? Why do they call you the Sun Queen?"

She sat back in her chair, her face serious. "It would be more correct to say *Suns* Queen. There are so many stars, you know. I have made Paris into a new art form. It's so hard to explain. It is made . . . to *experience*. It *is* the explanation. There are no other layers to it, outside of itself. You must *be* it."

"But—try and help me understand. What makes you want to do this? How were you able to do it?"

She frowned slightly. "Even now, I don't know how I did it. Just as I was never sure how I did a painting. Artaud and I were in a situation to which there was no way out. So we turned around and faced the peril directly. And once I did that, I discovered that I had the power to transform the situation. I had the power to change Paris into this . . . this art. I am still learning."

"But what about all these people?" he asked. "Why do they adore you so?"

Her grin was the old one he remembered. "They have fallen in love. Not with me. With my idea. But anyone who wants to is free to leave Paris. If they do, they receive a huge credit that would enable them to live in excellent style anywhere. If they stay, they contribute to the life of Paris, but they can remain as separate as they please or merge with the vision as much as they want to. As to what I'm doing . . . I'm not really sure. What is—that? Inside your jacket?" She reached forward and touched his lapel, gave him an apologetic glance. He realized that she could not move the jacket and he pushed the lapel aside, revealing the sculpture he now kept on a chain around his neck.

She stared at it. "Where did you find this?"

"In Bangkok. That's when I knew you were still alive. But Illian, what is it?"

She looked up at the sky. "I don't just want to communicate with other people. I want to communicate with the universe. With something out there. I feel as if I have something to say. That everyone does. That we are all saying it together, but that I am providing the framework. That"—she gestured toward the sculpture—"that is a small rough image of . . . the shape of my thought. It's *light* art. *Radio* art."

"And everyone here is being this? I too can be this 'radio art'?"

Her face was lit by a huge smile. "You are, dear Tamchu. You are now, just sitting here with me. And you have made me very, very happy."

Then she effervesced away.

Tamchu was not surprised. Nothing surprised him any more.

He gazed across Paris. The sun was setting and trees and buildings were burnished orange. The heat of the summer day had subsided, and a slight breeze stirred the air, carrying a perfume that perhaps came from the enormous flowers, which he saw—fully—for the first time.

From his high point, Paris looked like a garden for giants, laced with lights that intensified as the sky darkened. These lines of lights went everywhere, at angles that gave him a sense of rhythm. He stood, he saw as he looked directly below, on a framework of light.

No matter where went in Paris, he would be with Illian, even though he could not see her.

That was all that mattered.

He was free.

Kita insisted on spending day after day in Paris and commanded Hugo to stop pestering her to leave. "There is something stunningly important happening here." She sat at the café table she'd had dragged into their apartment. She parked herself there almost twenty-four hours a day, looking at her data, trying to stop her ears against Hugo's frantic mutterings.

Now he said, "What could be more stunningly important than whatever's happening now in New Orleans? Kita, I'm *beside* myself.

They could all be . . . wiped away—or whatever—by now. My contact in Hong Kong told me that she was positive that the Kyoto weapon, or plague, or whatever you want to call it, is now in the hands of the International Federation worldwide. The latest news from the United States is that Atlanta is under siege and that the Army is moving toward New Orleans—"

Kita withdrew her thoughts from her work with great difficulty. It was as if she was running down ten avenues simultaneously with glowing wires of powerful thought, braiding them together in a precise sequence, seeing the endpoint way out there in the distance. And then it was gone.

It was apparently necessary to make some kind of impression on Hugo. She pushed back her chair, stood, and slammed her fist down on the pheromone table. A rainbow washed chaotically across the tabletop. She allowed the stern voice of her mother to make itself useful for a change. "Let me try to explain one more time. Paris was attacked with the same plague that was loosed on Kyoto. By now, it has disseminated around the world through terrorist groups who probably have very little idea of what to do with it once it has had an effect. Apparently, this so-called International Federation falls into this category—a once-legitimate entity now governed by thinly disguised hoodlums and thugs who took over in a well-plotted international coup. Illian, the so-called Sun Queen, has rescued Paris."

"Who is Illian anyway?" asked Hugo impatiently. "She reminds me of the Wizard of Oz."

"I've never read that book," said Kita. "Americans seem very excited about it."

"Well, you never hear or see the great and powerful Oz until the end, and then you find that he's just an ordinary human being."

Kita laughed. "Illian is *not* an ordinary human being. For one thing, she has the unusual DNA sequence that has cropped up here and there around the world since the Silence. That might be pretty significant, though no one has ever seemed to figure out why, and I don't know a lot about it myself, only that it exists. But what is astonishing to me is that she allowed herself to be read, cell by cell, into the information system of Paris. This is a process people have been talking about since before the millennium—preserving consciousness by transforming it into another medium. Not into a dead record, like a book, but into a living entity—like a BioCity—in which the individual can continue to function mentally. It was very brave of her. Theoretically, I can see that it's possible, yet I would certainly never do it unless, maybe, I was about to die anyway. I'm not at all sure how she knew that this was possible. From what I gather, it was an intuitive endeavor, since the original Illian was an artist, not a scientist. During the initial transformation of Paris, it was even more plastic than it is now and much more vulnerable to such an act. She just seized the opportunity. But that's not the only unusual thing about Illian. By sacrificing herself to this transformation, she has done something to the city that protects it. Paris is not like Kyoto. Paris is free, vibrant, powerful." The memory of Kyoto drove Kita. When she was able to sleep, she often woke from a nightmare of Kyoto, where all minds were silenced, awaiting directions from whomever knew the key to providing them. "If I have any chance of saving New Orleans, the best way to go about it is to figure out what has happened here. Why has Paris been spared the fate of Kyoto?"

Hugo nodded as she spoke, obviously impatient for her to finish. "Well, have you figured it out? How much longer will we have to stay?"

" 'Well, have you figured it out?' " Kita mimicked. "Yes, of course I have, Hugo! Days ago. But I'm just enjoying my trip to Paris so much—" Again her mother's sharp nagging voice.

It's my voice now, Kita realized. And that's just fine.

"Look, Hugo. If you will just leave me alone, this might not take much longer. It has taken me a long time to understand how to access everything. But I believe that the key lies in rhythm."

"Rhythm?" Hugo's eyebrows shot up.

That, along with his new pin-striped shirt with rounded collar and bow tie, gave him a comical look that refreshed Kita immensely. Hugo was not a dull man.

"Yes. You know that Illian has proclaimed this a city of radio art, a city of cosmic light. She has configured much of the conduitry and other large metal objects, like rail tracks and so on, into a huge receiving array. She is also sending a signal toward space. I have no idea if the signal makes it out past the ionosphere. I don't know if it gets transmitted anywhere. However, she has spread this rhythm everywhere in the city. Everywhere you go in the city, musicians are playing music based on it. It all sounds different, because there are different instruments, different moods. But underneath, it's the same. She has set up flashing light displays everywhere. She screens movies in the theaters with this rhythm flashing subliminally."

"Quite a woman," said Hugo. "Or maybe, quite a monster."

"Well. A benign monster. A benevolent dictator? You might have some firsthand experience—just kidding!" From what Hugo had told him about Marie, she seemed to fit the same description. "Anyway, this rhythm stimulates a particular growth sequence in the brain. A chemical environment is set up. Musical thought in particular is a powerful environment for growth of dendrites, for facilitating new connections in the brain. Jazz musicians called on to improvise, for example, were observed long ago to use their brain in a different way than those musicians who simply read music and repeat what they see on the page. I am pretty sure that this particular rhythmic sequence is intimately tied to the release of certain brain chemicals. This constant inundation prevents the plague-inducing chemicals from locking in and proliferating. To use a rough analog, stressful exercise releases naturally produced opiates, called endorphins, which connect to receptor sites in the brain. This engenders an experience of bliss. Some people even report mild hallucinations."

"Sounds rather exhausting."

"Well, it is. I mean, if one were to keep dancing to this rhythm. It may even be that dance—have you noticed that Paris is full of dance halls and that Parisians are constantly dancing, Hugo?—also ties into the endorphin chemistry. But at some point the chemical environment needs to be locked into the brain, so to speak. Through what medium? Vitamins? Hormones?"

"Um . . . I think you're teasing me. Let me guess, Kita. Pheromones?"

"Exactly! But which ones? What combination? I've been running simulations until I feel as if my mind is turning to mush. But there is most definitely an airborne chemical process that can lock in this state of mind—this freedom from coercion, this strength of individuality. And that's what I need to find." Kita dropped back into her chair. "Could you please bring me some more coffee?"

"Sure. And when you find this bit of illumination, you're going to give it to Illian? Assuming that, as you say, she is doing all this . . . intuitively."

Kita was startled. "Illian? She could not care less. Freedom is not her goal here. It is just a side effect. I'm not really sure what her goal is. Her influence is very powerful within this system. I'm sure that she has the capacity to know much more now than she did when she was entirely human. I have never had such close contact with such an unusual being. I'm not sure if we could actually communicate with each other very effectively. It would probably be like a cat and a dog trying to agree on the nature of reality. I run into traces of her all the time within the system. Kind of like a flavor. Of course I will share it. I guess it would be like showing someone how their brain works. I'm not sure that she wants it. She is just generously allowing me to use these resources here. I really hope to be finished soon. I'm working as hard as I can. It would help if I were bothered a bit less."

Hugo said, "Sorry. I'm just pretty worried. I might be able to find a fast diesel sailboat on the black market to get us to New Orleans. We can't risk flying. Is that all right?"

"Whatever you want, Hugo. Just leave me alone, all right?"

Kita's eyes burned, despite her most chemically advanced efforts to stave off the effects of sleeplessness.

She jerked awake, hearing someone snore.

Oh. It was her. There was no one else in the dark room.

Her table glowed solid blue, in suspended mode. She must have been asleep in her chair for at least twenty minutes. This would not do. She tried to ignore the way her heart began to beat more quickly, the way her stomach tightened. If only she were smarter! It would be stupid to go on to New Orleans without taking advantage of this opportunity to understand the mechanism of Paris's salvation, but she was tired of getting nowhere.

She felt very much alone. Though Hugo, in theory, knew what they had taken from Tamchu, she was not sure that he truly understood its full import.

It was like the Holy Grail. Or the philosophers' stone; whatever that European medieval idea had been called. The alchemist's quest for a substance that could turn dross into gold—or something very much like it—had at last been achieved. It was the power humans had sought and lusted after for thousands of years, but it had not been discovered. It had been deliberately developed, created, in a wholly artificial and godlike process.

And Kita was convinced that it was something that humanity would need time to learn how to control. It held the potential of reassembling the world into bounty. At the same time, it was more dangerous than the atomic bomb.

And it could not, without more wisdom than could be scraped from a billion pages of philosophers' ramblings, reassemble the human mind so that it would know how best to use this power.

Perhaps that might be the worth of Marie's city-on-the-sea, her Atlantis, mused Kita. It might be a safe haven where we might, at last, reach to the roots of understanding where we have come from, what we have become, and where we might possibly go.

Kita got up, went to the sink, bathed her face.

"Are you making progress?"

Kita turned at the ethereal yet familiar voice. "Hello, Illian."

She saw a thin woman sitting on the kitchen bar that divided the room. She wore a yellow sheath dress, a red brocaded shawl, and had her blond hair pulled up in a French twist. Her legs were crossed, and she gripped the edge of the bar with both hands.

Kita could see right through her.

She looked around involuntarily, trying to find portals in the walls that might project laser beams. The wall was covered with flocked wallpaper. Lasers had long been reduced to almost quantum-sized beams, and the projectors could easily be embedded, in a city such as this transformed Paris, in every surface. Rearrangement at a molecular level was swift and precise, and wherever Illian wished to manifest, she could no doubt command the quick assembly of hologram projectors. Kita was still awed by the powers of Paris and wished again that she did not have to leave.

But she had responsibilities.

Illian continued, "I was thinking that perhaps I could help you. I heard you talking to the dwarf a few hours ago. There are things of great beauty in the databanks of the city. I know that I do not see them as you do. I use them in different ways. But look."

The wall near the sink lit up. Kita saw swirling nebulae and a running table of numbers scrolling down the right side of the image. Something about a magnestar and starquakes. Kita sat and watched them for a moment. "I don't know anything about astronomy. Where is this picture coming from?"

"These are old images from the Paris Observatory, from just before the first Pulse. They enchant me. But then—let me see—perhaps the chemical information from my hives. I have seen you come very near to accessing it, but something always holds you back. I think that it's some kind of identification code. The city does not recognize you as being fully vested. There is a great stubbornness about it; it knows that you are not French." She grinned. "I have managed to fool it completely in that regard. Here. Will this help?"

New information appeared on the wall.

Kita leaned forward. This made sense. She tried to study the chemical equations, but they blurred before her tired eyes. "Is there a way to convert this information into a bar graph?"

"Well, I don't know. I suppose."

The colors on the wall reassembled into a bar graph showing metapheromone concentrations in various quarters of Paris and their history since the Kyoto plague rained down on the city.

Kita leaned back, suddenly quite alert. It was like seeing a clear blue sky after weeks of storm. She wrote rapidly in her notebook for several minutes, suffused by relief.

Finally she looked up. She wasn't finished, but she was well on her way to understanding. "Thank you very much, Illian. This will do quite well. I have another question."

"I will try and answer."

"All of the physiological information from your previous physical body is in the city's memory banks and there is something very unusual about it."

"What?" asked Illian with a touch of eagerness.

"Many organisms have been shown to create magnetic maps as part of their development. They receive magnetic orientation information via the magnetoreceptors—which are basically comprised of magnetite and often intertwined with the same nerve receptor system used to sense pheromones. They are then sent to another part of the brain and compiled. I have studied honeybees extensively and they have this sense, as do many fish, birds, and even mammals. These organisms all use naturally generated magnetic fields for navigation. It is a learned process. I'm not sure if you know this, but the learning process—brain growth—can sometimes be very tumultuous and create a lot of strange symptoms. Your trigeminal nerve—a nerve that runs from near the nasal passage to the the anterior part of the brain—was magnitudes larger than that of normal humans, and this is the nerve used by most organisms to transmit magnetic information from the magnetoreceptors to the brain. The information is apparently gathered by the superficial ophthalmic ramus. In fact, your body contained a lot more biogenic magnetite than most humans."

Illian's voice was thoughtful. "That is interesting. I know that I am different from most people. I know that the lab that I ran away from when I was much younger was engaged in trying to analyze people like me. I was often very sick when younger, but Artaud helped me. My art helped me. And now the city of Paris is helping me."

"But what are you *doing*, Illian?"

"I don't really know. I didn't know what I was doing when I did my art on a more personal scale. I only knew that it was necessary and gave me a sense of satisfaction. It was like going down one path and finding darkness, then going down another path and finding light. I learned to take the path to light. This is where it has led."

"I wish that I could stay longer," Kita said. "There is much to learn here. But the information you've shown me about the metapheromone concentrations in Paris and the pathways you used to take the Kyoto Plague to a manageable level is what I need now. Hugo is very anxious to leave. Maybe at some point I will be able to return and learn more about the magnetoreceptors. I think that the fluctuations in broadcasting must have had a profound effect on you as you grew up."

Illian's laugh was much more hearty than Kita would have expected. "To say the least," she said and vanished.

Chromatic Passing Note

New Orleans | 2039

A knock sounded at the door of Marie's headquarters. Surprised, Marie walked over and hesitated a moment before opening it. "Who is it?"

The reply was muffled by the wood. "Jason Peabody. These guys checked me out."

She opened the door a crack. Neely, one of her trusted body-guards, nodded. She opened the door fully.

A young white boy stood there. Well, young by her standards. Maybe twenty-five. He wore jeans, a T-shirt, hiking boots. His hair was almost white, burnt by the sun, she surmised, for he had a dark tan and his face was peeling.

"Texas is pretty damned big," he said, "and NAMS is blocked around Dallas. I had to walk fifty miles in the sun before I could catch a ride." He grinned. "Jason Peabody, certified nanotech engineer. I'm looking for a job."

It was a quiet day in New Orleans. The Crescent City project—the floating city—was progressing as planned. Many of the nanotech-nologists, engineers, and other scientists that had shown up in re-sponse to Marie's ad were there, but she also had a respectable coterie of highly qualified people installed in the towers that lined Canal Street. One of the most glaring holes in the Crescent City plan was the fact that they had no space program. A small faction was constantly on her case about finding someone to establish a space agenda.

Marie had lunch with the young man so that she could check him out: raw oysters, caviar, and beer. These were wild oysters Marie bought from the same oyster supplier her grandmère had used. "At least the food programs are running pretty well," Marie mused. "The caviar is completely manufactured."

"Outstanding," enthused Jason. His pile of shells was much larger than hers.

"Thanks. But right now I've got a few problems to deal with." Marie pushed her plate aside. "Where are you from again?"

Jason shrugged. "All over, I guess. In the past few years, I've been in Los Angeles, San Francisco, Salt Lake City, and Houston."

Marie leaned forward, a frisson of excitement brushing her spine. "What's going on in Houston? I've heard rumors that the space program is taking a strange turn there."

Jason nodded, blotting his sweating forehead with a napkin. "They're planning a launch."

"A launch!" This was news, though not entirely a surprise. The International Federation insisted that all space programs were dead, crippled beyond repair by the lack of communications capabilities. But everyone hoped that the remnants of NASA were carrying on. Cape Canaveral had been hit by a killer hurricane ten years earlier and launches had been discontinued. The serious spacers had taken over NASA operations in Houston about that time, with, if rumors were true, all kinds of advanced nanotech capabilities.

"A lightship," he said gravely. "It will be their first launch ever at the new launch site. It's a gorgeous thing, really. Stage after stage of deployment and development right up to the time that it finds the source of the Signal. It evolves. That is, if it's ever completed, it will."

So, Jason was the real thing. He was informed and intelligent. Marie took in the young man's face—serious, excited, troubled. "This means a lot to you."

Jason nodded.

"And how close were you?" asked Marie.

"I was a janitor. I programmed the cleaning nan for the Space Center. The previous janitor had top clearance, but he'd died suddenly. Of course, they were terrified. It's kind of funny how important such a lowly job would be. I'd just mustered through two top-rated engineering training programs." His face was flushed; exhaustion showed in his eyes. "And while I was at it, I managed to figure out a way to hide my . . ." He stopped.

Marie opened her mouth to speak, then closed it. She didn't want to spook him with too much quizzing. "So you had something they needed."

"Yes. Very much." He leaned forward. "I managed to get the—"

Once again, he paused. "Is New Orleans everything that people say it is?"

And less, she thought. "What do you mean?" Marie wondered what he had managed to get. Something quite interesting, no doubt.

"Free. That's what people are saying. That's the rumor. That's why I came. Everywhere else, I ran up against barriers. They're embedded in the structure of every BioCity I trained in. I tried discussing them with my mentors and with other engineers and they all were of the opinion that these limits and barriers are necessary to enable the city to run smoothly." He leaned back; furrows appeared between his eyes. "The whole approach reminded me of something I saw as a child. Maybe I didn't go there myself, I don't remember; maybe it was some kind of educational thing. Yes. It must have been. Because I was walking around in a very dangerous place and my parents never would have let me do that. It was in Los Angeles, I guess. The people were really mean. They would kill you in an instant. Or you might get killed just by accident if you got in the way of something going down. That happened to a lot of people. A lot of children. And the thing was that at one time it was a really nice place. The people there owned stores and businesses and their own houses and knew all their neighbors. A lot of families had lived there for generations. Then some city planners came in, put through a freeway. They had the best intentions in the world, but didn't take into account human nature. They relocated people to kind of okay housing, but in the process tore up the web of relationships. In twenty years, everything was chaos. The freeway enabled people to live outside the city but come in to work. It funneled foreigners through the old neighborhood and cut everything into a good side and a bad side of the highway. I kind of felt like that in these cities. There's a good neighborhood—kind of an artificial place, created at the expense of . . . well, of full information. They can only function by pretending that certain kinds of knowledge don't exist. It's like a textbook that ends at some point or those old maps of the world that just had sea monsters beyond a certain point. Like true knowledge of nanotech would be too messy, too much for the common people that get receptored in to handle. To me, it seems like the perfect opportunity to increase the mass of knowledge—if there is such a thing. To have a society where knowledge keeps growing and growing. But that isn't what's happening in most of the BioCities. People in them accept the limits in order to have . . . well, whatever they feel they're getting. A good life, by their definition. Like they've been trained to never expect more." He gulped down his second pint of beer and slammed the mug onto the table. "Sorry. I mean, I don't care if that's how they want to live. I feel *sorry* for them. *They don't have any choice and that's not right.* Of course, they all voted to change to BioCities. Again, without full information. And they had to pay for it all to boot. They're still paying."

He gazed blearily at Marie. A goofy half-drunken smile flitted across his face. "There are rumors about New Orleans all across the country. I had to get around all kinds of military action to get here. The International Federation has got you locked up pretty tight. As far as I'm concerned, that's a good sign. You must be pretty dangerous."

Marie planted her elbows on the table and rested her head in her hands for a long moment. Then she looked into the boy's . . . no, the *valuable* young man's eyes. "I have to be honest with you. We have the same problem here. That's the plan, what you were talking about. That's what I want. But it hasn't worked out so far." She pushed back her chair, got up, and started pacing.

"We had to get the original package from the government. We couldn't have afforded it otherwise. No one can. It was really stupid of me. I was counting on getting information from one of the original designers of metapheromones."

"From Japan, you mean."

She smiled, well-pleased. "Yes."

"I'm pretty smart. Maybe I can help." He spoke in a neutral and informative tone that amused her. He wasn't bragging, just offering information. Marie had no way of vetting his credentials except by his results.

He was very young. But he seemed solid, committed, and, above all, extremely knowledgeable. He had fathomed the dark places where government programming lurked.

"I think we can use you here," she said. "And eventually I think we will create the kind of place you're dreaming of." She leaned across the table and looked into his eyes. "I've been dreaming of it too."

Marie clung to the bow of the *Erzulie,* filled with the effervescent joy a visit to Crescent City always brought. The navy blue of the deep sea lightened to translucent green as they entered a canal that cut through the breakwater surrounding the city. The breakwater was covered with lush orchards of papaya, mango, and citrus and rose in elevation until they were traveling in a narrow canal bounded by fifty-foot-high walls. Then the height of the walls descended rapidly and the canal opened into a vast lagoon, one of many that ringed the central towers. Schools of fish darted beneath the boat, and Marie saw that on the next lagoon over, spirulina harvesting was taking place.

The floating city was hexagonal in shape, comprised, like a beehive, of hexagonal sections. Thermal energy converters generated electricity via heat exchange, a process that had been perfected in the last few decades. Nitrogen thus brought to the surface nourished the spirulina farms, which in turn fed a growing web of life. The structure itself grew modularly around the buoyant converter towers, of which there were now five, providing twenty million square feet of living area, for each tower was fifty-five stories high.

Still, this was only enough space for a population of about ten thousand, since it had to supply all of their needs—indoor and outdoor, public and private spaces. She hoped to have enough room for at least fifty thousand people before beginning full-scale settlement. That would take about another year, according to their constantly revised timetable. Until then, she had to put up with the increasing instability of the mainland.

Marie had tried to squelch a rumor that some kind of Marcus Garvey island was being grown in the Caribbean, but three more rumors popped up in its place. Garvey, a visionary, had galvanized and divided the African American community in the first part of the twentieth century with his campaign to raise money for the project of establishing a Black Star Line to unite the black diaspora throughout the world and help former slaves to return to Africa if they so wished. Perhaps there was some kind of distant analogy between Garvey's effort and her wish to provide an environment free of government manipulation, but she could not claim so proud a lineage, philosophywise. Still, the spirit of the rumor pleased her.

But she feared Crescent City becoming a target for pirates, soldiers, or radicals. Right now about three thousand people lived here, but they were not trained in defense. They were the scientists, technicians, and sociologists that were making it work.

She looked up at the towers, blue-tinged against the blue sky, and envisioned the gardens and rooms within. On one of the highest levels, there was even a terraced coffee plantation, misted and cooled. Marie didn't know the name of the bacteria that lived on the red coffee berries, but she did know that it had some kind of important medicinal potential. She knew only a bare fraction of what the city was all about—an overview, seen from the perspective of a distant manager.

The *Erzulie* headed toward a sparkling white sand beach fringed with coconut palms, then cut toward a marina, almost readied for the process of loading the spirulina, cultured pearls, and seafood they would export in order to defray the cost of the city.

Kalina greeted Marie with her usual disdain as Cut Face and Shorty, now seasoned crew, brought the boat to dock. Four years at Harvard, a hallowed enclave protected from social uproar with a hefty dose of old money, had given her a sophisticated intellectual gloss. Her glorious black hair was pulled by the sea breeze as she tied off the *Erzulie*'s bow line and nodded curtly to Marie.

Harold, her chief engineer, had no such reservations. A short middle-aged man with a bald pate and a salt-and-pepper beard, he stood on the landing grinning, well tanned and wearing only shorts. A survivor of the Freestate disaster, he was the overseer of the entire project—knowledgeable and competent. He also had an unshakable faith in Crescent City.

He grabbed Marie's hand, pulled her onto the landing, and gave her a quick hug. "Hey, babe, welcome home. What kept you?"

"Problems, Harold," They walked down the dock beneath a cooling overhang.

Crescent City was stunningly beautiful. Too attractive by half, she thought. The ascending pavilions, filled with empty apartments and blossoming gardens, were a vacuum waiting to be filled.

"Things are tough all over," Harold said.

"I'm all ears."

After drawing pints of home-brewed wheat ale, they sat in an open cafeteria that one day would be brimming with the citizens of Crescent City. Now the wind blew through the empty space, bringing with it the scent of plumeria blossoms.

"One of the programs seems to have gone bad," Harold told her, both elbows on the table as he clasped his beer, his pale blue eyes focused on hers. "We're not generating enough manganese to bond with the magnesium and form the alloy necessary to finish the final segment. I think we'll need some hefty shipments of manganese in order to keep on schedule." He frowned. "Damned if I know how this happened. According to our records, our natural production should have been much higher in the last three months. Sorry I didn't catch this sooner."

Marie pulled her attention back from the beautiful greenness of the artificial lagoon with an effort. "Espionage?" she suggested.

Harold shrugged. "Could be. There are precisely four ways in which we ought to have known about this, and it looks like all of them failed. We got enemies?"

She laughed. "Plenty. Get me some figures on what you need, how much, and when. I'll see about getting it shipped to New Orleans as soon as we get back. One of the main NAMS lines was bombed by terrorists a few weeks ago, but I think it should be repaired soon."

"And after that, you can just buy a few thousand slaves to mine whatever we need, right?" asked Kalina, stepping up behind Harold.

"Got the whole world in your hands, don't you? A new world a-comin', right?"

"Why are you so rude to your mother, kiddo?" Harold asked.

"She's not my mother."

"Oh. Well, *that* explains it." Harold laughed.

"Listen, Harold," Marie said. "You—or someone here—need to start thinking more seriously about security. You tell me who and I'll have a talk with them. I want something heavy-duty in place pretty quickly. There's a lot of . . . trouble . . . out here. Zealots and terrorists just aching to find a place like this."

"Yeah, Marie." Kalina held her hair in one hand to keep it from blowing across her face. "Let's set up a standing army on the City of the Future. I think that would be the ideal basis to your 'pure democracy.' Kind of like, you know, a South American dictatorship. Get it off to the right start."

"At least a start," said Marie, pushing back her chair. "Harold, mind giving me the inspection tour?"

Harold gulped the rest of his beer. "Let's have at it."

A metallic clank woke Marie that night. In an instant, she was kneeling on her bed, looking down out her window onto the landing below.

A long low boat was tied up in the shadows. Two men unloaded a large black box from their fifty-foot-long flash boat and set it on the landing.

Her bare feet made no sound on the seacrete floor. Her nightgown flowing behind her, she hurried out the door and down the steps. She was not sure where the others were sleeping. She tried to tamp down the rage she felt. She'd waited too long to insist on tighter security. But it was her own fault. There was just too much to do . . .

Marie was pretty sure the box contained weapons—or perhaps explosives. She was angling for a better view when someone grabbed her from around the waist from behind and put a hand over her mouth.

She bit the hand and punched her elbow into her assailant's groin. She backed up and stomped on his foot. He cried out and she wrenched free, turning. They stared at one another, panting. He had his gun out.

"Who are you?" she said loudly.

"Who are *you*?" Then he stepped back. He was a white man with a shaved head. Tattoos writhed across his scalp. "I recognize you. Marie Laveau."

"That's ridiculous." She heard running feet.

He grinned. "Hell yes! It's really *you,* Miss black-as-the-ace-of-spades Voodoo Queen her*self*. Hoo!" He reached out and grabbed her heart stone, yanked it so that the chain broke, and examined it, shaking his head. She smelled his sweat. "Some idiots say your power comes from this. Some kind of cheap trinket, eh?"

She did not pause to tell him that her power came from the fact that she had nothing to lose. She kicked his gun from his hand and dashed for it as it skittered across the landing. She grabbed it as Kalina came around a corner. The dock lights glared on suddenly.

The man, still holding Marie's heart stone, pulled a derringer from his belt and took a step toward Kalina, who looked at her mother with fear-filled eyes.

Marie took careful aim at the man's chest and squeezed the trigger.

Blood spurted across the landing as he staggered backward, gasping, and toppled into the sea. Marie saw his flailing hand, trailing the chain to her heart stone, as she rushed to the ledge. Then it vanished beneath the dark surface of the choppy ocean. There was nothing below for almost a mile, except the heat-exchange towers and sea anchors.

Kalina screamed.

Marie saw that Cut Face and Shorty were scuffling with the other men. Several more shots were fired, muffled by surf pounding the nearby beach. "There may be more on the boat," she yelled, as Harold and a crowd of younger men and women arrived. They just stood and stared as Marie herself marched down into the boat and flushed out a cowering man in a black wetsuit. On the back of his hand she noticed a tattoo of two intertwined c's.

She prodded him onto the landing with the gun she still held and climbed out, her nightgown blowing against her. "What's going on?"

The man glanced around wildly. "There's not supposed to be anyone at this landing."

"Says who?"

The man pointed to a man sprawled on the landing. "Him."

Harold knelt at the man's side. "Callihan. Shit. He's dead. I fired him six months ago. Smart guy, but . . . I had a funny feeling about him. I wonder if he had anything to do with the bonding problem."

"Open that box," Marie directed the man with the tattooed hand.

"No!" He stepped back.

"Lift that box back into his boat," she directed Cut Face and Shorty. "Very carefully."

They did so, settling it behind the console.

"You," she told the man. "Get in the boat."

"But—"

"Now!"

"I'll tell you where I'm from—"

"I know where you're from. You're from New Orleans, you have ties to a terrorist group called the Caribbean Confederation, and you planned to take over this place by killing everyone. Now get in."

He climbed down into the boat.

Marie looked around. "And you." She waved in two injured men with her gun. "That's everyone? Start up the engine and leave. And you! Behind me! Go! Now!"

She waved the gun wildly and everyone retreated beneath the overhang.

Marie untied the boat and shoved it away from the landing.

The tattooed man looked doubtfully at Marie. "Turn the key," she directed.

He started the boat, turned it seaward, and opened the throttle, heading at full speed toward the breakwater.

After five seconds, Marie took aim and fired.

Her third shot hit the boat and it erupted in a tremendous geyser of water and flame.

Kalina stared at Marie.

Marie could not fathom her expression. Disgust? Admiration?

Or was she simply stunned at what she had just seen her mother do?

Marie dropped the gun on the landing and walked away.

She found an elevator and took it as high as it would go. She stepped out into a vast hall filled with shadowy shapes and walked toward the enormous arched window. Above was one of the new water-filled skylights, and it cast rippled moonlight on the floor.

Marie leaned out and watched the shards of fire out in the lagoon until they were extinguished.

For some reason, all that she could think about was the aching absence of the heart she had worn around her neck for all those years.

Agwe's heart.

Two weeks later, Marie, in an anomalous state of uncertainty, stood beneath a black umbrella in the pouring New Orleans rain. The chill darkness of the late-November afternoon seemed apropos. Her immortality had been precipitously withdrawn.

The reflection of the red neon ACME OYSTER BAR sign shimmered in the street, pocked by raindrops. Marie walked slowly toward the oyster bar, heedless of puddles, shook off and furled her umbrella beneath the overhang, and stepped inside, almost tripping over a huge burlap bag of oysters.

The old man pulled the sack behind the bar. He cut it open, grunted as he heaved it up, and spilled the rough gray oysters into a scarred wooden trough. He rapidly opened half a dozen and set them on a white plate, which was whisked away by a waiter. He turned his attention to Marie. "What can I get for you?"

Marie hoisted herself onto a stool. Her hat brim deposited drops of water on the bar, but she left it on. "Half dozen and a draft. Ale."

The ale was cold and bitter. The clatter and din of the room seemed to expand in rough increments. She watched raindrops trace the window with crooked, red-limned trails.

"I'll not mince words," Dr. Weinstein had told Marie. They sat in her office. A poster for the Louis Armstrong Centennial illuminated the wall behind her, called forth from the city's memory. "You're dying."

"Hmm."

"That's all you have to say?"

Marie nodded. "I thought so. How about that!"

"It may be difficult for you—"

Marie stood up and slammed her fist on the desk. "Damn it! So fix me! I'm too fucking busy to die!"

"Ah, that's better." Dr. Weinstein's frizzy black hair was pulled back in a tight bun, but much of it escaped around her light brown face. "You do have options."

"Go back in the tank, right?"

"Not exactly. But it will involve some downtime. Probably about ten months."

"Can't do it."

"Why not?"

"I have a bit of work to do."

"I rather thought so." Weinstein's voice was needling. "Well, then, it's a good day to die."

"Give me my alternatives."

Weinstein tapped the cube that held Marie's medical tests. "As we suspected, your nerves are atrophying at a pretty rapid pace. There is an underground regenerative drug available."

"You've done your homework."

"Enough to know that it's a quick fix, and dangerous, and that it works short-term."

"How short?"

"We don't know yet. You'd be one of the first test cases." Weinstein leaned forward, and her clasped hands slid across the desk toward Marie. "Use the tried-and-true method, Marie. You don't have nine lives. You'd be out for six months, max, and back on the road after four months of rehab, better than ever."

Without Hugo, there was no one to pick up the reins, no one she could trust to oversee New Orleans, the Crescent City Project—everything! Except . . .

Kalina was too young. And Marie was not at all sure that she had any interest in her mother's plots and plans.

Crescent City itself was coming along. On her last visit, Harold had proudly shown her the lineaments of what would be a truly revolutionary place to live, to survive, to ride out the rising chaos, and to perhaps find a way to go forward into a new era for all people.

But the next six months would be crucial.

Still, for the first time, Marie had doubts. Must she sacrifice herself for her city? "The technology for brain replication is not quite ready, I gather?"

Weinstein's laugh was sharp and short. "You really do live in a fairy tale. Although I've heard that you could try Los Angeles if you're interested in that sort of thing. Laveau, it's time to fish or cut bait. My advice is to cut bait."

The Acme Oyster bar man said, "Ma'am? Miss Laveau?"

"What?" Marie looked up sharply.

"You think you're invisible?" His eyes were sympathetic. "What is it? You remember me, don't you? Your grandmère use to come in here. Fine woman. I really appreciate what you have done for me and my family." He was a handsome man, his white beard contrasting with dark brown skin. He continued to shuck oysters as he spoke.

"Oh." Marie tried to remember but couldn't. She did remember that the factors that had dragged her in here were the redness of the sign, the necessity of eating and drinking. She looked at her ale, now at half-mast. "How many of these have I had?"

"Three."

"What have I—what have I done for your family?"

"Don't be modest. I went to Louisiana State. A lot of good it did me. When I was a young man, I couldn't find any job except this. I've left it many times, but I always came back. I shouldn't have majored in theater, I suppose." His laugh was deep; Marie could see him onstage easily. "I did a lot of local television commercials in the old days. In a few weeks, I'll be starting another stage production. So I'm happy, even though my wife wasn't all that excited about my career choice over the years. What I'm talking about is that my daughter and her husband and my three grandchildren have those receptors. I don't know what the world is coming to. But whatever is coming, I think they're prepared for it." He flipped out his wallet and leaned his elbows on the bar. Their pictures lit as he pressed the SCROLL key with his thumb. "Tunishia. She's my little doll. Only six. Already doing geometry. And Ellis. He's ten. He's working on some kind of cell design project. I do thank you, Miss Laveau. You have cared enough to make sure that their education is uniquely suited to their talents. I'm sorry that you're so troubled."

She gazed at the children for a moment before he flipped the wallet shut and returned it to his pocket. She was left with a vision of them perishing when homeless angry hordes swept into the city or when subversive elements from the government—or those pretending to be from the government—took over the city by overriding the frail protections she had put in place.

The news was not good. Outside of the cities, the country was becoming increasingly Balkanized. People routinely took justice into their own hands. The frail social contract that depended upon at least some forms of commonality had deteriorated, and great fear—fear of nanoplague contamination carried by food, water, or even by air—was rampant.

Marie took another gulp of ale and accessed the jukebox with a tap of her finger and flicked through the enormous library of sound now available in practically every space in New Orleans. The bar took her fingerprint, one of the many ways the city kept track of profit and loss. This was constantly analyzed by an algorithm that would tell her, eventually, whether this particular social experiment, this venture into a strange blend of capitalism and socialism, was working. She touched the dime-sized green light on the bar's surface with her finger. This prompted the appearance of a small screen on the bar's surface, via which she paid her bill, added a large tip, and found "Mood Indigo."

Its haunting strains insinuated themselves into the air and brought back stories of its era of composition, stories her grandmère had told her about when she was young and piloting boats to and from Cuba, eluding the Feds. About how Churchill's gathering cloud seemed very real and dark, pressing down on the world, extruding frantic, powerful art, and migrations fraught with fear.

This era seemed the same, except there was no safe haven, no country to which to flee, shorn of everything save bare life. *El Silencio* blanketed all, and on the horizon loomed the cloud of nanotech running amok and dismantling everything. The time was ripe for wild preachers, grave predictions, harbingers of doom. Rumor had it that the moon and Mars colonies were both lost—to aliens, to nanodeath, to *El Silencio*.

Marie finished her ale and Ellington continued. The powerful percussive opening of *A Drum Is a Woman,* a piece based on African rhythms, brought forth Agwe, and Agwe saw the golden city far on the horizon.

Agwe bought a pack of cigarettes and lit one. Agwe slid off the stool, left the Acme Oyster Bar, strode three blocks through the rain, slammed soaking wet into Dr. Weinstein's office, and demanded the potion that might prove deadly to Marie, the potion that might truly end her life forever after six months, a year, two years.

But it was Marie, in a warm dry robe, head cleared easily of hangover only half an hour later, thanks to a patch slapped on by Weinstein, who read all of the material, signed a release, and downed that which would heal and perhaps kill her.

And it was Marie who woke the next morning filled with energy, clear memory, full coordination, and urgency, who set her eyes on mothering the city that would preserve civilization for a new millennium.

Hard Bop Rip, Slow Spill

Zeb | Washington, D.C. | 2039

Zeb could tell it was hot by the way others looked at him as he strode down Twelfth Street, his—Craig's—overcoat swinging open and flaring out behind him like a cape. He liked its frayed weight. It actually seemed to cool him if he wore it this way, without a shirt. At the shelter, he had been forcibly sprayed with a permeable sheen of UV filters, which allowed him to bare skin to a presumable breeze that today did not exist. Zeb could barely see five blocks ahead; the trees were an unmoving sculpture of haze-dimmed green, gray buildings simply blended together as if in a hot fog.

He loved this weather.

Drenched in cooling sweat, admiring the colors of the wall next to him, on which an advertisement for domed Los Angeles danced, he failed to see a Social Snitch dart from a doorway and fasten her intensely sensitive hand on his arm. Thus pinioned, he was too startled to move while she flattened her other hand on his bare chest.

"Sir, you belong in Sector Five," she scolded. "I knew you weren't one of mine. You just turn around and march back to G Street where you belong."

" 'This is my country, land that I love,' " belted Zeb in a cigarette-roughened voice. He never knew when such impulses might well up. He wished he remembered more of the words. Must be something he learned in elementary school. He loved being in this mood. He grinned at the Snitch.

"As long as you refuse to register," said the Snitch, "this is not your country. But I'd be happy to register you." She dropped her hand and wiped it off on her flowered skirt. Her face was shadowed by a large blue bonnet.

Zeb pushed the bonnet back and looked into her eyes. "I don't remember voting for you. Can I buy you a cup of coffee?" He almost meant it. Her eyes were a lovely shade of pre-haze blue, punctuated by indigo triangles that wheeled around the irises in a pulsing rhythm. Hypnotic.

As they were meant to be. He jumped back as she pulled her right hand from her pocket and again tried to touch his chest, knowing that her palm held annealing that he refused as his constitutional right. Her swipe went wild and she yelled, "We'll see about you, mister!" as he walked down the street, once more savoring the flare of his coat. He took a deep breath of thick haze, said, "Ahhh!" and remarked to a man as he passed, "Lovely day, isn't it?"

It was lovely to be up to be alert to be full and happy and hazy and plus. Multiplied was better but for now plus would do. Minus was the bad part and he wouldn't think of it, not today. Traffic pulsed next to him, constitutionally filling the streets—a court-proven right to drive singly in a private vehicle—and all around him were concealed constitutional weapons and it was grand—grand—to be in a constitutionally correct area of mind. Since the International Federation had sent soldiers to the United States, the Constitution was much on everyone's mind. "I am constitutional!" he heard himself yell. It was never as if he actually slathered or spat or danced, but he heard and felt o yes, he tasted and saw . . .

A great splat of music held him stationary. From a door, like a cone expanding outward, dense and woven and fraught with a strange positivity. A solid cone, then gone. Then there again—blam—roaring through his brain and leaving it twenty degrees cooler than the weather, clearer, cleansed.

He ran his hand along the flat bar by the door, top to bottom, and his hand read THE HOPSCOTCH BAR in the instant before he was once more rearranged by sound. He combed his beard and hair with his hands for a second noticing in the glass reflection that he wore no shirt and, shrinking with embarrassment, that he was ugly-bearded and unwashed and oh scary too, bushy eyebrows he wanted to turn and run and apologize to the Social Snitch, but instead another blast of music drew him in like a million hands pulling on his neurons. Like space. Like . . .

Suddenly calm, he stepped into the cool dark of the Hopscotch Bar and merged with the intervals he'd so long ago discerned and memorized. They blended into him like silence, matching so perfectly that they almost made the world and time and space vanish so that he was no longer Zeb but everything at once and absolute and perfect, a clarity of matter.

The moment passed as the music lunged forward in exhilarating stupendous constructions apparently generated by a woman in a corner of the room, surrounded by gel-speakers, pressing madly on buttons and brushing various glow-colored pads with elbows, nose, and toes, part of a dance she did, long skirt twirling and contributing to the overall effect as it too brushed ankle-high sensing pads with fishing weights, tennis balls, a mad swirl of objects attached to the hem. With a flourish of her head, she produced a hail of tones with the ends of her braids, and all vibrated gradually into silence. She stood still, her face sweat-sheened, panting. Ten feet away, the bartender rubbed the bar with a cloth. Light rectangled through small high slit windows. Zeb clapped loudly for a long time and no one clapped with him, for he saw as his eyes adjusted to the lack of light, there were no other patrons. She smiled broadly, bowed lightly, and squeezed out through the enveloping array of sensing panels with a clatter of assorted amplified sounds, stepped down off the stage, and slipped into a pair of waiting sandals.

"Can I buy you a drink?" she asked. She was pale brown, with rosy cheeks and lively, large brown eyes. Her voice was like a cultured pearl, smooth and deep-toned. She was not very tall. Perhaps five feet three inches—and skinny.

"I don't know," said Zeb, at a loss. "I should buy you one." He felt in his pockets for nothing and she laughed a hearty three-toned laugh.

"Sit down," she said and pulled out a rickety chair for herself. "This is my bar. I'll treat you. This isn't a show yet. I'm just practicing."

"Meditating," said the bartender as he set large glasses of iced water in front of them, a reverent tone in his voice. "Miss Ra be meditating. What can I interest you in, sir?"

"This is fine," said Zeb, cooling his hands on the glass, marveling at how he'd been physically stunned by sound out of his morning's manic frenzy. In the dark quiet of the place, the buzz of his mind receded. "That Social Snitch outside almost got me."

" 'Social Snitch'?"

"Sure. You know. They touch you and know you're out of place and send you back to your sector . . ." He was silent for a minute. The fan above rotated slowly. Finally he said, "There aren't any Social Snitches, are there?"

"They call me 'the Healer,' " Ra said. She lifted her glass and upended it, poured water down her long throat, which undulated as she gulped. She set it down and took a deep breath. "I could sense you—sense you—walking down the street and needing healing. In case you were wondering about how good you feel right now."

Zeb said nothing. The word "nonsense" circulated weakly through his mind for a moment, then vanished, replaced by powerful paranoid thoughts that paralyzed him. How could they follow him everywhere? How did they know? Who were they; what did they want? They wanted, of course, everything he'd thought for the past fifteen years. They were damned clever. The Social Snitch, of course, and then they set this thing up pretty fast . . .

He was startled by Ra's laughter. "I've got your mind going in circles for sure. I can see you're not a Believer. We can fix that."

"Do you have a first name, Miss Ra?" managed Zeb. It was the polite alternative to getting up and walking out, but he could see that would be useless as an elusive ploy.

"Sun," she said.

"Sun Ra is the reincarnation of, you know, Sun Ra," called the bartender from his post. "A reinterpretation." Dusty light rayed out over the age-darkened pine floors as he spoke, as if with the mention of Sun Ra the sun itself had awakened.

"Sun Ra?" asked Zeb. But Ra, or Sun, said nothing. She leaned back in her chair and stared at Zeb. After the span of about two traffic light changes, she spoke. "It doesn't matter." She sighed, stood, rested her arms on the back of the chair, tilting the two bones of her arms against one another so that her elbow appeared strangely indented. She narrowed her eyes at Zeb. He'd never felt so closely examined.

"Excuse me," she muttered. Her eyes focused on the door so strongly that Zeb turned his head, but there was no one there. She started to walk back toward the stage. Zeb watched her cross the room as if it were a time-delayed movie. He realized that he couldn't stand hearing those intervals again. They brought back the pain of the past few years too clearly. *How* many years? That was the question.

"Why is this the Hopscotch Bar, then?" he asked.

She turned, a smile in her eyes, and the weights and tennis balls and . . . all manner of junk tied to the hem of her skirt whirled out and around, reversed direction twice with momentum, then finally stopped. She hopped twice on one leg, bounced forward on two, went back to one, letting the skirt speak its piece about physics. Zeb continued to watch her. Finally she pointed down to some chalk lines on the floor and said, "Hopscotch."

"Oh," he said.

"And the bar," she said. She walked behind the counter and rummaged around. The bartender said, "It's over there," and she straightened, holding a block of wood, a rectangular prism. She brought it over to him and sat at the table. "Here," she said, pressing it into his hand.

It was smooth. There was no sharpness to it, though he imagined when new it must have been painted or varnished. It was about three inches long and two inches wide and in its center was a cylinder of metal that rattled dully when he shook it. "What is it?"

"A hopscotch bar," she said, a patient tone to her voice. She took it back, crouched on the floor by the hopscotch drawing, rubbed the bar back and forth a few times, and sent it sliding.

He did not shrug, but he felt like it.

She took two long strides and caught it up. "You slide it to the number you're supposed to hit next. Then you have to go and scoop it up and bring it back. If you miss, you lose your turn. Heaven's at the end."

"Where did you get it?" Zeb asked.

"Stole it," she said. "When I was seventeen. I went back to my elementary school. I wanted to get my records and this man yelled at me for coming into school barefoot. I was pretty pissed and went out on the playground down these huge wide steps and the same lady was sitting there as when I was little. She had white hair and wore a white blouse and blue slacks. She sat on a wall next to a stone lion bigger than she was. She always kept watch over us when we were on the playground. She blew her whistle and it was time to go in. The kids ran inside and I walked around the playground and I saw that some-body had left this hopscotch bar outside. I should have taken it inside, but I didn't. I put it in my pocket." She grinned. "It's probably why I haven't been able to save the world yet. Not pure enough. Not as pure as I used to be."

"Pure enough," said the bartender from his ever-moving post, clanking glasses, as if participating in a call-and-response revival meeting.

"Why did you play what you played when I came in?" he asked. She had to be some kind of government agent.

"I just thought of it," she said. "My goal is to save humankind. I know it sounds corny, but there it is. You, for instance. You have such . . . bright edges. But then everything does. Have bright edges. So bright."

"Tell him," said the bartender. "You got to tell him. It's the pure thing to do."

She blinked and sighed and shrugged. She walked over to her squeezed music alcove and slithered inside to a low random cacoph-ony as parts of her touched the sensing devices. A synthesized assonance lingered as she grabbed a piece of paper and squeezed back out. She walked over to the table and handed it to him.

He blinked. It was a narrow flyer. Ranged down it like Morse code were the intervals. Lines, bars, and dots. Repeated three times. That was all.

She took it from his hand and sat down, smoothed it out on the table. "You have to admit it has a lovely rhythm. I fell in love with it when I saw it."

"Where did you get it?" he asked.

"From you," she said. "You were passing them out in the park last week. Throwing them at people, actually, big wads of them like confetti. You were yelling stuff about the secret of the universe. I guess you don't remember. Of course you don't. You were in a state. I was dragging the flowerpots out this morning when I saw you coming down the street." She giggled. "I admit it. I ambushed you. I wanted to surprise you. It's just so sublime. It's not quite finished. I was going to go find you when it was. I've seen you around for the past year or so. We even had coffee once in the old People's Drug store."

"People's Drug?" asked Zeb.

"Ra and me, we been around for a long, long time," said the bartender. "They call it something else now." He did something behind the counter and all manner of glowing lights came on—lines of purple and red that zipped around the crown molding, lights on the table listing PALE RHINO RED, CAPITAL ALE, and other local microbrews. "Tales of the City," a locally produced twenty-four-hour soap, appeared on screens around the room silently, paired with the replicator races that were the big betting draw nowadays.

Zeb smoothed the paper several times. Its texture did seem familiar. He did not quite believe her, though.

Some people came in the door—young people, laughing, asking for beer. More sounds and lights. Zeb looked at the form calling herself Sun Ra, a pattern of information. The pattern swept toward him, outward, he saw, like a wave, enveloping him, so he was once again in his familiar field, that of information.

He heard her voice as he rose from his chair and walked toward the booming light of the door, but did not stop.

Once outside, he raised his hand, holding the crumpled paper, and continued his interrupted stroll down the street. "The secret of the universe!" he heard a voice declaim, and it was his.

But he did not own it.

It was pleasant at the Hopscotch Bar. He could drop in any time he liked and Ra would make sure he had something to eat. Her patrons liked the Star Man too, and he regaled them with speculation, often using the one intelligent table she had to illustrate his points with diagrams or mathematical explanations. In fact, Zeb found that the Hopscotch Bar sufficed quite well as a work environment for him.

That fall and winter passed in a new fashion for Zeb. Ra gradually convinced him to spend a night at her house, then another; they became lovers. This was a new experience for Zeb and he moved into a state of gladness, amazed at Ra's insightfulness, her beauty, and by the fact that she'd used free clinics and university experimental programs without fear to keep her seeming physical age at a steady forty years old.

Most of all, she shared his passion for space. Like the original Sun Ra, she believed that "Space is the Place" and often had that motto running around the frieze of the Hopscotch Bar. She believed in him deeply. She believed everything he said. She did not think he was mad.

In January, Washington filled with even more soldiers. They were preparing for some sort of assault to the South, where Atlanta and New Orleans were defying the authority of the International Federation. Occasionally, they came into the Hopscotch Bar and sat sullenly, drinking alone, for no one liked them. Their English was often atrocious, for it depended on imperfect translation programs, and everyone was suspicious of them and of their intent. About once a week in the newspaper, Zeb read a story about how an International Federation unit had been wiped out in a surprise attack by a homegrown militia that believed they were the emissaries of a One World Government. Around Washington, they were known as the Bug Police, after the slang for nanotech devices, "bugs."

Then Zeb read that Atlanta and New Orleans had seceded from the Union and that New York would be next. Home rule for the District advocates gained new fuel, and riots were frequent. The United States was a member of the North Atlantic Nanotech Organization; NANO's treaty called for severe crackdowns on any nonlicensed use of nanotechnology. Such as was now occurring in Atlanta and New Orleans.

The mood of the city, and of the country, and probably the entire world, was ugly.

Zeb opened his eyes and did not know why. The clock said it was 3:48 A.M. But he felt uncomfortable.

That was not too unusual. He still was not used to sleeping inside, even though he had been with Ra for months. He missed the breeze, the flow of traffic; even, Ra teased him, the crash of breaking bottles. At first he didn't stir, not wanting to disturb Ra. He was capable of lying still for many hours, just thinking.

But . . . this was something different. He got up, picked up his pants from the chair and his cigarettes from the bedside, and went into the living room, shutting the door behind him.

Pulling on his pants, he lit a cigarette and went into the kitchen to make some coffee. Coffee always calmed him down. He'd calmed remarkably since moving in with Ra two months earlier. He was not sure why. It made no sense. He still had long stretches of utter insanity, but they did not come as often. He was grateful to Ra, though, for all that she had done for him. She was a wonder.

As he flicked on the machine, thinking that he might have to switch batteries, he remembered.

Rumors had flown all day at the café. Ra's performance had drawn a packed house, for her apocalyptic views seemed particularly of the moment. She'd been exhausted afterward, but more than that: grim. A lot of people were leaving town. "See if they tell us little people what's up," she grumbled as she toiled up the stairs only an hour earlier. "I don't know, Zeb. Want to leave?"

"I don't care," he told her truthfully.

He poured his coffee and went back to the living room. Car lights traversed the walls and ceiling in a constant flow. He pulled aside the curtain and looked down on a street mobbed with vehicles and people carrying backpacks and suitcases. The evacuation must be well under way.

Evacuation from what?

But he woke her. With little discussion, they left.

The streets were filled with madness. Zeb pushed through the static crowd as best he could, trying to break a path for Ra, but after an hour, of it he was shaky and the mood was beginning to scare him.

Fireworks filled the sky—bottle rockets set off from rooftops and all manner of illegal fountains and bursters. Children leaned from open windows in the chill spring night, holding sparklers, screaming with delight. Behind him Ra shouted out some sort of song that continued to form as she walked. Abandoned cars blocked traffic; many had been pushed onto the sidewalks and caused massive bottlenecks. They had passed two mobbed Metro stations, scenes of fighting and, at the last one, two gunshot deaths.

Zeb turned and leaned against the rough bricks of a town house. He heard one man say as he pushed past, "I heard it jumped to Anacostia." He wiped sweat from his forehead with his sleeve. His hand was shaking.

"You okay, honey?" asked Ra. She appeared to be miraculously unruffled. Zeb realized that compared to her nightly performances this had about the relative tension of a lullaby. "Only about another mile, don't you think?"

"You go on," he said, forcing the words out. "I'm slowing you down."

"I'm in no hurry." She swung her pack to her other shoulder and took his arm. "Now you sing along with me—'I'm the Star Man, I got star vibrations'—that's right—louder. It passes the time. I want all you to sing with me. Come on!"

And she had them all chanting and tramping. Amazing woman.

Zeb felt the pressure of her arm linked through his and flowed along like a dog at heel. His weariness vanished. The chanting was a great strong song, a river, and the fireworks flowers against the black night, in which he could see no stars. So this was it. This would be it. And it wasn't coming from the stars. It was coming from his fellow humans. He laughed, and no one noticed. Why had they been so worried about what might come from space? "We're worse than anything we might possibly imagine!" he shouted, and for a few minutes, some others took up the words as a descant.

Traffic was moving, just barely, by the time they reached Memorial Bridge. Ra stared up at the huge brass horses, glinting with dawn. Zeb stopped with her. He felt as if he might just fall asleep on his feet, standing there.

"Boost me up!" she said, and he obediently formed a step with interlocked fingers. Her bootstep was light and he gave a heave, hoping at the last minute that she wouldn't be hurt.

She grabbed the horse's neck and pulled herself up. In a minute, she was standing balanced on his broad back, head thrown back, singing. He could not hear what in the roar of the traffic.

A pickup stopped next to him. A woman rolled down her window. "Zeb?"

He turned. "Do I know you?"

The look she gave him shook him, though he did not know why. "I'm Annie." She set the brake and got out. People behind her cursed and honked. She opened the passenger door and pushed everything out onto the road. "Get in. Now!" she shouted.

"Ra!" he yelled. "Let's go!"

He caught her legs as she slipped down and carefully lowered her. She grabbed her pack and jumped into the front seat of the truck next to Zeb and slammed the door.

"I've always wanted to do that," she said. She leaned forward so she could see around Zeb. "I'm Ra. Sun Ra."

"I'm Annie."

Zeb leaned forward and punched the cigarette lighter.

"Zeb, where are your manners?" asked Ra.

"She knows my name," said Zeb, lighting a cigarette with a shaking hand.

"That's nice," said Ra with a puzzled look. "Why?"

"I don't know," said Zeb, his voice filled with despair.

They got across the bridge. Annie rolled up the windows and closed the vents. She turned toward Rosalyn and passed Roosevelt Island. She downshifted behind a bank of glowing red taillights. "Don't look now, folks," she said, eyeing the rearview mirror, "but I think our nation's capital is about to become history."

Zeb turned his head as best he could. He saw a flash shudder across the distant buildings. The Washington Monument glowed briefly, then darkened. That darkness seemed to roll outward, then to cross the bridge, to creep up over the riverside verge . . .

"Hold on," said Annie and drove off the highway onto a deeply slanted greensward. She was not the only one, but she drove faster than most, bouncing down beneath a highway ramp, gunning the engine to send the truck flying over a curb into a parking lot.

A dark alley angled away from the parking lot. She careened down it and crossed three lanes of traffic, leaning on the horn. "I think we're heading into the wind," she said, her voice hoarse. "If we can just outdistance it . . ."

She turned into a dark suburb that was deserted; no cars were on the street except for a van, which someone was putting something in. "Looters!" she laughed.

Ra held tightly to the sissy bar above the door, her eyes fixed on the road. "Police up ahead," she said.

"Right," said Annie. She drove even faster, smashed through a barricade, ignored the sirens.

"You're crazy," said Zeb. "Who are you?"

"Your niece," she said.

"Oh." Zeb was quiet for a minute. He lit another cigarette. "Maybe there's some reason we shouldn't go this way?"

"Hell yes, there's a reason. It's a reserved emergency route for government officials, the assholes. But they probably all left days ago."

"How do you know this?" asked Ra.

"Because I'm a fucking government official, that's why," Annie laughed. "Only I thought I might be able to fix things, so I stayed. Not to the last, though. Not to the last." Her voice was defeated. "It's pretty damned strange out here, from what I've heard. NAMS is down from here to Atlanta because of terrorist activity. Our soldiers, under the command of the International Federation, are laying seige to New

Orleans. But I'll take my chances out here. By now, everyone in the District has changed into a zombie."

"You're talking about like when a nanotech program takes over their minds, right?" said Ra.

"Yeah," said Annie sadly. "That's right."

Ra got them lost sometime after midnight. After they got past Manassas, they drove on the smallest roads that they possibly could, and by the stars, with which Zeb helped. One of the reasons he'd hated to move in with Ra was that he deeply enjoyed the nights spent lying on his back outdoors, watching the stars reel through the night sky. He generally fell asleep at dawn. Even though he was in a city, he'd been able to seek out the darker places, see what there was to see, and fill in the rest from memory.

The old roads, vestiges of wagon roads, roads that had been carved before the Revolutionary War through mountain passes, did not run by the compass, as did the roads of the Eisenhower Revolution. They cut down a mountain's flank like a surfer angling a wave's face and dove into small rills with switchbacks. Old metal signs were defaced with paint and bullet dings, so Ra's map-reading capabilities were strained to the utmost. "Hold that lightstick still!" she ordered Zeb every few minutes.

They drove through night-quiet Mount Jackson, perched on the river cliff, twice before Annie realized the mistake. Then she pulled over and they slept in the cab, Annie with her head on a sweater wadded up on the steering wheel, Ra held within Zeb's arm. He did not sleep, but stared at the small white town as the river roared below. Two or three cars passed them but did not slow. Annie woke with a start at dawn, slid out of the truck and peed behind a bush, let off the brake, and jump-started the truck as it drifted down Main Street, waking Ra, who said, "Oh!" Zeb saw the blue-gray line of the Shenandoahs, far across the Valley, and memory pierced and startled him. Zeb Aberly. Born down the Valley. The heart of the mountains his heart.

His lost heart. Lost because of some radio waves from space. That was it. But then, as Annie passed out baloney sandwiches for breakfast and poured coffee from a thermos, he lost that thread.

As morning progressed, Zeb sat by the open window of the pickup truck and the hot summer wind blew his hair back. It seemed to him that the wind was greenness itself, the very essence of the hedgerows and trees that crowded close to these little-used roads that traversed the Blue Ridge parallel to I-81 in the valley's floor. From time to time, they had a view of it, ten miles away, the cars seemingly unmoving, seemingly endless. Long brambled stalks of tiny hot pink wild roses sometimes whipped his arm, so close to the edge Annie drove, steering the wavy road with reckless speed, a look of distant concentration on her face.

Ra had a map propped on her knees and read out distances and the names of small towns as they came and went. "New Hope. Euphoria in six miles." There was usually a single white-steepled church, perhaps a general store, often nothing at all. A century had passed without leaving a mark.

"How come there's no subdivisions out here?" asked Ra.

"No work," said Annie.

Zeb let the years wash through him, wash from him. He realized that he was sitting in his own truck and this startled him, not the least because it had taken him so long to know it.

"Are we heading anyplace in particular?" asked Ra.

"New Orleans."

"Ah," said Ra with deep satisfaction. "I can handle that."

"Why?" asked Zeb.

"You don't know?" Annie leaned forward and looked over at him with amusement in her harried blue eyes and Zeb saw only Sally for a moment. Sally, laughing at her little brother. "I think it will be your kind of town, Uncle Zeb. Our great good government has no toehold there. Not anymore. It seceded from the Union. In fact, it's under siege. Some weird character has gathered all kinds of people there, from all over the world, to work on . . . now what did that damned thing that dropped out of the sky say?"

" 'Consilience through information,' " quoted Ra. "Seems they could have made it snappier." Someone had floated a blimp over D.C. a few weeks ago that had been shot down as soon as it was determined that it had no permit. The liquid within rained across a narrow swath of the city, briefly manifesting information in most mediums it touched. Sidewalks blossomed with the names of people who had come to New Orleans. People you might have thought were dead. Pictures of quaint streets combined with slogans like "Creating the next wave."

" 'If you're interested in freedom,' " quoted Annie and grinned bleakly.

Zeb sat back in his seat, closed his eyes. It seemed to him as if he remembered something about riding a raft down a river. Heading toward freedom. He laughed.

"Well, anyway," continued Annie, "I thought we could help. Or they could help us. We've been hearing a lot about how subversive they are down there. Trying to sabotage our grand plans for keeping the universe intact. Ra, are we getting close to that red dot?"

"If that was Canna Crossroad we just passed, it's about two miles. I think."

"Good. We're cutting it close. Now here's the drill, kids. You guys are from my office. Top security, that's all you have to say. If they ask. Zeb, get that .44 out of the glove compartment and load it, please."

Zeb pushed the button. The glove compartment flopped open and he indeed saw a .44 and a box of ammunition. Zeb dutifully loaded it. "I used to be a good shot, didn't I?"

"The best—with a rifle," said Annie. "Wild turkey and venison. Just slip that in your pocket. I have no idea how you can wear that nasty coat in this heat. I wish you'd throw it away. Only not right this minute," she added hastily.

"Where are we going?" Ra cleared her throat in a nervous fashion.

"The gas station." Annie's freckles stood out on her pale skin, and her straw-colored hair, pulled back with a rubber band, straggled around her face.

A faded billboard for MOON PIES sat off to the right of the road, almost obscured by kudzu. "This is it, I think. Gee, all those late-night memory sessions are sure coming in handy. I am so proud of my government."

" 'Hail Columbia!' " sang out Ra unexpectedly, and Annie laughed. Then she became serious. "Listen, guys, if anything happens—*anything*—you head for New Orleans. Don't look back. I mean it. Agreed?"

Ra and Zeb were silent. "I take that as a promise," said Annie. "It's very important. Believe me."

They came to a rusted gate with a cow guard. Annie had Zeb get out and open the gate. "Leave it open," she yelled out the window. They were on a narrow dirt road that smelled of damp earth and honeysuckle. "Keep in mind that the good guys might not be in charge," Annie said as he got back in.

"It's all relative," said Ra. "Is that thunder? Sky's clear."

They all listened over the wrenching squeaks of the ancient truck. As they topped a rise, the sky's tenor changed, darkening toward the south and giving the air an eerie glow. The wind picked up.

They rounded a curve and the road widened out into a meadow. A concrete wall ran crosswise, and in it an iron gate stood open.

"Hmmm," said Annie. As she approached, a thin teenage boy stepped out from behind the gate. He had a rifle trained on them. Zeb reached into his pocket. Annie said, "Wait."

The boy approached. He shouted, "Ya'll aren't from the goverment, are you?"

"I heard there was gas here," shouted Annie. "Any chance we could buy some?"

He lowered his rifle. "What you got?"

"What do you want?" asked Annie. "How about a watch for a fill-up?"

The boy walked over to the truck. He shaded his eyes and looked at Zeb and Ra suspiciously. "Where you from?"

"Roanoke," said Annie.

"Oh," said the boy. "What you doin' up here?"

"Came up to visit Gramma. Thought we might take her back down in the Valley. She wouldn't come. Stubborn old lady."

"Yeah, they get that way," the boy said.

Annie unstrapped her watch and showed it to him. He smiled. "This'll do. Come on in."

No one said anything as they passed through the checkpoint.

Inside the walls were two rows of black sedans and a tank. A bunker jutted up out of the ground. Heavy steel doors stood open, revealing elevator doors.

"Are those like, cannons, sticking out there, next to the elevator?" whispered Ra. A few heavy splats of rain hit the windshield.

"Pretty much like," said Annie, looking around.

"There they are," said Zeb, pointing to the pumps.

"Okay," said Annie. "Now I want you to stay real alert while I pump gas. I'm going to fill up all those cans in the back too."

She slid out of the cab, slim in her jeans. She fiddled with the pump and started to fill up the truck. A man emerged from the shadows of the bunker a couple of hundred yards away and walked toward them, his open shirt flapping in the wind. Annie finished with the truck, closed the cap, got back in the truck, and turned the key as thunder boomed.

"You're not going to fill the cans?" asked Zeb.

"Hold on," said Annie.

She drove straight at the man at top speed and he dove to the ground. She brought the truck around in a cloud of dust and careened back past the sedans. A heavy report behind them shook the ground. "Missed," said Annie as they zipped through the gate and down the dirt road, rapidly turning to mud in the downpour.

The boy was leaning against the concrete wall, his rifle propped next to him, shielding his new watch from the rain with his shirt and holding it in both his hands. In the noise of the storm, he seemed to notice them only at the last moment, looking up.

They squealed out onto the main road and Annie said, "Okay, Ra, I'm taking the next left. Tell me where it goes."

Her hands shaking, Ra squinted at the map. "I can't—okay. It'll be County Road 73."

"Here it is," said Annie. "Now, what's the next right?"

"Eleven."

"Too big. I'm taking . . . this one."

The truck careened around another corner, onto a narrow trace. It was paved, though, and hugged the ridge. "Hope we don't meet someone coming the other way," said Annie.

"What was that all about back there?" asked Zeb.

"I just didn't like his looks," said Annie. "They've obviously taken over the place. Can't say as I blame them. They've got a real gold mine there. Cars. Enough fuel to drive them all around the world. Provisions." She laughed. "Nanotech secrets. If they can figure them out, they'll have a little kingdom there. The works." She glanced in the mirror. "Shit."

Zeb woke soaking wet in a bed of brambles. His whole body ached. It appeared to be dawn. He groaned as he staggered to his feet.

His right arm was the worst. The sleeve of his coat was singed to charred rags and his skin was blistered and red. His head pounded. But he could still walk. He pushed through the briars, stumbling downhill because it was easier than going uphill. Then he caught a tree and stopped himself, staring through a skein of trees across fields of corn. Beyond, blue ridges rose like lines portraying lyric information in swaying rhyme, echoing one another, converging, parting, rising, falling. Above, the sky, so blue and plain, wiped clean of cloud.

It had been a fireball. His hands were burned. Something that the people following them shot at the truck, then zoomed past as Annie lost control and the truck careened off the road.

He'd pulled her and Ra out of the flaming truck in the pouring rain. He remembered that. But he didn't remember anything else.

He turned and made his way back up the mountainside. It was almost impossible to get through the brush. His hands were bleeding and he was terribly weak. He came to a small run and bathed his face and hands. Blackened skin sloughed off into the bubbling creek. He tried to scry his face, but the water did not mirror him, so quickly did it swirl. It carried leaves and sticks along with firm rapidity.

Nothing here was stuck. No rocks were positioned in such a way that stale eddies formed, keeping the stream's traffic of sticks and leaves from moving.

Despite the horror of the previous day, Zeb felt that he'd broken free at last. Not that his freedom would be mirrored in any sense by the outer world. But memories surged in, awakening his heart from its long sleep like a maiden's kiss.

He stood, dripping with sweat from his mad climb and cool creek water. He smelled the stink of the ancient coat he wore and cast it from him, leaving it in a black muddle next to the stream. He stopped, stepped back, rummaged through it, and took the gun from one pocket and his fat ragged notebook from another. Holding one in each hand, he trudged upward. It was easier here. He walked through a vale of bluebells.

Then he broke through to narrow black road and overhanging trees. The road was potted and unlined. He looked to the right and saw a bare curve. He looked to the left and saw the truck, its cab licked with soot. He trudged toward it, heart thudding.

He saw no bodies.

He walked around the truck. The cab was more or less intact. The bed was empty of whatever Annie had been keeping there. Must have been looted.

He spent several hours ranging up and down the road; climbing down from it, climbing up. Both sides of the road were wooded with scrub and blooming lilac. He wandered through the remains of an old farmstead, the tattered barn crazed and gray, the house just a brick foundation covered with morning glory vines.

He sat in the cab for over an hour, sunk in blackness, trying to go over the possibilities in his mind. Annie and Ra were both gone. Someone had found them and taken them to a hospital—obviously. Or somewhere.

He turned the key, pushed in the clutch. The truck worked.

He got it backed out of the ditch. He had to go forward a mile or so and then was able to turn around. For another hour, he drove around trying to find the place they'd gotten gas, almost in tears from tiredness and frustration. It dawned on him how very sick he was. The hair on his chest was white. He'd been relatively young when he last drove this truck. Now he was an old man. He didn't even know how old. He didn't even know if he'd remember thinking this an hour from now. His carefully delineated routes, the streets he'd come to love in Washington, surrounded him no longer. He was out in the country, out in the world.

Finally he gave up. He had to believe that whoever had taken Annie and Ra meant them well. Otherwise, they just would have left them to die.

It was late afternoon by the time he turned southwest again, following the line of the Valley. The gauge showed three-quarters full, and he could only drive the truck until he ran out of gas or until he found more. He doubted that he would find more.

He felt immensely stupid and helpless as he drove past deserted farms and short spurts of deserted strip malls. He fought down fear constantly until he dripped with sweat from sheer nervousness. Wind hot with another evening's storm rushed in through the open windows. Seeing another vehicle on his road sent him into a state of terror. That meant they were probably gasoline-powered, which meant that they might try and take his remaining fuel by force. He tried to summon up memories of how this state of things came to be and was frustrated by their sketchiness. Protests when gasoline-fueled cars were prohibited from production. The promise of dedicated solar roads that collected energy and constantly propelled your vehicle from below without the need for carrying heavy fuel or a combustion engine and so many magrails above and below ground that there would be no need for private transportation. Public outrage when such cars proved to be incredibly expensive and those holding the train patents edged the price too high for them to tendril into all the suburbs and small towns.

Most of the cars and trucks he saw were independently solar-powered; some were steam, homemade contraptions that worked nonetheless.

The long ridges on both sides of him seemed comforting, protecting. They paced him through the day, firm and radiating a palette of blues and greens, flat luminous planes pieced together and arching skyward. His life in the city had been one of rapidly changing scenes, as if sets were placed around him—colorful, loud, and distracting—leading him here and there, until he'd become a skittering manic idiot devoid of any kind of sustained focus. He'd been working, yes. One part of him, also manic, had filled a thousand notebooks with the abstract ravings of a lunatic. The settled unmoving mountains gave him momentary perspective. He had no idea how long it would last, but it was like a beacon in a dark night. For the first time in a long time he yearned for healing, yearned for normalcy. He was sick of whatever bizarre understanding, like abstract hallucinatory impossible shapes dancing in his brain demanding voice, had taken over his life.

The storm broke as he coasted into the outskirts of another small town. Ramshackle mansions in need of paint lined Main Street. An old man waved at him from the sidewalk. Zeb quenched the urge to yell out to him that aliens were coming and realized with a start that it was his standard greeting. Darkness washed over him. If they were coming, where were they? His whole life had been a tragic mistake. Out here, away from the sweat and distraction of the city, it suddenly seemed easy to see. At least for the moment. He knew that he'd forget this small realization. A small grocery store had its lights on and Zeb's stomach rumbled. But he had no money. The truck ran out of gas just as Zeb spotted a deserted gas station on the right. He pulled in, engine quiet, truck squeaking and clanking to a stop.

Zeb got out beneath the shelter of the gas pump overhang. Rain sheeted down around him; thunder boomed. Lightning streaked down and seemed to hit two blocks over. The station, with large letters that said JIFFY M RT above the door, was empty, and the door stood open. Zeb dashed through the rain and went inside, hoping against hope that a lone cigarette might have survived, but the metal shelves were empty and covered with a heavy layer of dust. He went back outside and, drenched, tried all the pumps, but if there was any gas in them, which he doubted, the pumps had no power anyway.

Zeb stood by the gas pumps, hands on his hips, and breathed deeply of the early summer air. It was cleansed; pure, with a chilled edge. The rain slackened and ceased. Out past town, he could see that the storm had cleared the ridge, leaving it blue-green, sunset glowing in a thin line sandwiched between upraised land and slate-blue thundercloud. Purple thistles sprouted next to the gas pumps.

He turned and got his notebook out of the truck. He unclipped the pen and wrote in large letters on the front NEW ORLEANS. That's where he ought to go. He knew that now, but might forget soon. Annie had been going there. If she and Ra were all right . . .

He was cold. He wished for a moment that he'd kept the coat.

Then he set out walking and was glad that he had not.

Zeb walked as evening deepened through a million mingled scents, brought out by the rain, that took him back to his youth. He hoped to catch a ride, but realized that he'd most likely have to get over to I-81 in order to do that. No vehicles passed him for an hour. He thought that as long as he kept walking, he wouldn't get too cold.

The depth of the darkness, without city lights, startled him. Just as the intense blue twilight vanished over the western ridges, he thought he saw a campfire up ahead. His pace quickened.

Long shadows loomed against a tiny—almost toylike—church. The moon broke free of clouds, golden and huge, and Zeb saw that the churchyard was full of milling figures. A large flatbed truck was parked nearby. He approached cautiously, but was hailed with friendly gestures and shouts and pushed near the fire.

"You're soaked," scolded a woman wearing a bedraggled business suit. "Don't you have enough sense to stay out of the rain?"

Zeb was confused. He looked around and saw that most of the men and women were dressed similarly, in business clothes. "Where are you from?"

"Annandale," said the woman. "My name is Sylvia. Our office had this truck set up and ready just in case. Kind of like an air-raid shelter." She giggled in a hysterical fashion. "I guess we didn't really take it seriously, but the other morning we were glad we did it. We gathered at the checkpoint and took off. Are you from around here?"

"No," he said. He looked at them more carefully. They were all young adults. "Where are your kids?"

A silence descended over the group. Finally Sylvia said, "That's kind of a strange question."

Zeb tried to feel his way into the situation, but couldn't grasp it. Had their children been trapped in a school somewhere? He sensed tragedy. "Why?"

"He's too old," said one of the men.

"Yeah, but—"

"I'm a bum," said Zeb bluntly. "I'm not well. I don't know what's been going on. For years."

"Oh," said Sylvia. "Well, a good number of adults in the D.C. area are sterile. And a lot of other cities too. Anti-population-growth terrorists put something in the water that mutates eggs and sperm. The Gaians took responsibility," she said, her voice bitter.

A quiet voice broke into their conversation. "I can heal you."

A woman dressed in black stood just outside the fire. Her jeans were black, her long-sleeved shirt was black, her boots were black. White hair stood out around her head, but her face seemed unlined.

"Who are you?" asked one of the men.

"Jonnie Cash," she said, and they all laughed. She smiled slightly. "I'm protesting injustice in the world. And I am the minister of this church. It is the New Pentecostal Church of the Valley. I welcome you to the grounds. Stay as long as you want. You may call me Mother Cash."

"We'll be leaving in the morning," said one of the men nervously. "Thank you for your hospitality."

"It's nothing," she said. "I would like to invite you inside for a service."

They muttered and yawned and said that it was late, they'd been traveling all day, it was time to crawl into their tents and get some sleep.

The woman looked hurt. Zeb said, "I'd be pleased to come to your service, ma'am. If you don't mind having it just for one."

Her face brightened. "One soul saved is worth a million services."

As he followed her into the small white church, he read the marquee next to the door. He remembered from his past life that these signs sat out front of practically every church, with witty sayings that were changed weekly. This one read:

CIRCUMCISE THEREFORE
THE FORESKIN OF YOUR
HEART AND BE NO
MORE STIFFNECKED

He stepped inside.

There were twelve oak pews in the tiny plain church, washed by candlelight from wall sconces. The floor was scarred and sagged in the center. An oak table covered with a flowered tablecloth sat in the front of the church, below a plain wooden cross that hung from one of the beams that crossed the room beneath the narrow sharp-peaked ceiling, shadowy above. Zeb almost expected to see an apple pie on this homely altar, but instead saw a torn loaf of homemade bread and a silver goblet.

"We will sing 'What a Friend We Have in Jesus.' You know it?" Mother Cash asked anxiously. She opened a hymnal for him and he squinted in the flickering light, following her lead, the tune coming back to him as he sang. She then told him to open the prayer book. The service was copied by hand into a small bound book and decorated with pictures of angels and demons. The demons frightened Zeb. He felt dizzy with hunger and hoped he wouldn't faint in the middle of the woman's service. It seemed so important to her.

As she spoke, her voice lost its quaver, became sure and strong. She allowed him to sit while she delivered a short sermon on the state of the world and how he must prepare his soul for the coming Armageddon, which would take place because of humanity's impurities.

"I do not have the power to pardon your sins," she said. "You must make your own peace with God. We will have a moment of silence."

To Zeb's surprise, memories tumbled forth. How he'd left Sally, and how she had searched fruitlessly for him. The death of Craig. The disappearance of Ra and Annie, both of whom had loved and protected him in their own ways while he tottered like a baby through life, trailing death in his wake through his own irresponsibility. He began to weep. He watched distantly as Mother Cash poured wine into the goblet from a dusty bottle she uncorked with some difficulty, set the wine bottle down, and picked up a small vial of cut glass that sparkled next to the bread and wine. From it she poured a few drops into the goblet and said firm words of blessing. Then she walked over to him and grasped his hand tightly. "Come forth, Son, and partake of Communion. I see that the Spirit is working through you. God will forgive you."

She asked him to kneel in front of the altar, and he swayed on his knees and grasped the edge of the table. She gave him a small chunk of bread and he chewed gratefully, wanting to grab the whole loaf and stuff it down. She tipped the goblet to his lips and he took a large swallow of sweet wine.

His mouth burned with it. It seemed to pour into his head and illuminate it. He saw a bright flash of light and passed out.

He woke in the morning stretched out on the floor next to the altar. What now? he thought, opening his eyes to stained sunlight patterning the white wall opposite him. He sat up, rubbed his eyes. He felt uncharacteristically clearheaded.

He wondered what she'd put in the wine.

He stood and looked into the cup, but it was clean and shining. The bottles were nowhere to be found. Even the bread, which he would have gladly breakfasted on, was gone. Even the crumbs.

He noticed that his burned arm was no longer blistered.

He walked out into the sunny morning. The truck and the unredeemed Annandalians were gone.

As was Mother Cash.

Later that morning, Zeb caught a ride with a man heading to Roanoke with a solar truck full of corn. He split the lunch his wife had made for him, a huge roast beef sandwich and some Cokes. "I trade hard for these Cokes," he said, jouncing along as he shifted gears. "Hear tell something strange has happened to Atlanta. Cokes are scarce. These here come out of a plant in Chattanooga."

Zeb was utterly grateful for the meal and just as grateful that the man had picked him up, shirtless and bedraggled as he was. He could scarcely believe how normal he felt, how good. The world did not waver and mutate. It did not give him the sensation of distant music, nor fill him with fear, nor with the urge to rant. He grasped the armrest on the door gratefully, feeling the omnipresence of matter. Matter was always here, always dependable, completely undemanding. A surge of appreciation engulfed him. He almost said, "Matter is the most wonderful thing about life, isn't it?" But he was able to realize that it was a strange thing to say and that it would mark him in this man's eyes as strange. Perhaps he would for the first time in his life achieve a balance. Perhaps he would be able to understand whatever it was he was born to understand without being overwhelmed by whatever chemical anomaly allowed this understanding.

Or maybe he was too old for all that. Maybe he'd left whatever genius he had behind in the gutters of Washington, D.C. Maybe it had evaporated along with steam from the winter grates.

No matter. He was going home.

* * *

It took him two more days of hitchhiking and walking to get to his farm.

He almost didn't recognize it. The trees and the gravel road were gone. The outlines of his old house were there, augmented by an addition that jarred him. The land was cleared and fenced and grazed by sheep. Hundreds of sheep, apparently. And recently. The grass was eaten down to the nub.

But they all lay dead, scattered across the hill. There was an awful stench in the air and a billion flies.

A sign hung at the turn: ANGEL'S REST FARM. NATURAL AND ORGANIC WOOL.

Two collies ran down the road to meet him.

He knelt and hugged them. They seemed happy to see him, though they didn't even know him. Collies were a happy breed, friendly and near-useless as watchdogs, though Zeb guessed that they'd be pretty good at herding sheep. They liked to tell people and each other the right and wrong of things.

Yet something was amiss here as well. The dogs were shaggy, their winter undercoats trailing them in great white gobs. He pulled some off thoughtfully. Anyone with a minute could keep them combed out in a rudimentary fashion. And beneath their fluffy coats, they were too thin.

He stood. The sign, tasteful in tones of cream and green, accented with a white stylized ewe, was cracked and peeling. The verge by the driveway was grown up in blackberry brambles, and the driveway was full of potholes.

Without the trees, the lay of the land seemed foreign to him, as if his past had been wiped clean. Even his antennas were gone. If it weren't for the collies, he would have had half a mind to pass the place by. It haunted him, and he was afraid. Afraid that his was only a temporary lull from madness, and that any kind of stress could bring it raging back. It always did. A sick feeling tightened his stomach.

He walked up the long driveway. It seemed strange to be able to see the low ridge behind the house cleared to the ridgeline. It was like seeing a loved grandmother naked.

He used the large brass sheep's-head knocker to raise a ruckus. No one came to the door. A small windowpane was broken out. The door frame was rotten, and paint peeled from the door. He knocked again, then tried the knob.

The collies followed, pushed around him, and hurried inside. Heavy curtains swathed the interior in darkness. "Hello?" he yelled. "Anyone home?"

He heard a sound and wheeled.

In the dim light, he heard the click of a rifle being cocked. "Get out of here!"

"I'm sorry," said Zeb. "I was looking for someone named Brad." His heart began to pound hard.

"This is my house, my name is Brad, and I'm about ready to blow your damned head off."

"I'm—Brad, I'm your Uncle Zeb."

He heard heavy breathing and wanted to leave badly, but was afraid to move. The voice was incredulous. "Zeb? You're a damned liar. Zeb died years ago."

"I didn't," said Zeb. "Though I might as well have. I've been—well, I've just been a bum."

"My mom spent years—*years*—looking for you." His voice was almost hysterical now. "She was always gone. Then she died. It was your fault."

"I'm sorry," said Zeb. "I'm terribly sorry, Brad." He paused. "How come all the sheep are dead?"

"You just want your farm back, don't you? After all the work I've done. Well, take it, then! The place is ruined. Stuff fell from the sky. Sheep died. Dogs went nuts. Most of 'em run off." In the dim light, Zeb saw him lower the rifle. He sat heavily in an easy chair.

"I don't want it back." Zeb saw the dim outlines of a room heaped with dirty dishes, clothes, and books. Brad—tall and thin—had a ragged untrimmed beard and shaggy hair. "How long ago did this happen?"

"Last week. Week before. Don't remember."

Zeb sat gingerly on the edge of an ottoman. "How long have you been sick?"

"I'm not sick."

"Don't try and kid me." Even now he wanted to run from the house, as if it might be catching, as if he'd just been imagining the surcease he'd been granted. "You're not too bad, really."

"The dogs kept me going," said Brad. "And then the sheep. I had to take care of them. Every day, no matter what. There was always work to do. After Mom died, Dad didn't do much. He died two, three years later. Annie was out of school, had that hot job in Washington. She didn't care. I went to the doctor; he gave me the news. But he was lying. I don't know why he wanted to lie to me like that. All the doctors do. Even the one at the county clinic. I thought she was my friend."

Zeb's eyes were adjusting to the gloom. He saw more clearly the room of his debacle, long-buried emotions coming suddenly to the fore—his failed marriage, the job and the life that he'd refused in favor of madness.

Now this lost boy sat here in his place. He frightened Zeb; frightened him with his own image. "There's medicine you can take, Brad."

"Why should I take medicine if nothing's wrong with me? Dad got me some of that shit once. I threw it away." He raised the rifle he still held vertically in his left hand and rammed the butt on the floor a few times. "Don't try and tell me what to do. In fact, you can just get the hell out of here. I know you really want your house back. It's what you came for. It's beautiful, isn't it?" He laughed. It was an ugly sound. "Yeah, I did okay for a lot of years. Sold lots of stuff through mail order. Gave work to all the neighbors. But all this nanotech stuff—I had to let my workers go. I had to take the wool to Roanoke myself to ship it off because my old shippers said it would take a while to get their delivery systems back up to speed after gasoline was regulated and they had to change over to solar. Guess nobody cared about delivering things anymore because they're starting to manufacture things on site with those little nanotech ovens. Real manufactured organically grown wool!" He cackled again. "I was still doing all right until they killed the sheep. Bunch of us started a network of Saturday markets where we could trade. I reworked the trucks and made them pure solar. None of this shit that only runs on their roads. That's the problem with this nanotech stuff. Big goddamned bottleneck." He fumbled around on the table next to his chair with his right hand and came up with some kind of bound packet. "I give out my booklet on Saturdays too." He tossed the packet over to Zeb and small heavy booklets fell out of their rubber band and rained to the floor.

Zeb picked one up and held it up to the sliver of light coming through a slit in the window. ALIENS LIVING ON MARS FOR THOUSANDS OF YEARS read the cover. He opened it.

Inside was an amazingly intricate map of the alien colony, as well as detailed pictures of their appearance. Their habits, their physiology, the society from which they sprang, and their ships were all there—down to the last tentacle and knob. The print was so tiny that Zeb really couldn't decipher it.

"You . . . thought this all up?" asked Zeb.

"No, damn it. I didn't *make* it up." Brad was on his feet, shouting. "It's true! I would have expected you to understand! Isn't that what you thought?"

"I . . . I had evidence of some kind of organized signals from an intelligent source. That's all. I drew no other conclusions."

"Some people came around about ten years ago," said Brad, still standing. "At first they thought I was you. I had to prove to them who

I was. Great country. They told me the truth about the aliens while they were at it. Guess they thought they'd scare me into admitting that I was you. After they knew I wasn't you, they threatened me. Said they thought you were alive and that I was hiding you. I could only remember that Thanksgiving dinner before you disappeared. That's what you said." Brad was panting. "It's true, I tell you. They killed my sheep because of this pamphlet. And it's all your fault! Everybody can just stay away!" He sobbed angrily between shouts.

He bent swiftly and swooped his rifle up off the floor. Before Zeb could move, he cocked the rifle and fired. The window shattered.

Zeb dove for the open door. He sprinted toward the two trucks he'd seen near the house. Brad continued shooting at him and screaming.

Zeb leaped into the first truck, feeling around frantically to find a method of starting it. There were no keys, but he found and flipped the big red ON switch and a quiet hum purred through the truck. He backed out, ducking, and drove as fast as he could up to the driveway. He heard a bullet ping into the back of the truck. He looked in the mirror and saw that the collies were running along behind, tongues out.

After turning out of the driveway, he stopped, opened the other door, and let the dogs scramble inside. He looked to see whether or not Brad was following him in the other truck, but he seemed satisfied with merely driving him away.

Zeb simply drove numbly for a while, past the familiar country-side, past the Zimmers' old house, past the turnoff for his antenna. He thought about going up, but the awkward step van wouldn't make it up there and no doubt it would just be an empty field now.

The dogs sat next to him, alert; panting. One was a tricolor, and one was slightly merled at the tips of her ears. He reached over to pet them and they crowded toward him, slipping on the slick floor as the truck jounced along the old deteriorating road.

Zeb drove for twenty-four hours, stopping only to get the dogs water and to let them go for a run. He drove on small back roads he remembered from his years in the mountains and was amazed that memory seemed undamaged, as if it were a pearl nestled beneath crushing layers of muck. In southwest Virginia, he drove right toward a man who stood in the middle of the road with a rifle trained on him; the man jumped aside at the last minute. In Tennessee, he picked up a middle-aged woman hitchhiking on a hilly road. She climbed in, thanked him, and pulled food from her pack that she shared with him.

"Where are you going?" Zeb asked.

She shrugged and split off a bit of sandwich for the dogs. "Away. I don't know. Maybe it's better to go north now. But Sister's in Atlanta."

"Why would it be better in the North?"

"Reason it's so hot is that a cold front up north is keeping this hot air down here. Along with the plagues."

"What plagues?"

She looked at him as if she found him odd. "You know. All the plagues. That make you believe one thing or another. Got loose from the Pentagon, they're saying. They've been developing them all along. With our tax money. Lord knows what they were going to do with them."

"I'm sorry," said Zeb. "I've been kind of—out of it for a long time. I've been a bum. A woman at a church up near Lynchburg healed me somehow, I think." He remembered talk in the Hopscotch Bar about these rumored plagues, about how they were testing them out on unsuspecting people. Whenever someone acted a little off, the joke was they must have a plague. "So what do these plagues do—exactly?"

"The paper said that they can make you believe certain things, whatever plague it is."

"Oh. I think I'm remembering." A night at Annie's apartment? When? And where was her apartment? All he had was that isolated night. When she talked about how they were developing plagues. "But why would they do such a thing?"

"Who knows why the government does anything?" she asked. She pulled a packet of cigarettes from her purse. "Smoke?"

She lit one and handed it to him. She leaned back and propped her booted feet on the dashboard. "Paper said some of them were developed as educational tools. Right. Nice of them to think of us."

Zeb let her drive after it got dark; he lay down on the van floor and used his arm as a pillow. It was a jolting ride, but he fell asleep quickly and didn't wake until he felt her shaking him. "Look!"

He sat up groggily. "What?"

"It's Atlanta. I'm not sure what to do."

Zeb made his way to the front of the van.

They were stuck in a river of vehicles. "Are we on the interstate?"

"Yeah," she said. "I got on at Chattanooga."

Well, he hadn't told her not to.

They were on a rise overlooking Atlanta, less than ten miles away. He looked at the sky and judged it to be about 4 A.M. People stood on the pavement and sat on a hill next to the road; it was obvious that these cars were not going to move for a long time.

"It's burning," said the woman.

"You're right," said Zeb after a moment.

He saw that the city seemed to be surrounded by a golden wall. Above towered buildings that nagged at his memory.

Again, he realized that he'd seen them with Annie on that strange, singular night.

They were eerily beautiful, as if designed by a grandiose, slightly mad architect.

The flames licking them were probably huge, he thought.

Dark shapes rose from the buildings, like dragons, like . . .

"The Bees!" shouted the woman. "I've never seen them. Only heard about them. I've got to find Sister!" She started running toward the burning city, her boots pounding on the pavement. Zeb tried to catch her, but she quickly vanished in the crowd.

A wailing siren sounded behind him. People began screaming. When he turned, he saw that huge caterpillar blades, apparently attached to tanks, were laboriously advancing, pushing cars off the road as they approached. "CLEAR THE ROAD," a voice said over a loudspeaker. "THIS IS A GOVERNMENT EMERGENCY ROUTE. CLEAR THE ROAD." But the tanks did not pause to allow anyone to try and retrieve their vehicle.

Zeb leaped back to the truck and yanked open the door. The dogs rushed out. He grabbed the woman's pack and fled, climbing the guard rail and dropping onto the grass on the other side. The screech and crunch of smashing metal filled the air, along with the smell of smoke.

He clambered down into a small gully; he and the dogs drank from the culvert at the bottom and climbed the concrete side. There he found a small twisting road that rose about a hundred feet above the other road, from which it gradually diverged. It was lined with huge dark warehouses. The dogs kept pace with him, panting, their nails clicking on the pavement. At one point, the road dead-ended and Zeb kept on in the same direction, using the stars. He passed through a thin stand of woods before striking another road, this one lined with strip malls. He went into a fast-food restaurant where lights still burned and found half-eaten meals on the tables and a row of wrapped hamburgers beneath warming lights. He fed the dogs and filled the woman's pack with hamburgers and containers of orange juice. During the balance of darkness, Zeb watched spectacular explosions light the sky and wondered what was going on. He decided that he must have led an active life in Washington, for he was not very tired; the hike seemed only to invigorate him.

Just past dawn, the road angled down into a neighborhood with large houses set in graciously landscaped yards of flowering bushes and trees. To his surprise, it was not deserted.

The first house he passed was white. A profusion of roses diffused a strong perfume. A man in a tuxedo and a woman in an evening gown sat in the front yard at a wrought-iron table, bathed in early morning sunlight. It looked to Zeb as if they were playing cards. He was cutting across the yard to talk to them when sprinklers came on. He retreated to the sidewalk. The man and the woman continued to hold their cards and to play them, prying them apart from one another as they got soaked. Zeb watched for a moment, decided he would get little information from them, and continued on.

Two blond children, a boy and a girl, rode tricycles toward him. He prepared to greet them, but had to jump out of their way. "Hey!" he yelled, but their faces were blank and they appeared not to have heard him. He ran after the boy, stepped in front of him, and held the handlebars of the trike steady. The boy just stared ahead and tried to move the pedals. When he found he couldn't, he stopped pushing but left his feet on the pedals. "Hello," said Zeb. He lightly shook the boy's shoulders, but got no response. Suddenly afraid, he stood. He let the boy go and watched him follow the girl down the street.

After that, Zeb walked more quickly. He saw a bicycle leaning against a tree in a yard and took it, jumping on and speeding away. The dogs ran next to him, stretching out in a fluid gait that looked like flying.

After about two miles, he got out of the subdivision and turned onto an empty main road. Below was a huge parking lot filled with cars, and in the center was a low building that said NAMS.

Zeb found his way down to the building and left the bike behind. The dogs followed him down an escalator that was not working, though lights were on down below. He studied a map and saw that he was on the green line that went into Atlanta. Two stops away, the train connected with the NAMS line to New Orleans.

Excited yet wary, Zeb waited for a train. After ten minutes, the lights on the platform began to gently glow; he heard the rumble of the advancing train. The door opened.

One lone old woman was in the car. She shrank back into her corner, training a pistol on Zeb as the door closed.

"Don't worry, I won't hurt you." Zeb sat facing forward, his back to her. He wasn't in the mood for conversation and neither, apparently, was she. The dogs lay flat on the floor, seemingly exhausted.

He and the dogs got off at the second stop; he turned and said, "Good luck." He saw that he had forty-five minutes to wait until the train to New Orleans stopped. If, indeed, it would. He sat on a concrete bench, but feared he would fall asleep. So he prowled the platform and found a newspaper kiosk stocked with two-day-old papers. The headline read: ATLANTANS FLEE PLAGUE

A stampede of people anxious to leave the city collided with the wave of refugees from Washington, D.C., heading south yesterday evening. Rumors of an approaching Pentagon plague spurred the escalation of the use of the popular *Gone With the Wind* program, which nanotech engineers have tried in vain to remove from the city's program menu. One city official, who asked not to be named, said that he believed that Revolutionary Independence, Inc., with the sworn goal of making Atlanta a sovereign country, developed and disseminated this program.

The International Federation has joined the National Guard in an attempt to contain Atlanta's Bees, which have the capacity to spread the program to the countryside, using any means necessary.

This action was not welcomed by Atlanta, which declared independence three months ago from what a Bill of Secession termed "an illegal and unconstitutional alliance between the United States and international powers." Mayor Jackson urged everyone to join the effort to defend Atlanta and her Bees, which are the property of the city, by use of the civil defense programs that every receptored citizen has access to. "If we all work together, we can keep Atlanta the beacon of civilization it has become in the past five years, since it voted to join the spreading ranks of BioCities throughout the world. If we fail, we fail ourselves and all others who believe in civilization." For the receptored, a hyperlinked version of this article is found at *atlantaconstitution.org.index.nationalguard.37459*.

If you have no receptors, the mayor reluctantly recommends evacuation. "We will not be able to take in any refugees, much as we might like to," she concluded.

The train was coming. Zeb felt a whoosh of air as it emerged from the tunnel; he hurried to the edge of the platform.

The first car was filled with people, but the door did not open. He pounded on it and was ignored. He ran to the next one; those doors slid open and he slipped through, holding the doors for the dogs. The car was full of black men, most of them asleep.

"Hey," said one of them. "I thought you were holding the door button, Nance."

"Must've dozed off," said the accused, looking at Zeb. "You'll have to get off at the next station."

"I'd be happy to pay for a ticket," said Zeb, and they all laughed, slowly waking and stretching. He noticed that several musical instruments were scattered around the car, which was long and luxuriously appointed. "That's not the point," said the first man.

"He looks harmless," said another. "I vote we let him stay."

There was some grumbling, but they finally assented. "Want something to eat?" Zeb asked. He opened his pack. "I have some hamburgers."

There was another roar of laughter.

A very good-looking man approached him, wearing tailored pants, suspenders, a buttoned-down shirt from which an untied bow tie dangled, and two-toned shoes. He had a thin mustache. Zeb looked at him for a long moment, then smiled. "You're Ed Street," he said.

The man tilted his head. "Are you sure?" he asked in a smooth, melodious voice.

"I'm sorry," said Zeb. "You're Duke Ellington."

The men applauded and Duke shook Zeb's hand. "Pleased to meet you, Mr.—?"

"Aberly. Zeb Aberly."

"Would you like some eggs Benedict? I was just preparing to breakfast."

He led Zeb into the next car back. A double row of tables covered with white tablecloths was occupied by black men and women eating breakfast. The air was filled with companionable talk and the sound of silverware ringing against china. "Coffee?" asked Street—Zeb was determined to think of him as Street—as they sat. The dogs lay down behind him.

Zeb nodded, thinking, Who's the crazy person here?

"So this train is going to New Orleans?" asked Zeb.

"If we can make it through," said Street soberly. "We're on a mission. Someone there asked for us."

It was as if a chime went off in Zeb's head.

"Is her name Marie?" he asked.

Street tilted his head and nodded, his warm luminous eyes curious.

Zeb said, "She asked for me too."

Zeb dozed intermittently in the club car as the orchestra rehearsed. He supposed it was rehearsing, but after a while it began to seem as if it was more like a creational effort shared by Street and the musicians. Zeb, sitting next to a sax player, watched as a sheet of e-paper registered notes; each chord or note jumped to life as played. Zeb realized that only their own orienting skeleton appeared on each orchestra member's page; otherwise, the paper would have had to have been huge.

Street was in charge of deciding what was saved and what was tossed. They worked out a movement during the afternoon. He began with a melodic idea, noodled out for them on an electric keyboard, and assigned measures and themes to various players. There was room for solos. It was fascinating to hear the piece evolve. A trombone or clarinet might play ten measures or so and then play the same interlude with two other instruments. Once in a while, someone would laugh in derision or say "C'mon, Duke, you can do better than that!"

After a while, Zeb slept. He dreamed that he was expanding through space in particular, very precise intervals. His body assumed impossible geometries; geometries that violated their own laws of existence; he knew and felt them to be impossible, yet there he was, being them. There was a target; a goal; he could reach it; it was a kinetic progression . . .

Suddenly he was wide awake and in the midst of rich, powerful blasts of sound. "That's it!" he yelled. "That's the way!"

"Right on, man," the clarinetist sitting next to him, awaiting his next entrance, said. "Jazz is the way!"

They played on. Street *was* Duke Ellington—suave, worldly-wise orchestra leader, directing; in control.

How did they know? Zeb wondered. How did they know these intervals, these relationships that he had beheld so long ago, when on the snowy bald? Even more fully than Ra, Ellington had woven them into music that held the core of Zeb's new understanding of the universe; contained the new thought that had reached the Earth twenty years before.

The piece stopped abruptly. Though the train was cool, everyone was sweating. They mopped their faces with handkerchiefs, pulled on bottles of beer, sat back.

"Nance, I want you to come up a little more quickly next time." Street alone looked cool and unruffled. "I see our guest is awake. How did you like it?"

Zeb, pulled back to the mundane world, managed to say that he liked it indeed.

"It's embryonic right now, but I think that it's what Marie wants. I think that it will reach a fuller evolution, once we spend a bit of time in New Orleans. Feel its pulse. She wanted me to incorporate certain information into it having to do with rhythm and tempo; I have found it an intriguing challenge. Not only that, but she has certain themes which she wanted me to express that run parallel to my own development as a composer; themes uniting history with the future. We both agree that it be called *Crescent City Rhapsody*."

Street didn't seem to require any comment from Zeb. He turned back to his podium and started moving e-notes around with something that looked like a pen. Changes appeared on various musicians' pages. Someone groaned and asked for a break; Street reluctantly agreed to one.

They filed out front and aft, while Zeb watched the flat plain landscape of Alabama roll past.

Zeb started awake as the train screeched to a halt. For seconds, he had the sensation of drifting through space; then, facing backward, he slammed into the airbag his seat back emitted. Instruments flew through the air.

Dazed, he watched as blue-uniformed soldiers paced next to the train. Row on row, they passed and finally stopped and turned sharply toward the train. A woman with short curly hair stared at him impassively, one out of a row that stretched forward and back as far as his angle of vision permitted him to see. Behind her ranged more like her, to a depth of about twenty-five soldiers.

Then in a bizarre wave each soldier turned to the soldier on her west and pressed palm to palm, both hands, as if playing a bizarre game of patty-cake, or the more complex hand chants, such as "A Sailor Went to Sea Sea Sea," described rather graphically in corrupt form by Ra one night as they lay in bed. As the wave passed eastward, a calmness seemed to settle upon them.

Inside the train, all was pandemonium. Ellington's cultured soothing voice cut through the chaos. "Sit still, sit still. The train will repel them."

The man sitting next to Zeb moaned, "It's the end, man. The living end." He laughed hysterically.

"Why?" asked Zeb, rubbing the back of his head.

"Look! Look! They're goddamned zombies."

"What?"

"They got the power to take this train apart molecule by molecule. Watch! Oh no—"

The line of soldiers advanced toward the train, holding out both hands, which glowed neon-green in patches.

"They do look determined," said Zeb. "But how can they—"

"You shittin' me?" The man's thin brown face turned gray. He choked out another hysterical laugh. "Hell. Might as well spend my last few minutes outlining how we're going to die. They have . . . I think that they're some sort of DNA computer embedded in their hands now. They passed the information up the line just now. It can sense the molecular composition of the shell of the train and turn it into its elements. It will kind of . . . melt."

"Really?" asked Zeb. "That's amazing." He leaned forward with great interest. "And then I suppose we too shall be decomposed in like manner?"

"You're kind of on the edge." The man sat quietly. "Maybe. Maybe we'll get to be like them." The rest of the car was pandemonium: people using instruments to try and smash open the windows and trying to open emergency exits. But nothing was responding. They were trapped.

Zeb stared into the eyes of the approaching woman, smiled, and waved. For an instant, he thought he saw startlement, an almost imperceptible stumble.

Then blue flames licked the sides of the train.

The line of soldiers shied back. The woman threw one arm up before her eyes. Her hair caught on fire. The rest of the soldiers were rolling on the ground. Those not engulfed in flames were—

Melting.

"No!" shouted Zeb, leaping up and pounding on the window.

"Damn," said his seatmate. The train began to move forward slowly. Water ran down the windows and steam hissed outside. Zeb imagined it was almost hot enough on its own. Well, that was an exaggeration. The outside temp monitor had only climbed to 99 degrees Fahrenheit so far today, and it was about noon. But the previous day had peaked at 101 degrees. Zeb sat back in the seat, battling the urge to jump up, scream, and try to join the soldiers. At least they weren't trapped inside this tube of velocity and music.

"Did you see that?" asked his seatmate excitedly. "On their foreheads."

"Blue letters," agreed Zeb. "What did they say? 'IF'? And a star?"

"International Federation," said the man with anger in his voice. "The star is their icon. Trademark, probably. The new world army. They got the right by treaty to come here. Here! Into the United States! Hell if I know what they're up to anymore. Dollars to donuts, they don't either. They just get bigger and bigger. And everybody was saying in Atlanta before we left that there were a lot of zones here."

" 'Zones'?"

"Yeah. Where you been, on the moon?" The man laughed bitterly. "Wish to God I was. They say there's a bunch of revolutionaries there. Peacenik revolutionaries. Won't have nothing to do with us. Lucky them. Yeah, zones. Just plagues, that's all. You never know. Columbus, Ohio, had some kind of James Thurber Plague. Just whatever." The man began to laugh hysterically again, bending over in his seat until doubled.

Zeb pushed past him and made his way toward the smoking car.

Behind him Ellington was commanding everyone to start again from the top. It was hot and stuffy. Out the window, to the south, smoke billowed from an unseen fire. They rolled through a flat rural land. Zeb saw in the distance a lone white shack as he settled into a smoking chair and ordered a cigarette of particular chemical composition from the table in front of him. After thirty seconds, it rolled down a small chute. Zeb lit it via a red-hot spot on the table, which then vanished. He drew smoke into his lungs and wondered why he was here.

THE FIFTH MOVEMENT

The Ellington Effect; Trading Sixes

New Orleans | July 2039

Marie, on her first distant glimpse of a fifteen-foot-high float of herself assembled from black roses, burst into laughter. Hysterical, gut-busting laughter that had her doubled over and gasping. She leaned against the door frame of the balcony wiping away tears. She figured that the humor-inducing properties of the float would last a long time. Humor was rare, she'd found, without Hugo. Her doses of mandatory amusement resembled acts of desperation more than anything else.

The giant rose Marie made its way up St. Anne Street from the river and turned west on Chartres and passed just beneath her. She waved, and a mighty cheer arose from the crowd.

The float turned toward the river again. Evidently they intended to go around and around the square and fête her. The Queen of Secession! Queen of an Independent New Orleans!

Like hell. Secession was a hollow victory: What was there to secede from? It was simply a gesture of necessary pride in the face of what was happening to Atlanta and any other city that didn't bow to whoever was in power in the disintegrating capital and conform to the increasingly strange demands that issued from various agencies. There were strong rumors that Washington, D.C., was no longer viable, and that whatever was done in the government's name had no backing at all. Congress had either fled or was now transformed by some plague, along with the rest of Washington. Certainly, the troops stampeding through the South were not Americans, though in the beginning some units of the National Guard were mobilized. But now, apparently, the

National Guard had turned on the International Federation forces. U.S. military forces had refused to cooperate with the IF despite their treaties and for a while she had hoped for rescue from them, but realized that the Articles of Secession might have confused matters somewhat. Local militias were being formed to fight the International Federation, but there was little central organization.

And now she was being fêted by the people of New Orleans. She didn't deserve their trust. She couldn't deliver. This grand Carnival was dust in her mouth. It was not that she minded taking the blame for disappointing everyone, for leading them down some sort of garden path. But the light she'd envisioned for so long was swallowed by a morass of doubt.

They were trapped in New Orleans. They would never get to Crescent City.

Marie collapsed onto a chair on the intricate wrought-iron balcony. She had taken over the Cabildo and the Presbytère, venerable centuries'-old buildings flanking both sides of St. Louis Cathedral and looking out onto Jackson Square, and beyond that, the Mississippi. This was her operations headquarters.

Since taking Weinstein's potion, Marie had little need of sleep. She was everywhere, on fire, nervously prodding Harold, Kalina, Jason, her legions of volunteers to work faster, better, leaner. She was a rack of bones and plagued by strange visual effects, but she didn't care. She could work—and work hard.

And it had paid off. Crescent City was ready, bastioned by a volunteer army, a well-worked-out initiation plan for the new citizens, already functioning for the few boatloads that had already settled.

Now was the moment for which Marie had worked and planned: the public unveiling, the celebration, the exodus. People had begun crowding into the French Quarter weeks ago for this two-week Carnival that would culminate in tonight's feast, the Festival of St. James and a celebration for Ogou, a *voudoun* god. Tomorrow the ferry was to have begun the first of its weekly runs to Crescent City. Those from outlying areas had come to the festival. Marie had been planning on revealing the existence of Crescent City to everyone, along with the choice of going there. So far, it was a secret. An open secret, perhaps, but she preferred that the government not have any kind of hard information about it—particularly not its location.

This moment—this celebration—was the gateway to all that she hoped would happen in the next few decades—a growing understanding of nanotechnology, as well as *El Silencio* and its many aspects, including that of the strange children generated in its inception. She suspected that Jason might be one. He was the right age. She had not mentioned it to him. Why spook the kid? He was astonishingly helpful.

Kalina, Zion, and many of the old Freestate children who now worked on the many facets of Crescent City had also come for the celebration. The nanobiologists and engineers had stayed behind to make sure that all would be running smoothly when the first wave of settlers arrived. When word came of the siege of Atlanta, Marie sent a frantic message to them to tell everyone to stay at the floating city.

Too late. The day after the boat from Crescent City arrived, the Mississippi was blockaded above and below with warships.

Just after dawn this morning, the ancient cannon from the museum had been used to shoot down a blimp hovering above flooded Algiers, the town across the river. Binocular observation ascertained that a snowy substance was drifting from it.

Marie feared the worst—the plague that her intelligence sources told her was enveloping the South in nanotech zones. Her zombie plague, sharpened by generations of sophistication; multiplied in volume a millionfold.

The night before a flotilla of personal watercrafts had been launched from New Orleans on the shore of Lake Pontchartrain, only to be machine-gunned and sunk by the IF. Fifty or more people had been massacred on the other side of the Canal Street Wall earlier in the day after they emerged in IF territory. The IF was determined to wreak punishment on them for "intent to misuse molecular manipulation devices," illegal under international treaties and grounds for swift and immediate action. It looked as if their ultimate intent was to draft everyone into a vast IF zombie army.

The Marie Laveau float approached her balcony again. A roar moved down the street, following the float, and apexed past the balcony from which Marie watched, waving again and trying to smile. It was a roar of approval. A roar of approval issuing from a mob of drunks, of course, but it was approval nonetheless; heart-deep and without reservation.

And thanks to her, they were now prisoners of a BioCity over which they had no deep control. The BioCity wall that had been grown around the city's core, from Canal Street to Lake Pontchartrain on the west and down Esplanade on the east, was also a pretty effective mechanism for keeping them all contained, along with the warships.

But there was no need for IF to stage a battle. New Orleans had no military capabilities whatsoever. Containment and infection with the plague of choice were all that was needed. If Hugo had returned with what he went to get, the picture would be vastly different. The city would be capable of manufacturing all kinds of weapons. Marie was aware that some people were forming a militia, with headquarters on Bourbon Street, and collecting all the weapons in the city, but she didn't have any hope that that would come to anything, and she was trying to discourage them. They would just be slaughtered.

A marching band blared past. Kids yelled, "Throw me something, mister!"

Marie stepped back into the coolness of the stone rooms. Though crammed with the latest generation of DNA computers, the original personality of the spaces was so strong that these present-day infringements seemed negligible as dust. The wooden floor gleamed, covered here and there by worn oriental rugs. Groups of comfortable chairs and sofas surrounded low tables like oases, and off to one side Marie's long war table glowed with a pale light, its informational surface flat; empty. She'd told everyone to take the day off. Have fun. They all knew, of course, that this might be their last day of life as they knew it. Surely that sentiment was fueling the celebration now at hand. Still, she knew that they trusted her to pull things off—somehow. That was the way she was. She inspired confidence and trust. Erroneous, deadly confidence and trust. Her hubris would destroy them all. There would be no one left to go to the floating city.

A model of the present BioCity, holographically generated, sat on another table nearby. The tallest building was a foot high, but she could change the model with a touch to the control pad. Members of the committee could go inside any room in the entire light-city, once they enlarged it, or they could travel down its pipes and other infrastructures.

They just couldn't change anything in the actual city. It was protected much more tightly than anyone had imagined.

What an idiot she'd been.

What would happen to all of them? Over the past few years, ever since her famous ad, people had flocked here. People in all kinds of disciplines, with all kinds of expertise.

Many of the airborne-plague experts had left two months ago when it was learned that a faulty plague, which would impel people to come to New Orleans, had been developed by radicals with intent to distribute. Those that followed the radicals hoped to intercept them, but surely they would be too late. The radicals had developed something they were calling the New Orleans Plague. It compelled its victims to raft down the waterways of the Eastern United States, filled with visions of *Huckleberry Finn* and early America. Apparently, it could be deadly.

That was on her head too.

She had invited the world to a siege, not a party; a war, not the intended knowledge-fest.

She watched a golden raintree catch a breath of breeze, its viney branches billowing like undersea tentacles in an exotic dance. She saw in its movement a doomed reaching out for others of its kind. She felt for her absent heart stone; she missed it constantly but felt as if something about its loss represented her standing with the universe. She had no heart, not even an external one. Her daughter hated her; she seemed to have sent Hugo to his death; the floating city was still not the New Jerusalem she'd envisioned those years ago; and for all her power, she had not even been able to free Cut Face and Shorty as her manbo had instructed her to do. New Orleans would soon become enslaved, and powerful forces were trying to destroy it.

She caught sight of herself in a tall mirror suspended on a wire that hung from the old picture molding, itself twenty feet off the floor. A gilded frame surrounded her image. In her extreme thinness, she thought she detected some sort of resemblance to the old manbo who had given her the heart stone, but she wasn't sure why. Maybe it was something about her eyes . . . some sadness that was new.

With a start, she realized that Hugo's hope had come true, the hope he'd had when he created Kalina behind her back.

She cared now. Desperately.

The mirror, she recalled, was from an old ballroom, where quadrilles had been held. White men picked their quadroon and octaroon mistresses at such balls, set them up for a season or for life, depending on their whim and on what their wives would allow. No doubt at least one of her ancestors had been such a mistress. And another ancestor had been the white man who chose her. She tried to imagine herself dressed in a frilly ball gown and could not. One age of domination had ended.

Another was about to begin.

A new sound rose from the streets. She pushed the window open as wide as it would go. Drums for the Rada Ceremony. Marie thought of the costume Nightwing had created for her, a richly colored African design, its large skirt gathered at the bottom into beaded points. The drums beat, as her manbo had said, in her blood.

What good could anyone do now?

Ten minutes later, she was costumed and at the door. She ran into Jason coming up the stairs.

"Where are you going?"

"To dance."

"Oh." He looked at her as if he thought her insane. "Mind if I try to get some work done?"

"Knock yourself out."

Jason was a good kid, as bright as any of those who had gathered in New Orleans to try and set up a new scientific community. Almost all of them were in Crescent City now. Jason had not wanted to go.

She paused. She yelled at him as he climbed up to the main room, "Need any help?" The fact was, she knew very little about the things one would need to know in order to help him. But guilt made her climb back up a stair or two.

He called back from the top of the stairs, "No. You'd only be in the way."

A minute later, she was out on the street.

Jason was glad to be alone in the control room. Most BioCities were equally distributed systems, but Marie was the kind of person that always wanted to know what was going on, always wanted to be in charge. It was very wearing to be around her. She seemed to never sleep and always had an opinion.

He had tired of how the Genome Project people, recent refugees from D.C. who had set up shop in New Orleans courtesy of Marie, kept pestering him for a blood sample, and he was moderately tired of Marie, but he never tired of oysters. He wished he had some now.

As he brought up the system and opened some information windows to track the contagion that had been dropped this morning, he thought of how strange it was that he might die here. He supposed that he might be able to make it past the IF guards if he went alone and was seriously considering it, but kept putting it off.

He kept hoping there was something that he could do.

Just after dusk, a sleek diesel sailboat hugged the Mississippi shore below New Orleans. It tied up at an abandoned tobacco wharf and a dinghy was quietly lowered. Three silhouetted figures climbed down into the dinghy and began rowing upriver, keeping to the mangrove banks, and silently passed the warship that loomed just in view of the city.

Kita was much more agitated than Hugo as they neared the landing. "Watch out. Are those soldiers over there?"

"Trees," said Hugo.

"What's all that noise?"

"A party." He and Tamchu rowed steadily.

"But what are all those drums I hear?"

She could not see Hugo's face in the shadows, but she could tell he was smiling. "*Voudoun* drums."

"You mean—like in witchcraft?"

"No," said Hugo, puffing. "As in Jungian archetypes."

"Oh. You mean, as in temporal manifestations of timeless elements of the collective unconscious?"

Hugo chuckled. "Right."

Tamchu said, "What are you talking about?"

"Shhh. We're almost there." They had reached a dilapidated wharf, which was lined with a row of deserted town houses.

"I don't know why we have to be quiet," said Kita in her normal voice. "I doubt that anyone could hear us if we shouted. Look. Do they have the river cordoned off?"

Hugo stopped rowing. The river pushed against them. As they drifted downriver, Hugo stood and caught a metal ladder that ran from the wharf to below the water. The boat swung around as he tied up to it. "Okay. Come on." He climbed up to the concrete wharf; Kita and Tamchu followed. They both wore jeans and T-shirts, but Hugo wore a beige linen suit he'd had made in Paris and a purple shirt of rough raw silk. Kita had never seen anyone go through suits so quickly. Maybe that's what Western men did.

"How are we going to get in?" It looked to Kita as if all the buildings a few blocks ahead were fused together into a wall. She saw the outline of roofs but no doors or windows in the solid surface.

"They're not trying to keep people out," Hugo said. "They're trying to keep people in." He was walking so quickly that Kita fell behind. The brick streets were ill-lit and a great din filled the air ahead of them. Kita was soaked with sweat despite the fact that it was well after dark. Maybe it wasn't sweat; perhaps it was just the river mist collecting upon her as she moved toward that beacon of light and sound. Just moving through the air here was like swimming.

"Who's that?" she whispered as a uniformed woman came out of the darkness, casting a lightstick here and there as she passed through the glow of a streetlight. Old dilapidated buildings with boarded windows added to the spookiness of the area. Hugo had already gone past her.

"Identification, please!" The woman's voice rang out over the music as she strode toward them. "This city is sealed by order of the International Federation."

Tamchu stood still until she was right in front of them. He pushed something that sparked into the woman's chest, and she collapsed onto the ground.

"Hurry!" he said. "She'll probably emit some kind of signal, so her fellows can find her. She did not seem to think that we might resist her. It is strange."

"What did you do?" asked Kita, short of breath, as they ran to catch up with Hugo.

"Just stunned her," said Tamchu. "She'll be all right. Look, there he is."

Hugo, in a streetlight's circle, turned and was waving his arm to urge them onward. They caught up with him and he led them left at the next corner. He pulled up what appeared to be a sewer lid. In seconds, Kita was climbing down into a damp tunnel. She was thankful that they emerged quickly on the other side of the wall into a dark deserted section of town.

"This is even more scary," said Kita. The music was still distant, but its tempo pulsed dimly from some of the components of the street—a random brick that glowed and darkened, a neon sign echoing the interval in light, the dance of a solitary drunk as she swayed in ragged clothing under the pulsing streetlight, her tattered scarves swirling as she moved. "It's the CEREMONY," she hollered at them, her voice hoarse, as they hurried past.

Hugo yelled, "Where's Marie?"

"Marie Laveau? Where else, my friend? At the peristyle! The dance stage in Jackson Square!"

Hugo stretched forth both arms as he sprinted onward. "Man, it's good to be home again!"

For fifteen minutes, they hurried through alleys and down deserted streets where houses rose from the edge of the sidewalk and where there were no trees. Kita said, "Are you sure you know where this place is?"

He laughed. "It's my own heart."

He turned down another narrow street. In front of them was a dancing mob.

Hugo waded into it.

New Orleans was aswirl with characters from Marie's dreams. Ghede nodded from a distance, so tall his head topped most of the others in the crowd, touching the brim of his top hat with a two-fingered salute. She gazed into the dark eyes of Erzulie and was washed with an unmistakable expression of deep compassion. *I love you,* breathed Erzulie into Marie's ear. Then the Goddess of Love dropped her glittering white mask for an instant and was Kalina before weaving away in the tightly packed crowd.

The energy of the crowd was growing. Marie felt as if the entire rich past of New Orleans was manifesting now: in these hours, in this dance, in this dense and potent Carnival. Was this the plague of the government, streaking through her brain like lightning?

It could not be. It was too real, too powerful, too *alive.*

Perhaps the Carnival was holding back the government's plague.

Legba was in Jackson Square, dancing on the wide stage. He was an old yet powerful man, flourishing his cane as *servitours* gave him food and drink. Of course. He was the Guardian of the Crossroads, and the Crossroads were here now. Drummers played the sacred drums, sacred back through centuries. The backbone, the resistance, the drums that were outlawed everywhere that slavery existed. Except in New Orleans.

And they must resist now. Let them dance!

To Dance is to take part in the cosmic control of the world.

Marie heard herself shout with the rest, her voice blending in chant. She danced through the sunset, danced into dusk. She danced as Agwe and knew still that she would take them to the New Jeruselum on a sacred voyage by sea. All of the gods of the *voudoun* pantheon danced in Jackson Square, danced in the streets of the city, danced on the roofs and in bars and on balconies.

There was even the brown dwarf, Gad, the guardian—

But—no!

"Hugo!"

And then Hugo was dancing with her, flinging his arms around as if in some mad Irish jig.

He grabbed her hands, reeled her around, and they danced in a ring like children in the mad hot night, dizzy and shouting and crying.

Very soon afterward, they trooped up the stairs to Marie's control room, sweating and laughing. The sounds of revelry were not quite so overwhelming after they entered the stone building, but the music and drumbeats and singing were still present.

Kita followed Hugo and Marie up the stairs, with Tamchu by her side, in the wake of excited chatter, astounded by their levity. Clearly, they didn't understand the seriousness of the situation. Even Hugo seemed to be infected by this bizarre party atmosphere. Marie had been glad to see her, yes, after all these years, but she was fawning all over Hugo—

Well. *She* had work to do.

"Hi. I'm Jason Peabody."

Kita turned at the voice and saw a young man whose blond-white hair gleamed in the light from the crystal chandeliers.

"Kita," she said, looking around. At least this seemed like a stunningly well-set-up environment. Marie had skimped on nothing. Kita began to examine the equipment.

"Oh! Are you number thirty-eight?" Jason asked.

She turned and stared at him. "How do you know?" Thirty-eight had been her code identification number when inputting information into the Apiary Project.

His smile was broad and boyish. "Marie has told me about you. I've been here for a few months. She said that Hugo had been sent to find you but hadn't returned. She described your work and it reminded me of the work of number thirty-eight."

Kita frowned. "I still don't understand."

"Sorry. I got my engineering license two years ago and I've been studying ever since. When I was in Houston, I came across a top-secret history of the Apiary Project. Every layer of input. I developed a kind of profile of everyone involved—"

"You *factored* the entire thing?" asked Kita, amazed.

"I guess," said Jason. "Anyway, your breakthrough on rapid morphing just blew me away. The one using isolate human olfactory nerves to govern matter mutation on a nanoscale."

"Ah." Kita smiled. "Thank you. Can you tell me what's been happening? They look pretty busy." She nodded toward Hugo and Marie, sitting opposite one another on two deep chairs, talking.

"Yeah, I think so. Today the International Federation dropped something just across the river. Quite a few spores reached New Orleans, over on Canal Street. I tried to contain them, but they're multiplying at a pretty fierce rate. I think that there will probably be some sort of flashover in"—he walked over to a screen he had windowed open on the interactive wall—"a hundred and forty-two minutes. At that point they'll flood the interstices and also be released into the air. That's about all I've figured out."

Kita pushed her hair back behind one ear. She pulled a cigarette from her T-shirt pocket and lit it. She looked at Jason's window. With her cigarette in her left hand, she used her right hand to get an analysis of the substance that was causing portions of New Orleans to mutate.

It was indeed the same process that had changed Kyoto overnight. The mobster terrorists had deeply infiltrated the International Forces around the world.

Kita muttered, not really caring whether or not Jason heard, "I was thinking that I could use my prototype city."

"What?"

She spoke a bit louder to be heard above the din of greetings. The entire population of New Orleans seemed to be trooping in the door and hugging Hugo. "I have a prototype city stored in my DNA. But it would take at least twelve hours to decompress the information and put it into a form that I can use." She puffed her cigarette rapidly, then pointed to Jason's window. "There's not enough time for that."

"Oh," said Jason, clearly disappointed. And—if he had more than an iota of intelligence—probably deeply terrified.

Kita said, "Well, I guess I have to do *something*." According to the monitoring system Jason had set up, the contagion that had caused Kyoto to be wiped out overnight was replicating right now in well over a thousand locations in the city. The rain of assemblers must have been extremely sparse, but it really didn't matter. One infinitesimally tiny nanotech factory could begin transforming matter at a fairly rapid rate. Though they started slowly, once these scattered patches reached a certain size, they would metastasize, so to speak, doubling their size quickly until everything in New Orleans—and probably everything for a good deal outward—would be utterly transformed and ready for the International Federation forces to move in.

"Is there anything that you you can do?" asked Jason, the tenor of his voice pushed up a notch. Now he indeed looked worried. As well he should be.

"I can try and use the Universal Assembler."

"The *what*?" Jason stepped back a pace. "It doesn't exist. No one would dare build it."

Kita felt compassion for this young man. Perhaps among all of them here, he was best qualified to understand what she was talking about. "I'm afraid that it does."

As far as she knew, though, the prototype had never actually been used. She was not sure what protections it contained—if any. There was a good possibility that plugging it into the system would unleash uncontrollable replication.

It might end the world as they knew it.

This was the fear of everyone associated with the development of nanotechnology. If a molecular factory was developed that was capable of transforming matter, fail-safes had to be designed into it, limits at which it would cease to reproduce. But since the Universal Assembler had been developed outside the auspices of international nanotech conventions and by the military factors that had used Dento as a smoke screen, she had no sense of assurance that it had been designed with safety in mind.

She raised her voice. "Hugo! Marie! Come over here."

They jumped up and hurried over to her. She said quietly, "Actually, there really is no decision to make. We have only one way to stop the spread of this. And it must be started immediately."

*   *   *

Ten minutes later, Kita was set up in a work station with a DNA computer interstice interface, a concentrated node of manipulative computing power. She stood before a narrow waist-high shelf that manifested touchpad controls. In front of her on the wall, she created a screen about two feet high and three feet wide.

On the table was the Universal Assembler and the spiral sketch pad in which she had recorded her Paris notes. It was less fragile than bits and needed no special equipment to access. She studied the pages as slowly as she dared, turning them until she came to the end. She went back and marked two of them with the paper clips she had requested. Then she flipped back to the beginning of that section and left the pages open flat.

She ran a few checks on New Orleans's configuration, remembering that Hugo claimed that it was a program hobbled in some regards. It did not take her long to find that he was correct. It was like a piano with several dead keys. She could not play it as it ought to have been played. It would take quite a long time for her to analyze its defects and rectify them, particularly since she was sure that powerful stops existed within the city to prevent knowledgeable people, such as herself in particular, from playing with the parameters so painstakingly installed.

Her only choice was to take the Kyoto baseline, which was now manifesting, courtesy of Jack and the other terrorists who had put it into the hands of the corrupt International Federation, and bring it to the same configuration as Illian's Paris system.

The Universal Assembler contained molecular manipulators that were independent of both the New Orleans and Kyoto BioCity systems. Theoretically, if all went well, Kita could direct them to take the Kyoto Plague and transmute it into the Paris configuration following the pathways Illian had forged. It was a transformation that Kita had studied in great depth and which she felt that, if she concentrated and kept cool, she could facilitate and control.

It had been done before. She had to remember that—and not lose her nerve. She had the template, carefully lifted from the record of Illian's transformation of Paris. But did she have the correct catalyst? Had she left something out? She thought she knew the steps Illian had unconsciously forged. But was the record complete?

Behind her and to her sides, a tense silent crowd pressed inward, peering over one another's heads. Someone coughed. Though the doors and windows were closed, the Carnival drums could still be heard. "Get out of my way," Kita said. "I need to be able to move freely." The crowd shuffled backward.

Kita picked up and examined the Universal Assembler that Hugo had placed on the table.

The philosophers' stone.

The stainless-steel case that contained it was about the size of a credit card, bowed slightly outward so that it had a concave appearance. The word DENTO was embossed on it and, beneath that, a skull and crossbones. WARNING, EXTREME DANGER was embossed on it in many languages. Kita also found an international patent number and shook her head. There was no way to actually get at the lab inside without destroying its capabilities—which might also set off a nanotech surge.

She looked at the plug. It was about a millimeter in diameter and female. On the side of the DNA computer, which was a rectangular prism about the size of a novel, were several ports. She examined them closely, looked back at the plug. "I don't think this will fit. Do you have any other cables sitting around?" There wasn't time to configure and grow one. The crowd around her dissolved as everyone ran to search frantically for cables, which were actually just delicate nanoscale wires encased in plastic so they would be manageable. She heard drawers and cabinets opening and, one by one, cables were brought.

The computer itself interfaced directly with the interstice system of the city. Once plugged in, the flow of information from the Universal Assembler would translate directly to the interstice system. Kita would be able to manipulate the molecules—theoretically—using the touchpad in front of her. The touchpad had a full alphanumeric complement, but it also had the international nanotech controls created by technicians and scientists. She would use them to quickly and easily manipulate the models she would see on her screen.

There was no way to disconnect the computer node from the rest of the city. Of course, she could probably set up some complicated firewalls if she had the time. But if the Universal Assembler was programmed to be a weapon, it wouldn't really matter. Once the information got into the computer—any computer, city-manifested or an old-fashioned, severely limited freestanding computer—it would immediately begin disassembly, which would progress to the touchpad, to Kita if she was touching the touchpad or if some of the disassembling molecules floated through the air and landed on her skin, and then to the table, the floor . . .

"It might be good if all of you left," she said, finding a cable from those piled on the table that slid into the Universal Assembler with a barely audible click. She had only to press the other end into the computer. She looked up questioningly. "It still might be possible to get away if you move quickly enough. If the worst happens, there is

a possibility that the surge might be contained by some natural parameters measured in distance or governed by the mediums it
encounters."

No one left.

Kita plugged it in.

The screen was flooded with images and language of warning.
Standing as if poised like an acrobat on a high wire, Kita touched the
pad deftly and brought forth the waiting menu images of New Orleans,
thankfully already established by Jason, with its flaring hot spots of
contagion.

Magnified models of molecular manipulators poured swiftly onto
the screen, showing that replication had begun instantly and was progressing rapidly. Kita tensed and willed herself to loosen up. She could
not panic. She heard gasps from those around her, heard people running from the room as they lost their nerve.

Adrenaline flooded her as one of the robot arms reached into its
blobby body and pulled out another like itself. That was imitated by
the newly formed blobs, and before she could blink, she saw a number
doubling rapidly on the screen: 16 . . . 32 . . . 64 . . . 128 . . .

A *surge*. A vision of the Kyoto train station filled her mind.

She was shaking. She felt Hugo's hands on her arms. "Relax,
kiddo," he said softly.

"I can't," she snapped, but her brain seemed to take in some
soothing essence, perhaps his scent, and her mind leaped forward.
She sensed that most of the people had left the room, leaving the
doors open so that cacophony of drums and music poured in. It did
not bother her. It even seemed to help.

With a flick of her finger, Kita rounded up the tiny nanotech engines that could create or destroy, contained them with a bar of light,
and demanded a chemical analysis. There was a free carbon bond.
She called up a cubic liter of oxygen molecules and loosed them into
the circle.

The activity slowed, then stopped. A minuscule amount of carbon
dioxide had been created. That was all.

"It wasn't an event," she said, almost choking with relief. "I'm
sorry. I panicked."

Glancing at her notes, she sent the precise, complex metapheromones that Illian had helped her analyze to the hot sites all around
the city. She focused on one such site, where the Kyoto Plague was
doubling its size every forty-five seconds, and opened a window that
gave her a real-time picture of the progress.

She realized that she was holding her breath. The Carnival sounds
were a background to the drama before her eyes.

The metapheromones intuitively manufactured by Illian when she entered the Paris BioCity system as pure intelligence surrounded the Kyoto Plague molecules. One by one, they linked to the Kyoto-type molecules and transformed them into Paris-type molecules.

Kita was weak with relief. She leaned on the table and bowed her head, noticing that she was soaked in sweat.

"Is it—all right?" asked Hugo.

She nodded. "I think so. I really think so. But we still have a challenge."

"What's that?" asked Marie.

"This new metapheromone mix is activated in human brains by the repetition of a certain strong rhythm."

"What is that?" asked Marie. "We can do rhythm."

Kita paged through her notebook. "It is—"

A low distant roar filled the room and everyone was quiet. Even the music outside ceased.

"What is that?" asked Kita.

"It sounds like a tornado," Marie said.

They all stampeded onto the balcony.

Everyone on the *City of New Orleans* was in a state of high expectation.

At the tail end of sunset, the train passed the first sign for New Orleans and a cheer went up. Bottles of vodka and rum were passed around. New Orleans was visible, distant and tiny, in the last rays of the setting sun, its buildings gleaming silver above an olive-green plain, hazed in the mad summer heat, shimmering beneath a pale new moon. Even Ellington was content to drop into a seat and watch as the glittering towers of the fabled city grew larger.

"I heard that there's some kind of wall around the French Quarter," said a woman across the aisle.

The tracks were raised above gleaming swamps where the plants were completely alien to Zeb, a prehistoric-looking mix of palms and moss-covered oaks. White herons flapped skyward as the train flashed past. The sky darkened rapidly in an afterglow of marbled orange and pink. Zeb returned to determining the rules of a new solitaire game he was creating, using his tray screen.

Then the bucolic setting was shattered by an explosion. The window in front of Zeb was plastered with mud. The train shook and Zeb crouched down in his seat.

Ray Nance, sitting next to him, patted him on the back. "Can't nothing hurt this train. And if it did, there ain't nothing we can do about it anyway."

The door at the front of the car slid open and a flood of people rushed in; from their shouts, Zeb gathered that the car ahead of them had indeed been breached, despite Nance's assurance of invulnerability. Zeb erased his game and searched for the screen that gave information about the train. The people from the forward car packed the aisles.

"More soldiers up ahead," said Nance, using his hands to cup vision through the dark window. "Damn, my drink spilled." He pulled a silver flagon out of his pocket and sipped from it. He offered it to Zeb. Zeb shook his head.

"I don't see them," said Ivie Anderson, the legendary vocalist of perfect diction recruited by Ellington. "It's too dark."

"Well, we sure know they're there now." Nance said. "That was the big news in Atlanta, remember? Nobody allowed into New Orleans by order of the IF."

"I'm not a citizen of any International Federation," said Ivie. "I'm a United States citizen. I'm tired of those people trying to push us around."

"So are the people in New Orleans," said Nance. "That's why the IF wants to keep everybody out. They're afraid of an uprising. Besides, New Orleans seceded, remember?"

Taut silence fell over the train car. Even Ellington, who usually had something urbane to add, was quiet.

"What else can they do?" asked Ivie.

"Oh, derail the train, bomb it, stuff like that," someone that Zeb couldn't see replied.

"What can we do about it?" asked Ivie.

"Not a damned thing," replied the same voice.

"Sure there is," said an unseen woman way at the front of the car. Her voice was thoughtful. It also sounded somewhat familiar to Zeb. They all heard the beep of system access, then silence.

"What are you doing?" asked someone else.

"Activating some really cool features of the train. Don't bother me."

Zeb touched his table back on, brought up the keypad, and wrote: OBSERVE DEFENSE PROGRAMMING TAKING PLACE. A side view of the train appeared on the table. Above it the box read: *Impact absorption and fire-retardant features enhanced.* REPAIR OF INSULT PROGRESSING AND SCHEDULED TO FINISH IN 10:16 MINUTES. FOOD SERVICE SACRIFICED FOR THE DURATION. IN THE EVENT OF NANOTECH EVENT, DEFENSES WILL BE SWITCHED ACCORDINGLY TO COMPENSATE.

This was replaced by some sort of exterior long distant views: a 180-degree fish lens of the approaching scenery, at a hundred and fifty miles per hour. As Zeb watched, the speed of the train inched upward until they were moving at two hundred miles per hour.

"Isn't that a little fast?" he blurted out loudly. "How are we going to be able to stop in New Orleans? It's only fifty miles away. We need to begin stopping now!"

"Seat belts fastening automatically," said the train. A belt pushed Zeb tightly against the seat.

The train shook from another shelling and water blasted from the swamp coursed down the sides. A gash erupted in the ceiling and debris scattered across the passengers. Sheets of music whipped out the hole. Zeb glimpsed buildings, then they rose and flowed over a huge arched bridge with a roller-coaster sensation.

Outside was just a blur of colors, then Zeb was thrown forward violently. His seat belt caught him. An air bag held him captive for an instant, then deflated. Through the hole in the ceiling he heard cheering. His arm bled slightly from a small cut.

Outside was a huge crowd, a stage, a park, a statue.

New Orleans.

And Annie. He was sure the woman in the front of the car was Annie. He thought he heard her yelling for him but the mob pushed him back toward the rear exit. The sprinklers came on and soaked them. Musicians cursed and tried to shelter their instruments as they scrambled from the train.

Marie watched the scene in horror, pressed against the balcony railing by the crowd behind her.

A maglev train approached on the old L&N tracks, roaring and spitting sparks and surely moving too fast to stop without plowing through the crowd. Its snub stainless-steel nose glinted as it shot through the corridor of streetlights lining the tracks. Waves of people pushed back in a great pulsing mob.

Amazingly, the tracks were cleared just in time. The massive train halted next to the recently deserted stage. It was battered and mud-splattered. The second car was almost completely destroyed.

All was eerily silent.

Marie waited for the soldiers to come leaping from the doorways.

Instead, a conductor jumped from the rear door of the third car and placed an iron stool on the pavement.

After a moment, a man wearing a shining white tuxedo and a white top hat stepped down, holding a baton. He smiled and waved a white-gloved hand, then walked toward the stage. The crowd pushed back to allow his passage.

Then a woman in a white evening gown was helped down by the

conductor. She paused and waved at the crowd, then followed the man in the white tuxedo.

More men, all wearing black tuxedos and carrying trumpets, saxophones, clarinets, and trombones, stepped down from the train and made their way to the stage. The white-tuxedoed man had spoken to someone and folding chairs were hastily carried onstage and set up. The musicians seated themselves.

"Ladies and Gentlemen," said the white-gloved man. His voice rang out clearly. He had the full attention of the crowd. "My name is Duke Ellington, and this is my orchestra. We are honored to be here, and of course, we love you madly. We would like to play for you a piece commissioned by Marie Laveau. We hope that she finds it suitable. And we hope that all of you will enjoy it tremendously. It is entitled *Crescent City Rhapsody*."

Primal, isolate, opening notes sounded, fifths of stacked clarinets and trombones. The effect was eerie. The lights of the city dimmed, as if someone had their hand on a switch.

The piece grew like an embryo or like a proof, building on itself. Rhythm pulsed through saxophones used as a bass anchor. Cornets blared in syncopated counterpoint to the saxophones, then both intertwined in a dizzying fashion and flew off on their own trajectories. The woman's voice rose above it all: piercing; haunting.

And then the piece moved from portmanteau to body. The band began to swing with a strange powerful rhythm. It seemed unbalanced, falling-forward, yet was superbly—if barely—contained by an arrangement of sheer genius. It created a sound as shattering as that of Charlie Parker and Dizzy Gillespie when they blew the first fast riffs of bop, as strange and new as Coltrain's sheets of sound. A scream rose from the crowd at its sheer audacity and spirit, and everyone broke into dance.

Kita, standing on the balcony, shouted, "That's it! That's it! How did they know?"

Hugo, standing next to her, said, "Perfect. Absolutely perfect."

Jason said, "I've heard this before." Then he slipped away. Kita saw him a moment later, dancing with the crowd below the balcony.

Zeb was ejected into a scene as bizarre as any that he might have imagined in recent years. It was so hot he thought he might faint; within seconds, he wanted nothing so much as to plunge into a tub of ice water. Dazed by lights and trembling in the aftermath of the explosions, Zeb shielded his eyes with his hands. There seemed to be a square in front of him, and Ellington was performing. The roar was overwhelming, comprised of voices joyful and angry, irritated and ecstatic. The people, in constant motion, looked bizarre, costumed in brilliant clothing that seemed much too hot to wear. The momentum of the mob shoved him forward.

Zeb found himself chanting with all the rest, their voices pulled forth in imperative sequence, part of the piece, as if in a channel determined by the deft composition. He was hoarse, ecstatic, and everyone was dancing, dancing in the streets.

But this was different than his years of madness. He was lucid, utterly clear. He was becoming clearer by the second, as if his mind and being were in reverse, moving with great rapidity back to that time of fierce correct intensity before he was felled by a biochemical twist of fate. He experienced an explosion in reverse, the shards of his being pulled back from the years in which they had embedded themselves, yanked by a magnetism begun by that woman in black only a week earlier . . .

The horns rang out his freedom. The orchestra swelled to a sweet singularity that lasted but a second, then rayed out in timed perfection into a new universe. Zeb was swept into it as on the crest of a wave inexorably nearing a shore.

He staggered, found his feet, and reentered Eden, tears streaming down his face, hugging some stranger who hugged him back, weeping equally.

"Damn, he's good," said the man, breaking the embrace and disappearing into the crowd.

Zeb swayed, infused by truth, then stood firm and gathered the lost years to him.

Cut Face and Shorty, commanded by Marie to go forth and celebrate, walked up Bourbon Street at about three in the morning, dropping into yet another bar and settling on stools. Shorty held up two fingers and they wrapped their hands around cold ales. The music was not all that loud in this dark room, but the band—an electric guitar, a drummer, and a bass—repeated the Ellington rhythm, which always seemed new because of its irregularity.

Shorty said, "How you be feeling?"

Cut Face took a sip of his ale. "Why you ask?"

"Because I be feeling—I don't know. Different."

"Yeah. Me too. Kind of like—I don' care what Marie say."

"You t'ink we free at last?"

Cut Face said, "Who knows it feels it, brah."

"Jah be forgiving us. Praise be."

They clinked glasses.

*   *   *

403

Hugo, minus his jacket and vest and sandals, leaned against the high carved footboard of Marie's mahogany bed; she sat crosslegged at the headboard. Between them a six-inch-high table sat on the bed. On it was a bottle of iced vodka, two glasses, caviar, toast, chopped eggs, and butter. They were stuffing themselves and laughing. Ellington's music was a distant backdrop.

"This is heaven!" said Marie.

"This is alcohol," replied Hugo. "Alcohol and caviar."

"Same thing to me." Marie slathered more caviar on toast and squeezed lemon on it. After she swallowed it, she said, "Why didn't you write?"

"I did. Many times. International mail is nonexistent now. I sent all kinds of messages. I got kind of laid up in Japan."

"I'll bet," said Marie.

"No, really. I had a serious injury. Want to see the scar?"

Marie held up both hands and screwed up her face in mock horror. "No thanks! But your healers worked? You don't really *have* scars, do you?"

"It was touch-and-go for a month or so. But I pulled through." He laughed. "I'll tell you what, Marie. It's damned weird out there. I think you're right. It's the end of the world." He sighed.

"Tell me about Tamchu. What's he wearing around his neck?"

"I'm surprised you noticed in all the hubbub."

"I've got sharp eyes. Hugo, what's happening in Paris? All we have are rumors. What does Kita know?"

"Just calm down. I'll fill you in on everything. If you're nice. You look terrible. Mind telling me why?"

"Weinstein prescribed some strong medicine to keep me going. I think that someone in Crescent City will be able to figure out the next step."

"So you're going to be all right?" asked Hugo.

"Sure," she said lightly.

"Don't lie to me, Marie."

"I'll make it so." She took a sip of vodka. "This Tamchu guy you were telling me about. I wonder if he might have some insight as to how we can deal with the Federation forces."

"It's a good possibility, but he's had kind of a religious conversion. You'd have to convince him that you're on the side of goodness and light. He swallowed my version of what we're up to, but once he meets you—ow! No fair throwing forks!" Hugo brushed chopped onion from his vest.

They looked at each other for a long moment while Claude Bolling held forth.

"Don't cry now," said Hugo. "You'll have me crying too and that would be pretty ugly."

"Stick around for a while, then."

"Nothing could make me happier."

"We're improvising now, Hugo. There aren't any notes written down. We've digressed quite a bit from the original melody."

"I'm with you all the way."

"We just might make it, then."

After his arrival, Zeb fell into a hallucinatory phantasmagoria quite the equal of his wildest imaginings for untold hours; he couldn't judge the time. Music blasted forth everywhere. No humans lived in this world where he'd landed, only fantastic birds, beasts, and creatures for which he had no name. They all danced as if they had no bones; twisting and bending, thrusting forth arms and legs, their fingers as expressive as those of hula dancers. He was caught up in parades every half hour or so and once he was pulled onto a float where all the planets revolved around a golden naked man holding a scepter, around which twined a huge white snake. There was nothing to drink except beer, wine, and spirits, which even came out of the drinking fountains. Eventually he found his way to a rooftop by climbing a fire escape. Though it was not empty, the people wore no costumes and spoke quietly in small groups. He did not join them; he simply lay on his back and watched the stars until he fell asleep. Sometime during the dim morning hours, he was roused and helped to stumble somewhere.

He woke in a small high-ceilinged room with swirling stucco walls that opened onto a courtyard with a fountain. It contained a single iron bed, a nightstand with a lamp, a pitcher of fresh water, and a glass. He fancied he could still hear the roar of partying in the distance, though a faint slash of light on the floor told him that it was past dawn. The dogs, lying next to the bed, jumped up. Zeb dimly remembered them jumping from the train and following him gladly all night, probably getting so much to eat that they'd been sick.

A part of Zeb wanted to hide in this cave until the storm of music, dance, and color blew over. But to his surprise, he found that another part of him wanted to brave the disorientation, to test his newfound balance. He sat up on the side of his bed, poured himself a glass of water, and prepared to dress.

He was startled by a woman's disembodied voice. "New Orleans is now in the preliminary stages of nanotech conversion. This public service announcement will inform you of your options."

Zeb looked around, his heart beating hard. Voices. He wasn't cured! Tears started in his eyes. With effort, he calmed himself, following a tenuous linkage of thought back to normalcy. This voice had the same quality as the one from the train. Brisk, efficient, anonymous.

It was not coming from inside his head. It was all right.

"What is your source?" he asked as he pulled on his pants.

"This is the audio function of a system that is distributed equally throughout the city. Memory will increase as interstices are reconfigured."

"What is an interstice?" asked Zeb, pulling on his shirt but leaving it unbuttoned. He looked around but didn't see his shoes.

"What level of information do you require?"

"The simplest, to begin with."

"Interstices appear in every room and on many city streets. Generally they manifest as brightly colored vertical lines. They are bounded by a tough membrane that instantly self-heals if insulted. Within is a liquid medium containing a specially developed strain of *E. coli*, one of the first organisms to have its DNA completely mapped. The DNA of this strain of *E. coli* is programmed to accept and transmit information generated by receptored human users in the form of metapheromones. These metapheromones are able to penetrate the membrane, where they are instantly transformed to DNA-based information. The user can also receive information in this fashion."

Zeb stood, went through french doors that opened onto a brick court, and watched the play of the fountain. The dawn-gray sky was clearing to blue. The showers that had drenched them periodically last night were gone. Outside on a table covered with a white cloth were a silver coffee urn, a pitcher of water, some cups, and a plate of some kind of donuts. "Keep talking," he said. "What are 'metapheromones'?"

The voice seemed to follow him as he walked out into the courtyard. The dogs' claws made sharp clicks on the bricks. He drew a cup of coffee. It was sharp and strong. He poured cups of water for the dogs and set them on the bricks.

"Metapheromones were originally developed by a Japanese nanotechnology firm. They are in wide use throughout the world. Kyoto, where the headquarters are based, was recently destroyed in a nanotech surge, and—"

"What is a 'nanotech surge'?" asked Zeb, settling into a cast-iron chair with pink-and-green-striped cushions. He remembered reading about them in *The Washington Post,* but the content was lost to him.

"It is the most feared of nanotech consequences. From a single nexus of specialized molecules, the conversion of matter spreads outward at varying speeds depending on the nature of the molecules the

406

process encounters. A map of a surge might look like this." At Zeb's feet a flowerlike map appeared, its boundaries wavy lines that advanced slowly. "Would you like a different view?"

"No, this is fine," said Zeb, starting on his third donut. "Is this any particular map?"

"This is actually a map of the conversion process occurring now in New Orleans. You are near point zero, so the process is about 10 percent complete."

"I thought you said that this was a feared process," said Zeb, finishing his first cup of coffee and rising to tap a second.

"The process is well controlled here. In Kyoto and in other places, it took the form of a surprise attack, an out-of-control event, or an accident."

"Why is it so well controlled here?"

"Do you always ask so many questions?"

"Well, here's another one. I'd like something more substantial to eat. Are there any good cafés around here?" He dusted powdered sugar from his hands, stood, and walked toward the arched wrought-iron gates, flanked by white urns filled with red and yellow day lilies. An enchantingly sweet scent infused the air. Zeb felt a wave of great contentment. He was happy. He loved New Orleans. Whatever was going on was magnitudes more calm and predictable than what his own head was capable of generating. As he opened the gate, he heard a woman's voice apparently using the same kind of amplification as the more neutral voice he'd heard before. This voice had character and nuance; it was rich and full. It sounded very happy.

"Hello. My name is Marie Laveau. Many of you already know me. If you have just arrived, welcome. I apologize for any inconvenience you may have suffered, as well as for the military actions to which we may be subjected in our quest for freedom. We have just regained control of the deep functionings of the BioCity program. It is my honor to welcome those of you who arrived last night to the Free Territory of New Orleans. Conversion updates are available throughout the city, as well as information about the receptoring process. At twilight, a celebratory ball will be held in Jackson Square; everyone is invited to attend." Her voice paused, and when it continued, Zeb thought it was choked a bit with emotion. "And before then, we invite all who wish to attend festivities in Congo Square."

Strange glad music began to play, a mixture of clarinets, trumpets, and clicking sticks, and a brief solo piano bridge, snappy and brisk. "Play it, Miss Lil!" shouted a distant small voice.

"What is this music?" asked Zeb, still standing in the arch, with the gates of oddly delicate wrought-iron design standing open on each side. The street before him was narrow and European-like, and down it strolled couples of every color and mix of sexes, many hand in hand, in wild headdress, subdued suits, or running shoes, shorts, and nothing else—women included.

"Louis Armstrong and the Hot Fives. They never played together except in the studio. They created seminal studio recordings of jazz in the 1920s." The voice was no longer Marie's, but a male voice, as if Zeb had accessed a different information track. He sensed a brief image of a small smoky room at about 3 A.M. that smelled of beer, where shouts accompanied the newborn form of jazz, which zigzagged into blues momentarily and then was nothing but deep drumming of an irresistible rhythm. Sunlight slanted into the street at a sharp angle. He turned and made his way to the main street and thence, following maps which manifested fairly often, made his way toward Congo Square until the drumming became louder and he realized that he was hearing it live. The press of the crowd was intense, as if everyone in the city was crowding toward this center. Zeb grabbed a sandwich from a stand as he passed and discovered it had fried oysters in it. He tossed a few to the dogs, who were on his heels, and ate the rest.

The crowd formed small circles as he made his way to the center, each with a surrounding a drummer seated on a barrel. The drummers, using hands or sticks to pound their rhythms, were invariably black, wet with sweat, and wore only shorts.

Dancers surrounded each drummer, their heads thrown back or forward, their hands and arms moving expressively, some of them talking wildly, some singing with eyes closed.

The drumming intensified. Zeb found himself drawn to the center of the field, where a tall, carved, brightly colored wooden pole served as the nexus for a vast crowd of dancers.

Then Zeb was dancing too. He had never danced in this fashion, though he had felt this way often—as if some other entity lived within him, through him. Yet the rhythm of the dance helped organize his being, whereas before whenever he had opened himself in this way, the result had often been disorganization and chaos. This was new. He was part of the crowd, part of the cosmos, part of space, organized and organizing pure being. He continued to move, propelled by the drums, the sensation of heat sublimed into the energy that moved him.

He was ecstatic, he realized. Out of his body. Yet in his body, deeply in his body. It was fascinating, mesmerizing, and he wished it would never end. He ripped off his shirt and tossed it in the air.

"Slaves danced here in Congo Square," said a low melodious voice right next to his ear. "They were in a place of power. They were united with their gods. They were in a magic space, at the crossroads of time and timelessness. Like us, Star Man."

He turned. Sun Ra was there, her lovely brown face shining with sweat, smiling the biggest smile he'd ever seen.

"Ra," he whispered, his throat choking his voice. Then he shouted. "Sun Ra! The Queen of Space and Time!" He grabbed her close to him and found he was crying, crying in a way that felt good, that was coming from the center of his being. It was the only way to express the depth of what he was going through and he could not stop. "Ra, I'm better now. I'm healed."

But it seemed to him that the final healing only flowed into him as she held him close to her, and around them the mythic great dance of fusion and creation was danced.

The evening of the day following the great victory, Tamchu stood on a garden terrace awash with brilliant flowers as the considerable heat of the day died down, balancing Illian's sculpture in the palm of his hand. He put his other hand atop it, hoping perhaps for the flow of some current, hoping to feel her essence generating within him the closing of a circuit through which her intensity, her very being, might flow. She had imbued it with some kind of information—but what? And how could it be accessed? He let it drop down on the chain that held it around his neck, an ungainly decoration. He sighed.

Illian was in love with this Artaud, who was actually a Bee, and half a world away besides. She had no need of him.

At least she was alive.

With this thought, the world came alight again, as if all he saw was animated by a powerful and beneficent thought. Never had he thought that he might see her again; certainly, he would not have believed that she would engender the worshipful attitude that caused this great ache in his chest.

He surveyed the brick streets below, half on guard for an assassin, half not caring if he should meet with one. He still did not know what he was doing here in this hot city. Kita and Hugo were very busy. They had used the device he had given them. Hugo had told him that it had helped in transforming the informational base of the BioCity program. Well, that was good, he supposed.

On the other side of the globe, the General was drilling her girls and perhaps even plotting some kind of vengeance, planning a future devoid of humans—or at least beings who bore little emotional resemblance to humans. He had briefly met Marie, but that was it. There was no purpose for him here, no reason. Hugo had persuaded him to come here, but what for? He already felt restless and confined. He had learned that the city was much smaller than it used to be, because the great river that bounded it had risen and overflowed across the land on the opposite shore. Huge dikes had been built around the central part of the city here, and outside the wall were graceful neighborhoods where people lived in the upper floors of old rotting mansions. A row of tall flower-crowned glass towers, like those of Illian's Paris, contained inhabitants living with the help of a strange hodgepodge of technologies. The French Quarter, an area of about twenty square blocks, was all that remained of free New Orleans.

He did not intend to stay much longer. He might as well return to Paris and live on whatever crumbs Illian might be able to spare for him. Or perhaps he ought to try and return to Tibet. The entire world had changed; maybe that was possible now. If not, maybe he could be of service there. Perhaps he might learn how to be a Buddhist again and learn how to want to save all beings, even though he was surely chief among those who needed saving.

His stomach growled. At least *that* was easily remedied here.

He found his way to Jackson Square. On one corner was a large open-air café. He looked at the name and realized that this was where he was supposed to meet Hugo and Kita and Marie this evening. They were not here yet. Perhaps they would arrive soon.

He found a table by the iron railing where he could watch the sidewalk. Hugo had told him that everyone in the French Quarter would stroll past this café during the course of the night. Tamchu was sure this was a great exaggeration. He ordered coffee and jambalaya without shrimp. Its virtue was that it contained rice.

He pulled the chain over his head and once again studied Illian's sculpture. He never tired of looking at it; it generated thought after thought, as if his eyes and mind followed one line only to be pulled aside into another, beginning a new relationship. What he was thinking of he could not have said. His order came. He slipped the chain back over his neck and sipped coffee, took a bite of spicy rice.

A man came close to his table and he started, ready to draw his knife from its sheath on his belt and defend his sorry life. Then he relaxed, amused at himself. The General would not send a man for this task!

"Excuse me," the man said. "My name is Zeb. May I sit down?"

Tamchu forced himself to be polite. "Of course."

The man placed a bedraggled notebook on the table and sat. His beard and hair were gray. "I couldn't help noticing that thing you're wearing around your neck."

Thing! "This is a work of art created by a very great artist." Tamchu suppressed the urge to hide it beneath his shirt.

410

"It . . . it reminds me of something," said Zeb. "Would you mind if I looked at it more closely?"

Tamchu looked at him, seething with suspicion. "Why?"

"Where are you from?" asked Zeb.

Tamchu said nothing. He bowed his head and continued eating. Maybe this man would just go away.

"Let me show you what I do," said Zeb and opened his notebook. He turned it around so that Tamchu could see two pages of numbers and symbols. "I'm trying to figure something out. That . . . work of art makes me think of it."

"Why would that be?" asked Tamchu, feeling unaccountably jealous.

Zeb looked at the piece hungrily from across the table. "It's something about the proportions. Almost as if it were . . . an edifice of thought. Perhaps even . . . directions."

Studying him, Tamchu relaxed. The man's eyes were thoughtful, yet sharp. They were friendly, honest, open. His weathered face told Tamchu that his life had been hard, yet to have a hard life and still have eyes not marred by hate or malice . . . that was unusual in Tamchu's experience. He had a clear center to him, a place where anger and revenge had never existed. That showed in his eyes. He allowed Tamchu to look into his eyes for a long moment, and this too was unusual. Sometimes eye contact elicited resistance or might be a show of force or intent. His gaze was an act of revelation and trust.

Tamchu lifted Illian's sculpture from his neck and handed it to Zeb.

Zeb held it and looked at it for a while. Then he closed his eyes as his fingers explored it, turning it this way and that. He opened his eyes and smiled. He looked exceedingly satisfied, perhaps even a bit astonished. He said, his words slow, "It is . . . a map of a galaxy."

"What do you mean?"

"A galaxy is—"

"I think I know what a galaxy is. A . . . neighborhood of stars."

"I guess that will do," Zeb's smile was gentle and not the least condescending. "This has distances and angles. But different somewhat than what they are today. Shortened. Maybe a bit skewed."

"What do you mean?" Tamchu did not know what to think of this. Illian had studied the location of stars in a galaxy and mapped them? Well, it was not that surprising, actually, not half as surprising as many things about her.

"I surmise that this is a map from light-years ago—or at least light-minutes. A great time ago. It will take me a while to figure it out. And there are some interesting additions as well." The man's hands trembled slightly. Tears stood in his eyes.

"Are you all right?" asked Tamchu, sorry that he had been rude to this man, who was actually quite extraordinary.

Zeb began to laugh then in a frightening fashion, wild and high. He shook his head silently for a few moments, without stopping, as if he could not stop, then changed abruptly to a nod. "Oh yes, yes, I am perfectly all right! Perfectly! I've been perfected, you see! It's just been so long. So very long. And it happens in such interesting stages. As if I'm still growing. You know, like you have stages of growth you go through and when you think you're grown up and an adult there are still stages that you can't possibly see and perhaps there are more human stages and possibilities . . ." He mopped at his face with his napkin. The waitress brought a glass of iced tea and looked at Zeb with concern.

"Why do you cry?" asked Tamchu as the waitress walked away.

"I have a lot to be sad about," said Zeb. He squeezed lemon into his tea and took a long drink. "And I have a lot to be happy about. Sometimes I cry because I'm very happy. It's kind of equal, I think, the sadness and the happiness. But I've had very few moments in my life when everything seemed perfect and this is one of them." He sighed deeply and smiled once again at Tamchu, leaning back in his chair.

"I think that I can understand that." This man was like the Buddhist nun for Tamchu. Something flowed from his eyes and the world was alight again, the particles burning with an inner fire. He was here, and it was all right.

He had helped this man by making this long trip, and it was enough. He needed no other purpose. Zeb's perfection was generous. It reached out and pervaded him as well.

Jason sat in the café, sipping a cold beer and eating raw oysters. The smells of hot grease and spilled beer mingled. A spasm band on the corner sent the beat of that captivating, yet liberating rhythm through the open doorway. He could not remember having ever felt this way, and the feeling continued to last. It was one of slow controlled euphoria. But it was more than that. Things were coming together in his mind that he didn't even know how to express.

Yet, no matter how euphoric he felt, there was a new sharp loneliness that he did not understand.

He pushed aside the basket heaped with empty shells. It looked as if he still had some time to kill. Marie had asked him to drop by the café, saying that she wanted to have a meeting, of sorts, and treat everyone to dinner. She'd intimated that she had something important to reveal. But he'd gotten hungry a bit early.

Something caught his eye a few tables away. Two men were looking at a strange sculpture that sat on the table.

He stared at it. How was it possible for this spatial thing to echo this rhythm? Yet it did. And not only that, it had been made by someone else, someone who understood.

Someone who had felt the same rhythm, perhaps, as long ago as he had.

Maybe Abbie had been right.

He pushed back his chair and got up. He slowly approached the other table, thinking that he might be wrong, thinking that it was really too far to see and that his mind was playing tricks on him.

But no.

"Can I sit down?"

The man that looked Asian frowned, but the other man, an American, said, "Sure. Pull up a chair. I'm Zeb. This is—Tamchu?"

Tamchu nodded. Zeb held out his hand and Jason shook it. Tamchu reached for the sculpture.

"No, wait," said Jason. Tamchu looked familiar. He realized that he had seen him last night with Kita and Hugo. "Do you mind if I look at this?"

"I suppose not," Tamchu muttered.

"What do you think?" Zeb asked Jason as he picked it up and examined it.

"I don't know. Why are you interested?" asked Jason.

"It seems to me that it possibly represents directions." Zeb sighted down one angle, then another.

"'Directions'?" Jason mistrusted the word.

"Yes. Directions to the source of the Signal."

"What do you mean," asked Jason, "'the Signal'?"

Apparently, Zeb did not notice Jason's sarcastic tone, for he continued in his friendly enthusiastic voice. "The original pulse cleared the way for an incoming signal, most of it out of the range of what we use for radio and television. It appears that different variations are still coming in from time to time. Here." He pulled a notebook from the pack next to his chair and opened it. He turned to one of the pages. Jason noticed that each page, front and back, was full of equations written in a small careful hand. He turned the notebook to Jason and said, "Here. See this angle—" He pointed to a nexus on the sculpture. "Now look at this. This is one of the relationships that I got out of the original incoming data."

413

Jason looked at the equations and it was as if his mind was engaged and moved into high gear. "Mind if I look through this?"

"Not at all."

Jason felt the rhythms from the street merge with this man's pure ascetic thought as he examined one page and then another. It was a powerful dose of truth, the truth that he had run from all his life. The truth he did not want to know. The truth that did not really matter. What mattered was life on Earth, the beauty of being human, the attempt to understand all there was to understand, here. To make things work. To help people. To do something real, instead of flying after some dangerous dream. He was only capable of catching a glimpse of what this man had discovered, uncovered, and spread out here like a glorious fireworks explosion of interstellar intelligence and where it might be coming from.

After ten minutes of slowly turning pages, Jason said, "I think that it would take me years to understand this." He tried not to feel angry. One should not feel angry at the truth.

"It took me years to write it."

"But where did you get your data?"

Zeb looked at him sharply. "You're not from the government, are you?"

"God, no!" Jason started to laugh. "You're not, are you?"

Zeb shook his head. "But a lot of this was classified and I . . . well, someone gave it to me. I don't know what happened to him."

Jason said, "You know, don't you, that Marie Laveau, the boss of this whole shebang, is planning to someday go into space, don't you?"

"No. I just got here last night."

"I think she would find you very interesting. She's built a city out in the Caribbean that she hopes to eventually enlarge enough to support a space program. She's amazing. She wants to find out what happened to broadcasting. She wants to establish a city of free scientific inquiry."

"I've heard that," Zeb said. "You say she'll be here later? I'm supposed to wait here for someone. Maybe I could meet Miss Laveau." He took back his notebook and closed it. "Thank you," he said to Tamchu and returned the sculpture.

Tamchu slipped the chain around his neck.

"Where did you get that?" Jason asked Tamchu.

"A friend made it."

Jason continued to look at the sculpture from across the table, though he was aware that it made Tamchu uncomfortable. Whoever had made that sculpture might well be the same as himself and Abbie.

The part of him that he'd tried so hard to deny might be the most important part.

The gas lights came on, and the iron gates of Jackson Square were thrown open. A jazz combo was setting up on a stage beneath the statue of Jackson on his rearing horse. Jason saw Marie crossing the street, heading toward the café, and he waved. She saw him and waved back. Accompanying her was a tired-looking man wearing a dress shirt without a tie and black slacks.

They entered the café and made their way toward the table. Jason got up and pushed two tables together. He wondered who Marie's guest was. He felt as if he'd met most of her inner cadre in the past few months. This man must have just arrived quite recently. He was unshaven. His shirt had streaks of dirt on it.

As the man approached, his face paled. He stared at . . . Zeb, that was the guy's name. He stared at Zeb as if he were seeing a ghost.

Zeb didn't see him; he was studying a page in his notebook.

Jason watched with interest.

Marie continued on, then, realizing that the man had stopped, turned back. "Craig? Are you all right?"

Zeb's head jerked up. He looked at the man with Marie. He stood suddenly, knocking his chair over.

Marie looked from one to the other. "Do you know each other?"

Craig approached the table. "Zeb? Is it really you?"

"Craig? But I thought you—"

"I'm not dead," Craig said gently. To Jason, the man's haggard face said that he almost wished he was.

Marie stepped between them. "Introduce me, please," she said to Craig.

"This is Dr. Zeb Aberly. The radio astronomer . . ."

"Oh," said Marie thoughtfully. "Sure. I remember. The man you told me about. I sent Hugo to fetch him. Years ago."

She smiled—much less aggressively, thought Jason, than she usually did. She looked downright gentle. "I'm Marie Laveau," she told Zeb, holding out her hand. "Glad you could make it. Craig just got here too. But he's been here before. He's told me quite a lot about you."

Looking very confused, Zeb shook Marie's hand. "I'm sorry. I don't really understand."

Craig made his way around the table and picked up Zeb's chair. "Sit down."

Zeb resumed his seat and looked at Craig warily. "Any, uh, tracking devices in my shirt?" He grinned weakly, but only for a second.

Craig reached over and pulled Zeb's notebook toward him. He

dropped into the chair next to Zeb and flipped through a few pages. He ran one hand through his hair and sighed. "Amazing."

His face was almost babyish, yet Jason was sure he was about the same age as Zeb, who looked weathered and old.

Craig said, so softly that Jason could barely hear over the jangle of the rapidly filling café, "Want the rest of the collection?"

Zeb stared at him. To Jason's surprise, tears filled Zeb's eyes. "Ellie had them, Craig. What the hell are you talking about?"

Craig looked away.

"Are they the reason she died?" The veins on Zeb's neck stood out. "*Tell* me, damn it!"

Craig was silent.

Jason didn't know who Ellie was, but something seemed to flow out of Zeb at that moment. His face lost its animation, became slack and blank.

Finally Craig began to speak. "I'm so sorry about . . . everything, Zeb. I did the best I could. I had to go into hiding. I think that I told you why. Remember that day on the bus? People in my own division got all whacked-out about that alien thing—"

Jason's face warmed. He felt as if his cheeks must be flaming. He looked from Zeb's face to Craig's. He said, "What—?" Then he stopped himself.

They paid him no attention.

Craig continued. "Evidently, their obsession was caused by an early prototype of information nan, a precursor of what's causing the Information Wars. Some jerk doing research for the NIH thought that we weren't taking the alien threat seriously enough and had someone spike the punch at a New Year's party with something he called 'X.' His cohorts infiltrated the worldwide intelligence community and pretty soon the meme of the deadly alien infestation that had to be rooted out had made its way around the globe."

Zeb shook his head. "So all that alien stuff was nonsense."

All that alien stuff was nonsense. Jason stared at the two men, wanting to believe it. Everything—the sculpture and what it implied, the long, long chase that had taken his parents as casualties, Abbie's fool conspiracy theory that made them part of a group of victims— dropped away. A powerful sense of relief and disappointment spread through Jason. Suddenly his world was normal.

"No." Craig was emphatic. "It wasn't nonsense. Not at all. But the way the government—and other governments—handled it was."

And with that, Jason's heart was beating as fast as a rabbit's.

Marie was as riveted by the conversation as Jason. She kept glancing over at him as if expecting him to say something.

Suddenly Kita and Hugo arrived. They began to greet Marie, but she hushed them with a gesture. They sat down and Hugo stared at Zeb for a moment, then whispered something to Kita.

Marie cleared her throat. "Zeb, Craig told me that you're working on a Theory of Everything. A unified field theory. That you have an idea about what the Silence might be and what the incoming signals might mean."

Jason couldn't contain himself any longer. Who were these men who knew so much that had been kept from him, from his father and mother? "What about the—the aliens?" he demanded.

Craig seemed startled. He looked at Zeb, whose face was stony, and shrugged. "This is what we surmise might have happened. We believe that zygotes around the world—probably no more than several thousand—had DNA that was somehow mutated by the incoming signal following the first Silence. The only commonality that we could ascertain among all of the mothers we could find was that they all had a virus that seemed to manifest in no way other than to affect their fetus in such a way that their DNA was mutated. They all still had the virus. The only symptom, in some of them, was a slight cold when they first contracted it. It was not contagious."

Jason felt Marie's eyes on him.

She knew.

She must have always known. Ever since he came to town.

"But why?" asked Marie. "Was it a natural virus?"

"It may have been sent here," said Craig. "But we don't really know."

"*What was the result in the children?*" asked Kita, her black eyes intent, her cool sharp tone commanding their attention. She tossed down the match with which she had just lit a cigarette and took a deep pull. Her question hung in the air. No one said anything.

Beneath the table, Jason clenched his hands together to keep from jumping up and punching Craig. And he bit his tongue—hard—to keep from shouting out with rage and sorrow at what had been done to his family.

Craig glanced at Kita. "This . . . has been classified for practically forever. It's very strange, but we really don't know what the significance might be. One result was that these children have a much stronger concentration of magnetite in their magnetoreceptors. These are sensorial cells that are intertwined with the cells that sense pheromones and other scents. They are exquisitely sensitive to electromagnetic phenomena. When they were young, they became very ill when broadcasting worked."

"Like Illian!" shouted Tamchu. He jumped up, his coppery face alight. He continued in a low excited voice, stumbling a bit. "She—she was always sick when the radio worked. She made this." He held his sculpture aloft. "And what are you saying?" he demanded of Craig. "That she is from outer space?"

Kita leaned forward, looping her shining black hair behind her ears. Her glance touched each of them in turn, as if including them in a seminar. "I've never heard this. I mean, I've heard about the DNA anomaly, but . . ."

Zeb interrupted, his voice low and so hushed that they all had to strain to hear him. He seemed to have regained interest in the conversation. "This—Illian? must know. Somehow, *she must know*. She made the map. But *how? Why?*"

"Perhaps," said Kita, lighting another cigarette from her spent one, her hands trembling a bit as she did so. "Perhaps . . . there was something about the incoming signal that caused her brain to develop in certain ways. Like training. I can't tell you how much work I've done in that regard. So if, as Craig claims, these children were ultrasensitive to magnetic phenomena, it could be that . . . you know that it was proven years ago that vertebrates such as fish and turtles, whales, and mice, and even insects create a magnetic map within their brains which is one key to their navigational powers. So," she continued, blinking rapidly and fanning smoke from her face, "it could be . . . that Illian really could sense magnetic phenomena in a more intense way than the rest of us because of her mutated DNA. It seems hard to believe that she deliberately created what she knew to be a map of the cosmos. She's an artist. I worked and spoke with her quite extensively in Paris and I didn't really get any particular hint that she knew exactly what she was doing."

Marie was sitting back in her chair with her arms crossed, an extremely satisfied look on her face. She had gathered all these people together on purpose. Zeb was apparently a happy accident. Icing on the cake. But he was not entirely necessary. This guy Craig, Kita, and *himself* . . . Marie, with all her snooping and spying, had put all these human puzzle pieces together and was just waiting for her goddamned *synergy* to happen . . .

And Jason couldn't stand it any longer. *"She doesn't!"*

The shout burst from him in spite of himself, in spite of the long years of hiding, the early training burned into him, the imperative to lie low, to remain secret. He jumped up, spilling drinks as he jarred the table, and held on to the edges of the table with both hands as tightly as if it were saving him from drowning.

They were all staring at him now. It was a moment suspended in time for Jason. A jazz trio down the block and a reggae band in the square were an undertone to the other conversations in the café, which continued unabated. He smelled magnolia blossoms and wondered crazily if they were in bloom now or just someone's perfume . . . "I mean—"

"What Jason means is that he doesn't know either," said Marie, her face alight with something Jason couldn't read.

"That's right," said Jason, mopping his forehead with a napkin he grabbed from the table. "*And I'm one of those fucked-up—mutated—things* that you guys tracked down." Now he was shouting directly at Craig. "You killed my father! You drove my mom nuts! I hate all of this shit!"

Craig stood, his furrowed face even more defeated-looking, and reached a hand toward Jason. "It *wasn't me*. Really. I was trying to—"

Jason ignored Craig's hand. "I don't care." He shoved through the welter of chairs toward the sidewalk. He didn't stop when one fell backward with a clatter.

"Where are you going?" Marie stood up and looked as if she were on full alert.

"Away."

Marie came around the table and held him by the shoulders in a light but steely grip. He'd never been so close to her. Her eyes and face were oddly intoxicating, powerfully compelling. Now he knew how she kept everyone under her thumb.

"Jason, *please* don't go. If you stay, you can help us understand what's going on. Don't you see? This is what Crescent City is all about. Learning. Trying to find out what's happened. Trying to get through the difficult times ahead. We need people like you. Even if it weren't for this, we would need you. I've come to depend on you. Please."

Jason slipped from Marie's grip. He stopped at the end of the table and surveyed the strange assortment of people in front of him.

Tamchu, who knew another woman like Abbie, like himself, who seemed to have taken a completely different turn. Kita, who almost singlehandedly developed the strange and marvelous Flower Cities that were becoming the shelter from the storm of barbarism and ignorance out in the wasteland the world was becoming. Craig, to whom he could never imagine speaking civilly. Zeb, some kind of strange genius working on the source of the delicious musical signal that had haunted and twisted his entire life. Hugo, whom Marie called her Billy Strayhorn, her collaborator. And Marie, who had moved heaven and Earth to build this new citadel that she called Crescent City.

He had to hand it to Marie. Somehow she'd pulled this off. Everyone at the table knew a lot more than they had ten minutes ago.

Including him.

"I really . . . don't have anything to add." His throat was sore from shouting. He took a sip from someone's water and gestured toward Tamchu's sculpture. "I don't know anything like that. I'm just human. That's what matters. Making *this* world a better place. Not turning into a form of light, like my mother did." He blinked back tears and continued, his voice stronger. "Not flying off into space, like my lover plans to do. You've got plenty of help. The rest of the world doesn't. I want to help the *rest* of the world. You have a hundred engineers better than me in Crescent City."

"But—"

Jason had never before seen Marie look desperate, even when the city was falling apart.

He wavered for only a second. He shook his head. "I won't be used, Marie. I don't want to be understood. I don't want to be studied. I don't want to disgorge whatever I might know, which is nothing. I've been at the mercy of this persecution all my life and I just want to forget it. I want to grow up. I want to be a part of the world I've always been separated from. I don't want to live on an island. I've *always* been on an island. Don't you understand?"

"I understand," Tamchu said.

Jason was completely wrung-out. He stood for a second, thinking that there was something he ought to do. Then he unbuttoned his shirt pocket and pulled out a laser sphere wrapped in the customary felt pouch. He reached past Hugo and Kita and gave it to Zeb.

"What's this?" Zeb asked.

"It has a lot of information from the Houston Space Center in it. It might come in handy."

"I guess," said Zeb, barely glancing at it. "But—"

"Nice meeting you," said Jason and walked out of the café.

He heard Marie call his name but did not turn around. Two women veering into the café almost knocked him down. One said to the other, "Annie, look! There's Zeb, right where he told me to meet him. He'll be so excited to see you."

It was getting dark. Jason walked four blocks, trying to shut his ears to the music, the beat, the euphoria that echoed through his body, threatening to make him believe that the most important thing in the world was to leave it and to spend the rest of his life figuring out how and where to go.

Jason arrived at the towers flanking the French Quarter on Canal Street. The levees had been built up so that much of the year the streets were dry, but it did not take a very heavy rain or much of a rise in the river to flood the streets. These skyscrapers were linked by high barricades. They were Flower buildings. Most of the city's information was generated and exchanged here, though interstices ran throughout the city and many blocks had their own Flower.

He took the elevator to the sixth floor. He walked to the Genome Project door and opened it.

As he expected, several clerks and lab assistants were at work. Most everyone in New Orleans was on a twenty-four-hour shift schedule. They had probably ignored the crisis, the soldiers, and the Carnival here. They were pretty no-nonsense.

A young man at a reception desk asked, "Can I help you?"

"I want to add my genetic information to the project."

He beamed at Jason. "Good! I'll call up the form for you." He sat at a console and in a minute rose and told Jason to take the seat. "There. Name, date of birth, all that. Just put your finger there."

Jason rested his finger in a depression, felt a slight needle puncture, then the sting of antiseptic. Next to NAME he entered JASON PEABODY. He filled in all the blanks.

By the time he finished and stood up, a light was flashing above his console. The attendant rushed over. He looked at Jason. "Can you please wait here? This is very important." He hurried away.

Jason left and closed the door behind him. He took the elevator to the ground floor and pushed open the emergency exit on the west side of the building.

He stepped into the street as alarms sounded and made sure the door was locked firmly behind him.

He was Outside once again.

The street was empty beneath the full moon. He walked a few blocks, saw flickering firelight and soldiers playing cards, and turned north for a block or two. He crossed under an empty interstate bridge. Water lapped beneath it; he headed north again until he came to the tail of the flooded area and went around it, picked up the road on the other side. It was pleasant; much cooler than during the day. Most of this area had been wiped out by flooding. After a mile or two, he came to a low rise on which stood a row of deserted shacks. They made him nostalgic, in an odd way, for all that he'd seen while bumming around the country.

A bike leaned against the front porch of one of them. Jason yelled into the shack, "Anybody home?" But of course everyone was long gone.

He hopped on and was delighted to find that it had a generator light that brightened as he pedaled.

He continued north. It felt good to be back on the road.

Stars. Silence. A distant destination.

He settled into the rhythm of flatland pedaling.

Ride Out

Tamchu was very happy to be back at work.

The night was moonless; the rush of the river loud. It drowned the dip of his oars. He enjoyed using his expertise to silently board the warship, to deal with the two soldiers who tried to stop him, to find his way to the air circulation unit where he sprayed the filter with a metapheromone cocktail of Kita's design, which, within fifteen minutes, would infiltrate the rooms of all the sleeping soldiers. He then made his way to the operations room, where, as planned, his cohorts had taken care of those on watch. They were, as he suspected, of a variety of nationalities, male and female. They sat or lay in attitudes of restful ease, soon to wake happy in the service of Marie Laveau. He made the hand-slapping gesture with his colleagues that showed solidarity. They began installing the new virtual reality training program at one end of the room; he looked at his watch and counted down the seconds. He switched on the microphone for the ship's speaker system, which was exactly where it had been in his virtual run-through, and spoke into it.

"Hello. I am your new captain. You will now obey me. If any one of you betrays any sign of disloyalty, your messmates will kill you. You will enjoy obeying me. Muster out."

Marie had told him that she wanted him to go Singapore. That suited him. He was excited about it. She had shared some of her plans with him; they had to do with using nanotech to travel to space and reestablish radio communication. She had been wild with gratitude for the information he'd brought from Illian. Marie envisioned a *vou-doun* galaxy, in which everyone lived in some place she called the crossroads, some sort of intersection from what he gathered. He envisioned a Buddhist galaxy. Perhaps they might not be so different. At any rate, Marie was alive. He knew, because the particles of life were on fire for him and burning with a white light, that she did not think so. He read on her face the record of some tremendous failure. But to be human was to fail. The grander one's plan, the easier it was to fail. Her plans were the plans of life, not the plans of death, and he was deeply glad that Hugo had found him and brought him here.

He saw through the window the troops gathering below on the enormous deck. He removed from his pocket the list of commands they were to carry out and leaned over the microphone.

Thirty-six hours later, Marie watched the USS *Columbia* set off toward Crescent City, overflowing with passengers. Many jokers were still smashing bottles of champagne across the railings of the boat and practically everywhere—a boat much more antique than she'd expected to find in this day and age. It meant that the IF and the National Guard consisted of a lot of posturing. They lacked a lot of important technology. Perhaps much of it had been destroyed when Washington had surged.

Yet they could still be deadly, and she didn't want to underestimate them.

Over the course of two weeks, the warship made four round trips. The *Be Happy* cruise ship was preparing to leave on its fifth and final trip on a blue-skied morning of astounding clarity. A morning that put fear in Marie's heart.

She and Hugo were breakfasting on the roof.

"Hugo, remember the morning before Alexandra hit?"

Hugo put down his poppyseed muffin. "Oh."

"I'm not saying that this resemblance means that we'll have a hurricane within thirty-six hours. Or less. But the barometer is dropping too."

"I hear that up north they're setting up some kind of trading network. Going to call it the Rural Network. Maybe we ought to set up something similar in the Caribbean. At least to trade weather information." Hugo was silent for a few minutes. "Marie, come with me today. Please." He finished his muffin and wiped his hands on his napkin. He swigged the rest of his coffee. "There's really no reason for you to stay. Even for a few days."

"I'll think about it." She felt a pang about leaving her headquarters. Its spacious rooms and landing-facing balcony were both soothing and efficacious. She was able to keep an eye on things. The Flower atop her building was an orchid. Or at least it looked like an orchid. The air was still and unusually cool.

"What's that sound?" Marie stood and went to the railing. "There they are." Approaching the landing was a rough raft, about twenty feet on a side. In the center was a torn, mud-stained wigwam that looked as if it had been made with an old white sheet. On it, half a dozen people stood, waving with tremendous excitement and shouting. "More rafters with the New Orleans Plague. Good. You can take them to Crescent City. I hope that our plans to rescue the ones that come after we leave work out."

Hugo responded predictably. "Marie, they are not your responsibility." He said that several times a day.

"Bullshit," she said, straightening.

"You didn't create the New Orleans Plague."

"I engendered it, more or less."

Hugo joined her at the railing and pointed downriver. "There's the *Columbia* coming around the bend. Right on time. But that sky looks almost green. Look. There on the horizon."

"It's your imagination."

"I don't think so. How many people are left?"

"Oh, not many." Her smile felt strained even to her. "A skeleton crew. Look. They're retrieving the rafters. Good."

"Too bad they're all incurable," said Hugo.

"Well," said Marie. She sighed. "We'll find a cure. At some point. Until then, they'll just have to imagine that they're on a raft with Huck Finn, riding into the heart of America."

"Like him, they won't find what they expected."

Marie had never seen Hugo furious before. He was usually completely in control. But now he was screaming from the bridge of the *Be Happy* through a megaphone. "Get onboard, Marie! Now!"

The wind was rising. Unmistakably. In the past eight hours, the sky had clouded over and now heavy drops splatted on the landing. Marie's long thin dress blew back against her.

"Cut Face and Shorty and I will come on the ketch!" she yelled back, though she knew he couldn't hear her. He knew the plan. He just hadn't agreed to it. "The storm will be over in a day or two!" Her straw hat blew off her head and skidded across the landing into the river.

Hugo would leave. Kita was now in Crescent City, and she was pregnant. Though smoking no longer held the same deadly potential as it used to, she had stopped smoking once she knew. Marie was as thrilled as Hugo. She'd taken to calling him Pops. It really irritated him. Everyone else was there too—Craig, Zeb, the invaluable nano-technologist Annie, Sun Ra . . .

Everyone, she thought a bit sadly, except Jason.

Kita had carried with her the astonishing Universal Assembler. She hoped to create an environment in which she could study it and its powers safely. She was still astounded, she said, that all had come out as well as it had, but attributed it to good design and forethought rather than to luck.

Marie gave a last wave as the ship pulled away ponderously from the landing. No matter what the storm might dish out, the ship could take it, as long as it was in deep water. But it could make good speed. She was pretty sure that it would make it out to the city before the storm's swirling fury reached its peak.

She turned away from the boat, no longer able to hear Hugo's imprecations, and walked through deserted Jackson Square. Birds escaping the storm flocked overhead. Sycamore trees released their dry leaves and bent beneath the wind; palms flailed. Cut Face emerged from a café where loud reggae music was playing.

"Hi, Robert."

He grinned and saluted her. "Damn good job, Marie. After de storm, we head on out, eh?"

"I wish you'd left on the boat."

"Now you know that is not what we choose to do. So you jus' sit tight now."

"This area is pretty low."

"We be heading for Magnolia Tower soon, eh?"

"Yeah. If I don't see you there in two hours, I'll come and drag you over there myself."

A Bee blew past overhead. They always reminded her of the woman bicycling through the sky in *The Wizard of Oz*. So incongruous. But everything was—now.

She took her time walking to her apartment, savoring every step. She'd walked to school as a child down these streets. Gone for ice cream with her mother and Grandmère, three generations of women on an evening stroll on a hot summer's evening while the sun sank low on the Mississippi River. Even though every detail had been re-created in Crescent City in a tiny quadrant of its vast area, it did not sit on holy ground. There really wasn't any point. It was a fantasy re-creation for the benefit of others. It did not fool her.

In the St. Louis #1 Cemetary was buried the original Marie Laveau, her namesake. Marie smiled. No doubt her life had seemed just as tumultuous, just as much lived on the edge. African culture and iden-

425

tity were fading into ancestral memory during her time, and she fought to keep them alive and to give them power and majesty. Louis Armstrong had fired off a gun a few blocks away on a fateful New Year's Eve and been sentenced to the Waif's Home, where a strict bandmaster gave him the discipline to help him bridge the gap between amateur and professional and where he had for the first time in his life been assured of eating regular meals every single day. Untold numbers of krewes had labored over their costumes and floats. Slave ships from Africa had put in here, and their chained surviving human cargo sold like cattle. That was here too, and she didn't care if that sank along with the entire South, but that suffering and that will to survive and that strength was in her blood and in the very African-laid bricks on which she walked.

Her daughter, Kalina Marie Laveau, was in Crescent City now and ready, after a long teenage rebellion, to pick up the reins should it be necessary. Marie had great faith in the power of Crescent City, the power of human knowledge. But if that could not be done, she had made her peace. She had done what she had set out to do.

Marie arrived at the home in which she had been born, opened the gate, pushed open the door, and stepped inside.

These thick walls had weathered countless hurricanes and floods. She touched the swirling plaster for a moment: cool, and she seemed to know the lines of the swirls by heart. She smiled. Probably because she'd colored over them when she was a child to illuminate their pattern and had received a good switching from Grandmère.

She ignored her rooms of antiques, all of which were programmed into Crescent City now. Anyone could have one of these very Queen Anne chairs in their very own quarters if they wished, with identical upholstery. But then what was the point? Perhaps a simple celebration of form instead of rarity. Funny how the age of nanotechnology delivered both more and less than she had ever imagined that it might. But they were still only on its threshold.

She climbed to the top floor. Her office; her citadel. She had not been here in ages. She threw open the french doors to let in the fresh air. They slammed back in the rising wind.

She sat once again in the chair, the very chair in which she had sat when this all had begun. When she had passed out of the old world and into the new.

She did not activate Petite Marie's holograms, nor did she have to. They had not been replicated in Crescent City. They were etched in her memory, and she was the only one to whom it mattered. Petite Marie danced infinitely in her heart. Merry and naughty. All that she ever would be. Each one of us was interrupted at some point, Marie mused, and at that point death rounded us into a kind of perfection, a finished work.

She sat there for a long time, thinking.

A window shattered, waking her from reverie.

She stepped out onto the balcony. Wind no longer allowed her tendriled golden raintree to dance, but pulled its viney branches horizontal to the street. She figured it to be forty-five, maybe fifty miles an hour.

She looked down on the street where so long ago Cut Face and Shorty had juggled their guns and killed her. Was she even in the same universe? Had it perhaps all been some sort of postdeath dream?

She held tight to the railing and knew its truth.

Then she was startled by an explosion.

It was dull, deep, and huge. It was the result of massive explosions. Dynamite.

As in the destruction of earthworks.

She heard more explosions. The Federation must have blown the levees.

It wouldn't be long before the river's surge reached the city.

Cut Face and Shorty were in a low part of town. In a low part of town and partying with the aid of unlimited beer.

They were too far to reach before the surge would arrive. She sent a message via the interstice, which still glowed, telling them to get to safety. Then she ran to her desk and called up New Orleans. It popped up holographically.

She knew it by heart.

She pulled on her programming gloves, trembling. Be cool, Marie. Now, of all times in your life, be real, real cool.

She picked up the building on the corner of the block where they were and set it on top of theirs. That was the best she could do in a hurry. It was not sophisticated. But it indicated that matter was to be transferred to that building. That it was to grow, and with all possible speed without melting. The pelting rain would keep it cool. The goddamned flood would cool it too. She touched the SOLIDIFY command pad. It said, "Do you really want to do this? Let me inform you of the possible—"

"Yes!" Marie shouted. "I want to do this!" They would be able to climb to the top of it, perhaps—

Then the door to her room slammed open. Cut Face and Shorty rushed in.

"Damn, Marie, we thought you still be here," said Shorty. "Because you so crazy."

"They've blown the levee," she said. "We'll be drowned."

"Nah," said Shorty. "We got a plan. Hurry now." He yanked an old jacket out of her closet and flung it at her. She pulled it on and followed them to the roof. A rowboat with a small engine sat there, seemingly attached to the roof by some sort of skirt. Of course, it had been grown. But who had initiated it?

"How did this get here?" she asked.

Shorty laughed. "You t'ink you be da only one who knows how to use da city? We grew it from da bar. Started it a few hours ago. We know you probably be lingering here too long. Didn't know da damned soldiers would blow da levee, though. Now get in." He heaved the canvas bag he'd been carrying over the side.

"It not be quite finished," said Cut Face, looking underneath. "Still attached." He pulled out a pocketknife and began cutting the membranous connections through which the matter of the boat had flowed.

Marie looked off across the city in astonishment. "It's coming," she said, but could not hear her own voice over the wind.

A tremendous gray wave, beneath a gray sky, crested toward them about half a mile away. It moved like the coil of a snake, ponderously, building on the river and rushing outward across the recent swamps. Cold rain slashed her face; soaked her dress.

Shorty grabbed her arm and made her climb in the boat, which they'd loosened from the roof. She settled on a seat, looked down, and didn't see any holes. Maybe it would float. She smiled at Shorty, who was facing her, and picked up one of the oars with both hands. Cut Face squeezed next to her and picked up the other.

"Ready?" she asked. Suddenly she felt wonderful.

Brown water filled the streets swiftly. It rose to the top of the building and flooded over it in a large swell, lifting the boat. For an instant, Marie was afraid that they might be swept down into the street on the other side of the block as if they were going over a waterfall, but Shorty held fast to a rope tied to something she couldn't see. He lashed his end around one of the seats. For ten minutes, the water rose steadily and then the main swell had passed, leaving only a rushing current of water that was several feet higher than her roof.

Then the rope snapped. They swirled crazily over Bourbon Street and almost smashed into the top floor of her Uncle Rob's old bar.

"Now what?" she screamed, trying to overwhelm the wind's shrieking.

"Row like hell!" shouted Cut Face in her ear.

They slowly made their way toward the nearest tower, which was swaying. Bees were pushed helplessly through the sky; the bioinformational petals were stripped from the gathered interstice cables. A huge sheet of glass popped out ten stories above them and glided downward, landing on the water with a loud smack a hundred feet away. "I don't think this is a good idea!" Marie shouted.

Cut Face nodded and they changed tack.

The wind and current brought them near the bell tower of the St. Louis Cathedral on Jackson Square. Marie pulled with all her might and they managed to smash right into it. Marie hooked her arms over the open ledge and scrambled in; in a minute, they were all inside. Shorty untied the boat's rope from his waist and tied it around a stone pillar. He pulled the boat close and retrieved the bag he'd flung inside.

Above, the bell tolled sonorously. They climbed to the highest level, about thirty feet above the water, and looked out.

Marie felt the brunt of the wind. It would probably get worse. If they were lucky, this sturdy old tower would not crumble. Below her only the top stories of the old houses were visible. Perhaps no one would ever live in them again.

But they had been well lived in, in their time.

She listened to the tolling of the bell, fancied that its regular tones took on a new rhythm, the rhythm of one of the passages of *Crescent City Rhapsody*.

A rhapsody was a work of many pieces stitched together. That was what New Orleans had been.

And that was what it would be again. Stitched together out of what was best in this strange transmuting world.

She envisioned her shining city, far out in the sea, a place of refuge and a place of consolidation. A place of hope. A springboard to the future. A link to the cosmos.

"This is my l'wa," she said, not shouting, but talking to herself. "I didn't lose my heart. It was always here. And I have always served it." She stared off into the distance, which was all hard rain and whitecaps breaking on roofs.

"Who you talking to?" yelled Shorty.

"My manbo," yelled Marie. They grinned at each other.

"Thirsty?" Cut Face pulled a bottle of champagne from the bag and popped the cork.

They passed the bottle around.

And after a while, they danced to the music of the wind.

Final Note

It was night when the *Be Happy* gained its first view of Crescent City.

Zeb stood on deck, holding the railing tightly. Ra was next to him. The city rose from the dark sea in swooping lines of light.

He looked up at the stars. Deep contentment washed through him.

There were mysteries in the heavens. There always had been. No matter what he discovered in the new life ahead, there always would be.

What joy.